D0834309

Nationally Bestselling Author
PAMELA MORSI

WINNER!
Romance Writers of America RITA Award
Romantic Times Reviewers' Choice Award
Georgia Romance Writers Best Historical Award

"I'VE READ ALL HER BOOKS
AND LOVED EVERY WORD."
Jude Deveraux

"ABSOLUTELY DELIGHTFUL"
Heartland Critiques

"WARM AND WONDERFUL"
Laura Kinsale

"MS. MORSI BRINGS A HEARTWARMING
TOUCH . . . GENTLE HUMOR AND
DEPTH OF CHARACTER . . .
TO HISTORICAL ROMANCE."
Rendezvous

PAMELA MORSI

THE LOVE CHARM

AVON BOOKS ◆ NEW YORK

THE LOVE CHARM is an original publication of Avon Books. This work
has never before appeared in book form. This work is a novel. Any
similarity to actual persons or events is purely coincidental.

AVON BOOKS
A division of
The Hearst Corporation
1350 Avenue of the Americas
New York, New York 10019

Copyright © 1996 by Pamela Morsi
Front cover art by Liz Kenyon
Inside front cover art by Doreen Minuto
Published by arrangement with the author
Library of Congress Catalog Card Number: 96-96759
ISBN: 0-380-78641-9

First Avon Books Printing: November 1996

AVON TRADEMARK REG. U.S. PAT. OFF. AND IN OTHER COUNTRIES, MARCA
REGISTRADA, HECHO EN U.S.A.

Printed in the U.S.A.

RA   10 9 8 7 6 5 4 3 2 1

For
Donna Caubarreaux,
who opened her house to me and
shared her laughter and her lovely family with me,
introduced me to her four-legged clients,
and was so welcoming, I forgot I was a stranger.

And for
Alma Reed,
who answered my most ignorant questions,
informed and entertained me,
showed me the sights of Eunice, Louisiana,
and made me eat a stuffed ponce.

Prologue

Southwest Louisiana
Spring 1820

The wedding pirogue that eased down the gentle current of the Vermillion River was festooned in blooming vines of honeysuckle, bright purple water hyacinths, and delicate swamp lilies. Like everyone else on the bank, Armand Sonnier shouted and waved at the young couple on board until they disappeared from sight around a bend in the river. His older brother, Jean Baptiste, was a married man now and poled the little boat home with his new bride.

"It's so romantic!"

The words were accompanied with a soft girlish sigh and Armand turned toward the pretty girl by his side. She was sweet and dainty in a pink pinafore, her dreamy gaze still focused upon the river. At fifteen he was no longer much interested in playtime, but for Aida he made an exception. She was an only child and Armand thought she was probably lonely. He often talked with her and found her delightful imagination and scatterbrained silliness to be funny and entertaining.

1

As the rest of the crowd turned back to the church-yard, where the food and dancing and frolic would go on until dawn, Armand was drawn to his young friend sitting in the grass.

She had gathered up a few of the scattered flower petals that had been strewn at the feet of the newly-weds. She was stowing them in her handkerchief along with a dollop of river sand, a tiny crawfish claw, a heron feather, and a piece of linen string.

Armand took a seat beside her, watching curiously.

"What are you doing?" he asked. "Making mud pies?"

"Mud pies!" She frowned at him disdainfully. "That's for little girls."

With her rosebud mouth, her round cheeks, and her shiny black curls peeking out from beneath her sunbonnet, Aida Gaudet looked to be exactly that. Armand couldn't resist the urge to reach out and give her hair a playful tug.

She didn't allow him to draw her into the game.

"Someday I'm going to be a bride," she declared.

Armand shrugged in agreement. All the girls in Prairie l'Acadie married eventually. "I wouldn't be surprised," he said.

"I'm going to be the most beautiful woman on the Vermillion River and I'll choose the most handsome man in the parish as my husband."

"You seem very certain," he pointed out.

"Oh, I am absolutely sure," she declared, her voice lowered with mysterious intent. "Because I am the greatest hoodoo woman in all of Louisiana."

"Oh really?" he asked, familiar with her girlish games of pretend.

She nodded soberly. "I make cows come fresh, keep rats from your corncrib, and can make the moon pour silver coins into the river if I so choose."

Armand grinned. "I tremble in fear just to know you."

"As well you should," she told him.

"And great hoodoo women get to marry handsome men?" he asked. "It seems Madame Landry had no husband at all."

Aida shrugged in tacit agreement. "But I will," she said. "I will have the man I most desire, because I have made this love charm and no man can resist it."

She tied a knot in the handkerchief and held it up for his inspection.

"Very nice," he assured her, laughing.

"When I decide who is most handsome and deserving of me, I will bestow this gift upon him and he will be mine forever."

"Forever?"

"Forever."

"Whether he wants to be or not?"

She stuck her tongue out at him. "Of course he will want to be. I told you, I'm going to be the most beautiful woman on the Vermillion River."

"Aida!"

She startled slightly at the sound of her father's voice. "I've been looking all over for you," the man said. "I told you to wait for me at the church door. We are to take supper with Father Denis."

The bright-eyed youngster looked momentarily horrified.

"Oh Poppa, I forgot!"

"You always forget. Now hurry! Hurry!"

She shoved something in Armand's hand as she rushed away. Momentarily he gazed down at what he held and then shook his head. Armand Sonnier held in his grasp the love charm.

Un

Destiny, a divine plan and a game of chance.

The gleam of moonlight on the dark water of the Vermillion River illuminated more than the broad expanse of Prairie l'Acadie. On the porch of the Sonniers' sturdy half-timbered house near the outside stairs, three men sat around an overturned wood-slat washtub, their faces serious and unsmiling in the yellow glare of the lantern.

Jean Baptiste turned over the last card he dealt himself and looked into his opponent's eyes. "Trump is clubs," he said evenly.

Armand glanced with feigned carelessness at the card and surveyed his own hand once more. He forced his insides into a deliberate calm so that his face would reveal nothing.

Armand's best friend, Laron Boudreau, sat silently observing the two brothers. He had bourréd on the last hand, requiring him to ante the value of the pot. He'd thrown in all he had, but it wasn't enough to earn him another play. The huge pile of coins and paper notes on the washtub was enough to make a man's mouth go dry and his heart beat faster. Bourré was a dangerous game for a gambling man; big losses were common even for a skilled player. Big stakes,

5

however, always drew the interest of young men still in their twenties, still with plenty to learn, yet confident in their own abilities.

The two Sonnier brothers, Armand and Jean Baptiste, were alike in many ways, the same light brown hair, the same fair complexion, the same bright blue eyes. Armand was like a miniature version of his brother. While Jean Baptiste was of medium height, stocky and broad-shouldered, his brother was a man of small stature and fine-featured. He carried not an ounce of extra fat upon him. It was only the strength of his jaw that kept his face from appearing delicate.

"I will play," Armand announced finally, raising that prominent chin deliberately, almost in challenge. He had gambled against his brother many times and he knew well that any show of his own confidence was sure to make Jean Baptiste reckless.

Jean Baptiste gazed back at him, his face so much like Armand's own, and nodded slowly. "Dealer plays also," he said.

Cards were casually tossed, one at a time, toward the center of the overturned washtub. Armand took the first two tricks with the ace and queen of clubs. Jean Baptiste took the third and looked across at his brother. Armand's stern concentration wavered as a smile took over his features.

Jean Baptiste made a sound that was almost a groan as he led his best card. Armand bested it and took the trick. Armand then led and Jean Baptiste threw in his last with a sound of disgust. "Take it, go ahead, take it," Jean Baptiste moaned. "It's only money, the root of evil, and I never have enough to matter."

THE LOVE CHARM · 7

Armand laughed delightedly as he pulled the winnings toward him. "Don't worry, big brother, if your gambling gets so bad you can't feed the family, I'll always make you a small loan." He grinned conspiratorially toward Laron. "Five for ten is prime terms for this bayou."

Laron nodded as if the suggestion seemed reasonable.

Jean Baptiste huffed. "My own flesh and blood, devil-bent on usury!"

"As the old men say," Laron teased, "never play against a wiser man."

Jean Baptiste nodded. "And I can never remember that my baby brother is the wiser man!"

The three laughed together companionably. Bourré was serious card playing, but once the money was lost, all could be philosophical. And it was not as if the cash would be stuck in some wily Creole's money pouch and taken down to New Orleans. Armand would hold the coins until next week's game, when he'd probably lose what he'd won this night, if not more.

It was late, very late. Jean Baptiste set the washtub against the side of the house. Armand straightened the cards and returned them to their wooden box.

Laron fished a small bag of tobacco out of his pocket and all three men took turns filling their long-stemmed clay pipes. They rearranged their hide-seat ladderback chairs to face the wide stretch of bayou given the auspicious name of Vermillion River. Jean Baptiste raised the chimney tin of the lantern and lit a sprig of dry palmfronde. He passed the fire to Laron and Armand before sparking his own smoke. The smell of home-cured tobacco filled the air around the porch with a familiar masculine aroma. They stared out into the darkness of the evening, relaxed.

They had been friends forever. Armand and Laron were the same age and had stuck together tighter than mud on a wagon wheel since childhood. The brains and the brawn, people called them. And for good reason. With a small, almost frail, appearance, the result of childhood illness, Armand had a bright mind and a gift of speech that bordered on the eloquent. Laron was big and sturdy and muscular. He was the first man you'd call upon if you needed a stump pulled or a sunk raised. Folks said that for all the scrapes the two were involved in, the reason they never got into trouble was that if Laron couldn't bust them out, Armand would think and talk them out.

Jean Baptiste joined them as companions as they grew older and the three years' difference in their ages ceased to matter. Now the three sat together, quietly smoking in the stillness of a late autumn night.

The Sonnier family, Jean Baptiste's wife and children, were all abed inside the house. The peaceful breathing of a mother and children sleeping on the far side of the curtain-covered doorway was accompanied by the sounds of the night. The buzzing mosquitoes, the scratchy call of crickets, the chirp of tree frogs were punctuated by the occasional splash in the water as a big old turtle or maybe even a gator made a late-night swim.

Contented and quiet, the talk moved from cards to crops and cattle. Cotton, they thought, would be good next year. Cattle even better. Sugar; sugar was too much work, they all agreed. Not a fit crop for small farmers, *petits habitants*, like themselves.

Ultimately the subject turned to one often favored by young healthy men on this prairie—a subject favored by young men on *any* prairie or bayou or city street. The subject of women.

"I hear that old man Breaux has a niece up in Opelousas," Laron said, glancing toward Armand. "He says she's no bigger than a minute."

Armand shrugged with good grace and offered a fatalistic sigh. "There is not a wide selection of women on the bayous in any case," he said sadly. "But when a man's own height decrees he must confine himself to the females that grow no taller than swampgrass, the choice becomes limited indeed."

His brother and friend chuckled.

Armand's lack of stature was a long-time joke with the three. From a childhood of being called "short-bread" and "knee-high," Armand had developed not just a thick skin, but a confidence in himself for his other qualities. Still, when it came to courting, a man wanted a woman to look up to him. Most of the young ladies on this prairie would have to sit down to do so.

"And so you laugh at me, my friend," he accused Laron good-naturedly. "Here I pine away for want of a wife of my own while you are affianced to Aida Gaudet."

"Ah," Jean Baptiste commented. "Some men are forever lucky."

The lovely Aida was almost a legend. Armand's once funny little friend was now described as *belle chose,* inordinately beautiful. And it was no fib. Aida Gaudet was the most beautiful woman on Prairie l'Acadie, perhaps the most beautiful girl on the Vermillion River, maybe even the most beautiful in Louisiana. Her fine figure, perfect pale flesh, and glossy black hair set pulses racing in every man still strong enough to stir a stick.

Unfortunately, Armand Sonnier was no exception. He was in love with her. And she had promised to marry Laron Boudreau, his best friend.

"I am a fortunate man," Laron admitted, and then told Armand, "Do not worry. The right woman will come along for you."

Armand agreed, sighing a little. No one knew that his heart was already ensnared. And no one would ever know.

"It must be the biggest irony ever among two friends," Armand said. "That I would marry tomorrow if I had a woman to choose. And my best friend has been engaged nearly two years and still no wedding in sight."

"When *are* you getting married?" Jean Baptiste asked. "Last winter you said in the spring. In spring you said in the fall. Autumn is on us now and we haven't heard a whisper of your plans."

"We will marry in due time," Laron assured him. "It is not a thing that a man needs to rush into."

"I heard old Jesper is getting very restless," Armand warned. "He has asked Father Denis to intercede and press you two for the reading of the banns before cold weather sets in."

"A Frenchman in robes is not likely to rush me to the altar," Laron told him. "And he won't be any more likely to persuade Mademoiselle Gaudet than her father has been. That young woman does exactly as she pleases. She always has, and Lord help me as her husband, I suspect she always will."

Armand chuckled. "Do you think she will manage you as easily as she wraps that old man about her little finger?"

"I hope not quite," Laron answered.

"I'm surprised that Jesper even mustered the courage to ask Father Denis for help," Armand said. "He must be getting desperate."

"I can't imagine why. Do you think he's unwilling to feed the girl another winter?" Jean Baptiste asked.

"What is another mouth to him?" Armand replied. "He's doing so well even the priests would be jealous. That mill of his has him set up fine and proper. And his fields are as green and prosperous as any I've ever seen."

Jean Baptiste sighed with feigned wistfulness. "Ah, beautiful and wealthy, too. It is more than a man should expect in one woman."

The other men chuckled in agreement.

"And no fellow in greater need than my friend Laron," Armand added, teasing.

His friend nodded at him, conceding the point. Laron Boudreau was virtually landless, the youngest son of Anatole Boudreau's fifteen children. The law of Louisiana stated that upon death a father's property must be partitioned evenly, with every portion to have water access. Once old Anatole's moderate holding of ninety arpents was divided, Laron found his own farm to be a strip of land so narrow that a thirsty cow on its way to drink from the bayou would probably cross onto the property of his brother a half-dozen times.

"What truly amazes me, Laron," Armand said, "is that you have the prettiest, wealthiest, most sought after mamselle on the river and yet you seem loath to marry."

Laron took a deep draw on his pipe and shrugged. "I'm not the first man to get gooseflesh when the talk turns to wedlock."

"Is that what it is?" Armand said.

"Don't ride him, brother," Jean Baptiste piped in. "He is right to hesitate at the idea of marriage. A man must do it, but it is truly no bargain."

Armand turned to look at Jean Baptiste in curious disbelief. "Is my hearing playing tricks upon me?" he asked. "Is this my brother, Jean Baptiste? Jean Baptiste who was so eager to wed that he could hardly wait for his chest to fur before he tied the knot? Our Jean Baptiste, who carved Félicité's name on a tree before he even knew how to spell it! Tell me, Laron, is this my brother who speaks ill of holy wedlock?"

Laron quickly joined in. "Old married men are always sighing and complaining," he answered Armand. "Pay the worn-out old poppa no regard."

The two younger men were laughing. Armand noticed that his brother was not.

"You are serious," he said incredulously. "Whatever is wrong with you?"

Jean Baptiste glanced back guiltily at the curtained doorway behind him. He answered in low, regretful tones.

"Marriage is different than I thought it to be," he told them in a soft whisper.

"Different? How so?" his brother asked.

Jean Baptiste shook his head, his brow furrowed. "I

thought I was so much in love. Now I think I was just . . . I was just eager to take a woman to bed."

"There are whores aplenty down on the Bayou Blonde," Laron pointed out. "You didn't want to *take a woman to bed*. You wanted Félicité."

"Are you thinking you don't love her?" Armand was genuinely shocked. "What nonsense! Of course you love Félicité."

Jean Baptiste shrugged. "I entered into marriage too soon. Now I am stuck for a lifetime."

"Stuck for a lifetime?" Armand's expression was disbelief. He laughed without much humor. "You have as kind and gentle a woman for wife as any I know. Not many men would describe such a circumstance as being *stuck*."

Jean Baptiste shrugged off his brother's words. "Yes, yes, of course Félicité is a fine woman," he agreed. "But having a wife is not like pursuing a woman. There is no excitement in it. No real pleasure. How I envy you both. You both have fun and freedom and anticipation. You may dance and flirt and steal sweet kisses. I have only work and trouble and responsibility. One day looks to me just like the next. Oh, how I envy you."

Armand was shocked into speechlessness.

Laron was confused and uncomfortable with his friend's confession. "How can you speak so, Jean Baptiste? Félicité is a wonderful wife and devoted to you."

Jean Baptiste did not dispute him. "But you see that is the point, she is a *wife*," he said. "Wives, by their very nature, are neither exciting nor pleasurable."

Laron scoffed. "She must be somewhat pleasurable, my friend," he said. "You have three children and another due to arrive before Christmas, it seems."

"I like children," Jean Baptiste admitted. "But four in five years is too many. The woman has been fat nearly from the day we wed."

"Fat!" Armand howled in disbelief. "She is not *fat*, Jean Baptiste, she is once more and again with child."

"I know the cause, my brother, but the truth does not alter the face in the mirror or the size of her girth."

"In case you did not realize this"—Armand's words dripped sarcasm—"the begetting of those babes can be put as squarely at your doorstep as at her own."

The elder Sonnier brother shrugged. "Still," he said wistfully. "I would that I had not wed so soon. Could I do it again, I would have stayed a bachelor much much longer."

He grinned and shook a finger at Laron Boudreau. "At least long enough to try my chances at routing you for the hand of the beautiful Aida."

"You think you would have had a chance for her?" Laron asked, deliberately making his words light. "I'm not sure the taste of the mamselle runs to worn-out old married men like yourself."

Jean Baptiste laughed then. "No, I suspect not," he admitted.

"Of course not," Armand concurred. "There has never been any question that she would choose any man but Laron. It is completely like her."

"What do you mean?" his friend asked.

"We have all known Aida since she was in braids," he said. "A more foolish featherbrain was never seen on this prairie."

Armand's opinion of the most beautiful woman on the Vermillion river was well-known. He made certain that it was, since his scorn was the mask he held up to cover his feelings.

"You will get no argument from me on that," Laron said with a chuckle.

Armand nodded and continued, "Aida Gaudet chose her husband the same way she would have chosen a bolt of store-bought fabric. Value and durability come second, my friend, to what pleases her eye."

Laron laughed out loud. "And you think I am pleasing to the lady's eye?"

Armand only shrugged. There was nothing further to say. Truth was truth and Armand had faced it a long time ago. Laron's thick black hair, tied loosely at the nape of his neck with leather cord, his strong features, and his perfectly straight white teeth spoke for themselves. He had the looks to take a woman's breath away.

His friend was tall, strong, and attractive. Armand was short and very ordinary. He could still recall Aida's girlish declaration. She would be the bride of the most handsome man in the parish. Clearly his best friend, Laron Boudreau, was that man.

"I know why Aida Gaudet chose you," Armand stated firmly. "But what continues to puzzle me is why you chose Aida Gaudet."

Laron tipped his chair back on two legs and stretched out to rest his bare feet against the porch rail. He folded his arms across his chest and perused his best friend with speculation.

"My brother is truly crazy," Jean Baptiste piped in. "Every man wants her, Armand."

"Laron does not."

"Why would he not?"

"Because he has a *veuve allemande* to keep him warm through winter nights," Armand replied.

Laron's expression turned stony. The front legs of his chair banged against the floorboards.

"I have no idea what you mean," he said flatly.

The coldness of his friend's reply did not deter Armand Sonnier in the least. The quiet contemplation of the dark night and the aching of his own heart somehow brought forth words that he had never in his life intended to speak.

"I mean exactly what I said," he answered evenly.

It was common knowledge on the river that Laron Boudreau had taken up illicitly with the *veuve allemande*, the German widow. Some even said that Laron was father to her youngest child, a pretty three-year-old. Armand didn't believe that. He knew his friend too well. But he was aware that Laron spent every spare moment in the widow's company. And the very furtive nature of those visits left little doubt that the two were not merely passing comments about the weather.

"I mean exactly what I said," Armand continued. "While I am a poor bachelor near-starved for a woman's touch, my friend Laron has set up a bower as warm and lush as any married man's."

Laron's jaw was tightly set and his voice was cold. "I will not have the name of Madame Shotz spoken ill, even by my closest friend," he warned.

"And I would not speak ill of her," Armand said quietly. "I do not know her, but I do know you. If you respect her, so do I."

Laron accepted his words as apology.

"I meant merely," Armand explained more lightly. "That you seem as much at peace with your life as any man I know on bayou or prairie."

Laron hesitated a long moment before he replied. "I have found a measure of contentment with Helga," he admitted finally.

"I know that," Armand said. "And it is why I worry about your lengthy engagement to the fair Aida. It will be difficult to cast off that ease for the certain *misery* of husbanding a woman that you do not love."

There was silence between them.

"It will only be misery in the daytime," Jean Baptiste piped in quickly with a sigh of longing. "Nighttime with Aida Gaudet would surely be paradise."

His humor broke the tension between the two other men and they relaxed.

"Truthfully, you have the right of it, my friend," Laron admitted. "Helga is woman enough for me, but a man must marry."

None contradicted that statement. Like birth and death, marriage among the Acadian people was expected. Only the priesthood exempted a man from such duty. Laron Boudreau was no candidate for the priesthood. And he couldn't marry Helga Shotz.

Though she was known as a widow, Helga was already married.

Her dress was too plain and the neckline too high. Aida sighed sadly, but there was no help for it. Were she the daughter of a rich Creole, she could clad

herself in crinoline and lace and show the swell of her
bosom with impunity. But her father was a simple
Acadian farmer and Acadian women dressed modestly in homespun cottonade with an occasional
decoration of linen or crochet. At least it was colorful,
bright and cheery with wide stripes on the skirt and a
vest corset of vivid indigo with red ribbon laces. She
looked well enough, she thought.

And besides, as Father Denis would tell her, shaking his finger menacingly, vanity is unbecoming of
womanhood. Easily she pushed away her mild disappointment. It *was* Saturday night and vanity or not,
she *was* the prettiest girl on Prairie l'Acadie, perhaps
the prettiest girl on the Vermillion River, maybe the
prettiest girl in Louisiana.

At least, that was what people said.

Aida tried to hold that thought to herself with
comfort. Carefully she inspected her teeth, especially
the tiny chipped corner of her right incisor. At age ten
she'd tripped on her own skirts and fallen against the
porch. No one remembered the incident or ever
mentioned the imperfection, but Aida remained ever
aware of it. The chipped tooth was, she thought, her
only flaw. And she knew it was her own fault. God
had denied her a fine wit or a true purpose in life.
He'd intended her for perfect beauty; any less than
that was her own failing.

Aida had schooled herself not to smile broadly,
laugh with her mouth open, or display any other
expression that might draw attention to the broken
tooth. If men found her tiny wavering tilt of lips
intriguing and alluring, well, so much the better.

"Aida, *ma petite*, it is time that we go," her father

called from the doorway. "I can hear already the music begin to play."

"Coming, Poppa," she answered. "One minute more."

She gazed at herself again in the mirror. Her thick black curls were tied away from her face and secured beneath her lace-trimmed cap. But the length of it was twisted and balled at the nape of her neck to remind the gentlemen, if they were wont to forget, that her hair was long and luxuriant and certain to be prized by the man who married her.

Aida was thoughtful. A prize. That's how most saw her. A pretty, gaily wrapped prize. A thing to be won and displayed like a sixteen-point deer head or a fourteen-foot-long alligator hide. Aida didn't want to be a man's trophy. She wanted to be loved.

Father Denis had scolded her. Almighty God, the priest told her, had given her much. She had a good home, a devoted father, plenty to eat, and fine things to wear, and she was the most beautiful woman on the Vermillion River. Did she dare to ask heaven for more?

"No good can come of your romantic lingering," he'd warned her. "It is your duty to marry and bear children. You hesitate over some foolish female notion; God is not pleased."

What God truly thought, Aida did not know, but she suspected that Father Denis had not been pleased with her for some time.

"You are a vain, undutiful daughter," the priest had charged. "You are selfish and spoiled!"

That's what Father Denis always said. And Aida had to admit that it was the truth. She never suggested that the good father was not absolutely right. She always made her confessions and sorrowfully she did her penance, but she didn't really reform.

How could she? She really wanted to be a better woman, a better person. But could a person really *not* put herself first? Could a person truly say, *I only wish to do my duty and I will find happiness in that*? Perhaps another, a better person could say that. Aida Gaudet could not.

Aida was not evil, but she knew that she was not at all saintly. She also knew that beauty was not enough upon which to base a marriage.

"Aida! Are you coming now?" her father called out.

"Yes, Poppa, I'm coming," she lied.

Most Acadian farm girls began dreaming of weddings and trousseaus while still dressed in pinafores. A wedding was the pinnacle of a woman's life, the measure of her success. Aida, too, had dreamed of a beautiful wedding, flowers and ribbons and every eye upon her. And she had dreamed of a handsome man standing beside her. She dreamed of love. She dreamed of being loved by a husband. With a little shake of her head she remembered a long-ago wedding when she'd gathered up some flower petals and flotsam and made herself a love charm to ensure that happened. Vaguely she wondered what had become of that silliness wrapped in a handkerchief.

Aida was to marry Laron Boudreau. He was handsome, kind, hardworking. Everyone in Prairie l'Acadie thought the two of them a perfect match. The most beautiful woman on the Vermillion River should be won by the most handsome man.

That's what people thought. Aida's choice, in fact had nothing to do with Monsieur Boudreau's good looks. Laron had not money or property to recommend him. To Aida his lack of finances worked in his favor. She'd thought it all out carefully. Laron would come live with her at her father's house. Though he would be her husband, it would still be her *father's* house and he would always work her *father's* land. For that he would, of necessity, be grateful for his marriage. Gratitude was not love, but it was closer than admiration. If he could need her, then he could love her, *her* and not the most beautiful woman on the Vermillion River.

Of course there was the German widow. Aida tapped her teeth thoughtfully with her fingernail. She doubted that Laron realized Aida knew about her. Aida wasn't hurt or worried about that alliance. She wasn't even certain that she would object to it continuing after they had wed.

The German widow was Laron's mistress. Aida allowed the thought to flow over her like water, testing the feel of it. It was not bothersome at all. Aida thought that it *should* bother her, but it didn't. That he held another woman in his arms, that he probably did with her unspeakably intimate things, was not disturbing or hurtful, but merely a curiosity.

If Aida never acted as if she noticed, no one would ever suspect that she knew. Surely he couldn't love the German widow. Her brow furrowed unhappily at the suggestion. Aida didn't mind Laron having a mistress, as long as he didn't love her. When Monsieur Boudreau finally began to love, Aida wanted to be the recipient.

She pushed away the troubling thoughts. She was young and pretty, and tonight, just up the river, music was playing. Somehow, some way, her husband would come to love her. She was Aida Gaudet, young and beautiful and ready for a party.

"Aida!" her father called out impatiently once more.

"Coming," she answered as she began looking around for her fancy kid dancing slippers. She bit her lower lip, worried. Where were they? It was one of the terrible realities of her life; Aida was likely to lose things. Well, perhaps that wasn't exactly true. She would simply forget where they had been put.

"She would forget her head, were it not attached," the old women joked of her. Unfortunately, it was probably true. Somehow she could not seem to recall what she was supposed to do when. Where things were or why. Or even if she had done what she was required to do.

Frantically she began searching the room, sorting through the worn old sea chest, searching through the unstraightened bedclothes, kneeling to look under the bed. By complete chance she spotted them. The slippers of aged buckskin dyed with poke salet berries were hanging from the rafters. The rains had been bad last week and she had feared the damp floors would ruin them.

She climbed up on a chair and brought them down, grateful for their safety. Brushing them lightly to assure herself they were not dusty, she slipped them into her sleeve for safekeeping. She grabbed her guinea feather fan and hurried from her room, through her father's, and into the main part of the house.

Her wooden sabots sat next to the door and she slipped her bare feet into them. They clomped against the porch boards as she made her way noisily outside.

The dancing slippers could not be risked to the damp dangers of water travel. If a shoe became muddy or lost in the water, it should be a wooden one, easily replaced.

"Coming, Poppa," she called out to the gray-haired man waiting rather impatiently at the end of the dock.

The Gaudet house, like most on the Prairie l'Acadie, was built on the natural rise of land beside the water. The stream facilitated travel, whether for visiting neighbors or for transporting goods to market. Water access meant prosperity.

But water could also mean flood. The whole area was low and wet. Good for game and crops, but people and their possessions needed to be high and dry. As if God understood this wet paradox, all along the bayous and rivers, thousands of years of sediment deposit built up along the banks, making the areas near the water the safest in time of flood. So even with huge areas of open space behind them, the residents of Prairie l'Acadie lived bunched together on the natural levees in close proximity to the river and its tiny tributaries.

Jesper Gaudet was wearing his best cottonade *culotte* tied just below the knee and his striped blue *chemise*. His face was shaded from the last of the afternoon sun by a wide-brimmed hat woven of palmetto.

"We're going to miss everything," he complained as he helped Aida into the long narrow boat known in the bayous as a pirogue. She ignored his words and settled herself comfortably in the narrow, seatless hull, her cherry-striped skirt billowing around her like a frothy soufflé, as her father pushed off from the dock and began the slow, laborious task of poling the pirogue upstream.

"They've been playing and singing for seems like half a day already," Jesper continued to fuss. "All the good food is likely gone."

"Oh, I'm not hungry," Aida told him lightly.

"Well, I certainly am," the old man complained.

With a little O of surprise and shame, Aida covered her mouth. She had forgotten once more to fix Poppa any supper.

It was near sunset. The light was low and filtered through the thick line of aging cypress and tupelos on either side of the broad expanse of water. The outstretched branches of the trees were draped and weeping with Spanish moss. And the quiet serenity of coming evening was disturbed only by the call of crickets and the buzz of mosquitoes.

The loud hungry squawk of a heron caught Aida's attention and she watched the bird's smooth graceful flight just above the water as it searched for prey. It was beautiful. She admired beautiful things.

The pirogue cut a neat swath through the bright green duckweed, so thick and verdant, it looked as if a person could simply walk across it to the distant banks where the knobby knees of the trees were visible above the water. The river was light and color and beauty. It was home.

They came around a bend in the waterway, and the sounds of song and merriment grew more distinct. Up ahead the glow of lanterns was visible in the distance. Aida sighed happily. This was life, this was what life was meant to be, *joie de vivre*.

Deux

The whine of bowed fiddles and the pounding of dancing feet against cypress planking filled the air, mixing with the smells of boiled shrimp, *gumbo févi*, and fresh baked *miches*. It was Saturday night and for Acadians that meant dancing and laughing and fun.

Fais-dodo was what the people had jokingly begun to call these community outings. The term, meaning "go to sleep," was coined from the practice of putting all the babies together in a bed at the back of the house. Children, typically much beloved and coddled, found suddenly that the parents who normally were content to converse with them for hours on end now only had one phrase to say: "Go to sleep!"

It was a phrase that Armand Sonnier himself uttered as he helped his sister-in-law get her three children tucked into the Marchand family's low-slung four-poster. A half-dozen children already reclined there, boys and girls alike wearing the traditional shapeless knee-length gown.

His niece and two nephews were healthy, rowdy, and active, much too much for his sister-in-law to handle alone.

Félicité Sonnier was heavily pregnant again. Her once pink, pretty face was round as a plate and splotched with the faint brown mask of childbearing. Her formerly lustrous brown curls were dull and limp and wound rather untidily about her head. And below the hem of her skirt her feet were so swollen no shoes would fit her and it appeared she had no ankles at all. Her best dress hung around her massive body like a tent, the shoulder stained with baby spit-up. Félicité Sonnier was tired. Armand knew by the sounds of her sighs that she was very tired.

"You rabbits get down in your den," Armand told the three curly-headed children. "And I don't want to hear a one of you calling out for Maman."

"I'm too big to go to sleep," four-year-old Gaston complained with a yawn.

"Me, too," his three-year-old sister chimed in. Little Marie's words were hard to make out as her thumb was already tucked firmly in her tiny little mouth.

"You two must lie here with Pierre," their uncle explained to them with great seriousness. "The baby needs his rest and you must watch over him."

Ten-month-old Pierre, wide-eyed, gurgling happily, and as fat as a sausage, seemed the only one of the three who wasn't really sleepy.

"All right," Gaston agreed with a sigh as he snuggled down into the bed. "I'll lie here and take care of Pierre."

"Me, too," Marie echoed.

Armand kissed all three and waited beside the bed as he watched Félicité do the same. The two older children were already dozing off as he took his sister-in-law's arm and urged her away from the sleeping room.

"We must find you a place to sit," he said. "You are so near your last gasp, I really should carry you."

Félicité giggled. She was a head taller than he and outweighed him by half again as much.

"I'm just fine, Armand. You'll spoil me with this treatment. It reminds me of your brother when we were expecting our first."

"A little spoiling wouldn't hurt you," Armand insisted.

She laughed. "Truly, I am getting used to my delicate condition. I've been having a baby, just had a baby, or having another baby for years now." She leaned forward as if to whisper conspiratorially. "It seems to be something that I'm good at."

Armand grinned back at her. "Along with cooking, cleaning, sewing, and sister-in-lawing. Let's find you a place to sit and rest awhile and I'll bring you something to eat."

Jean Baptiste had been tying up the pirogue and was still standing at the end of the dock, engaged in a deep discussion with Emile Marchand. Armand didn't mind fending for Félicité. As a single man in her household, he was routinely provided good cooking, clean clothes, and a tranquil home life. Armand was grateful to her for those things. He also simply liked her ready wit and empathy for others. They were fine qualities in a woman, qualities he someday hoped to find in the woman he chose for his own bride.

An empty chair was finally located on the north side of the house next to Madame Hébert. The woman, a close friend of Félicité's, welcomed her eagerly, ready to talk. She was one of Laron's many sisters and had his handsome good looks, plus ten years.

"Doesn't he look slicked and pressed?" Madame Hébert said to Félicité as she pointed in Armand's direction. "Must be a lady on his mind."

Félicité nodded in agreement. "Yes, Yvonne, I have to agree. When a man combs back his hair and puts on a clean shirt of his own volition, there *must* be a woman on his mind."

Armand laughed and shook his head. "I only dress for Saturday night, *mesdames*," he assured them. Unlike most of the men present in their knee-length *culottes*, Armand wore trousers. He thought that the longer pants made him appear taller. "Even the most careless swamper shines up for Saturday night."

"So you have no interest in women?" Madame Hébert asked, disbelieving. "My husband has a cousin in St. Martinville. She is just turned fifteen and very petite I hear."

Armand smiled broadly at her. "Perhaps I must find an excuse to visit St. Martinville this winter," he said.

"He is planning a house," Félicité whispered excitedly.

Madame Hébert's eyes widened and Armand would have gladly stuck a stocking in his sister-in-law's mouth.

"I had not heard this," Madame Hébert declared.

"He has just been talking and dreaming about it with Jean Baptiste," Félicité explained. "When a man starts thinking of having his own house, you know he must be thinking of having his own wife."

Tutting with concern, Madame Hébert was shaking

her head. "Does my brother know this? Poor Laron wishes his own house, I know. On his land it would look more like a bridge than a home."

Armand laughed. "Your brother knows all about it," he said.

"He will not need a house," Félicité pointed out. "Once Laron and Aida are married, they will live with Jesper."

Madame Hébert nodded. "Still a man always wants his own house, does he not?"

"Laron can share my house," Armand said. "In fact he has offered to help me build it. He says I needn't despair to live in it alone. If no woman will have me we will live as two old bachelors together."

"Two bachelors in a house!" Madame Hébert giggled. "Father Denis will worry about every female in the parish."

"Truth is, that I do hope to wed," Armand told her. "I just need to find the right woman, as my brother did."

Félicité laughed again. "Any woman would be lucky to get you," she said.

"And every man on the river has a bet on who it will be. Oops!" Madame Hébert covered her mouth with her hand, horrified at her own words.

"Are they truly betting?" Félicité asked.

Madame Hébert looked chagrined. "You know these men, everything to them is a horse race, even romance."

Armand laughed, unoffended. "You well may be right, madame." He glanced once more at his sister-in-law. "Let me get you something to eat."

Félicité looked toward the line of people waiting to be fed. "Oh, it is too much trouble," she told him.

Armand shook his head. "Nonsense, I have nothing else to do," he insisted, adding with a teasing smile to Madame Hébert. "The woman of my dreams could be watching me at this very minute. I do so want to make a good impression."

The two women laughed like young girls. Armand bowed smartly to them and took his leave. The smile lingered on his face as he made his way through the crowd. The Marchand homestead was prosperous enough, with a sturdy double-house on the levee and several smaller outbuildings around the back. On the river side a broad cypress dock stretched out into the river, providing both easy access to water and a wide storage place for ready-to-ship goods.

Tonight that dock was being used as a dance floor, and a quartet of couples, some in bare feet, others in dancing slippers, were moving with lightfooted exuberance through the movements of the *Lancier Acadien*.

Armand watched them enviously a moment. He loved to dance but rarely did. The young ladies, all of whom had known him since childhood, were always polite and willing, but he could tell that they were less than charmed to be partnered by a man whose stature made him most likely eye level with their bosoms. And of course he felt strange himself. When a fellow pulled a woman close, she was supposed to look *up* into his eyes.

The swirling dancers were like the brightest flower garden in springtime stirred into wild motion. He watched with longing. To be young and in love and dance away the night.

He pushed away the frivolous thought. He knew about being in love. He could not recall with accuracy the day that he knew he loved Aida Gaudet. It was like owning to the day he knew that he loved the river, his family, his life. He felt he had always loved her, even when she was a young girl. And from the first moment in his life that he felt desire, it had been exclusively for her. Her smile, her laugh had entranced him and he had dreamed of her, sighed after her ever since. But he could never have her.

He knew her too well. Aida was sweet and often kind, but she was also giddy and featherbrained. She loved beautiful things, clothes, ribbons, flowers. She surrounded herself with loveliness. It was only natural that the man she would call her own would be perfect.

Armand was clearly imperfect: short and plain and ordinary. And she saw him only as another of the legions that desired her. She no longer flirted with him, of course. He refused to allow it. He might not be special to her, but she was special to him and he would not let their friendship be otherwise.

Once he had wished for her, longed for some magical charm to win her. But it had never occurred. And when Laron declared his intention for her, Armand had put away his hopes completely. She was to be his best friend's wife.

Someday there would be a woman for Armand. He knew that. Someday a shy sweet girl, just as high as his chin, would look up to him as if he were the tallest man in the world. He would be a good and faithful husband, devoted and loving. And perhaps, perhaps eventually, he would forget about Aida Gaudet.

He wished that day would hurry up and arrive. Armand made his way back toward the food tables and cook fires at the far side of the house. The whine of Ony Guidry's fiddle resonated and the voices chatting and visiting were raised loudly above the sound. All around the area of the house, under each tree or open space, gatherings of friends and neighbors flourished.

A circle of farmers was standing together swapping stories amid laughter and guffaws. They could tell jokes from sunset to sunrise with hardly a break for a cup of coffee. Many of the jokes were about Creoles, the other French-speaking people of Louisiana, who were generally disliked and distrusted. Creole ancestors had been nobles or those aspiring to nobility in the West Indies. Acadians were descendants of yeoman farmers, pioneers who sought freedom and egalitarianism. The two groups did not mix well.

Occasionally jokes were told about Frenchmen, who were thought to be much like Creoles. But most often the subject of Acadian humor was the Acadians themselves.

Oscar Benoit called out Armand's name and waved him over to a small group standing near an overgrowth of *lilas*. The man was already laughing as he slapped Armand on the back.

"Tell them that new joke that's going around," he said. "You always tell these things better than I can."

"Which joke?" Armand asked, refusing an offer of tobacco.

"You know," Benoit insisted. "The one about the farmer who called his wife by the mule's name."

Armand shook his head. "I don't know it."

"Oh but you must, you always know them."

Armand shook his head once more.

"Oh well, I must tell it myself."

He motioned for the men to gather around him as

he began. Armand listened eagerly along with the rest.

"The madame was to throw her farmer out of the house," Benoit told them dramatically. "For while they were loving he called her by another woman's name."

The men gathered made collective sounds of humored horror.

"She was furious!"

Many nodded. One of the Acadians whistled in understanding of the seriousness of the mistake. All, along with Armand, leaned closer, grinning in anticipation as Benoit continued.

"The farmer swore he was innocent of any wrongdoing, saying to her that the name was not the name of another woman but only the name of his mule."

A couple of the men snickered.

"So she said she would forgive him, because she knew that he talked to that worn-out old mule all day as he worked. But she told him she thought that it was very strange that he would make such a blunder at such a time."

The group around Benoit nodded in grinning agreement.

" 'But dear wife,' the farmer said to her. 'Your face was turned from me. From that direction any man might have mistaken you for my mule.' "

Hoots exploded from those gathered, but Benoit was not yet finished.

" 'And,' " he continued. " 'I spend a lot more of my life staring at hers than staring at yours!' "

The roar of laughter was nearly deafening. Armand chuckled along with the rest, shaking his head.

"You fellows with your stories of marriage misery are going to rob me of my dreams," he complained.

"If they are dreams of women," Emile Granger shot back quickly, "only death can steal them."

Armand laughed along with the others before continuing on his way.

He noticed a heated quorum gathering. Father Denis was right in the center of the verbal fray and Armand had the good sense to immediately put some distance between himself and the good father. The old priest was bound to try to draw him in and Armand wanted no unpleasantness to ruin his Saturday night.

Finally he made his way over to an old woman sitting in front of a big black cauldron. She seemed almost lost in thought as she stirred the mixture of fish and vegetables in the dark, rich roue.

"Are you cooking up something good for me, *Nanan*?" he asked.

A grown man's use of the childish nickname for godmother might have made another woman's eyes twinkle and another woman's lips curl in a smile, but Orva Landry merely looked up and gazed at him critically.

"You have not been to see me," she said simply.

Armand bowed his head slightly by way of apology. "I did not realize that I was neglecting you," he said.

"I have heard your name," she said, looking at him intently, her rheumy eyes serious and purposeful. "I have heard your name on the water."

Armand was momentarily taken aback.

Orva Landry, some said, was older then the bayou. She was a cold and mostly silent person whom few thought of as a friend. But she was held in great respect by the people of Prairie l'Acadie. Orva Landry was *la traiteur*, the treater.

Born in the place the English called Nova Scotia, she had lived through the Grand Derangement, the time of terror when women had been pulled from their houses, children captured at play, and men herded from the fields. They were forced onto English boats that carried them away from the land they had tended and toiled upon for one hundred and fifty years. All for their failure to swear allegiance to an English king.

According to local legend, Orva, a frightened little child, had been separated from her mother and father, her sisters and brothers, and never saw them again. But as God is often wont to do, when He taketh away He also giveth. Orva Landry was given the treater's gift. Where the young girl, now an ancient crone, had learned the secrets of charms, gris gris, and hoodoo, no one knew. But she could heal both man and beast, had treatment for any ailment, and heard the voice of Joan of Arc speaking to her on the river.

"You have heard *my* name, *Nanan*?" Armand asked, disquieted. Perhaps more than any human on the Vermillion River, Armand Sonnier knew Orva Landry as a person. Therefore he feared her less than most. But he never for a moment doubted her gift.

Armand had been born frail and feeble. He had come into life feet first and too early, and his mother was too weak to properly care for the sickly child.

Armand's father had wrapped his baby son in a blanket, laid him in the floor of the pirogue, and poled down the river to Madame Landry's tiny house.

The old woman tended the child and was credited by one and all for keeping him alive. The Sonniers named her as Armand's godmother and throughout his life he sought her out when he was ill. Armand knew Orva Landry. And if she said she spoke to voices on the river, Armand knew that she did.

"Are you sure it was *my* name that you heard?"

Madame Landry glared at him impatiently. "A human does not get so deaf that she can't hear *the voices* clear," she said gruffly.

Armand apologized. "What do they say, *Nanan*?"

" 'There is uncertainty on the wind,' " she quoted. "Swirling around us now on this prairie is change, unexpected. And you, *mon fils*, you are at the center of it."

Armand's brow furrowed. Although everyone knew that Madame Landry spoke with the revenant specter of Joan of Arc, the saint's name was never mentioned. Superstitious and fearful, people spoke of her euphemistically only as *the voices*. To his knowledge *the voices* had never before spoken his name. It was disconcerting even to think that they knew it.

Armand shook his head thoughtfully. He knew of nothing, no one, with whom he was in conflict. He glanced around the gathering. His gaze paused momentarily at the little irritable-looking crowd speaking with Father Denis. Perhaps the trouble was there.

"Did they mention Father Denis?" he asked.

"Father Denis!" Orva huffed with disregard. "The voices care not for rich Frenchmen, even those who wrap themselves in robes."

The two spiritual leaders of the Prairie l'Acadie had very little mutual respect.

"Then what can this vision be about?" Armand asked.

The old woman stared at him for a long, thoughtful moment, then nodded in the direction of the river.

"It's about her," Madame Landry said quietly.

Armand turned in the direction she indicated just in time to see the most beautiful woman on the Vermillion River alight from her father's pirogue. Her dress swirled around her like a pool of lilies in a summer breeze and her voice was as cheering as music on the water. The music had ceased as if by design. Laughing and lovely, she had every eye upon her.

A twinge of shock stilled Armand's body and he involuntarily swallowed.

"It's about Aida Gaudet?"

The old woman didn't answer immediately but continued to study Armand.

He felt the heat rise to his cheeks. She couldn't know. He was sure of that. Madame Landry couldn't know how he felt about Aida.

"What about her?" he asked quickly.

Orva tutted in disapproval and continued to stir her brew. An uncomfortable silence dragged between them. Armand waited.

"A careless word spoken is like a tree falling into a mighty river," she told him finally. Raising her chin, she looked him straight in the eye. "Most times the tree merely lies to rot and be swept away. But sometimes when the water is low and the yonder bank delicate, the river will swirl around the tree with some force, wear away the weak side, and cause the flow to meander in a new direction."

"What are you saying, *Nanan*? That a careless word of mine has changed the destiny of Aida Gaudet?"

Madame Landry nodded as she lowered her gaze to the boiling pot of aromatic gumbo. "She will not wed the young Boudreau," she said quietly.

Armand was surprised. He remembered speculating to Laron that if he married a woman he did not want, he would be miserable. Could it be that Laron would take his words seriously? Armand found the thought lightening his heart. But he rallied against the wishfulness. Separating Aida from Laron would not turn her in his direction. Aida was flighty and carefree. She liked handsome, dashing men, and Armand was forever short and plain. But he hoped Aida would find a husband whose heart was not engaged elsewhere.

"I find that news not disquieting, but welcome," he told the old woman.

She huffed in disapproval. "Well, perhaps you should not," she said. "Altering the fate of one alters the fate of all."

He knew the admonition was true. Laron could never marry the German widow, of course. And they could have no legitimate children. But he would be a good man to her, loyal and true as any husband, and even a fine father to the little ones she had. Those would all be positive things. Armand could not see any bad consequences. Of course, there was the jilting.

"What about Aida Gaudet?"

Orva nodded approvingly as if she could see his thoughts coming full circle. "Soon she will cast her heart in a new direction," the old woman said.

"And in what man's direction will that be?" he asked.

Madame Landry ceased her stirring and slathered a helping of the broth and fish on a large piece of bread in a wooden trencher. "This is for your sister-in-law, isn't it?" she said. "She should eat, she will need her strength."

He accepted the dish, but continued to watch his godmother curiously.

"Who is the new man for Aida Gaudet?" he asked more forcefully.

Orva Landry raised her eyes to meet his gaze directly, but her words failed to satisfy his curiosity. "Someone I am sure that you would never suspect."

From the moment Aida stepped upon the Marchands' dock, she was determined to have a wonderful time. She did not immediately see Laron and she would not deign to cast her glance into the crowd for him. She knew that he must be there and that he was undoubtedly looking at her.

It was Monsieur Marchand himself who helped her from the pirogue. Her wooden sabots scattered behind her in the boat as she attempted to slip her dancing slippers from her sleeve. She was certain that she had put them right there, but inexplicably she could not locate them.

"I've been hardly able to hold my feet still since the last bend in the river," she confessed breathlessly to her host. "If I could just lean on someone strong like you while I hurry into my slippers . . . where *are* my slippers?"

Somehow the prized kid dancing shoes had disappeared in the sleeve of her gown, and with her other arm completely inside the covering of its opposite, she could not locate them.

"Where on earth . . ."

"I believe, mamselle," Monsieur Marchand said gallantly. "That perhaps they are in the left rather than the right."

"The left?"

She glanced down and could clearly see the telltale bulge in the other sleeve.

"Oh, they *are* here!"

Aida laughed gaily, as if it were a good joke, and amazingly, the gentlemen laughed with her.

"Indeed yes, mamselle," Emile Marchand agreed, holding himself very tall and straight. "It is an honor to be your champion."

Aida giggled as if the older man had said something quite clever and then braced herself against him as she bent to put on her shoes. To her surprise she found a gentleman at her feet.

"Monsieur Sonnier?" Her eyes were wide with feigned confusion. "It is very polite to bow to a lady, but it is not necessary to drop to one's knees."

Jean Baptiste laughed delightedly. "You tease me, Mademoiselle Gaudet. Your humble servant wishes only to offer assistance."

He took Aida's red slippers from her and placed one on each small foot as she leaned upon the sturdy shoulder of Monsieur Marchand.

"Thank you very much, gentlemen," she said when she was properly shod and standing unassisted once more. "You are both too kind."

"I am not too kind to ask a reward, mamselle," Jean Baptiste told her.

"A reward?"

"When the music starts up again, could an old married man beg a dance with the loveliest lady present?" he asked.

Aida batted her eyelashes at him. "Oh monsieur, I do hope that Madame Sonnier doesn't hear you say such a thing."

Jean Baptiste laughed lightly. "My good wife would never dispute the truth."

Aida batted him lightly on the sleeve with her guinea feather fan as if to scold him for his words. "All right, monsieur, I must risk your lady's wrath, for I fear I have no other partner," she told him.

He offered his arm and led her out among the dancers. They joined three other couples in a set. As soon as they took position, the music began once more as if Ony Guidry had been waiting just for them.

Aida curtsied to Jean Baptiste and he bowed to her. She turned and did the same to Pierre Babin, who was partnering his sister Ruby. The couples and corners of the square clasped hands and the intricate steps of the dance began.

Aida followed the well-learned steps and spins and turns and bows with natural grace. She did not have to think about the dance, the movements came to her as easily as a smile.

Jean Baptiste was an excellent dancer and he was tall and looked good beside her. But the man she expected beside her was not. As she circled backward in a handclasp with the other girls, she spotted Laron in the crowd. His face was visible for only a minute, but she knew that he was watching her. When she turned back to Jean Baptiste, she deliberately flirted with her eyes and giggled prettily at him.

A little tinge of jealousy wouldn't hurt her fiancé one bit.

When the music ended she laughed gaily and applauded as if Guidry's music wasn't just exactly as squeaky and slightly off-tune as last week and the week before.

Giving Jean Baptiste a nod of dismissal and the little half-smile that hid her chipped tooth, Aida grabbed Ruby's arm and pulled the girl close to her, giving her a gentle hug.

"*Comment ça va*, Ruby?" she asked. "How are you?"

Ruby accepted the hug with enthusiasm and smiled with shy delight at being noticed.

"I'm fine," she answered politely. "And how are you?"

Aida answered positively and waved away Ruby's awkward younger brother. "You go on, Monsieur Babin," she told Pierre. "Your sister and I have lots of girl talk and gossip to catch up on."

He gave a sigh of relief and nodded gratefully, hurrying away as if in fear that Aida might change her mind. She did not. She smiled warmly at Ruby.

"Don't you look sweet tonight!" she said.

Ruby's face nearly glowed.

In fact Ruby did not look sweet at all. Thin to the point of emaciation, her features were so sharp and pointed, they gave the appearance of meanness. Ruby Babin was one of the least attractive women on the Vermillion River. Perhaps if she had been witty and clever, or sweet and lovable, that would not have been a problem. But Ruby was none of those things. At the age of twenty-two she was an old maid. Her mother despaired of ever finding her a mate and her brother spent an inordinate amount of his own youth escorting her around.

It was all so unfair, Aida thought. Ruby was hardworking, often kind, and always dutiful. She deserved to have a husband and family as much as any other woman.

Aida couldn't give her that, but she could give her a bit of opportunity. Men swarmed around Aida like bees finding the last flower of summer. She could dance with only one at a time. And she wasn't interested in any of them. So she made it a point to share them with Ruby.

Another women might have kindly offered a short prayer in Ruby's name, but Aida was a young woman of action. If another person was starving and you had bread, you did not pray that they would get some, you shared with them what you had. Why would having an abundance of gentlemen be any different?

"How was your week, Ruby?" It was a question that neighbors always asked one another and Aida had found that it often set the other person to gabbing.

"Mama's felt real good. That tea you sent her has kept away those awful flashes of heat," Ruby answered. "And my little hen laid for me every day. Those are the best chickens I ever had."

Aida smiled. Ruby was no better at conversation than she was at anything else. Fortunately the two were both comfortable just to stand and smile at each other and let those around them lead the talk.

The would-be beaux had gathered eagerly. They treated Aida as what she was, the most beautiful woman present. The fact that she was engaged didn't deter their interest. Why should it? Her fiancé never showed even a speck of jealousy.

As the sets began reforming, Aida was snapped up by one of the quickest of the young gallants. One of the less hasty brethren politely requested Ruby's hand.

Aida danced with deliberate delight, refusing to allow herself to become annoyed. Laron always waited until well into the dancing to claim his chance with her, and although they were betrothed, he never danced with her more than twice. The fact that Laron was so considerate of her reputation was noted favorably by the old gossiping women. Aida herself would have flaunted convention. Laron was, by far, the best dancer. It seemed grossly unfair that she should not dance with him as long as she cared to. At least, she told herself as she was partnered adequately by Placide Marchand, one of the host's younger sons, Laron wasn't dancing with anyone else.

Aida danced and laughed and giggled with Ruby through several sets. She was nearly breathless and glowing when Ignace Granger, a young man of not quite twenty, led her to the food tables.

If there was anything that Acadians appreciated more than music and dancing, it had to be food and coffee. Monsieur Granger passed her plate along the table and it was soon piled high with rice and roux and vegetables.

Aida's eyes widened with delight as it returned to her.

"Oh monsieur," she scolded playfully. "Do you wish to fatten me like one of your fine cows?"

"Impossible, mamselle," he assured her. "Such beauty as yours could never be marred."

On the other side of the table Estelle LeBlanc snorted in disgust. "Never heard yet of a woman who didn't get fat when she married or loose her looks with old age," the woman declared.

Young Granger was momentarily struck dumb by the comment.

"A bright young man would pick a woman for her worthiness as a helpmate and housekeeper," Madame LeBlanc continued haughtily. "Aida, your poor father declared earlier at this very table that you forgot completely to cook for him today. And he confessed to us that he often finds dishes half-washed and beds half-made, and claims that since the death of your mother, no pot of beans has ever been cooked in your home without scorching."

Aida flushed. The teasing of the young men, the outrageous compliments were fun and a frivolous pleasure. The reality of her featherbrained ways was forever her cross to bear. She tried to remember things, to do things right, to stay with one task until it was done. But always her mind would wander and her work would be left unfinished and her beans burning over the fire.

"I feel very badly about Poppa," she admitted, accepting a huge slice of bread from the woman. "I wish I were a better daughter. He deserves better, I know."

The woman huffed, still disapproving. But Aida knew that it was difficult to continue a disagreement if one person resisted the impulse to disagree.

At that moment Father Denis approached the table,

in the middle of what seemed to be a heated argument with Oscar Benoit and Clerville Pujal.

Aida welcomed a chance to slip away from the table and Madame LeBlanc. Plate in hand, she headed for the leafy overhang of the *lilas*. Her eyes searching the crowd for Laron, she was startled when she bumped into a figure in the tree's shadow.

"Oh pardon!" she cried, startled.

"It is my fault," he apologized.

Aida turned to find herself eye to eye with Armand Sonnier. Like nearly everyone else on this prairie, she had known Armand Sonnier all her life. They had grown up together. Aida remembered him being ill much of the time as a boy.

"Any day that child could sicken and die," she had once heard one of the old women say.

Aida had been stunned and frightened at the prospect. Her mother had died, though Aida hardly recalled it. One day she was there and the next not. Father Denis said that her mother had gone to a better place, and at four years old Aida had accepted that. But when the little brown-faced calf had been killed in a drowning bog, she had been inconsolable. She'd cried for a week. How much more it must hurt, she surmised, to lose a friend than an animal. From that day forward, she had always run to Armand first, eager to assure herself that he was well and strong and that she would see him again tomorrow.

After he grew out of his poor health and joined the other young men in fun and frolic, Aida had tagged behind and pestered him. He was clever and funny and patient with her. Although she was rather silly

and not smart, he treated her kindly, as if he really
liked her. He was not big and brawny, but he always
took up for her when she was teased. He was quietly
her champion. Her smile brightened at the sight of
him.

"Monsieur, I did not see you here," she said.

He nodded. "I'm sure you did not."

Armand Sonnier, looking fashionable and elegant
in black Creole trousers and a long blue coat, stood
privately in the darkness of the chinaberry tree. He
had once been her hero. Now he was only the best
friend of her fiancé.

"Are you avoiding your escort?" he asked.

"What? Oh no, I mean . . . I forgot about Monsieur
Granger," she admitted as she raised her generously
laden dish, offering him samples of the dinner fare.
"Would you care to join me? I am hiding from the
matrons at the table. They find fault with me tonight."

"And why is that?" Armand asked, taking only a
tasty corner of roux-soaked bread.

Aida shook her head shamefully. "My poor father
arrived here hungry once more. I cannot seem to
remember to cook for him."

"Perhaps each morning you should tie three strings
upon your fingers," he suggested. "And when all are
gone at the end of the day, you will know that you
have fed your father adequately."

"That might work," she agreed with a little giggle.
"If only I could remember where I keep the string."

They ate together companionably for several minutes. Armand devoured the crawfish and cabbage
while Aida merely picked at the capon pasties. It felt

strangely intimate; his long, sun-bronzed hands choosing juicy tidbits from her plate, the warmth of his nearness, the scent of soap from his hair. Aida began to feel a sort of vague discomfort, as if her bodice had suddenly become too small. She glanced over at the man beside her. The familiar blue eyes were not recognizable in the dim light of the distant torches, but Aida could feel the heat of them upon her. Her heart seemed to catch in her throat. There was something distinctly disconcerting about being able to look a man straight in the eye. There was something distinctly disconcerting about standing this close to Armand Sonnier.

Thankfully he stepped away and Aida released the breath she hadn't realized she was holding.

"Are you enjoying the *fais-dodo*, monsieur?" she asked, suddenly desperate to fill the gaping silence between them.

"Of course, mamselle," he answered. "Although no one ever seems to enjoy themselves as much as you."

The words were slightly sharp, hinting at disapproval. Armand Sonnier had once been her champion, but he was that no more. Four years ago he had changed, or rather she had. She had stopped being a child. Her waist slimmed down and her figure blossomed. And the people of Prairie l'Acadie all began to look at her.

The boys who had formerly ignored her were suddenly drawn to her presence like flies. The men shook their heads appreciatively and chuckled. The women clucked and whispered behind her back. Aida had changed. And when she did the world changed around her, including Armand Sonnier.

He decided that he no longer liked her. She knew the exact day, the exact hour when it happened. It had been at the Tuesday Ball when she had just turned fifteen. Armand and Laron had both been *cavaliers masqués* and had spent the day running *Mardi Gras* from house to house collecting chickens, guineas, and provisions for a supper of rice and gumbo. The food was "purchased" by the singing of songs, and payment always included a "glass of encouragement" for the riders. By the time of the ball the two young men were tired, laughing, and more than a little inebriated.

Aida had been excited about the ball. She had a new dress in vivid blue with bright rose piping. It was a woman's dress and Aida felt like a woman for the first time. She had laced her vest corset as tightly as breathing would allow. That made her small waist appear incredibly narrow and her new budding bosom seem positively robust.

She could hardly wait for Armand to notice her. In fact she didn't wait. She caught up to him on his way to the barn.

"Good evening, monsieur," she called out to him. Aida was delighted to be "too grown up" to use his given name.

She placed her hands on her hips and raised her shoulders slightly. She'd discovered in her glass that such a pose showed off her new figure to best advantage.

Armand turned, a smile already on his face, as if he had recognized her voice. Then the smile faded. As a silly scatterbrained girl, he had thought her amusing. But in that moment, he had seen her as a woman.

And clearly a foolish one. Aida had frozen in embarrassment.

It was as the old women said. A silly brainless woman did not appeal to a serious man. Aida had flaunted her body at him, thinking to impress him with her feminine curves, to capture the attention from him that she so easily drew from others. She deserved his punishment, which was the loss of his friendship.

He looked at her now as he had then. And she felt his rejection just as keenly. It was as if she had offered herself and been found wanting. His cold words chilled her. Humiliation darkened her cheeks.

"Yes, mamselle," he said. "You seem always to enjoy yourself more than anyone else."

"There is no sin in laughing and dancing, monsieur, even Father Denis does not believe it so," she said, raising her chin in challenge before firing back. "But perhaps you are more priest than he."

She watched his jaw harden and knew her shot had wounded. "I am no priest."

"Then why do you never dance?"

His gaze narrowed with displeasure.

"Perhaps there is no one with whom I'd care to dance."

It was a direct cut.

"I love to dance no matter the partner," she retorted, lightly. "I am always willing to have fun with my friends and family."

"So I see," he said. "Another woman would save such frolic for her fiancé."

His criticism was unfair and she did not like it. Laron was the one reluctant to dance, not she. She would stay on his arm all night long if he permitted. But he showed no inclination.

"Monsieur Boudreau does not mind that I enjoy myself," she said.

"No, he does not," Armand agreed. "But a young woman who is so silly-minded that she can lose her shoes, her gloves, her hair ribbons, even her prayerbook, might discover that with such behavior, she can lose her fiancé as well."

Aida's pride was crushed at his words, she felt her eyes well with tears, and she turned her back to him.

"You are in a foul mood, monsieur," she said. "Perhaps I should take my leave."

A moment of uncomfortable silence fell between them.

"My humble apologies, Mademoiselle Gaudet," he said at last, sounding sincerely regretful. "Indeed, I am cross and unkind. You look lovely and have every right to enjoy yourself."

He thought she looked lovely.

"Thank you, monsieur," she replied. "I will leave you to your privacy then."

He gave her a slight bow.

Without another word she hurried away from him and into the crowd. His words disturbed her. His anger hurt her. Why did she feel so wonderful and comfortable with him and so miserable and uneasy at the same time? Why could they not be friends as they once had?

Aida did not seek her laughing companions or the gentlemen with the lavish compliments. She was looking for Laron Boudreau, the man to whom she was promised to wed.

He did not love her. She knew he saw her as only a trophy that he had won. But he wanted her, he admired her, and she would make him love her. She had to. She wanted love so much, and she was going to put her mind to getting it, starting now.

Laron was standing alone near the dance floor when she found him. It was all she could do not to throw herself in his arms.

"Good evening to you, mamselle," he said with vague formality. "Would you care to dance?"

She nodded and felt a little better. Her fiancé liked and approved of her. And it was her fiancé that she had to please—no one else.

Laron was a perfect partner for her. Tall and strong, he stood handsomely beside her. Work in the hot Louisiana sun had hardened his thick, masculine chest and darkened the tone of his skin. His jet-black hair was pulled tightly into a queue that hung down in back in one thick, perfect curl.

Gratefully Aida took his arm and he led her into a forming set.

She noted that as usual his manner of dress was as unstylish as her father's. Rather than the trousers and *bretelles* popular with many of the younger men, Laron dressed in traditional knee-length *culotte* and Acadian shirt and jacket. She would have preferred more fashionable costume, but at least the man's bare leg was well-curved and attractive. She glanced toward him as the circle joined hands. His dark eyes shone brightly in the torchlight and his smile gleamed pearly and white. He was big and handsome and darkly masculine. Exactly the sort of husband that she should wed. And as he led her through the steps of the dance, he smiled at her with appreciation, but nothing more.

Unlike his friend Armand, Laron had never paid her much regard as a child. And even when courting her and since they became affianced, Laron showed little interest in her habits or even her interests. Perhaps he thought she had none. But that would change, she assured herself. Once they were wed and living together, he would grow to appreciate her, to love her. Surely he would. Especially if she could remember to cook three times a day. Maybe she would try the string trick.

As the set completed and he took her arm to lead her from the floor she whispered to him under her breath, "I must speak with you."

"Certainly," he answered. "I will bring you coffee."

"No, I must speak to you privately," she insisted. "Let's walk away from the light."

He raised his eyebrows. "You cannot leave the dance with me." His tone was scandalized. The Boudreau family was known to be sticklers when it came to rules and conventions. But, Aida thought to herself, a man who would carry on a not-so-secret affair with a married woman should be a little less rigid.

"We are engaged, Laron," she told him firmly. "No one will think anything of a moment alone."

Truthfully, Aida could think of little she wanted to say to Laron; her mind was whirling with the sound of Armand's words in her ears.

"We will slip away quietly," Laron agreed, but he didn't look happy about it.

They walked silently toward the riverbank and then disappeared around a curve. Most of those present did not even notice.

Aida walked beside him in silence and tried to gather her thoughts. All she could think to say were the benign phrases that she always said. Oh monsieur, you are too kind. Oh monsieur, you flatter me so. Oh monsieur. Oh monsieur. Giggle. Giggle. These words were not conversation and they were not what she needed to say.

Laron stopped abruptly. She looked up at him in question.

"This is my pirogue," he said. "If someone finds us here I can say that I was bringing you here to see it."

His concern with the proprieties miffed her slightly. It was almost as if he was afraid that through some breach of etiquette he would be forced to actually marry her. Another man might be trying to get her alone so that they would have to hurry to wed. Even Armand Sonnier didn't shrink from talking to her in the solitary shadow of a tree.

Deliberately Aida reminded herself that his hesitation to be alone with her, trying to kiss her or flatter her, was a quality that she liked. It meant that he was not completely overwhelmed by her beauty. It meant he might appreciate her.

"Poppa and Father Denis told me to speak with you," she blurted out.

He stared at her for a long moment. "And?" he said finally.

"They are ready for us to set a wedding date."

He nodded slowly. "And when would you like to wed, mamselle?" he asked softly.

"Oh, I . . . I am ready when you are ready," she insisted quickly.

"Yes, well then we should do it soon."

"Soon? How soon?"

"You are hesitant?" he asked, seeming surprised.

"I was hoping that we would . . . that perhaps we would have time to get to know one another."

Laron chuckled. "I have known you all of my life, of course. You are no different today than a week before, are you?"

"Certainly not." She had no idea what further to say. Fortunately, he did.

"But like yourself, I am much in favor of long engagements. It has only been two years and you are still so young."

"Yes," she agreed quietly. Her heart was hammering like a drum. "What should I tell them?" she asked.

"Tell them . . . tell them you wish to wed in spring," he said.

"The spring?" Aida was stunned. The spring was not soon at all. "Should . . . should we wait until spring?"

"I think that we must," Laron said. "Do you not want a pirogue decorated in flowers for your wedding procession?"

"Oh that would be lovely," Aida agreed.

"Flowers are only available in the spring. All women want a pretty pirogue. It is a thing a woman remembers her whole life long," he said. "Surely the most beautiful of women must have the most beautiful pirogue."

She didn't want a decorated pirogue, she didn't

need a memory of it her whole life long. She wanted to be married, to simply be Madame Boudreau. To be valued for herself as a person. But she didn't know how to tell him that. She thought of the German widow.

"Nothing will have to change in your life when we marry, monsieur," she said. "Nothing."

He looked at her curiously, puzzled.

"Of course nothing will change," he answered. His words softened and he took her hand in his. "I will still be the lucky young man who captured the heart of the most beautiful woman on the Vermillion River."

Aida's heart sank and the taste in her mouth was bitter.

"We should—" she began.

A sound in the brush behind them startled them both. Laron pushed Aida protectively behind him. Bears and wolves were rare on this prairie but not impossible. Pirates, wild Indians, and escaped slaves were just as rare, but equally dangerous. And Laron was not carrying his gun.

Both sighed with relief that was close to laughter as Jean Baptiste stepped onto the bank.

Sonnier was almost more surprised to see them than they were to see him.

"Pardon," he said hastily. "I was . . . taking a walk."

Obviously embarrassed at being caught by a female on his return from answering nature's call, he moved to make a hasty retreat. Laron called out to him.

"My friend, could you escort Mademoiselle Gaudet back to the dance," he said.

Aida looked up at him, surprised.

"I must travel upriver tonight," he told her. "It is late already. I have only stayed this long that I might dance with you."

"But—"

"I will dream every night of the sight of you, my bride, riding in a pirogue of flowers," he told her, laying a feather-light kiss upon her knuckles.

She nodded slowly. "It must be spring then." Her tone was flat.

"Good, then that is settled," Laron said. "It is time that I head out. Monsieur Sonnier, if I might trust this lady's safety to your arm."

Jean Baptiste bowed with such enthusiasm that Aida managed a natural smile at him. He was safe. She didn't mind taking his arm.

As they walked toward the sounds of music in the distance, Aida heard, rather than saw, Laron boarding his pirogue. He had dutifully danced his one dance with her. He didn't want to marry *her*. He wanted to be married to the most beautiful woman on the Vermillion River. And he didn't even want to do that until spring, he said. In spring he would be suggesting the fall. In fall, the spring once more.

He was heading upriver. As he did every Saturday night, for a no longer so secret rendezvous.

He hadn't said, and she would never admit that she knew. But without question, he was heading upriver to see the German widow.

Trois

The distance between the *fais–dodo* at the Marchands' and the homestead of the German widow was significant. But Laron poled the pirogue with enthusiasm. Up the wide Vermillion to tiny Bayou Tortue, guided by the light of the moon on the water to the lonely, desolate outpost of the woman he loved.

The spring, Laron thought to himself. He would wed in the spring. He hoped the good father and Aida's poppa would accept that. He could hardly blame them if they did not. Two years was a very long engagement indeed. If he was very lucky he could hold off his marriage until spring. But no later. In spring he would be the husband of Aida Gaudet.

Aida Gaudet. He shook his head as he thought of her. She was so pretty, too pretty. It was that prettiness that had originally attracted him. That, and the sense of challenge. All the men on the river wanted her, but Laron had been the one to make the catch. And what had he caught? He wasn't sure that he knew.

Laron had no illusions about the beautiful Mademoiselle Gaudet. He had no real interest in her, either. But she was to be his wife. He knew appealing to her vanity was the way to delay the wedding. She couldn't resist the image of herself in a pirogue bedecked with flowers poling to the church, with every man, woman, and child on the river watching with awe from the bank. In the spring, almost certainly, he would be forced to go ahead and wed her. And in the spring when that happened, he was also certain that he would no longer be welcome on this bayou.

Up ahead he could see the glow of light from the Shotz cabin. It was a welcoming sight, one he was hoping for. He hadn't told her to expect him, of course. He never said when he was coming or going. It was not their way to speak of it. But then perhaps that was because in the beginning, it was not their way to speak. In fact, in the beginning, they could not speak. Helga's French had been minimal and Laron knew not one word of German. Some things did not require talk.

Laron eased his pirogue next to her dock in the darkness without even bumping against the wood. However, the minute his foot creaked upon the cypress boards, he heard stirring from inside the house.

The curtain covering the doorway was thrown back and a pair of small bare feet hurried down the planking.

"*Oncle! Oncle!*" a tiny voice called out in French. "You are home at last."

Jakob Shotz threw himself in the direction of Laron Boudreau, confident that he would be caught, and he was.

"*Tout-petit!* You should be abed already," he told the child.

The little boy rewarded him with a wet baby kiss right on the mouth.

"I was in bed," the little one said in flawless French. "But I was not asleep. I'm a big boy and don't get sleepy."

"You are getting big," Laron agreed as he secured the child upon his hip. "I'm not sure if I can carry you and these provisions as well."

The little boy's eyes widened appreciably as Laron retrieved the heavy weighted sack from the pirogue.

"What did you bring me?" he asked excitedly.

Laron feigned confusion. "Bring you?"

"What did you bring me? What did you bring me?"

Laron laughed as he began walking toward the house, sack over his shoulder, child in his arms.

"What did I bring you?" Laron repeated the question. "Hmmm. Muskrat hide?"

"No, no." The little boy shook his head. "Something else."

"Haunch of venison?"

"No, no, something else."

"A pound of coffee?"

"No, no *Oncle*, it must be for a boy," Jakob explained.

"Oh for a boy!" Laron exclaimed with the appearance of sudden understanding. "Then it must be the sweets I brought."

"Sweets?" The child's eyes were wide as he licked his lips.

"Pralines," Laron answered. "My sister made them, and she makes the best ones on the river."

"Pralines!" the little boy called out. "He's brought pralines!"

Laron laughed at the child's enthusiasm. He

glanced up to the porch. In the doorway stood a young girl of eight. Her long blond braids hung down on either side of her head; her blue eyes were bright with excitement.

"*Bonsoir, princesse,*" Laron said to her, bowing low and feigning a threat of dropping the little fellow in his arms. "How is Her Majesty on this lovely moonlit night?"

Elsa giggled and offered a curtsy in reply. "As well as any girl might be when she has two brothers," she answered as she drew aside the doorway curtain. Laron followed her into the cabin. The interior was fragrant with the scent of tarragon, thyme, and burning tobacco. "One of my brothers is a baby and the other a brute," Elsa announced.

"I am not a baby!" Jakob protested loudly.

The twelve-year-old *brute* sitting on the floor next to the smoldering hearth did not dispute her. He was looking faintly bored and tapping a corncob pipe.

"Hello, Karl," Laron said. "Have you taken up smoking?"

The boy didn't get a chance to answer; his sister did it for him.

"He's smelling up the whole house with that thing. It makes me sick!" she complained.

"Dumb girls get sick at everything," he replied.

"I never hardly ever get sick!" his sister shot back.

"Then my smoking shouldn't bother you."

"Men usually smoke on the porch," Laron told him in a tone so factual it was free of any hint of reproach or even suggestion.

Laron turned his gaze to the far side of the room and made immediate eye contact with the lady of the house. Helga Shotz stood before the table, which was piled high with cowpeas being sorted for drying. Her dark blond braids were twisted like heavy ropes across the top of her head. The plain blue dress of Attakapas homespun she wore matched her eyes. The bell-gathered skirt, which only partially disguised the width of her hips, was covered with an apron of sunbleached cottonade. Helga was a large, sturdily built woman of thirty-one years. With strong features, broad shoulders, ample proportions, and an abundance of feminine curves, she would never have been described as pretty or dainty by any man. Laron Boudreau knew her to be beautiful.

He nodded to her slightly in greeting. She replied likewise.

"I have brought you supplies, Madame Shotz," he said.

"We are very grateful, Monsieur Boudreau," she answered. Unlike that of her children, Helga's French was heavily accented with the guttural sounds of her native tongue. Some might have found the sound harsh. To Laron it was an intriguing, exciting sound. He found this woman endlessly intriguing and exciting.

Laron crossed the room and moved beyond her to the larder and began stowing the items from his sack. The children near the fireplace were arguing. Elsa was now insisting that her brother should smoke outside. Karl was loudly informing her that he was not her hired man. And little Jakob was warning both that the pralines were meant for him and him alone.

Squatting to reach the lower shelves, Laron turned slightly and surreptitiously patted the ample backside of Madame Shotz.

She slapped at his hand and blushed furiously as he grinned up at her.

"Missed you," he whispered.

"I missed you, too," she answered. "How was the *fais-dodo*?"

"Lonely."

She shook her head as if she didn't believe him. "There must have been lots of pretty girls there."

Laron shrugged. "None of them was you."

Helga blushed with pleasure.

The sounds of the children's disagreement increased in volume. Laron gave a nod in that direction.

"Difficult week?" he asked.

"One of the worst," she admitted.

"Your son is growing up," Laron said.

Helga nodded solemnly. "More than you know."

He finished his unpacking, stowing all the goods he'd brought in their rightful and familiar places. Finished, he stood, taking a long leisurely stretch, his hands nearly high enough to touch the ceilings before he nonchalantly took his place beside her.

"Thank you for the supplies, Monsieur Boudreau," she said. "I do hope you remembered to bring the salt. I am out completely."

"I brought it." Laron leaned forward slightly as if to get a better look at the abundance of pale green legumes with their very black nubs. He whispered quietly into her ear. "Sweet madame, I have also brought something else, much more exciting."

Helga covered her giggle with a hand to her mouth.

Any more conversation was lost as the children's disagreement increased in volume.

"You are mean and hateful!" Elsa declared loudly.

"And you are stupid and ugly!" her brother shot back.

"Mama make him—"

Elsa was not allowed to finish her complaint as her mother held up her hand for immediate silence.

"Enough!"

The three quieted immediately, but her elder children were still looking daggers at each other.

"I think it is time that you went to bed," Helga told the three of them in German. "Monsieur Boudreau is probably tired and he did not bring his boat this long distance to hear children quarrel."

"*Oncle* must put me in bed, no one else," Jakob demanded in French.

"*I* will put you in bed," his sister told him. "It's my job."

Helga nodded. "And you must go right to sleep, my baby," she said. "Remember tomorrow is Sunday, and since Monsieur Boudreau is here, we shall have *beignets* for breakfast."

Little Jakob licked his lips in anticipation and then sighed with acceptance of the good-night ritual. He allowed Elsa to lead him to the loft ladder. The sounds of their feet overhead could be heard before Helga spoke once more to her eldest son.

"You also, Karl. You need your rest as well as the others."

The youngster continue to puff on his pipe. "I am not tired," he said in French. Then in German he added, "And I know exactly why Monsieur Boudreau has traveled in his boat this long distance."

Laron did not understand the boy's words, but from the tone of his voice and the shocked reaction on his mother's face, he knew the comment had been hurtful. She lowered her head not quite fast enough to hide her distress.

He wanted to come to her defense. He wanted to demand to know what was said. He wanted to wash young Karl's mouth out with soap. He wanted to do something. But he didn't know what it could be.

"I brought my cards," Laron piped up, pretending to have missed the undercurrent in the room. "I promised to teach you bourré. If you aren't tired, we can play."

Karl hesitated a long moment. Finally he shrugged. "All right, I have nothing else to do."

Laron pulled out his cards and smiled at Helga. "You go ahead and finish with your work," he said. "We men will do our best to stay out of your way."

She raised her eyes, which still glistened brightly. "Karl has said many times that he wanted to learn the cards," she said, forcing a smile.

Laron nodded and stepped past her.

"Let us go outside," he said to Karl.

"Why?"

"I want to smoke my pipe," he answered. "And I would never offend your mother by doing so inside her house."

Walking outside alone, Laron waited on the porch, wondering if the boy would follow him. The way things were going the last several weeks, he would not have been surprised if the boy was too stubborn to even do that.

It was simply a part of growing up, Laron reminded himself. Karl was young and confused and testing the waters. Boys grew up early in the bayous. And a boy with no father grew up quicker than most.

The youngster did come out to the porch, still puffing enthusiastically on the hand-hewn pipe. They seated themselves on slat-back chairs before a low table.

"Where did you get the pipe?" Laron asked.

"Traded for it," Karl answered.

"Hmmm." Laron nodded with interest.

"The Arceneaux brothers, Jacques and Duclize. I gave them a couple of fine turtle shells."

"Seems like a fair trade," Laron agreed.

"They know you," Karl said, looking at him closely.

Laron raised his eyes to look at Karl directly. "Yes, they are my cousins. They are a little older than you."

Karl shrugged and puffed heavily on his pipe. "I'm old enough," he stated.

Laron didn't argue. "Let us play," he said.

He spread the cards out upon the table and showed him the four suits and identified the face cards. Neither could actually read the printed numbers, but both could adequately count the hearts, diamonds, clubs, or spades printed there.

Laron showed him the trick of shuffling to make the cards stack randomly. As the boy practiced the new skill, Laron lit his own pipe and watched.

After several minutes the boy set the cards in a stack in the middle of the table.

"I'm ready to learn," he said.

Laron nodded. "First the rules," he said.

"All right."

Laron reached across and took Karl by the wrist. His hold was not bruising or confining, merely firm. The boy looked up, startled.

"Rule one," Laron said quietly. "A son does not say things to his mother that make her cry."

Karl's eyes narrowed and his jaw firmed.

The moment lingered, dark brown eyes staring into blue ones. The intensity growing to unbearability before it began to wane.

"I am sorry," Karl said finally.

"You should say that to her and not to me," Laron pointed out.

After a long hesitation the boy nodded.

"Deal."

He did.

An hour later Karl was yawning into his cards and Laron called the game to a halt. When they returned to the interior of the cabin, the boy didn't relight his pipe, but he did sprawl into a chair.

"Aren't you going to bed?" Helga asked him.

"No, I'm still wide awake," he proclaimed, although his eyelids appeared heavy.

Laron and Helga exchanged a disbelieving glance. She shrugged and began bustling, rather tiredly, around the kitchen once more. Laron looked longingly at the comfortable rope-sprung bed in the corner of the room and then turned back with purpose to the boy yawning before the fire.

"I must tell you the story of how my people came to this place," he said.

"I've heard it," Karl answered, his tone sarcastic and bored. "You've spoken of the Grand Derangement many times."

"But it is a story that must be told many times, lest anyone forget."

Seating himself, Laron began to talk. His words were low, almost monotone. Karl, his head propped up on his elbow, feigned listening as the older man spoke at great length about the history of the Acadians.

"As a people we were scattered to the four winds. Exiles in places where our religion was reviled and our citizenship unwanted."

They were the stories Laron had heard all his life, told by parents and elders since the days when he could still find a comfortable perch on an old frail lap. Deliberately Laron left out all the tales involving adventure, danger, and excitement. Those had been his favorites at Karl's age. This night he concentrated fully on the factual and mundane.

He had just gotten to Théophile Peyroux's visit to the Spanish ambassador when the first little snore escaped from Karl's mouth.

Slowly, with big quiet movements, Laron turned to see Helga sitting with her elbow propped on the table. She was hardly able to hold up her own head. But when she saw his face and glanced over at her now sleeping son, she immediately became alert.

Laron grinned broadly, but put a finger to his lips, signaling silence, and pointed to the back door. She nodded and soundlessly the two crept out, keeping a watchful eye on young Karl until they were down the back steps and into the yard.

Laron grabbed her hand and they took off running. They were out of sight of the house when, breathless and laughing, they stopped to catch their breath at the trunk of a hardy old tupelo. "I thought he would never sleep!" Laron told her, chuckling.

Helga was shaking her head. "When you started reciting which boats headed for which ports, I thought I would be snoring first."

Laron wrapped his arms around her and pulled her tight against him. "But I would have awakened you, madame," he said.

He bent his head and leaned down to kiss her. She met his lips with her own. Warm. Eager.

His hands roamed her body.

She pulled at his clothes.

"Love me! Love me!" she begged him.

He did.

The Sonniers' pirogue, crowded with sleeping children and tired adults, bumped lightly into the dock in front of their home very late that Saturday night. Armand held the boat steady with the pole as his brother tied it securely to the cypress posts.

Jean Baptiste squatted on the dock. "Hand them out," he said.

Félicité lifted the baby to him first. The little one was awake and fussing. Jean Baptiste laid him on the wide cypress planks and then stretched his arms toward his wife once more. The two older children were passed into their father's arms. And then, rising to his feet, he assisted Félicité, who was huge and ungainly.

"I'll take care of this," Armand assured them, indicating the now empty cook pot, old tablecloths, miniature sabots, and sack of spare clothing, diapers, and needments required for traveling with little ones. "You two get the babies to bed."

His brother and sister-in-law made their way up the planking toward the house. Jean Baptiste carried Gaston and Marie, who hung like rag dolls from their father's broad shoulders. Félicité carried the baby, Pierre, who was squalling now in earnest. Armand suspected that it was near time for the little fellow to be put at his mother's breast.

He watched their retreating backs for a moment and then returned his attention to collecting the cargo of the pirogue. The evening had been a long one. He could not quite shake the worry and concern he felt at his godmother's words, despite talking with many other people through the course of the evening. At one point Armand had sought the solitude of the big chinaberry tree and allowed his gaze to wander around the crowd.

As always his attention settled upon Aida Gaudet. He watched her from afar as she laughed and giggled and flirted with every male still breathing.

Madame Landry had said that Armand's words were destined to change Aida's life. She would not marry his friend Laron. But then whom would she marry? Clearly she and Laron were perfectly paired. They were equally matched in grace and good looks, and he was head and shoulders taller than she. Her dainty feminine charms enhanced the appeal of his masculine strength. Anyone looking in their direction would note immediately what a handsome couple they made. They looked as if they belonged together.

Were his careless words about to drive them apart? Was his unsolicited opinion about to cause upheaval to people he cared about? And, most disturbing of all, was it his own selfish, unrequited passion that had caused him to speak?

Laron Boudreau was the closest friend he had in the world. Armand wanted what was best for him.

Armand had been thinking himself wise and helpful when he'd given his opinion on marriage without love. Wise and helpful. But now . . . now . . .

Armand shook his head furiously at his own conceit. He had urged his friend to give up a genuine opportunity to wed in order to continue an illicit union with a strange foreign woman of low morals. A woman Laron could never marry because she was still the legal wife of another man.

And Aida Gaudet would soon be seeking a new beau.

At first he'd thought this could be a good thing. When she had found her way to his tree-shaded hiding place, his heart had taken up a hurried pace. She was beautiful, of course. But there was more about her, more about Aida, almost a glow that surrounded her. It was what drew men to her side, Armand was sure. Many women had fine figures, handsome hair, and shy beckoning smiles. But Aida Gaudet had some unique indefinable something that seemed always to cheer the heart and brighten the day. And Aida was so guileless and uncomplicated, she remained unaware of the real source of her attraction.

Armand was not unaware. She was like the warm glow of an autumn fire, hard for any man to resist.

"Someone I'm sure you would never suspect."

Orva Landry's words, when he'd asked whom Aida would set upon for a new romance, now had an ominous ring. Aida Gaudet was a beautiful and desirable woman. But if she were not safely bound to Boudreau, she would surely seek out another man. And because she was not very bright, her choice might well be an unwise one.

It was just as he had told Laron; Aida would choose a man the same way she chose cloth, for the prettiness of its aspect rather than the durability of the fabric. Laron was the best-looking young man on the river, but here in Prairie l'Acadie, Armand knew what man might well come in second place.

The image of his brother Jean Baptiste kneeling at her feet helping with her shoes came to his mind.

"It was nothing," Armand muttered to himself. A still, frightening coldness settled about his heart. "It was nothing." And indeed it was nothing, helping her with her shoes. A public gesture with much joking or teasing; no one present took it seriously. But then no one present had heard Orva Landry's warning. No one present had heard his brother's dissatisfied complaints about married life.

And with any luck at all, no one present had seen the two of them sneaking back from the privacy of the woods.

With fear distorting his reason, Armand thought of poor Félicité swelled with child. He thought of Gaston and Marie. He thought of little Pierre, gurgling happily as was his nature.

He closed his eyes and swallowed hard against the fear that filled his throat. "Please God," Armand prayed into the quiet stillness of the Louisiana night. "Please don't let this be happening."

Armand hadn't seen them leave. He'd turned away from the sight of the festivities when Laron had swept her into the dance. They were such a handsome couple. It hurt him to look at them. He made his way to a group of men swapping hunting stories, telling jokes. Hippolyte Arcenaux had warned him that Father Denis wanted to speak with him and Armand quickly made himself scarce.

He was near the edge of the woods when he heard

the familiar tinkle of laughter. It had surprised him. Although, as an engaged couple, Laron and Aida would have undoubtedly been allowed an occasional private walk in the moonlight, his friend virtually never took advantage of that privilege.

A movement from the corner of his eye caught Armand's attention. In the distance, out on the river, he spied a man poling his pirogue upstream. He didn't even need to squint to recognize Laron Boudreau. His friend, as on every Saturday night, was on his way to visit the German widow.

Immediately Armand's heart began to beat faster. The man in the trees with Aida Gaudet could not be Laron. It might well be the new man, the man Orva spoke about. The man whose arms Armand's careless words had sent Aida flying to.

As footsteps grew nearer Armand thought to himself, surely it must be Granger. Granger or Marchand, it really didn't matter. He didn't care if it was young Babin or even old toothless LeBlanc.

He saw her first. Aida Gaudet, dainty and dazzling and desirable.

Holding her arm in his own and gazing down at her, blue eyes wide as a lovesick calf's, was his brother, Jean Baptiste Sonnier.

"Please God, don't let it be," Armand said to the silent night.

"Well, it *is* already Sunday, but don't you think you ought to save that for church?"

The words came from behind him. Startled, Armand turned to face his brother.

"I figured you were already abed," Armand told him.

"Thought I'd sleep up in the *garçonnière*," Jean Baptiste said. "If you don't mind me invading your territory."

"You're not sleeping with your wife?"

Jean Baptiste shook his head. "She's so big now and restless. She gets up a half-dozen times a night. I'll get more sleep upstairs in one of the extra beds."

He started up the stairs at the far end of the porch, but turned back toward Armand. "Are you coming up?"

Armand felt momentarily rooted to the spot.

"Yes," he said finally. "Yes, yes, I'm coming."

He hurried up the stair behind his brother. The so-called *garçonnière* was merely the floored space under the eaves of the roof. It was generally used only by young men because it was accessed by the stairs from the porch. The steep pitch of the roof made standing a thing done only in the middle, but the space around the edges was well-utilized by low-lying rope sprung beds.

Normally the room was Armand's alone. Laron stayed with him frequently, as did other young men, neighbors and cousins, when they visited. Even little Gaston had spent a night or two up there. But Armand could not recall his brother spending the night with him since his marriage.

Jean Baptiste picked a bed across the room from his brother. Armand was thoughtful as he readied himself for the night.

"You made quite a scene with Mademoiselle Gaudet," he said finally.

"Helping her with her dancing slippers?" Jean Baptiste chuckled. "It was a bit of fun, wasn't it?"

"It's a good thing that you're married," Armand

pointed out. "Otherwise she might have gotten the wrong idea."

His brother laughed as if the thought were a pleasant one. Stripped down to his smallclothes, he stretched out on the bed and stared up at the roof beams.

"Her feet are just as tiny as you'd expect them to be," Jean Baptiste said thoughtfully. "Dainty and pretty, just like the rest of her. And the scent . . ." Jean Baptiste took a deep breath as if he were breathing it in once more. "I couldn't quite place it. Was it was lilies or roses or . . . or something else?"

"Well," Armand pointed out, "most women smell good."

Jean Baptiste sighed and offered a noise of agreement as he rolled over on his side, punching at the moss-fill pillow to get it just right. Yawning and sleepy, just before dozing off he added, "Félicité smells like milk. I swear she's not going to get the last baby weaned before the next one is here."

Armand lay awake a long time.

Quatre

The rough dark gray bark of the tupelo scratched Helga's backside, but she paid it no notice. Her arms and legs were wound tightly around Laron, but her passion was spent.

They held their position for as long as they could. Eventually the strength of his legs gave way to the waves of relaxation that settled upon him and he eased her feet to the ground.

"Your *drawers*, madame," he said, finding them on the ground and shaking them out before he handed them over. His teasing tone was typical. Acadian women wore no such garment and Laron had declared them to be a needless, silly affectation of clothing.

"Drawers are the fashion now everywhere," she had assured him. "Only the most poor of peasant women would go around with their buttocks unsheathed."

Laron had laughed at that. "With all of the skirts you women wear, I hardly think that you are very close to nakedness."

He had not convinced her to give them up. Instead he teased her relentlessly about wearing them.

"So when did the smoking start?" he asked. "And why on earth is Karl so unwilling to go to bed?"

Helga hesitated momentarily. "The smoking began on Wednesday, I think," she answered. "He came home from fishing and was green as duckweed. The smell of supper had him puking off the back porch."

Laron chuckled and shook his head. "I remember that first time myself," he said.

"I didn't see the tobacco until Friday," she continued. "We had a bit of a row. Or at least he did. I refused to discuss the subject and he lit up very defiantly, as if he were trying to force me to lose my temper."

"You and Karl argued?" Laron seemed surprised.

"He just . . . well, there are things . . . we do not always agree."

His expression slowly changed from confused to amused as he gazed down at her discomfiture.

"*We do not always agree,*" he quoted her. "So you have made your home a democracy these days, madame? The influence of consorting with the Acadian men, no doubt. And I have always thought of you as a very autocratic German empress."

Helga was grateful for his humor. "I still say what goes on under my own roof and you had best not forget it," she told him.

He grinned. "You may have total dominion of the roof, madame, if I may have an equal say under the bedclothes."

She smiled back at him as they reached the porch. "Nothing will go on under those bedclothes tonight, monsieur," she told him. "As long as my son lays in the chair by the hearth, you and I will lie as chaste as nuns."

"As nuns?"

They stepped in through the back door. Young Karl was where they had left him, still sprawled uncomfortably in a chair that was never meant for sleeping.

"Maybe I could carry him upstairs," Laron whispered.

Helga looked up at him. "And if he wakes are you ready to sit until dawn continuing your history lesson?"

Laron made a disagreeable face. Helga stifled a giggle.

Stalling, she silently straightened the items stowed on the kitchen shelves as Laron divested himself and hung his garments on the hook beside the bed. There was virtually no light within the cabin and she couldn't see the man across the room from her, but she didn't need to see him. She knew the width of his back, the length of his thigh, and the breadth of his shoulders with more familiarity than she knew her own life. He was her man and she loved him. She had never meant for that to happen but it had.

The creak of the ropes sounded as he crawled into the bed. She moved toward the sound. He had scooted to the far side and held the blanket open welcomingly. She leaned forward and kissed him on the forehead.

"I must look in on the little ones," she whispered. "Go on to sleep."

He didn't argue as she made her way across the room and up the ladder to the loft. In the dim light seeping through the shuttered window she checked on her son. He slept peacefully on his mat, his sweet blond curls tousled around his head. She squatted down beside him and gently removed the thumb that was tucked so securely in his mouth.

Quietly she made her way to the larger sleeping mat. Elsa, too, was lost in dreamland.

Helga began removing her own clothes and hanging them beside her daughter's. She loosened and undid her braid. Finding Elsa's brush, she began drawing it through her hair, not bothering to count the strokes.

"I know why Monsieur Boudreau travels all this way."

In her heart she heard Karl's words once more. She had never meant for her son to know. She had never meant for it to go on this long. She had never meant—but what had she meant? A simple thank-you. That should have sufficed.

Helga put the brush aside and lay down with her daughter. She was eager to sleep but knew it would not come easily. She listened intently, hoping to hear the snores of her lover. Laron expected her to come to bed. If he fell asleep he would not know that she had not.

She hadn't meant to fall in love with him. She hadn't meant to take him as a lover. She had only been saying thank you to the man who had saved them after her husband deserted her.

Helga closed her eyes, willing sleep, but none came.

She had seen him first on the day Jakob was born. She had been far along in labor when a very frightened Karl had brought him into the house. By his manner of dress she recognized him immediately as one of the Acadians that lived on the river.

"Lazy, worthless people!"

That's what her husband had called them. And Helmut certainly should know lazy and worthless when he encountered it, they were so much his own personal traits.

But this Acadian had proved his value when her child came into the world and into his arms. She remembered those first moments watching him hold her son, cooing to the child and speaking to him in French. She wondered tiredly if the Acadians were like the Gypsies she'd heard stories about. Did they perhaps steal children? Might being stolen possibly be the best thing for Jakob? She wanted what was best for her baby. She wanted what was best for all her children.

It had been less than a year before Jakob's birth that Helmut had dragged them to this place. He had said it was a farm, but it had been only a decrepit hut in the wilderness.

She knew that they must be hiding out. Not she and the children, of course, but Helmut. He must be hiding out again from a judge or a posse or an angry citizen whom he had cheated. Helga had spent much of her life with Helmut hiding from someone. They had lived in a half-dozen places in the strange new country. Helga would settle in, try to start a life, and then it would all be over. Someone would be robbed or cheated and they would hurry away in the dark of night.

But never again. With two small children and one on the way she had said, "No more!" And Helmut Shotz had taken his gun and their stores and merely rowed out of their lives.

It hadn't taken long for Laron Boudreau to realize that they were hungry and desitute. He began to provide for them. He brought salt and flour, meat and game. He taught them to fish and forage and get by in the wet inhospitable climate that was Louisiana.

But she had had things to teach also. He had been an innocent, inexperienced young man of barely twenty. She had taught him to be her lover.

Cinq

Fall was branding time in Prairie l'Acadie. Traditionally all herds, cattle and hogs, were set free on All Saints' Day to winter as they would. For this reason careful marking would ensure that all animals would be returned to their rightful owners when spring was upon them.

Armand loved working the cattle. The horses were well-trained to turn and cut the cows from the herd. As drover, Armand sat high in the saddle, letting the fine bay gelding do the work of separating the animals out one by one.

Then all that was left to do was to throw a lasso around the cow's neck, a skill at which Armand excelled. Once it was roped, Jean Baptiste or Laron or one of the other men who were larger and stronger than he would throw the animal to its side, tie up the legs, and endeavor to keep it still while the white-hot metal of the brand was sizzled into the tough hide of its flank.

A half-dozen men had come at dawn to help with the branding, with more joining them as the day wore on. Friends, neighbors, those who had just needed or would soon need help themselves. The women, as expected, were cooking up a feast to reward them. And children cavorted and played as if the day were a celebration rather than merely hot, hard work.

The Sonnier brothers were considered highly successful cattlemen with a combined herd of nearly a hundred head. They had always worked together since the day their father had gone off to fight with Andrew Jackson to liberate New Orleans. The two boys had stood together at the dock as he packed his pirogue. Jean Baptiste had been twelve, already lanky and tall, his skinny legs still clumsy for him. Armand had been nine, very small and thin, but sturdy, his father insisted. Armand had grown sufficiently sturdy.

Sonnier kissed them goodbye and spoke to them as men.

"It is duty that bids me go," he said. "A man must always follow his duty."

The boys nodded, too young to fully understand.

"It is my duty to go and your duty to stay and care for this farm and for your mother."

"I will, Poppa," Jean Baptiste promised.

"And I can help," Armand assured them both.

He had nodded proudly. "A man is lucky who can count on such sons," he told them. "I trust you to do your duty until I return."

The boys did as he had bid. But he was never to return.

It had been a frightening time and a crushing blow to two young boys. And the grief of their mother had been harrowing to witness. The brothers, who for most of their lives until then had been separated in age and experience and temperament, now clung together solidly to do their duty as they had promised.

They cared for the farm, the land, the herd. And they had dutifully, lovingly cared for their dear maman until the day three years earlier when they laid her for all time in the solemn silence of the churchyard.

Perhaps these experiences made them closer than other brothers. Whatever the reason, the two worked well together in the saddle, cutting and moving the herd with dexterity.

A scraggly young bull slipped around Jean Baptiste's horse unexpectedly and was headed with determination for the safety of the brush. Armand heard his brother's curse and set chase. The young bull had too far a lead for his own horse to cut it off. Skillfully Armand twirled the rope above his head until he was certain of its velocity and threw the looped end true and right around the animal's neck.

There was a cheer of approval as Armand led the bawling angry miscreant toward the branding fire.

"Well done," Jean Baptiste congratulated him.

"We'd best make a steer of this one," Armand suggested. "Or we might not catch up with him next year."

Jean Baptiste considered a moment and then shook his head. "No, I rather admire the ones that try to get away. He'll make us a fine breeder bull in a couple of years."

Armand bowed to his brother's decision, although something about the reasoning bothered him. He returned to his work, only to be distracted a few moments later by the arrival of Aida Gaudet.

She was in the midst of the gathering, laughing and looking pretty and capturing the attention of all the men. Armand doffed his hat and gave her a polite nod, then he quickly looked over at his brother.

Jean Baptiste had ridden up to greet her formally and to look down into her eyes and tease her. Mademoiselle Gaudet was delightfully attentive and giggled several times. Armand felt his entire body tense. He was thinking to speak to her, to distract her, to distract his brother when a movement at the corner of his eye caught his attention.

"Sacré!" he cursed. His nephew Gaston and little Valsin Hébert had moved in close to play a game of "I Am Not Afraid" with the teeming cattle. Armand raced over to scold the boys and scoot the little ones back away from the dangerously unsettled herd.

The drama caught everyone's attention and not a moment later Armand heard his brother's voice raised in anger.

"Madame Sonnier!" Jean Baptiste called out to his wife. "Can you not watch your children?"

Armand turned to see the flushed face of his sister-in-law. She hurried the children back to the relative safety of the cooking women beyond the fires.

Her husband continued to scold and curse as he returned his concentration to the herd. Armand moved closer.

"You should not yell at Félicité, Jean Baptiste," he said for his brother's ears alone. "The boys always want to be near the cattle. We were just the same. Drovers must keep an eye out for that. It was not her fault."

"She is my wife, Armand," Jean Baptiste answered him. "Who else am I to yell at?"

It was not a reasonable answer and Armand kept looking at him.

Jean Baptiste shrugged. "I was frightened," he admitted. "You know I often yell when I am alarmed."

He nodded; it was and had always been his brother's nature to fight fear with anger. "Go easy on your wife," Armand suggested. "Félicité just looks so tired and so . . . so pregnant."

Jean Baptiste chuckled with agreement. "Indeed, she looks like one of the cows. Try not to rope her by mistake."

His brother was still laughing at his little joke as he headed back into the herd. For Armand there was nothing funny about any part of this situation. Jean Baptiste loved his wife; he had always loved her. But this newfound enmity and ridicule was unsettling.

Orva Landry's words of warning echoed in his head. He glanced back toward the crowd by the cook fires once more. Unerringly his gaze found Aida Gaudet. He recalled her smiling up delightedly at Jean Baptiste. She was foolish and naïve, but surely never would she be so unwise as to become involved with a married man.

Even if her fiancé was involved with a married woman . . .

"Armand! Armand Sonnier!"

With a sigh and a heavy heart Armand turned toward the speaker. He dug heels into the bay's flanks and loped over toward the wooded area away from the herd.

"Father Denis," he said, forcing a smile. "How are you this beautiful day?"

Armand eased the horse over to where the fat priest stood and resisted the desire to pull his hat from his head. Father Denis greatly disapproved of men wearing their headgear in his presence. When Armand was a child, the good priest had caned his palms so frequently for that very offense that even now he could feel the burn on the inside of his hands. Deliberately he asserted what Acadian men thought was their right to show deference to God alone and not to the men who merely serve Him.

"I am very well, Armand," the priest answered.

Father Denis was robed in the traditional garb of his order, making no concessions to the humid Louisiana weather. He eyed Armand's hat, still upon his head, with some displeasure, but today he said nothing.

Clasping his hands together before him, he spouted thankfulness that resonated more pompous than prayerful. "I am grateful, this day as every one, to our Most Righteous Father and Blessed Mother for both the state of my health and the fairness of the weather."

Armand gave the priest a wan smile. "That is good to hear, Father," he said.

No one knew what unfortunate alliance or political faux pas had sent a promising young French Jesuit into the Louisiana wilderness twenty years ago. While most of the prairie and backwater parishes made do with the prayers of laywomen and annual visits by a circuit priest, Prairie l'Acadie had been blessed with the constant presence of clergy.

And Armand was more closely tied to him than most since as a boy he had studied both French and Latin with the father. He was kept upon his knees for hours on end. His education was broad and his discipline harsh. It was the priest's assumption that his young charge was being readied for a life in

the church. Nothing could have been further from
Armand's desire. The boy's stubborn rejection of a
monastic vocation and his overwhelming interest in
the secular life had proved a stinging disappointment
to his teacher. Still, the good father considered his
former pupil a useful link between him and the other
parishioners.

"I've been hoping to speak with you about a
concern of great importance to you and the community," Father Denis said. "I have made several inquir-
ies with your friends and family."

"Oh?" Armand feigned ignorance. A lie, however
small, came with difficulty from young Monsieur
Sonnier's lips.

The priest didn't bother to question the younger
man's pretense of ignorance. Armand dropped the
reins of his horse, knowing the well-trained bay
would stand where it was until Armand returned.
With the priest at his side Armand began to walk
away from the boisterous crowd of chattering friends
and neighbors. Away from the dust and heat of cattle
branding.

Father Denis gazed with near-theatrical majesty
into the heavens above them and began a deep-
throated, well-rehearsed oratory. "I have asked myself and my Heavenly Father what work I might
humbly apply myself toward in this parish," Father
Denis continued, "and I believe now at last that my
prayers have been answered."

Armand waited with expectation.

"And do you know in what direction He has led
my footsteps?" the heavily robed cleric asked him.

Armand did not know and shrugged in lieu of

reply. Fortunately Father Denis did not require an answer.

"I have been led in the direction of enlightenment," the old priest said dramatically. "Enlightenment. One of God's finest gifts." He sighed and turned his gaze to Armand once more. "Not my own enlightenment, which I seek unceasingly, of course, but the enlightenment of this parish."

Armand personally considered the parish sufficiently enlightened already, but he kept his silence.

"I inquired meekly of my Lord," Father Denis continued, his voice gaining conviction. "What can I do for these most lowly people? And the answer was sent me in His Holy Writ. Do you know the answer, my son?"

Armand shook his head mutely.

"The children. It is the children."

"The children?"

"Yes, the only way to enlighten this parish, these people, is through the children."

Armand felt a wave of uneasiness settle upon him. "What is your interest in the children, Father?"

"I want to teach them."

The wave of uneasiness became a churning in his stomach. "Teach them?"

"All of them. The way that I've taught you." He paused dramatically. "I want to begin a school."

Armand's jaw dropped in shock. There were schools in Vermillionville and large parishes in towns, but there were no schools among the small farmers of the prairies. There was no need for them.

"We will build a school by the church. All the boys in the parish will come here to learn their letters."

Armand shook his head, gathering his thoughts. It seemed to him that the old priest was going to be mightily disappointed.

"I'm not sure that *all* the families would be interested in schooling," he said.

The old man nodded sagely and patted at nonexistent lint on the length of his robe.

"That is why I have sought you out, Armand," he said. "I have talked to a few of the parents and, as you say, there is some resistance."

Some resistance, Armand thought to himself, was undoubtedly an understatement.

"Many cannot spare their boys for school," he told the priest diplomatically.

Father Denis huffed in disapproval. "Well, they certainly will learn to. We shall *require* that all attend."

Armand's brow furrowed.

"Require them?"

"You are the judge, remember? You can make laws."

It was true. Three years earlier, Father Denis had approached him with a writ from the office of parish governance in New Orleans. According to new laws local citizens could serve the state on the parish level as sheriff, assessor, ward constable, police juror, and justice of the peace.

Armand had not been particularly interested in any job. He felt that as a farmer and cattleman, he had no need for other vocation.

"You are an educated man," Father Denis had told him. "It is your duty to use your knowledge for the good of your people."

He had still been hesitant but had agreed.

Truly it had not been so much to ask. He read and ruled on contracts and wills, negotiated with the state government, and represented his community on matters that concerned them. It was better than letting some Creole sugar planter be appointed to the position.

"You simply file a declaration and compulsory education becomes the law," Father Denis stated proudly. "Then all the boys will be *required* to attend school."

Shaking his head with alarm, Armand disagreed. "I accepted that post to deal with traders and tax collectors," he said. "I am no judge to tell the people what to do with their own farms or with their own children."

"But you *can*," the priest told him. "You have the legal authority to do so. And the moral right."

"But—"

"Every boy between eight and twelve years of age will be obliged to attend during the winter months," Father Denis said. "That will be no great hardship upon anyone and within another generation, every man in the parish will be literate."

It was not an evil intent. Still, Armand could not see himself requiring his friends and neighbors to obey.

"Father Denis, I cannot tell a man how to raise his own children," he pointed out. "I have no children. When I do, I will make decisions for them. Until I do, a parish school is none of my concern."

"It most certainly is," Father Denis insisted. "As the most literate person in this parish you have an obligation and a duty to those around you."

"I have heard this argument before, Father. I help

whoever and whenever I am needed," he said. "I do not see that I am needed here in this."

Father Denis ignored him. "I have talked to several of the fathers already. And I can tell you that I have been shocked and disturbed at what I've heard. It is as if they have no interest whatsoever in education. And they have shown no inclination to encourage the formation of the school."

"Perhaps it is because they don't see the need for a school."

"How can they not see the need? Do they not want better for their sons than they have for themselves?"

"No, they do not," Armand answered. He shook his head and sighed heavily. "Father Denis, how can you have lived among us so long and still not know us?" he asked. "We want our children to have the *same* life that we have. It is a good life. We have our families, our traditions, our homes. We want nothing more."

"What about prosperity?"

"Who needs prosperity when there is balance?" Armand asked. "Two bales of cotton is not enough to sustain a household. But four bales is too big a crop for a family to manage. So we plant three bales. We have enough to live without making life too much work."

"It's God's will that men should prosper," the priest said emphatically. "Your people ask too little of themselves." The expression on the face of Father Denis hardened into displeasure. "I am counting on you, Armand Sonnier, to convince these people that this is America and 1825! In the new world reading and writing are not the province only of priests and aristocrats."

"Father, I am certain that we will always have people like myself to read," Armand answered. "My nephew Gaston has already shown such an interest. I teach him myself. As long as some know, not all need to learn."

"One person to read contracts and write letters is not enough," the priest told him. "Can't you see, Armand, that only by educating these boys can we raise the aspirations of the whole community?"

"I have spoken plainly, Father, that I do not believe our aspirations need to be raised."

Father Denis scoffed in disgust. "You are all *petits habitants*, small farmers, barely scratching out a living. A few cows, a few pigs, and some chickens are all that keep you from scavenging like swampmen."

"We furnish our own needs. No one goes hungry."

"No one goes hungry!" the priest shot back sarcastically. "While all around you the blessings of world are being poured out in excess. There is opportunity here as never before. The world is changing and we must change with it."

"*Our* world is not in great need of change."

"How can you say that? Look at how you live. Your shacks are built with more moss than brick. Your clothing is made from homespun, your medicines rendered from herbs. And your knowledge is little more than superstition."

"It does not seem so bad to me."

"Last month I read in the New Orleans paper that there are more riches and rich men in Louisiana than in any other state in this nation."

Armand sniffed with disdain. "Creoles and Americaines."

"All up and down the rivers, field after field of cane

and cotton. They live in fine houses, wear beautiful clothes, and build magnificent churches," Father Denis said. "And they are able to do that because they have enlightenment."

"Enlightenment?" Armand's tone was dangerous. "Enlightenment! They live in fine houses, wear beautiful clothes and build magnificent churches, Father, not because they have enlightenment, but because they have slaves."

The priest blanched.

Armand's words were low, his eyes flashing with anger. "If enlightenment means the owning of another man, the buying and selling of him like an ox or a mule, profiting from his labor, taking his daughter to bed and seeing the fruit of one's own seed born into a life of chains, if that is enlightenment, then may God curse me forever to darkness."

"Slavery is naturally abhorrent—"

"But the Church does not condemn it," Armand finished for him. "We are poor people, our ways are our own, and we keep to ourselves. But we have our self-respect, and that is what we want most to leave to our children. We have no need for the world beyond and if our descendants never venture outside, so much the better."

Armand turned and walked away. Normally he was a man of even temper, but he was fuming. Twenty years Father Denis had lived here. Twenty years and he still did not understand the first thing about them and their lives. The only thing that mattered, the only thing that lasted, was the ties of family.

The invisible, unbreakable ties of family.

Armand walked back to the cattle herd and retrieved his horse. Most men were dismounted now, standing around the cookstoves, eager for dinner. He spied his brother, laughing and smiling, his talk animated and happy.

His conversant, once again, the lovely Aida Gaudet.

Six

Laron rolled over and immediately reached for the woman beside him. The bedclothes were chilled. He opened his eyes, surprised. The smell of breakfast was already in the air. It was the middle of the week. He did not often visit her then, but today was a special day and there was much work to be done.

Again last night they had waited and waited for young Karl to go to sleep. When he finally had and they had taken to bed themselves, their lovemaking had been strange and strained. Something was wrong, very wrong. Karl was growing up and being difficult. But there was more, much more. And Laron was loath to face up to it.

As morning light filtered into the room, he heard quick footsteps in the loft overhead. The children would be down shortly. He jumped out of the warm comfortable bed and hurried into his clothes. It was a bit of fiction that they portrayed, he and Helga. They never allowed the children to see him in her bed. And therefore they could pretend that the children would never know that the two slept there together.

He was still shirtless and adjusting the knee ties of his *culotte* as Karl appeared on the stairs.

The two looked at each other.

Laron nodded. "I hope you slept well," he said. "There is lots of hard work to be done today."

The boy nodded, rubbing his neck as if it ached.

Laron finished donning his clothing and caught up to Helga at the fireplace. He leaned down to kiss her on the cheek and then grabbed a basket for gathering eggs.

More footsteps sounded on the loft ladder as Elsa and her baby brother hurried into the room.

"Good morning," she said to both of them. "It looks to be another beautiful day. And a good one for rice, I think. Much hard work today will make for full bellies this winter."

The children looked upon the coming day's work eagerly. They knew that they would be working, working very hard. But working together as a family was much preferred over the solitary chores that filled their everyday life.

Buckets and baskets were taken up all around as the man and the children hurried to tend the hens and hogs and the milking before breakfast. Young Elsa rushed to the outhouse alone. The three males stopped in the weeds near the edge of the yard to relieve themselves before beginning their chores.

The morning was a fair one. The chinaberry tree at the north end of the house was already bright yellow, foretelling a coming frost. The distant sky was bright with pink clouds, pretty and predictable.

"It is going to rain tomorrow," Laron told the boys.

He gestured toward the eastern horizon and the boys noted the color.

"A bad storm? A hurricane?" Young Jakob sounded almost excited.

They had reached the bank and as Laron bent to fill his buckets he chuckled and shook his head.

"Just a rainstorm," he assured Jakob. "That will be good to have now before cold weather sets in."

"Why?"

"If the grass is too dry when it gets a heavy frost and then is thawed by warm rains it will rot," Laron explained carefully and with respect. Karl and Jakob might be only boys, but even boys, Laron thought, should expect to be spoken to without condescension. "The pasture needs to be wet when it freezes."

"But the cattle aren't even here," Karl pointed out, his voice questioning and surly.

"They are around somewhere," Laron answered, unconcerned. "And as long as there is grass they will not stray far. Jakob, take this water to your mother. Karl and I will tend to the chores."

The little fellow hurried back toward the house, spilling nearly as much water as he managed to carry. An inordinate amount of smoke was now drifting up from the chimney as Helga started the fire.

She would warm the water for him to shave, she would present clean clothes for him to wear, and she would fill his belly with good hot food. She was like a wife. But she was not his wife. She was his . . . his . . . even in thought he was troubled by the word. She was his whore. The term stung him. She was more to him, so much more.

He hadn't intended the relationship they had. He was not raised to consider such unseemly conduct.

"A man's seed is not to be sown illicitly," his father had declared one long-ago afternoon as the two, along with his brother three years his senior, set lines from their pirogue.

"The marriage act outside of marriage is a grievous sin and brings shame and ruination upon the man that consummates it."

Laron had had very little understanding of the marriage act or even how to consummate it. He was in fact a little young for the talk being given, very near the age that Karl was now. But his father, who was perhaps more rigid in his beliefs than most, did not relish the necessary father/son discourse required upon approaching manhood. On this occasion with his youngest sons, he thought to let one talk do for the two.

"There may be temptations set before you," he had told them. "But you must resist so that you would bring yourself as clean and whole to your marriage bed as you would expect of your bride."

"But if the women keep themselves pure, where would these temptations come from?"

It was his brother who had asked the question. Laron had had a similar thought, but was far too embarrassed to voice the question.

"There are women, even among us, who can be led into sin," his father answered. "A man intent upon a path of evil can always find the way. You must resist the unsanctioned desires of your body. Your reward will be much pleasure in marriage without the guilt of sin."

Pleasure without guilt. That was a thing to be sought after, Laron now knew.

Perhaps if his father had warned him about German widows, but no. No warning could have prepared him for his Helga.

The first time he'd seen up a woman's dress, it had been hers. Of course, she'd been giving birth to little Jakob at the time and truly there had been nothing sexual or seductive about the sight.

Her screaming had literally terrified him. He well understood the fear the little boy had shown when he'd coming running toward him on the bank of the river. He hadn't understood the boy's frightened words, but he'd recognized panic when he saw it.

He'd followed Karl back to the cabin and discovered the woman about to give birth. He had known about the German who had lived there. He had seen the man a few times and knew that he had a family. But it was said that the man had left for points downriver. It had never occurred to Laron that he might have left his wife and children behind.

He had been beside her while she gave birth. He couldn't say that he'd helped her. He'd mostly just wiped the perspiration from her brow and whispered coaxing endearments to calm her screaming. When the child had arrived in his arms, it was a miracle he could not believe. Perhaps he had begun to love her right then.

He hoped that it was his concern for his fellow human being and the hungry mouths of two innocent children that had kept him coming back to that cabin. He hoped that that was what it had been and not the occasional glimpse of pale female flesh when Helga took the baby to nurse.

He had never allowed himself to touch her, not even to brush against her accidentally. He just wanted to be near her. And he believed that she needed him. He could hardly stay away. Several days a week he headed up her bayou bearing stores and game and meat.

He remembered the evening he'd brought her the first of her guinea hens. He'd traded one of his brothers a half-cured deer hide for the pair of them. If his brother had wondered about his need for guineas he hadn't asked. Laron had loaded the two in separate sacks as if they were fighting roosters and carried them on the pirogue.

She had been delighted. Oooing and giggling over them as if they were satin shoes or hair ribbons.

"Thank you, thank you, thank you," she'd said to him. It was the first French she had ever spoken, obviously taught to her by her children.

He had been pleased to hear the sounds made uneasily by her pretty lips.

She'd fixed him a wonderful meal. That was one of the first things he had learned about her, that she was a marvelous cook. He could bring her anything, woodcock, squirrel, even possum and she could turn the meal into a dinner more luscious than wild turkey and sweet potatoes. That night she'd fixed a soup of fish with very strange but tasty bread. He'd never had such a thing to eat, but he decided that he liked it. He liked it a lot.

He had brought her coffee, but she knew very little about it and made it more like a tea. He brewed it for her as she got Karl and Elsa up to bed. The baby slept peacefully in the basket she'd woven for him from salt-soaked reeds.

Later as they'd savored the dark rich coffee, she suddenly seemed distracted and ill at ease.

Why should she not be? he had thought. The little

ones were all asleep. It was if they were completely alone in the cabin. And it was not at all the thing for a woman to be alone with a man who was not her husband.

He should go, he decided. But he lingered one more minute. It was one minute too long.

"Thank you, thank you," she said again.

He shrugged as if it were nothing.

She couldn't sit still and got up to pace before him momentarily, wringing her hands.

Her distress was evident. It was clear that he should go.

"Madame Shotz—" he began.

She dropped to her knees in front of him. He was startled. Was she going to pray? Was this some kind of homage, kneeling to him to express her gratitude. It was not necessary. He wanted to tell her that. He did tell her that. But of course, she couldn't understand his French.

She moved closer to him, her teeth biting down on her upper lip as if steeling herself for something painful. With no warning she reached into his lap.

"Madame!" he'd said, rising to his feet in shock.

Her hands were on him then, on the front of his pants. Touching him there, there where he was already growing to fit her hand.

And afterward they knelt together on the cabin floor, his arms around her, laughing together.

And then he kissed her. She tasted of him and herself and of the sin they had committed. It was a better taste than even her cooking.

Laron smiled to himself as the tender memory washed over him. He held the curtain aside and allowed Karl to precede him into the cabin. They carried eggs and milk and were hungry as bears.

Elsa and Jakob were helping their mother. Or at least Elsa was; Jakob seemed to be more employed in laughing and scampering about the room.

He and Karl emptied their buckets and poured the milk through a straining cloth. Laron leaned more closely to dip himself water from the big black pot that hung on the firehook. Then using the punch on the end of the poker, he eased the hook over the flames.

Helga was setting breakfast on the table. She had already washed with last night's water, her hair carefully braided and once more atop her head. She looked tidy and neat, and Laron wanted to walk across the room and kiss her. But it was full daylight and the children were there, so he did not.

"Beignets!" Jakob called out as if it were a battle cry.

Helga had learned to fry the sweet Acadian treat to please Laron, but her children enjoyed the hot, sugary cakes as well.

"And eggs, too," his mother answered. "The guinea hens have laid four this morning. That seems much abundance for this family to share."

The word *family* caught momentarily in her throat and Laron could not help but notice it. Something was wrong. Something was very wrong.

"It is a wonderful day outside," little Jakob announced to anyone who had not heard already. "A storm is coming. Oh I wish, how I wish that after breakfast we could go fishing in your pirogue?"

Laron shook his head. "Not today," he answered. "Today we harvest that providence rice down in the swampy bog. We've left it almost too long already. It's going to turn cold soon and we might lose it altogether before I return."

Jakob nodded, not wholly disappointed.

But surprisingly Karl turned surly. "I don't want to work in the rice," he complained. "I work here all week every week, while you come and go as you please. It's your rice; you should harvest it yourself."

The boy's attitude was more than disagreeable; it was disrespectful, and Laron opened his mouth to tell the boy just that. To his surprise, Helga unexpectedly interceded.

"Perhaps Karl can borrow your pirogue and catch us a big fish while we cut and stack the grain," she said. "With me and the children helping, you should be able to get the rice in without him."

Stunned almost speechless, Laron hesitated to reply, giving Helga a long curious look before he nodded and answered. "Of course," he said. "We can do it ourselves."

Karl puffed up like a toad fish and gave Laron a look that was positively defiant.

"You want to go fishing with me, squirt?" Karl asked his brother, one eye on Laron, almost daring him to speak.

The little fellow seemed startled by the invitation. Karl usually treated him like an unwelcome pest. Jakob hesitated, momentarily tempted. The tension at the table was palpable, undoubtedly even young Jakob could feel it.

"*Non*," he said finally. "I want to be with *Oncle*."

Karl looked daggers at Laron.

Laron looked questioningly at Helga.

Helga looked down.

Laron took his place at the table, still puzzled and uncertain. Without Karl to help, cutting the rice would put more work on Helga and Elsa and take all day at least. But Karl was Helga's son and she raised him as she saw fit. But clearly, something was wrong. Something was very wrong.

Aida was horrified when the Sonnier family arrived in their pirogue shortly after dawn. They towed a skiff piled high with sacked corn.

Aida hastily covered her mouth as a little exclamation of dismay escaped her throat.

"Bonjour," her father said, greeting them. "And what a beautiful morning for travel."

He hurried down to the end of the dock to help them alight. Aida followed and soon found herself holding fat little Pierre as Madame Sonnier was handed out.

"You look surprised to see us, Jesper," Jean Baptiste commented.

"It's my fault," Aida hurriedly explained, turning with embarrassment to her father. "Monsieur Sonnier asked me at the cattle branding when he should bring his corn for grinding. I said today would be fine and then I didn't remember it again until I saw them from the doorway."

Momentarily everyone appeared uncomfortable. Aida wished bitterly that the earth would open and swallow her up. Why hadn't she remembered? Once more her foolish feather brain had failed her and other people were embarrassed as a consequence.

"If this is not a convenient time," Jean Baptiste said. "We can come back another day."

Jesper waved his words away. "Non, non. It is a

perfect day for grinding corn. Not so damp that it will take on moisture and later spoil and not so dry that the turning of the stones will scorch it."

"I am so sorry for forgetting." Aida looked anxiously at the men.

"No harm done," her father assured all of them. "With Jean Baptiste and Armand to help me, it won't take any time at all to hitch up the team."

The men began unloading the skiff. The children, curious and energetic, began running up and down the dock in bare feet, their shapeless gowns slapping against their knees.

Aida still held little Pierre and the fat happy baby gurgled contently.

"Please come inside and I will fix coffee," Aida said.

Félicité accepted gratefully. "I should rightly feel guilty to rest myself while the men work," she told Aida. "But in truth, I am such a great cow that just getting from place to place seems a worthy effort."

The two commiserated as they made their way up the bank to the house, leaving the men to take up the challenge of turning a year's worth of corn into meal and flour.

In many ways it was the height of luxury to have corn mechanically milled. The Gaudets' *moulin à gru* could grind a year's worth of cornmeal in the time it took a woman working with mortar and pestle to pound out a day's ration. A man could rightly be proud of taking this burden from his womenfolk. And he could also be certain that if it was not ground to his satisfaction, he could complain about it hours on end without incurring his wife's wrath.

"I was just sorting some sweet herbs," Aida said as

they passed through the curtained doorway. "My little garden has really produced this year."

Félicité followed to the table where she sat down heavily in one of the leather-seated ladder-back chairs. Aida handed little Pierre to her and she set the little fellow on the floor beside her. The baby immediately grasped fistfuls of his mother's skirts and pulled himself into a standing position.

"He's going to walk soon," Aida said.

Félicité nodded. "I'm hoping he'll wait until this one is born. I'm in no condition to be chasing him now."

Aida began poking the ashes in the fireplace and urging new kindling to light.

Madame Sonnier looked around curiously, surprised.

"You've had no fire yet this morning?" she asked, clearly puzzled. "And you are sorting herbs before breakfast?"

"Breakfast?" Aida repeated the word as if she had never heard it.

Her eyes widened and she glanced down at her right hand, chagrined to find circles of thin cotton cord neatly tied on three of her fingers.

"Oh no," she wailed, sitting back on her heels. "I remembered the string, but then forgot to look at my hand."

Félicité's brow furrowed, confused.

"Poor Poppa," Aida explained, shaking her head. "He's out there working on an empty stomach."

Leaning forward, Félicité patted her shoulder, offering comfort. "Well, we will take him some bread and coffee," she said. "Men find that welcome any time of day."

"Yes, oh yes. Can we do that?" Aida asked. "It seems almost like cheating. Like pretending that you remembered a meal when you didn't."

"I don't imagine anyone will mind," Félicité assured her. "If you put on the coffee, I'll slice the bread."

"Bread!" Her whispered exclamation was disheartened and fatalistic. "Yesterday was bread-baking day, but I forgot all about it. So I thought I would just bake this morning. But then I got started with the herbs and—"

"We'll make biscuits," Félicité interrupted.

In less than a half-hour the two women headed out the back door of the Gaudet house carrying a huge basket of hot biscuits and a pot of hot coffee.

Jesper Gaudet had fashioned his grist mill, his *moulin à gru* with grinding stones bought downriver. It had taken two weeks and nearly ruined a team of horses to pull them upstream. But Gaudet told anyone who asked that it was the smartest move he'd ever made.

Jesper's three mules were hitched to long poles connected to a center axis. The grist mill was housed in a well-built shake-roof shed that sat on a raised dais just outside the horsetrod. Each creaking, groaning circle pulled by the mules created about one hundred revolutions of the stone wheel.

Inside, the great stones lay one atop the other. Aida's gaze was immediately drawn to Armand who stood in the shed, shirtless and straining as he and Jean Baptiste attached the long bull-hide band that connected the spindle that turned the top stone to the pulley that transmitted the power that was generated by the walking of the animals.

It was tough, heavy work and both men were slick with the grease they liberally smeared upon the stem. Aida swallowed a strange sense of nervousness inside her as she watched him. The muscles of his arms and chest were tight and flexed against the smooth pale flesh so faintly shaded with soft brown hair. There was no burliness or brawn upon his frame, but Armand Sonnier appeared sturdy and stalwart and somehow breathtakingly masculine.

The two had just managed to get the belt eased in place when he glanced up to catch Aida watching him. She felt the warmth of color rush to her cheeks. He jumped to the ground and hastily donned his shirt.

"What have we here?" Jean Baptiste called out. "The ladies have brought us a reward for our effort."

Aida's father headed toward them with an eager step. "It's good you caught us before the grinding began."

To her great relief, he didn't make any joke about her failure to fix him a breakfast and no one complained about stopping to accept a bite of refreshment.

Félicité seated herself and the children in the grass near the mill shed and spread the biscuits of little Gaston and Marie with jellied mayhaw.

Aida carried the coffeepot and saw that the men's mugs continued to be full of the thick black brew.

"Mmm, Mademoiselle Gaudet," Jean Baptiste said dramatically. "These are the best biscuits I ever tasted."

"Madame Sonnier helped me," Aida responded modestly. "I usually forget either the salt or the baking powders."

"You didn't forget a thing with these," Jean Baptiste assured her. "This daughter of yours is amazing, Gaudet. Not only is she beautiful, but she can cook, too."

Aida couldn't quite disguise the blush of pride that his words brought to her cheeks. She smiled happily at Armand as she walked over to fill his cup.

The younger Monsieur Sonnier, however, was not smiling.

"My brother is quick to offer a compliment," Armand noted.

Aida nodded almost shyly. "He is very kind."

"The biscuits *are* good," Armand assured her.

"*Merci*, monsieur," she replied, gleefully dropping a little half curtsy.

He had removed his hat to wipe the sweat from his brow. The morning breeze tousled his hair attractively. Aida barely managed to resist the impulse to smooth it down. Armand was smiling at her now, smiling, friendly, but there seemed something almost troubled about his expression.

"My brother is very charming always," he said. "But he is not so attractive as some men."

Her eyes raised in question and Aida turned to glance at the older Sonnier standing with her father at the far end of the clearing. To her, Jean Baptiste appeared very familiar and in fact very dear, because he looked like Armand.

Her gaze drifted back to Armand beside her. In truth, she had never thought whether he was handsome or plain. He was simply Armand, kind, patient, and oh so intelligent Armand. Aida loved beauty. She loved beautiful things and that included people. But she was not so shallow that she could not appreciate a person for his heart and mind rather than his face. A person could be even more beautiful inside than out. That is what she thought of Armand, inside he was beautiful.

Shockingly, a saucy little thought intruded into her ruminating. Although Armand was decently covered, she could still see in memory the very masculine chest now hidden beneath a coarse homespun shirt. From what she had glimpsed earlier, some of his inside beauty had worked its way to the surface as well. She felt a treacherous warmth of humor and . . . and something else. It was that same curious excitement that his closeness had conjured up under the lilas tree.

"On the contrary, monsieur," she answered with a teasing lilt to her voice. "I think the Sonniers are very handsome men."

Armand stilled immediately and with a narrowed gaze his blue eyes avidly searched her face. Aida knew that somehow she had said the wrong thing.

She knew from her own experience that beauty was, in women, associated with foolishness. But she had never thought men to fear such attractiveness. But perhaps Armand did. Maybe, because of his sickly childhood, he worried overmuch about what other men thought of him. Aida had never noticed that to be so. But there must be some reason why he kept her always at arm's length. He was the only man on the river that failed to flirt or tease her.

"A man can be attractive," she continued, trying to reassure him. "And a woman notices that. But women do not choose a man by his looks alone."

He continued to look at her, worried. Aida sought to give him an explanation. Her first thought was of Laron. He was very handsome, yet his handsomeness was not why she planned to marry him. His poverty and need for her father's land, figured much more heavily in her decision. But she couldn't say that. It was far too private to divulge, even to a friend. A movement at the corner of her eye caught her attention and she watched Jean Baptiste hoist baby Pierre in the air, causing the baby to laugh and gurgle. Aida had her example.

"Take your brother, Jean Baptiste," she said. "He is very handsome to look at, but it is his hard work and generous nature that set him apart from other men."

Armand's expression darkened and he threw out the rest of his coffee with a jerky motion that was almost angry.

"He is also a good husband and a fine father." His words, spoken harshly, were a puzzle to Aida.

"Yes, yes he is," she agreed. "I have always dreamed to someday be as happy as Félicité."

On that same day it was very late in the afternoon before all the available rice had been cut and stacked. As Laron piled the grain into the waist-high shocks for drying, Helga and the children searched along the edges of the *coulée* and into the nearby woods for isolated patches that had grown up among the pickerelweed and swampgrass. One of the balancing features of providence rice was that, although the farmer expended little effort cultivating it, he had to get his feet wet trying to find it once it was grown.

Helga found and cut a small clump that had been

nearly hidden by an overgrowth of mudbabies. She carried her bundle to the drier strewn piles.

Laron was there, sorting the cut rice and stacking it into shocks. His thin cottonade shirt clung to his sweat-soaked back as he bent and lifted the damp cut grain. He looked up as Helga approached, and he grinned. She smiled back at him, trying to match his mood. But he wasn't fooled.

Laron straightened and looked down into her eyes, warmly and with love. The slanted rays of the sun glistened on his hair and cast a shadow in her direction.

"I think this must be the last of it," he said as he took the bundle of cut grain from her arms. "Two weeks' drying in the shock and you'll be able to thresh out enough rice to keep those children's little bellies full all winter."

Helga nodded. "Yes," she said. "This year they will not starve. You've taught us how to feed ourselves. It has been an important lesson."

"It's about the only claim to education most Acadians would own up to," he admitted.

"We would never have made it without you," she admitted quietly. "I don't know what would have become of us if you hadn't come into our lives when you did."

Laron's smile faded and his expression became serious. "I'm glad I was here, Helga," he said. "I'm glad for your sake and the children, but mostly for myself."

Helga looked up at him, so strong and dependable and loving. She could count on him. She knew that. She could count on him for food, for shelter, for protection. She could count on him to love her and to provide for her children. She could count on him— but she could never have him.

And the whole situation was starting to hurt her oldest son.

"What's wrong?" he asked, apparently having read the sorrow in her expression.

She glanced around to assure herself that the children were out of earshot. Elsa was near the far end of the *coulée*. Jakob was much closer, but his attention had been captured by a small toad that was hopping through the muddy field.

"Tell me what is wrong," Laron repeated.

"Nothing."

"Nothing?"

"Nothing is wrong."

She'd made the statement adamantly. Not because she wanted him to believe it, but because she wanted not to have to talk about it. She wanted to delay for another day, another hour, even another minute.

But she could not.

"We should not see each other anymore," she said. "It is time you stopped these visits to me."

Laron paled visibly and his expression was stricken. He reached for her. His hands upon her shoulders, he held her firmly, securely, as if he feared she might run away.

"Helga, no. I cannot—"

"The time has come for this to end," she interrupted. "It has been three years. Three years that we have ignored our beliefs, ignored what is right. You know that I have always cared about you, but this liaison can continue no longer."

He was silent, frighteningly silent for a long moment.

"You have heard about Mademoiselle Gaudet, haven't you," he said finally.

Helga's brow furrowed. "Mademoiselle Gaudet?"

"I . . . I am betrothed," he admitted.

She couldn't have been more stunned if he'd slapped her. Helga thought herself already sufficiently wounded to be numb, but his words penetrated painfully. "No, no I had not heard. I recall you have said that she is a rare beauty. Congratulations."

"We have been affianced for well almost two years."

Helga's eyes widened in disbelief. An angry rebuke came to her lips, but she didn't speak it. She could not complain that he did not tell her. She was his leman, his convenience. She had no right to know or intrude on his life, his plans, his future.

"I wish you happy, Monsieur Boudreau."

Her answer was as unfeeling and formal as if she were only the most casual of acquaintances.

"We are not to wed until the spring."

Helga maintained a noncommittal mask. "It is a long time for a bridegroom to wait."

"This bridegroom could wait forever," he answered softly. "Helga, I love you. Perhaps I have not said that enough. I do love you. But a man . . . a man must wed. If you were free I—"

"I am not free and I have never been." Her tone was harsh, deliberately cold.

He nodded.

"Don't cast me out yet," he said, quietly pleading. "I knew you would not conscience me as another woman's husband, but I am not yet wed. Let me stay beside you until spring. Let me . . . let me love you until I take vows to promise not."

She shook her head. "It is not your vows or your bride that I am thinking about," she told him. "It is my children."

"Your children?"

Helga dropped her gaze, not wanting to face him. She purposely and deliberately kept her mind blank, her thoughts free, and her voice calm.

"Karl . . . the boys that he met, the Acadian boys, told him . . . they have told him."

"They are just boys, Helga," he assured her. "They swap stories and smoke tobacco. They know nothing of what is between us."

"They know the words, Laron," she said. "They know the words and they have taught them to my son, in French and German. To my face my son called me whore."

Laron's jaw hardened angrily. "That is too much! I will take a belt to his hide!"

He turned as if to go, but she grabbed his arm. "No, you will not. He is not your son. And I *am* your whore."

"Helga, no."

"You must go, Laron." She could not bear to look at him, she could not meet his eyes. "My own shame I could bear. But I cannot put it on my children. You must go and never come back."

He didn't answer. He didn't speak a word. Helga continued to stare at the stubble of rice at her feet and the silence stretched unbearably until she could stand no more. She raised her head to look at him.

Laron's young handsome face was now wretched

with pain. He hurt as she hurt. As in so much
together they were totally attuned. His eyes were
bright with tears. When he finally spoke grief dis-
torted his tone.

"I am sorry," he said simply. "Helga, I am so very,
very sorry."

She nodded.

He turned from her. He walked away.

"I caught the frog! I caught the frog!" she heard
Jakob say as he hurried in her direction. "Where goes
Oncle, Mama? May I go with him?"

"No darling." Helga's voice was almost a whisper.
"He's going away."

"Going away?"

Helga nodded. She stood another moment, silent.
Her child was at her side but she felt at once so very
alone. In the heat of a late Louisiana afternoon she
was chilled.

Sept

At Mass the sounds of Latin had a distinctive Acadian cadence, flavored with a French so old that it almost seemed a different language.

Armand mumbled the responses, but his mind was not on them. And his eyes were not on the priest as he blessed the cup. His eyes were on her. Her. Aida Gaudet. Men often looked at Aida Gaudet since she was beautiful. Truly beautiful. Any man who ever looked at her knew her to be so. And she was even more so when a man believed himself in love with her.

Armand believed he was in love with her. Selfishly he had allowed his careless words to undermine her bethrothal to Laron Boudreau. And now the fates had levied a price. A high one indeed, since it seemed it would be paid by his brother and his brother's family. And Armand had no one to blame but himself.

As Father Denis read the sacred words, Armand and the rest of the congregation knelt. Sunday Mass was an obligation. Armand was a man who lived up to his obligations. His obligations to God, to his community, to the land, and to his family.

Over the top of his prayerfully clasped hands he studied the smooth, alluring curve of Aida Gaudet's neck as she gazed toward the heavens in supplication. When she was little more than a girl he had fallen in love with her sunniness, her sweetness. But now, grown up, she was beautiful. She was magical. And he feared that she was almost irresistible. Armand's jaw tightened.

It was not his obligations to God or to the community that troubled him now. The obligations that concerned Armand this morning were those to his brother, Jean Baptiste.

Deliberately Armand took control of the direction of his thoughts. Jean Baptiste and Aida Gaudet. On the slippery slope of disillusion, a man could go way too far, too fast.

His brother was still sleeping in the *garçonnière*, and still singing the praises of the lovely Aida.

"How any woman can manage to look fresh and pretty in the dust and heat of branding day is a wonder," he'd commented. "And wasn't it charming the way she brought out food to us in the middle of the morning."

Armand's eyes had narrowed. His brother, his beloved brother, was entranced and ensnared, and Aida was now voicing her admiration and praise of a man who could never be hers. It had all the makings of a prairie tragedy.

A marriage could not be thrown over just because a husband developed an attraction to another woman. If the fair Aida succeeded in luring Jean Baptiste away from his wife, the sinful couple would never be able to live in Prairie l'Acadie. The two would have to relinquish friends and family. They would have to flee to a place where none would know them. Aida would never see her father again. And Jean Baptiste would have to walk away from his home and his farm. But that was nothing in comparison to walking away from his wife and three, soon four, children.

Armand surreptitiously glanced sideways toward his sister-in-law sitting near the end of the pew. Of course he would always take care of her, and he was sure Jean Baptiste knew that.

Armand prayed for wisdom. So far nothing had happened between his brother and Aida Gaudet. He was as certain of that as he was of his own name. *The voices* on the river had given him fair warning. But as certainly as winter followed autumn, if he did not take action, something would.

He glanced up to see the beautiful dark-haired girl, her hands clasped prayerfully and her chin lowered in submission. Emotion clutched at his heart.

Armand must keep his brother safe. To do that he must ensure that Aida Gaudet was not even tempted to look his way. She must marry Laron Boudreau and she must do it soon. Armand had set this course adrift, he would have to shore it up once more.

"Amen," he whispered in response to the benediction. If his tone sounded more determined than those around him, it was not really surprising.

The congregation began filing out of the pews and heading for the door. Armand also headed that way, helping to usher his niece and nephew as he went. The noise level in the small brick-between-timberframe building rose tremendously as they neared the open entryway. The naturally high-spirited Acadians managed the quiet reverence of the churchhouse with difficulty and only for short periods. By the time they stepped out into the open air, most could have easily followed the example of their children, who whooped, hollered, and ran in celebration of their freedom.

Armand relinquished control of the children, set his palmetto frond chapeau upon his head, and began to walk toward Aida Gaudet. He had not yet formulated a plan of action, but he knew that speaking with her privately would be a good first step.

It was a beautiful day in late fall. The sky was as blue as blue could ever be. The light breeze in the air was cool, but held not even one hint of a chill.

Somehow it was easy to spot Aida Gaudet, even in a crowd. Her skirts of indigo-dyed blue homespun cottonade were little different from those of any of the other ladies. The contrasting upper portion of the dress was vivid red and trimmed in yellow striping. The same yellow adorned her broad-brimmed bonnet with its shoulder-length sunshade. Her clothing was similar to that of all the women around her. Still she appeared distinct, unusual, exemplary. As if somehow her beauty did not contain itself upon her person, but radiated out around her.

Armand sidestepped a question here and a greeting there as he followed in her wake. He wasn't sure exactly what he was going to say, but it felt necessary to do something.

The light trilling of her voice sent shivers down his own spine. Shivers that had nothing to do with his brother. Armand turned his gaze toward the sound. Aida Gaudet.

She stood near the two large cape jasmines near the walkway to the churchyard *cimetière*. He immediately set his step in her direction. He had not yet decided what he was going to say. But he had to speak to her.

Perhaps there was a way to restore her previous destiny and save his brother's family.

A private word with the beautiful Mademoiselle Gaudet, however, proved to be difficult. Placide Marchand and Ignace Granger stood on either side of her, both calf-eyed and flirty. A beautiful woman, even one betrothed, was most often the recipient of the attention of single men. It was the pattern to practice one's wit and charm upon the unattainable until a man set his goal on the woman with whom he wished to share his life.

"Mademoiselle Gaudet," Armand said, tipping his hat to her politely. "You are looking very lovely today, as usual."

Aida smiled, appearing inordinately pleased at his words, and managed an attractive little cursty.

"Thank you, Monsieur Sonnier," she said in the low sweet voice that was somehow both innocent and enticing.

The two gentlemen at her side kept the conversation moving. The young beauty mostly smiled and giggled and flirted behind her fan. Armand watched her with interest. It was no strain. He had been watching her most of his life. She was exceptionally beautiful. It was easy to understand why Laron thought to marry her. It was easy to see why his brother would feel attracted to her.

But Aida Gaudet was out of the reach of his married brother. And out of his own reach, literally as well as figuratively. In the back of his mind lurked the temptation to win her for himself. Laron did not want her. Jean Baptiste could not have her. She should be his. He pushed the thought away as unworthy of him. It was unlikely that a woman such as her would come to love a man like him. She was bright and beautiful in all the ways that he was dull and ordinary.

They had once been very close. Now Armand treated her with deference and distance. Even before she was promised to his best friend, he had known her to be singularly unsuited to the life he would have to offer a bride, the life of a quiet, conventional scholar. And if in the darkness of some lonely night he imagined the soft curve of her breast against his hand or the plump, pinkness of her lips raised to him in a pretty pucker, he had never nor would ever, give evidence to those dreams.

His brother's marriage was in danger and he must do what he could to save it. There was no time to waste upon his own foolish fantasies. Aida Gaudet was not for him. It would take a miracle or a magic spell to capture her attention.

But she already cared for Laron. She already wanted to marry him. Armand had to make sure that she did.

"Will you be holding court upon your porch this day?" he asked her directly, referring to the accepted practice of receiving gentlemen callers on Sunday afternoons.

She lowered her lashes. It was a pretty gesture, one that on another female might indicate shyness, but everyone knew that with Mademoiselle Gaudet it was flirtation. "I do hope so," she said. "A young lady would be bereft should she sit Sunday upon her porch alone."

"As if such a calamity could ever befall you, mamselle," Granger piped in effusively. "I intend to spend a pleasant hour in your company, if you please."

"And myself also," Placide added. "I would not enjoy Sunday did it not include you, Mademoiselle Gaudet."

Aida blushed prettily. "You are always welcome," she told them. "I will be there and my dear friend Ruby has agreed to come and sit with me."

"Ah Ruby!" Granger exclaimed. He glanced toward Armand. "Dear Ruby, she is such a sweet thing and so devout."

Marchand was also gazing pointedly in Armand's direction. "Yes, Ruby is not so tall as some of the ladies and would make a fine wife for any man."

Armand felt his face flame with embarrassment and humiliation. Did they think he was setting a *tendre* for Ruby? Armand would readily admit that he was shorter than any man on Prairie l'Acadie, but lack of height did not mean desperation.

"I assume that Laron will be there," Armand explained quickly. "I need to speak with him about a personal concern."

"Of course my fiancé will be there," Aida assured him. "I should be quite put out if he were to neglect me."

"And he would be quite the fool to do so," Granger said.

"But he is already quite the fool to have delayed the wedding for so long," Placide blurted out.

Aida visibly paled.

Guiltily, as it were more his fault than his friend's, Armand came to her rescue. "*You* are the fool, Marchand, if you think it is Laron who puts off this wedding. Of course it is Mademoiselle Gaudet who hesitates to tie herself to such a knave as Boudreau."

Placide shifted his feet.

Aida glanced at Armand, grateful. He smiled back broadly. "I admit my friend is a knave," he told her. "But I speak highly of him just the same." Armand gave the other two men a long look. "He is the best of knaves at least."

Aida giggled out loud.

Armand found himself more than a little pleased that he'd eased over Placide's gaffe. Now if he could only undo the thoughtless words that he himself had spoken, the much more serious ones that put the happiness of his own brother and this lovely young woman in jeopardy.

The porch at the home of Aida Gaudet was crowded. Ignace Granger and Placide Marchand were in attendance, each trying to outdo the other with gracious compliments and clever conversation. Pierre Babin had brought both Ruby and her mother and seemed to be enjoying himself.

Hippolyte Arceneaux and his wife had been poling by on their way to visit their grandchildren when Madame Arceneaux spotted Madame Babin on the porch. Nothing would do but for her to drop in for a bit of gossip. Hippolyte had been sent ahead to tell his daughter-in-law why they were late. He returned shortly with the young Madame Arceneaux, her husband François, and her two little sons.

The older women were interested in the babies. Francois was interested in Jesper's grain mill. Jesper was interested in explaining its operation at great length. And Hippolyte had no hesitation about offering his two cents' worth of advice on any subject.

The younger men, Placide, Ignace, and Pierre, were chagrined by the topic of conversation and tried valiantly to turn it to more frivolous banter suited for

Sunday afternoon. When that proved impossible, the two merely commenced a rival conversation.

That worked for a while, but ultimately in order to be heard over Jesper Gaudet, the younger men spoke up a bit. Then Hippolyte, fearing that Francois and Jesper would not concede his point, raised the level of his voice also. That caused Placide and Ignace to speak even louder. The babies began to wail and the mother and grandmother began to coo. The crying woke Jesper's old dog, who set up a howl. Within minutes the Gaudet front porch became as noisy and confusing as the Tower of Babel.

Aida sat beside Ruby on a long wash bench, smiling occasionally at Ignace and Placide. Their attempt at conversing about more simple subjects was certainly commendable when compared to the behavior of Armand Sonnier. He sat on the steps, serious and silent, his back propped against the porch, gazing out at the river.

He was obviously disgruntled. Aida watched him out of the corner of her eye with distress. He was not one of her admirers, that was clear. Unlike younger, less learned fellows like Marchand and Granger, he undoubtedly found her silly and boring. Everyone knew he was the smartest man on the river, and he had come there to speak with Laron Boudreau. She had told him that her fiancé would be there, but he was not.

Sitting amid the near-deafening clamor, Aida pretended that she was not concerned. She pretended she was not embarrassed. Or even humiliated. She pretended that a fiancé's failure to appear on Sunday afternoon was not unusual.

Deliberately she smiled her little half-smile at the

young men. She was dressed as prettily as was permitted for a Sunday on the porch. And she had managed, after nearly a half-hour of struggling, to get her hair to hang in one long thick black curl down her shoulder. It was not altogether proper, but so far none of the women had commented on it. Of course they had another juicy bit of gossip to chew upon. Laron's absence.

Aida held Ruby's hand, as much to give the other girl courage among the company as to take some for herself. She flirted, tittered, and giggled at moments that seemed appropriate. Purposefully she tried not to think about the only thing that she could think about. Laron had not shown up.

This was not the first time that he had failed to sit Sunday on her porch. There had been other Sundays, however rare, when he had failed to appear. She had not been happy then. And she was not happy now.

She knew her father would be asking questions later. Madame Arceneaux and Madame Babin would be whispering the fact to anyone willing to take a half-minute to listen. And somehow Father Denis would find a way to blame her. But worse than his mere absence was the gossip, brought to the Gaudet porch with some embarrassment by François, that Laron Boudreau was down on the river somewhere. And that he was drinking. Unusual behavior indeed—and especially for a supposedly besotted bridegroom.

She smiled. She laughed. She entertained her guests. But inside, Aida Gaudet's stomach twisted and churned. She surreptitiously laid a soothing hand against the raw, burning pain. It wouldn't do to show her discomfort. Young ladies took to their beds when they were not feeling well. But if she took to her bed, everyone would think she was wretched over Laron. They would all think that she was sorrowing and fearful that he no longer wanted to marry her. They would all think that she suspected him and the German widow.

Aida laughed lightly and shook her head, casually calling attention to the one long thick black curl hanging down her shoulder.

"Oh you silly *farceur!* What a joker you are!" she exclaimed, tapping Ignace lightly on the sleeve with her fan. "How can a woman know when you are telling her the truth or when you are fooling her?"

Ignace didn't get a chance to answer.

"Walk out with me."

The words came abruptly from the mouth of Armand Sonnier.

Every voice on the porch was suddenly silenced.

For a moment Aida eyed Armand with disbelief. Armand Sonnier wanted to walk out with her? Then reality set it. It was a poor choice of words. She cast a quick warning glance to her father. *Please don't say anything,* her eyes begged silently. *Please, please.*

Armand, of course, hadn't meant he wanted her to "walk out with him" as in walk alone so he could sweet-talk her, but simply that he wanted a private word. Belatedly he realized what he'd said and appeared almost as dumbstruck as those sitting on the porch.

"Of course, Monsieur Sonnier," Aida answered lightly, rising to her feet. "I do not believe that I have shown you my herb garden. And I am sure, being as close to Madame Landry as you are, you must surely have a great interest in cultured plants."

He must wish to discuss Laron, Aida thought to herself. It *must* be that he wished to discuss his friend. Otherwise she was certain that Armand Sonnier would not have made such a suggestion.

She rose to her feet and he offered her hand.

"If I do say so myself, monsieur," she continued brightly, "I have a way with gardening."

Determinedly she allowed him to lead her down the steps. She refused to look behind her at their audience as she took his arm and strolled beside him. She began to chatter.

"It's . . . it's a lovely day," she said.

"Hmmm? Oh yes," he said.

She glanced over at him. He was gazing off into the distance, obviously lost in thought. His light brown hair was not slicked down with sweet grease like that of the other young men. It had a tousled, wind-blown look that was attractive in a sort of disheveled way.

"It's neither too hot nor too cold," she continued. "It seems that this might be the best weather that we've had in several months."

He nodded.

"But of course winter is coming," Aida rattled on. "Why, the sky this morning looked like bad weather heading our way soon."

She heard herself prattling aimlessly, but couldn't seem to stop. The late-afternoon sun threw their long lazy shadows along the grass as they walked. The cool slick grass under her bare feet was soothing; still her heart fluttered nervously.

Armand Sonnier was Laron's best friend. He was also without doubt the smartest man in the parish. What in the world could she have to say to him that would be interesting or entertaining? He probably spent his days thinking about things that she could never understand. Talking about things she'd never heard of and shaking his head in pity at foolish young women who have nothing more to recommend them than a pretty face and spend half an hour fixing a long thick curl of black hair.

"Of course, I love winter almost as much as fall," she told him. "All the seasons have their own specialness, I suppose. I love the prairies in springtime when they are full of wildflowers. The bayou is at its best in summer when the hyacinth and lilies bloom on the water. In autumn the leaves on the trees change to red, yellow, and gold. And in the winter, well I suppose that it's the absence of all that beauty that makes us recall it with such wonder."

Armand stopped still and turned to look at her. His blue eyes studied her intensely. He was no taller than she was. And it was strange, unusual, to look a man straight in the eye, just as if . . . as if he were someone just like her.

Aida flushed and glanced away. Of course he was nothing like her. He was a literate man. Her own father counted on him in trading with the Creoles and Americaines and he was the judge, the representative of the state of Louisiana in the parish. He was not at all like her.

"And winter is nice also because there is much time for dances and *fais-dodo* and get-togethers," she added.

He nodded and remained silent, his expression still pensive.

What was he thinking? Aida couldn't help wondering that. When he kept his silence for so long was his mind a blank or was he having an involved conversation with himself? A conversation about truth or religion or life? Did he agree with himself? Or were arguments going on in his head? Aida could only imagine. Momentarily she floundered as she sought for another topic for conversation. The weather had been stretched about as far as it would go. Had it been Ignace or Placide, she would have merely talked about herself. Somehow she didn't think that Monsieur Sonnier would be interested. With him she could not get away with a pretense of frivolity. He knew her too well.

Armand was so smart, so serious, so sober. Of course it was quite true that he could tell a good joke. But he never seemed to feel like laughing when he was with her. He must consider her a silly scatterbrain. Most of the Acadian men liked her silliness. Armand Sonnier obviously did not.

It was unfortunate that he was not more like his older brother, Jean Baptiste. She remembered how charming he was at the *fais–dodo* when he helped her with her shoes.

"How is your brother?" she asked, delighted with herself at coming up with such an agreeable subject. She liked Jean Baptiste, and Armand obviously cared about his brother. Exchanging views on their mutual regard for him would be easier than discussing the weather.

To her surprise Armand's expression took on a guarded, almost hostile look.

"He is well," he said. There was a gruffness to his voice that discouraged her.

Aida was unsure.

"He's a very good dancer," she said. "He partners me at nearly every *fais–dodo*. I always feel like I'm simply floating on his arm."

"*Laron* is the best dancer on the river," Armand stated flatly.

"Why yes, I know that he is," Aida admitted. "But perhaps I am partial in my judgment. Your brother is very good, too. I remember watching him dance with Félicité at their wedding. I was so envious. She was so lovely and I was so very young and gauche."

"But that's all changed now, hasn't it?" Armand said. He was looking at her so sternly that she was confused. His words were, she assumed, meant as a compliment. She was no longer so young and gauche. She was the most beautiful woman on the Vermillion River and everyone knew it. Still, he said it in such a way that made it sound almost as if he were angry at her for growing up and being pretty.

"Yes, I guess things have changed a bit. I have grown older, after all," she said.

His eyes narrowed. Her answer obviously did not please him. They stood at the edge of the small herb garden that grew by the side of her house. They were still in plain sight of the others. Aida could feel the curious eyes on her back. But they were completely out of hearing range.

"Are you and Laron making plans to wed soon?" he asked her.

Aida's brow furrowed. "Why, why yes, we are," she said, somewhat taken aback. "We discussed it the last time we spoke," she told him.

"Oh?"

"We are . . . we are going to wed in the spring."

He hesitated for a long moment, watching her. It was as if he were assessing her, gauging her.

"Laron is a good man, hardworking and honest. A

woman could hardly do better than to have him as husband."

She glanced away, embarrassed at the intensity of his look.

"You need not trouble yourself to convince me," she answered. "I decided some time ago that Monsieur Boudreau would suit me perfectly."

He nodded solemnly. "Yes, you two are a handsome couple."

Aida felt a moment's irritation. She wanted to explain that although Laron was quite attractive, that was not why she was marrying him. Laron needed her. He needed her father's land and he needed the prosperity that marriage to her would offer. And because he needed her for those things, he might learn to love her for herself. She said none of that.

"I don't think the spring will be soon enough, Mademoiselle Gaudet," he continued firmly. "I think that you and my friend should marry soon, very soon."

Huit

"Where in the devil have you been?"

Armand Sonnier's angry words echoed painfully through the groggy haze that seemed to envelope Laron's brain. He looked up from his position on the foul-smelling bed tick in the corner of the Hébert barn and squinted.

"For God's sake, don't shout," he answered.

Laron rolled out of his sleeping place and onto his knees. His head pounded and felt ready to crack open from the pressure inside. He noted with amazement that his brother-in-law's barn seemed to tilt abruptly and his stomach nearly rebelled at the motion. He reached over for the bottle, knowing it to be both cause and cure for his ailment.

"What is that?" Armand's question was incredulous.

Laron took a healthy swig before answering sarcastically. "It is liquor, my friend, strong drink, *la boisson*. A particularly fine product made from homegrown Acadian corn."

Rising to his feet was not as easy as Laron had anticipated and he fell forward. Armand caught him roughly.

"You're as drunk as a robin eating chinaberries!" he exclaimed.

"No robin has ever been this drunk," Laron told him.

It might well be true. When Laron had left Helga's farm he had been stunned, numb, in shock. He'd spied Karl, hurrying home with a stringer full of fish, and the reality of what was happening seeped in. The boy called out to him, showing off his catch. Laron had managed a nod of pride, but had not spoken. He had simply boarded his pirogue and headed down Bayou Tortue, his thoughts in a whirl.

He would never again share a quiet moment with the boy. He would never again tease Elsa. He would never again hold little Jakob in his arms. And he would never again feel Helga beneath him, breathless and quaking as he pushed her over the edge of pleasure and felt the spasms of her body clutching at his own.

He'd gone directly from Helga's farm to the Bayou Blonde. The Bayou Blonde was a rough and wicked place where the dregs of Acadian and Creole society consorted with low-life Americaines and escaped slaves, consumed strong drink, and gambled away their livelihood. He didn't know how many days he'd stayed there. He didn't remember how he'd managed to make it home.

"You always said you hated the taste of alcohol," Armand reminded him.

"I still do, my friend," Laron agreed. "I still do. I hate the taste, but I love the oblivion."

"Come on," Armand said, wrapping his arm around his friend's waist.

"No, I can't move," Laron moaned. "I can't move. I can't walk. I don't think I can live."

"Well, you are damned well going to have to," Armand insisted.

Laron was nearly twice the weight and an ax handle's length taller than the man who supported him, but Sonnier managed to drag him out of the barn and down toward the river. They stumbled along together with Armand talking constantly, his words part encouragement, part castigation.

"Liquor doesn't solve anything," his friend told him. "It merely makes you behave foolishly and causes your family to worry. Keep moving now, you can do it. It's a good thing your father's no longer alive. He'd probably still think to take a strap to you for this."

Laron concentrated merely on staying upright and keeping his stomach from heaving.

When they reached the bank Laron knelt expecting to splash his face with cool water. Instead, Armand dunked him, head and shoulders, into the river. Laron came up sputtering and then did lose the contents of his stomach.

Armand dumped him in the cold water again, this time almost to his waist.

"Are you trying to drown me!" Laron sputtered, his hair plastered to his head.

"It's an easier way to die than drinking yourself to death," Armand told him. "Your sister was frantic when I spoke with her. She sent her husband to Bayou Blonde to fetch you. What on earth were you doing there?"

"I can't seem to remember."

Laron collapsed on the ground. The cool grass

against his back and the rich fragrance of damp earth somehow soothed him. It was the middle of the day, the sun was high, but the chill in the air kept it from warming the wetness of his shirt. His own smell assailed him and it was extremely unpleasant. His life was extremely unpleasant.

"I'm going up to your sister's house to get some coffee," Armand told him.

"I can go with you," Laron assured him, attempting to stand although the ground swayed dangerously when he had risen only to his elbows.

"Don't bother," he answered, pushing Laron back down on the grass. "It's too far for me to drag you. Besides, I don't know who is up there now. And I'm sure your sister wouldn't want her children to see you this way."

"Oh no," Laron agreed. He was sure his friend was right. His straightlaced Boudreau parents had never allowed liquor in their house and Laron and his brothers had been warned against it on many occasions. He was fairly certain that the Hébert household, his sister's home, was equally intolerant.

"I'll be right back," Armand said.

"Fine."

"Don't roll over and fall in the river."

Actually that sounded like a pretty good idea to Laron.

"Just get the coffee," he answered.

As his friend hurried off, Laron lay still in the grass. He tried closing his eyes, but the spinning grew worse. He gazed up at the gathering clouds in the blue sky above him. It was a beautiful day. The kind of day made for weddings—or maybe funerals.

He folded his arms across his chest like a corpse

and imagined himself laid out on slats. Of course, this time of year, cool as it was, his family would probably still be able to keep him in the house. He'd rather be outside, he decided. If he waited to die in summer he could have that advantage. But was it really worth waiting that long? His life was over already.

Bayou Blonde had been wilder, dirtier, more pathetic than he'd been led to believe. There was gambling. But he hadn't bothered. He didn't have much money and what he had he'd spent on liquor.

There had been a woman, a woman with big dark eyes and a front tooth missing. She'd said he was "so pretty" she would let him do it for free. She'd changed her mind after he'd vomited on her skirt.

Helga! The name repeated in his mind. *Helga no, don't send me away.*

He had thought himself so worldly. He had his life, his plans; and he had his German widow. He'd known from the beginning that his illicit liaison with Helga could never last. Then he had so callously, thoughtlessly, become involved. He knew eventually he would have to leave her. He would have to marry. He'd even settled on whom and when. Had he thought that it would be so easy? Had he thought his heart was not involved?

Somehow he hadn't truly thought that he would have to do without her. Perhaps he secretly imagined that she would still welcome him when another woman shared his name. Perhaps he believed that her love for him would override all other considerations. Perhaps that belief had made it possible to affiance himself to Mademoiselle Gaudet.

He shook his head at his own idiocy and then

moaned with pain. He should have known better. Helga was as sweet and as worldly wicked as a woman could be. But she was also, in her own heart, as duty bound and decorous as his own mother had been.

His mother? The image came to him of his mother sitting so primly in front of the fire, speaking of her husband as Monsieur Boudreau, never as lover or husband, but more as a gentleman with whom she had a respectful acquaintance. And he remembered his father standing in the pirogue explaining to his two youngest boys about the facts of life, and looking unhappy and uncomfortable. Surely those two shared nothing of the sensual magic that was part and parcel of his relationship with Helga Shotz. His mind rebelled at the thought.

Still, it could not be overlooked that his parents had managed to produce fifteen children in a marriage of twenty-seven years. Such did not occur by keeping distance from each other.

Was it possible? Was it possible that his parents had loved as he loved? Was it possible that they might have understood why he did not want to live without Helga at his side?

"Sit up." The order came from Armand. "Your sister has sent a whole pot of *petit noir*," he said.

"Good, good," Laron said, forcing himself up off the ground. "I have made a mistake drinking so much."

"Well you certainly have the right of that," Armand agreed.

"A man must have a clear head when he makes momentous decisions."

Laron's hands trembled so much, Armand had to

help him bring the cup to his lips. The coffee was hot and dark and aromatic. It did not have the potency to truly clear his head, but it did have the power to make him believe it had.

"I love her," he said to his friend after he'd successfully downed the first cup.

"Your sister?"

"No, I mean, of course, but . . . but I love Helga."

Armand's brow furrowed. "The German widow?"

"I love her, Armand," Laron declared. "And I am going to marry her."

"My friend, the liquor steals your good sense," Armand said. "The woman is already wed."

"I don't care," Laron answered.

And he didn't.

Armand braced himself in his high position out on the limb of a big cypress. He extended his arm to reach as far as possible. The hook on the end of the long pole that he held caught a big clump of greenish-gray Spanish moss.

Below him, balancing himself with one foot on either edge of the pirogue's sides, Jean-Baptiste reached the lower hanging bits and maneuvered the boat into place.

With expertise, Armand eased his catch off the end of the pole, causing the moss to fall directly onto the growing pile already stacked in the pirogue.

"I'd like to know," he hollered down at his brother, "why, after all these years, I am still in the tree and you are still in the boat."

Jean Baptiste grinned up at him and laughed. "You should not ask me, but Father Denis or Madame Landry," he answered. "Everyone knows the smaller man climbs the tree. Whether it is, as Father Denis would say, 'God's will' or as Madame Landry would believe, 'your destiny,' the fact is, my brother, that you are shorter than I. And unless a gator comes to chew my legs off, you will always be so."

Armand glanced up and down the river and shook his head. "Where are those gators when you need them?"

Gathering moss was an important side business for the brothers. Long ago people had discovered that the spindly hanging swags were perfect for pillow fluff and mattresses filling. Mixed with mud the moss created a house plaster called *bousillage* that was strong, easy to work, and made good insulation. But most often it was gathered in large quantities and floated downriver to Creole and American factories that used it for upholstery stuffing. The demand for this cash crop was greater and more profitable than for their cotton or corn.

Now that winter was nearly upon them, the cattle and hogs already loosed to take care of themselves and the harvest put by, the Sonnier brothers had time to devote to piling moss.

"I'm littler than Uncle," Gaston declared from his perch atop the moss. "I should be up in the tree."

"And so you should," Armand agreed. "Jean Baptiste, hand that farmer up here."

Laughing, the elder Sonnier hoisted his young son up to the first big branch of the cypress. Armand moved lower to join the child. His knee-length shapeless dress hampered the boy's natural climbing ability.

With the pole in his right hand, Armand locked his legs tightly around the tree limb and wrapped his left arm around Gaston's waist, holding the little fellow securely to his chest.

"Are you afraid?"

The little boy looked down at his father several feet below.

"Your uncle Armand won't let you fall," Jean Baptiste assured him. "But even if he did, Poppa will always be here to catch you."

Armand felt the child's little body relax.

"It's pretty high up here," Armand said.

The little boy looked around, getting his bearings. "I like it," he said finally. "I like climbing trees and this is the biggest tree I have ever climbed."

Armand grinned at him and kissed the side of his brow.

"Being in the tree can be very wonderful. Look how far downstream you can see."

Gaston craned his neck.

"How far away do you think that is off there?"

The little boy shook his head in wonder.

"Perhaps we can see as far as La Pointe or Vermillionville. Do you think we can see as far as the bay?"

The boy squinted off into the distance. "I don't know," he admitted.

Armand smiled at him, pleased. "Shall I show you how to use the pole?" he asked.

Gaston nodded.

He had the boy grasp the pole just below Armand's hands. "Just ease it out," he said. "Get it just into the center of the swag and then gently pull back."

The two managed to hook a good-sized piece. Carefully they brought it around until it hung high over the pirogue. Then with a twist of the wrist, it fell into the towering heap that already heavily loaded the boat.

"I did it!" Gaston cheered himself loudly.

Both adults made the proper congratulations.

"I can gather moss just like you and Poppa," he declared proudly.

"My father, your *grandpère*, used to gather moss in this bayou. Maybe from this very tree," Armand told him.

"Truly?"

Armand nodded. "And someday you and Pierre will gather moss here, too, just like we do today."

"Me and Pierre?" Gaston was skeptical. "Pierre's just a baby."

"But he will grow up just like you will," Armand said. "And you two will be farmers like your father and I. And you will do things together and help each other because you are brothers. That is what brothers do. And the difference in age won't seem like anything important at all."

Gaston accepted that idea thoughtfully. "I'll be the big brother, like Poppa. So I will stand in the boat to get the ones hanging low."

Armand shrugged. "Maybe so. But you can never tell who will grow to be biggest."

"Oh *I* will," Gaston assured him. "I want to be tall like my poppa."

The two looked down at Jean Baptiste, who was smiling proudly.

"It's a good thing to be a big man and strong," Gaston said.

"It's a good thing to be happy with whoever you are," Armand told him.

"Uncle Armand, are you happy being small?"

Armand looked at the boy for a long minute and then leaned closer as if to put a secret in his ear.

"I get to climb the trees," he whispered.

The pirogue was low in the water as the Sonniers made their way home. With the weight of the moss it took both of them to pole the huge craft. Armand took the fore and Jean Baptiste the aft. They moved in unison aiding the pirogue on its downstream journey and keeping it within the deepest channel where it would not snag up on some unseen debris.

Young Gaston slept soundly, peacefully atop the heap, even though it was only noon. They had risen at dawn to complete their task before the heat of the day.

"How is Laron?" Jean Baptiste asked, breaking the contemplative silence.

Armand sighed heavily. "I don't really know."

"His family was very surprised and upset about his running off to Bayou Blonde."

"The German widow has bid him pass no more time with her," Armand said. "He is taking it very hard."

Jean Baptiste shook his head.

"It is for the best though," Armand continued. "She was why he was so hesitant to wed. Now he can go ahead, begin his life, have his family as he's always planned."

"Yes, he should get on with his life. He will forget the German soon enough. A beautiful young woman like Aida Gaudet could make any man forget the past," Jean Baptiste said appreciatively. "Even a past with one that he thought he loved."

Something as cold as fear and as hard as stone settled in Armand's chest.

"So have they pushed up the wedding date?" Jean Baptiste asked.

"Not yet. Laron is not yet reconciled."

"What do you mean he's not yet reconciled?"

"He still thinks to have the widow," Armand answered.

"How can he do that? She is widow in name only."

Armand sighed heavily. "He cannot. He doesn't accept it, but of course he will. He will have to."

Jean Baptiste nodded.

The last few days with Laron had been difficult ones. His friend was just becoming impervious to reason. He was going to have Helga Shotz and no one else.

Armand's own guilt about this multiplied innumerably. It was he himself who had first suggested this idea, after all. It was he who had said that perhaps Laron could be happy merely living with the woman that he truly wanted. He had spoken from his own heart, selfishly. Now he feared to reap the harvest of those careless words.

Having heard the whole story, he found that he now greatly admired Madame Shotz. With her little children to raise, the German widow was not about to openly live in sin with Laron, reviled by the community, an embarrassment to the Boudreau family. And now that her oldest had come to an age of understanding, she was not even willing to continue the clandestine relationship of the past.

Laron must see that he could not have her. And he must turn once again to Aida Gaudet. Armand had deliberately sought her out on several occasions in the last couple of weeks. He had spoken at length about Laron's good qualities and what a fine husband he would make for her.

She remained vaguely noncommittal. And the gossip about Laron's activities in Bayou Blonde had not helped, he was certain.

"You sound as if you have been chosen as his protégé," Aida told him, speaking of the tradition of a man other than the would-be groom proposing to the bride.

"Laron is my dearest friend," Armand said. "I want him to be happy."

He only hoped that the words he spoke were the truth.

The day before he'd gone by to check on Orva Landry, and the old woman had shaken her head and pointed her finger at him accusingly.

"You stir and stir," she told him. "But you can't make a chicken from soup. Just let the pot boil and accept destiny as it comes."

Armand glanced behind him at his nephew, asleep on the moss pile, and his brother, steady at the pole.

Armand knew from his own experience what it was for two brothers to grow up without a father. Would Gaston and Pierre share that fate? He thought to himself that some destinies must be avoided in any way possible.

Swallowing his anxiety, he purposely concentrated on the peace and beauty that surrounded him. There was almost no breeze upon the water. The occasional plop of a fish or splash of a turtle were the only sounds except for the gentle wake of their own pirogue. The morning had been cool, almost chill.

And there was a bite to the air and a fragrance in it that said winter was close.

All up and down the banks the verdant greens of summer grass and trees were giving way to the muted browns, pale yellows, and occasional vibrant splash of fall orange.

Winter was coming and winter was a good time for Acadians. There was little work and much time spent in frolic and family gatherings.

Old man Breaux had again spoken to Armand of his "tiny little niece" who was coming for an after-Christmas visit. Armand wanted to feel a sense of anticipation for his future, but the present worries of the people that he loved too much overwhelmed him.

Up ahead the sound of splashing water caught his attention. It was too loud to be turtles or gators. Was someone swimming? As they rounded a curve in the river, they spotted a woman doing laundry.

A long rough-hewn plank extended from the bank out into the river where the woman sat strad-dled, her bare legs in the gray water. The mid-morning sun gleamed down, showing her in relief against the dark shaded woods behind her. With the square wooden *battoir* she pounded the clothes on the end of the plank mercilessly. The strong, rhythmic motions were born of much practice and competence, the task somehow passionate and feminine in its aspect.

"*Bonjour*, madame!" Armand hailed her, politely not wishing to come up on her unexpectedly.

It was only when she turned to look in his direction that Armand realized the woman was Aida Gaudet. He was momentarily taken aback. He should have realized; certainly this was very near her father's home. And of course he knew that Mademoiselle Gaudet would have laundry to do for herself and her father, just as any other woman would. But somehow he did not imagine her, had never imagined her, as she was now. Garbed in a loose-fitting, near-threadbare work dress and with a *gardesoleil* sun-bonnet so functional and unattractive it was only describable as ugly, she labored hardily at such a mundane task.

"Messieurs Sonnier!" she called out gaily, as if she were at a party rather than scrubbing dirty clothes on the end of a plank. "How are you?"

Armand waved back silently and would have passed right by, but realized as the pirogue began to slow that Jean Baptiste was steering them closer. He answered her greeting.

"Well mamselle, and you?"

With an ease that belied the weight and clumsiness of the cargo, they pulled to a stop only a few feet from the end of the young woman's wash plank.

"How lovely you look this afternoon," Jean Baptiste said to her. "With the sun shining down on you, you are beautiful as a painting in church."

Armand had thought the same thing, but he was disturbed to hear Jean Baptiste say it.

Aida giggled as if he told a great joke.

"Thank you, monsieur," she said with exaggerated formality. "What you see before you is the very latest in laundering fashion. All the best clothes must be washed, so alas, the worst must be worn."

The two laughed together easily. Too easily, Armand thought. It was no problem for Aida Gaudet to joke about her appearance, he realized. Even clad in such clothes, she was inordinately desirable. Her rolled-up sleeves allowed a man to feast his eyes upon the smooth, sun-pinked skin of her arms, prettily rounded with not a hint of skinniness, and the delicate femininity of her narrow wrists, small enough for a man to hold both in his own.

It was upon her arms and wrists that Armand concentrated his attention because he was much too aware of her bosom, heavily spattered with water, the thin cottonade clinging to her abundant curves with unrelenting accuracy, and of the exposed flesh of her naked legs, only partially hidden in the murky water of the Vermillion River.

Of course it was impossible for a woman to wash clothes without rolling up her sleeves and tying up her skirt and getting wet. But did a woman converse with men in such attire?

To be fair Armand did recall several times when he conversed with Félicité as she did the wash. And of course he'd watched Orva Landry do hers. But that was not at all the same. Félicité was his sister-in-law and Orva Landry an old woman. He had spoken briefly once with Madame Hébert in much the same position that Aida was at this moment. But that had not seemed at all . . . at all the way that this seemed.

They should move away. They should not speak with her any longer.

Jean Baptiste kept talking. He kept smiling at her.

She kept giggling.

"Most women do their wash on Wednesday," Armand pointed out.

Aida's cheeks brightened with embarrassment. "As do I, too," she admitted. "But yesterday, well, I . . . I just forgot that yesterday was Wednesday and then Thursday was upon us and . . . and so I have to do Wednesday's laundry on Thursday."

As Armand listened to her explanation, it was all he could do not to shake his head in disbelief. The woman was completely devoid of any sense of reality. She must spend her life in a haze, unaware of anyone else.

She did, however, have other qualities. Unerringly Armand's eyes were drawn to her bare knees just breaking the surface of the water. They were spread apart by the width of the plank. She was completely covered by the bunched fabric of her skirt. There was nothing inherently immodest in her pose. Still Armand's throat went extremely dry and his body tense. Her knees were spread on either side of the plank. Parting Aida's knees, spreading them apart, wide . . . The idea sizzled through him like grease on hot coals.

He jerked his hat off his head and held it in front of him, ostensibly to run a hand through his hair.

Aida looked at him, smiling shyly, as if nothing was amiss.

"How is it going with Madame Sonnier?" she asked Jean Baptiste. "Her time draws near, I think."

"She is well," he answered. "Her limbs trouble her somewhat, they are badly swollen it seems. Much more so than any of the other times."

Félicité's limbs? Armand nearly scoffed aloud. Anger mixed unevenly into the heat of his arousal. His brother was thinking about limbs all right, but not swollen ones. He was looking at Aida Gaudet with her legs astraddle that plank and he was thinking the same thing that Armand was. Armand was sure of that. But unlike Jean Baptiste, Armand did not have a wife at home who loved him and cared for him. Jean Baptiste had no right to allow his mind to stray in such a direction.

And she, since the most handsome unattached man was ignoring her, was encouraging the most handsome attached man.

"Perhaps she should try some catmint tea," Aida suggested.

"Catmint tea?"

"It's said to help with swelling."

Jean Baptiste offered a polite thank you. "I shall ask Madame Landry for the herb next time I see her."

"Oh I can give you some," Aida told him quickly. "From my little garden. I grow my own herbs."

"I didn't know that," Jean Baptiste told her.

"It's just a girlish pass-a-time," she assured him. "I showed my garden to Monsieur Armand the Sunday he came to my porch. I enjoy watching the plants grow and flower. And I love the fragrances."

"Ah! So it is then no wonder that you always smell so sweet, mamselle," Jean Baptiste said.

With a pointed nod she accepted his compliment. "It will only take me a minute to get the catmint."

She scooted back along the plank and then rose to her feet and dropped her damp skirts in one smooth nimble motion that revealed nothing untoward.

"I will be right back," she called as she turned and raced up the path into the woods.

Armand listened to Jean Baptiste's pleasured sigh. "She is as graceful as a deer," he said wistfully. Then he shook his head. "Poor Félicité moves like an ox."

"*Poor Félicité* is your wife!" Armand almost snarled at him. "It would serve you better if you spoke of her with greater respect."

Jean Baptiste turned to look at Armand as if the younger brother had suddenly grown donkey ears.

"What in the world—" he began.

"Poppa, are we home?" a sleepy Gaston asked from the top of the moss pile.

"*Non, petit,*" Jean Baptiste answered. "We have only stopped to chat with Mademoiselle Gaudet."

Aida hurried up the woods pathway to the back door of her house. She wasn't sure how she was feeling—partially elated, partially embarrassed. Ostensibly she chose her washing site because it was close to the fence line where she hung the clothes to dry. But the fact that she was rarely seen there and that those who did pass by merely hailed her from a distance had always been a substantial side benefit. Laundry was not a pretty chore and it was difficult for a woman to look her best while doing it.

Now today, when she was not only garbed in her worst but splashed and spattered, the Sonnier brothers had deliberately sought her out for conversation.

Jean Baptiste was not difficult, at least. He was such a warm and agreeable fellow. Félicité was certainly a lucky woman to have him for a husband.

Armand, however, appeared today rather grim and humorless. While Jean Baptiste chatted and charmed, Armand looked at her as if she were a rodent caught in his corncrib. She had seen so much of him lately and it seemed inevitably when she was saying or doing something that made her seem like a fool. Compared to him, of course, she was not at all smart. He could read and write and he understood all about money and governments and the world outside. She didn't know any of that, but she did know that her engagement to Monsieur Boudreau was on a shaky foundation and getting more so everyday.

And she wished she could talk to Armand about it—not only was he Laron's best friend, but as children they had been close.

Laron hadn't so much as darkened her doorway since that Sunday that he failed to show up on her porch. A few days later Ruby had told her about Laron's trip to Bayou Blonde.

She had no idea what had set him off in that direction or what his feelings now might be. But he had not hurried to beg her pardon. He'd apparently sent Armand to do it for him. A half-dozen times since then his best friend had offered a recitation of her fiancé's virtues.

Aida's mouth thinned unpleasantly. Maybe because she had never made demands upon Laron, he thought that he could treat her without respect. Well, she was not about to be publicly humiliated by him. She was not going to be made a laughingstock. If Laron couldn't even be bothered to come speak for himself, she seriously doubted that he would be eager to make vows with her. And if the betrothal was to be broken, Aida knew without question that it was she herself who was going to break it.

Skirting the henhouse and the back shed, Aida made her way into the yard. Near the center of the cleared, nearly grassless area, used for household tasks and chicken scratching, was the tall circular-shaped cistern where rainwater was caught for drinking and cooking.

Aida dropped to her knees and opened the lower

store below the tank. There in that cool damp shelter she kept those roots, herbs and preserves that required such storage.

In a near corner on a small shelf sat a sturdy cedar-lined box. She pulled it out on the ground in front of her and opened it up. Inside, packed in small earthen jars with wide cork stopper lids were the fruits of her labors, her harvest of herbs.

Aida had always been interested in plants and flowers. Practically from babyhood she had kept a little garden of her own. There was something so purposeful, so reassuring in seeing the tiny green sprouts force themselves out of the dark earth to grow strong. Not content with cannas, zinnias, and marigolds, Aida had soon been planting lavender and rosemary and verbana, the fragrances of pretty girls.

She had become seriously interested in herbs when a bee stung her cheek. Her face had turned red and raw and swelled badly, temporarily disfiguring her. Aida had been frightened. And her father, very worried himself, had poled her down to see Orva Landry.

The old woman had been calm and self-assured. She'd crushed fresh savory and rubbed it over the injury.

"You'll be fine in a few days," Madame Landry had said with complete confidence.

She had been right. Within a week all evidence of the horrible sting vanished. Aida was impressed with that. But even more, she was impressed by the old woman's confidence. She envied the certainty that a person could have if she held knowledge within her grasp.

It sparked an interest in the medicinal herbs. Gradually she had come to plant them in her little garden. She would pretend that she was a famous hoodoo woman, blending them together for make-believe charms and cures.

Little by little she learned about the herbs used to treat her or her family or friends. She grew a little hyssop to ease her father's breathing when the scent of elm was in the air. And a plot of dill that soothed the ache in her tummy when she got overset. She raised lemon balm for headache and licorice to make the bowels move. Each season she added something new and the portion of her garden set aside for herbs had enlarged and spread until there was little room left for the pretty flowers that she once cultivated.

She sifted delicately among the contents of the herb box. Each bunch of blossoms, bundle of leaves, or stash of seeds had been carefully dried or crushed or mashed into paste to keep it until the spring arrived.

Aida easily found the catmint jar. The pale violet flowers inside were now faded to bluish-gray. The scent was pungent, almost spicy. The jar was completely full, Aida did not suffer often from female difficulties and holding water. She would send it all to Félicité, she decided quickly. If the poor woman's limbs were so swollen that her husband complained about them, then she was certainly in need.

She held her crisp white apron out by the corners and emptied the jar into it. Folding back the corners, she ensured that unless she tripped and fell upon her face, she could transport the herbs without fear of losing any.

She closed the chest and put it back on the cistern safe shelf. As she began to shut the door she spied an arrowroot tuber. After a moment's contemplation she placed it, too, within the folds of her apron.

Aida shut the door and carefully reset the raccoon-proof latch. She hurried back down the woods path. The Sonnier brothers were waiting. They undoubtedly had not had a meal since breakfast and she should not hold them up unnecessarily.

A meal? She glanced down to see two strings still upon her fingers. She must hurry to finish with her laundry. Her poor father must be famished already. She hoped he didn't show up at the water's edge and tell the men that she had forgotten him once more. Armand would truly be disapproving.

Her brow furrowed once more as she considered the younger Monsieur Sonnier's incessant insistence that she and Laron marry as quickly as possible. If she did not know better, she would wonder if he was speaking for her own father or the parish priest. But Armand was supposed to be Laron's best friend. If that was so, why would he push so rigorously for a quick wedding? It was a troublesome question.

"Here you are, monsieur," she called out as she came through the trees and spotted the men waiting on the pirogue.

The little boy had awakened and he waited excitedly.

"*Bonjour*, Mademoiselle Gaudet," he called out.

Aida couldn't help smiling back at him.

"And a good day to you, young sir," she replied.

The boat was pulled in as close to shore as the Sonniers would dare with such a load. Since Aida was dressed in her laundering clothes and already wet, it made perfect sense that she should wade out to them.

She was barely ankle-deep in the water when she heard Jean Baptiste speak up. "Stay where you are, Mademoiselle. I will come to you."

Aida opened her mouth to tell him not to bother, but didn't have time. With a hearty splash, Armand Sonnier was standing in the water.

"I'll do it," he said to his brother.

Aida watched with disbelief as Armand Sonnier made his way through the waist-high water toward her. When he reached her side he was dripping wet.

"I was going to bring it out to the pirogue," she told him by way of apology.

"I didn't want you to have to lift your skirt again."

From his face, the reply seemed to have escaped him unexpectedly. Aida's jaw dropped open in shock.

"I mean I—" He fumbled for an explanation.

Aida felt as disconcerted and uncomfortable as she had ever felt in her life. Hurriedly she unhitched the apron from her belt and handed it all to him in the bundle.

She chattered quickly. "The catmint will make a fine tea, but tell Madame Sonnier not to overboil it or it will be bitter to the taste."

Armand nodded. He appeared unhappy and discomposed. And somewhat irritated to be feeling that way.

"She needn't concern herself with straining it too carefully," she continued. "Even consumed whole, it's not dangerous."

He was standing too close to her, she thought. Well, maybe not too close, he was at least an arm's length away. But there was something distinctly intimate about being able to look directly into a man's eyes. It made her feel as if he could see right inside her. As if she had nowhere to hide.

"I've put an arrowroot in there, too," she said, trying to cover her discomfort. "It's good for thickening a roux or a stew and it is said to build up the strength."

"I will tell her," he said.

"That's all the catmint that I have. If she needs more, perhaps Madame Landry will have some," she said.

Armand raised an eyebrow at her. "Yes, and perhaps it is Madame Landry who should be prescribing teas and roots."

Aida felt the heat of embarrassment flame her cheeks. "Of course Madame Sonnier should follow the dictates of Madame Landry," she agreed quietly. "I . . . I only thought to help."

Her modesty seemed to check his annoyance and he appeared visibly to force his rather angry expression to soften.

"Yes, well, I'm sure you did," he admitted finally. "When you showed me your herb garden, I had no idea that you had such a talent."

"It is, as I said, just a pass-a-time."

"But it is an admirable one," Armand said. "Laron will be pleased to hear that his bride-to-be has such interests."

Aida secretly doubted that statement. She chose her next words carefully.

"I am not altogether certain that pleasing Monsieur Boudreau is any longer my concern," she said.

She saw his eyes widen.

"Whatever do you mean, Mademoiselle Gaudet?" he asked.

"Not having seen or spoken to the man in some time, I have no knowledge of whether he is even alive or dead," she told him.

"He is very much alive, mamselle," Armand said. "Although he has not . . . he has not been feeling quite himself. I expect him to be paying you a visit any day now. Perhaps you can make up a tea from your herbs to treat him, too."

Neuf

The last of the year's cotton crop had been too late and shaded for the sun to open it white and fluffy on the stock. Before the rain and cold could set in and the hulls rot unopened, the men gathered them in baskets and stored them to dry.

Now, with chill and wet and cold in the air, the women gathered together for a hulling bee—a party of sorts to break open the bolls and retrieve the last of the cotton that might have been lost.

Because Félicité was so close to her time, the bee was held in the Sonnier house. Great woven frond baskets filled the room as the women sat around in a gossipy circle. The little ones were sent up to the loft. The older ones watched the younger as they played and allowed their mothers the privacy to share secrets and talk woman talk.

The house was dark and gloomy as the rain drizzled outside. The fireplace popped and crackled, more for the sake of illumination than warmth. The bright yellow lantern hung down from a chain in the center of the room, but could not dispel the bleakness of the afternoon.

Breaking the hard spindly bolls and picking out the fine fibers of white and ecru contained inside required dexterous fingers and was hard on the hands. The women all wore sturdy gloves for the occasion. The fingers were straight and well-fitted for painstaking work, the palms were padded with moss to protect even the roughest and most work-hardened feminine hands from the sharp, slicing hulls that surrounded the cotton.

Aida, of course, had been unable to locate her work gloves that morning. Félicité had allowed her to borrow a worn pair of Jean Baptiste's. The extra padding kept her hands safe, but made her clumsier than usual in working with the cotton. She worked half as fast as any woman present and she was more than mildly embarrassed by the fact.

"And so I simply told him," Madame Doucet related to the group in general and Félicité specifically, "a healthy girl and a pair of sons, *twins* no less, that should be enough for any man." Madame Doucet's florid face was stern in expression. "I said, you, monsieur, just take yourself up into the *garçonnière* for nightly rest. And don't you come back down to my bed until I'm past my prime."

Yvonne Hébert, Laron's sister, leaned close to Aida and whispered into her ear. "He must be back down by now, don't you think?"

Aida disguised her giggle with a cough and covered her smile with her heavily gloved hand.

She had felt a little uncomfortable when Yvonne sat down next to her. Although she had yet to make her decision, as each day passed she became more and more certain that Laron Boudreau would never be her husband.

"Father Denis says that a woman should bear every child she is able," Madame Benoit said.

There was a murmur of concern among the women.

Orva Landry snorted. "What does a fat man with no family understand about feeding a houseful of empty bellies every winter?"

The women of Prairie l'Acadie were devoted to Church and faith, but they also were pragmatic. The lines between the secular and the spiritual were not always clearly defined, but the practical solutions to problems inevitably won out in their lives.

"Are there not herbs or charms that ward off pregnancy?" young Madame Pujol asked.

"There is pennyroyal," Orva answered. "Though it's not a thing I would recommend. It will kill you just as likely. The only certain way is to keep to yourself."

The older women nodded in agreement.

"Well there must certainly be something," Estelle LeBlanc suggested. "Something perhaps the Germans know. The *veuve allemande* has borne no children since her husband left."

Beside her Aida heard Madame Hébert gasp. With great care she put an expression of studied curiosity upon her face. She glanced around and, as she expected, every eye was looking her way. Aida smiled at them. Being known as slightly scatterbrained and forever flighty did have its advantages.

"I hope you are not asking me!" she said with a little giggle. "It is true that I do grow a few herbs and flavorings, but I don't even try to keep in my head what they are or what they are for."

There was no audible sigh of relief, but Aida could feel the tension within the room ease. Of course they would believe that she was too dumb to know. Too silly to realize what every person on the river knew; that her fiancé was involved with another woman.

She glanced across at Ruby, who was gazing at her with a puzzled expression. Fortunately she had the good sense not to speak what was on her mind. Of course it was certain that these women would think Ruby even more stupid than Aida herself.

"Yes Aida, I heard you sent catmint for Madame Sonnier," Orva said with a gesture toward Félicité.

Aida was partially grateful for the change of subject, but shriveled slightly under the scrutiny of Madame Landry. The older woman, who routinely spoke with *the voices* and could probably see right into a person's mind, was giving her a serious, lengthy perusal.

"Monsieur Sonnier told me of her troubles. I thought it might help the swelling," she said gently. She clasped her hands together in the heavy men's gloves to keep them from shaking. "And I sent arrowroot to build up her strength. I . . . I thought that would be what you would do."

"Indeed it is," Orva answered. "I arrived here this very morning with a parcel of catmint, some arrowroot, a dripping of holy water and birthing sachet." The old woman leaned forward a bit more, continuing to gaze at Aida. "It was good to know that dear Félicité had already begun her treatment."

"Poor Jean Baptiste," Félicité said, shaking her head. "I have been so uncomfortable and disagreeable with this one." She rubbed her heavily rounded belly lovingly. "You would think I would be used to it by now. The fourth one should be as easy as snapping beans. But I have been so cross and grumbling. I declare that my husband has been nearly a saint to put up with me."

Orva spoke evenly. "Each birthing is different. Nothing from the last can prepare you for the next. From each child we are taught different lessons. Some things can never be taken for granted."

"Yes, of course you are right," Félicité agreed easily. "I will just be grateful when it is over. Undoubtedly Jean Baptiste will be, too. I'm so puffed up, I wonder that he can recognize me!"

Orva patted Félicité's hand. "His eyes may not, but his heart always will," she said.

Then, surprisingly, she turned the attention toward Aida once more.

"I am pleased that you have an interest in herbs, young woman," the old treater said. "Why am I just now to know of it?"

"I never thought it worth mentioning," Aida said.

Orva huffed with disdain, then added with wry humor, "Must I wait for *the voices* to tell me everything?"

The other women stared askance, none daring to find amusement in anything about *the voices.*

Aida flushed with embarrassment. "There is nothing to tell, Madame Landry," she said. "Herbs are merely a pass-a-time for me."

"Merely a pass-a-time?"

"Yes, madame."

Nervously Aida tried to occupy her hands with the cotton but continued to fumble. One boll shot out of her hand as she tried to crack it and hit Madame LeBlanc squarely upon her ample bosom.

"Oh I do beg your pardon," Aida apologized, horrified.

Orva gazed at her intently. "Do you know how old I am?" she asked.

Aida was startled.

"Why no," she answered, wondering if she should hazard a guess. "No, madame, I do not."

"And I am not about to tell you," Orva replied tartly. "It's almost a sin against God to be able to count that high."

There was a titter of laugher around the circle.

"I am old enough, young lady, that it would not be an unholy expectation to anticipate seeing me laid out in a shroud."

Aida swallowed nervously. Surely she was not supposed to respond to that.

"And when I am cleaned and wrapped and put to ground," she continued, "who among these women will treat the ills?"

The room was suddenly very quiet. To Aida's dismay, every eye now looked upon her with both skepticism and hope.

"Not me, madame," Aida assured her hastily.

"I have been waiting forty years for a woman to take an interest in the herbs," Orva said. "I admit that I would never have thought that woman to be you." Madame Landry shook her head in wonder. "But the ways of grace are mysterious."

"Aida Gaudet as a treater?" Madame Doucet whispered the words in shocked disbelief.

The rustle of murmurs went through the group as the women sought to accustom themselves to the idea. Orva Landry's gaze on Aida never wavered.

"I . . . I could not do it, Madame Landry," she said.

"And why not?"

"It is a calling, not a pursuit," she said.

Orva waved that away. " 'Many are called but few are chosen,' " she quoted.

"The . . . *the voices* have never spoken to me." Aida hesitated to even mention them aloud.

"And why should they with me still living?" she asked.

Aida felt her anxiety and embarrassment growing.

"I am not smart," she admitted, lowering her eyes. "It shames me to say it, but you all know the truth. I could never be trusted with such a responsible task."

Orva hooted with laughter. The sound brought Aida's head up sharply. She was not alone. Every occupant in the room was staring startled at the old woman.

"Heaven does have a sense of humor," Madame Landry said, still chuckling. She directed her comments to those around her. "Here sits the most beautiful female this old woman has ever beheld. And what does she feel?" Orva continued to chuckle. "She is distraught because she is not much for wit. Around her the rest of us, all prideful in what we perceive, would trade, each and every one of us, for a fraction of this young woman's beauty."

There was a sputtering of high-minded dissension among the group. But not one woman contradicted Madame Landry's words.

"Heaven has disguised you from me," Orva said. "I am not the only one who has need of a lesson in humility."

No one knew to whom she referred, but there was

no ignoring the inference of her words. Aida continued to shake her head in disagreement.

"I could never do it," she insisted with certainty.

"You have done it," Orva said. "You have done it for Madame Sonnier and I will teach you to do it for others."

Aida's heart was pounding with wild anxiety. "As long as you are here for me to ask," Aida agreed. "Then I could follow your orders. But after you are gone? Oh, madame, how could I remember? I cannot remember where I left my gloves or which day is Wednesday or even to cook supper each night for my poppa!"

The truth of that statement stopped the discussion. Aida was flighty and featherheaded. Everybody knew that. She couldn't remember where to find the beans, much less when to put them on the fire. She would never be able to keep in her silly brain all the cures and charms necessary for the welfare of the people in the parish.

"Armand could write them down."

The surprise statement came from Félicité.

"What?" Orva's interest was piqued.

"While you apprentice Aida as treater," she said. "You must keep Armand with you. He can write down in words all the mixes and spells."

"But a man can't be a treater," Madame Marchand pointed out.

"And he won't be," Félicité said. "Aida will be treater and when she can't remember what to do, Armand can read it to her."

"All the cures written down in words?" Madame Doucet wasn't certain.

"After you are gone," Félicité said, indicating Madame Landry. "After Aida is gone, even after Armand is gone, the words would still be there. My Gaston is learning to read the words," she admitted proudly. "Other boys will learn, too. They can read them for the next treater and the next and next."

"The men write down laws and contracts," Madame Hébert piped in. "Why should not the women have those things important to us kept in ink and paper?"

Orva was nodding thoughtfully. "Writing it down. Having Armand write it all down. Yes, that would work," she said. "That would work very well indeed."

Outside of the hulling bee, standing along the riverbank in a dripping rain, the menfolk cast their fishing lines. It was a women's occasion. And it was not so much that the men felt unwelcome as they just felt unnecessary. They were expected to load, unload, transport, and carry. But when females got an opportunity to sit together, the farmers were supposed to make themselves scarce. A small fire pit blazed under the protecting limbs of a *lilas parasol*. A pot of strong black coffee was the only comfort being afforded.

Armand watched the end of his cane pole with a substantive concentration that could have snapped it in two. He'd already caught a stringer's length of fish that morning, but he had no heart for the sport this day. All around him he heard light-hearted conversations in which he did not participate. His mind was troubled.

Laron continued to be reluctant to go ahead with his wedding plans. He still insisted that he would have Helga or no one. Armand wanted to support his decision, but he could not. Not with his brother's happiness in jeopardy. Not with Jean Baptiste still sleeping in the *garçonnière*.

Aida Gaudet was much too dangerous for that. He'd nearly gotten into an argument with his brother the day they had caught her doing laundry. Armand remembered well his own reaction. He'd gotten hard as a stone just looking at her that day. And when he had waded in to stand beside her, it had been all he could do to keep himself from reaching out to touch the white skin on her arm, the loose lock of hair on her cheek. She was beautiful, desirable, and almost available. For any man that was a temptation. For one suffering a weakness in his marriage, it could be a damning combination.

Jean Baptiste continued to sing her praises while sighing with disappointment about Félicité.

"What is wrong with her face?" Jean Baptiste had asked Armand just this morning.

"I don't know what you're talking about."

"Félicité's face," his brother continued. "Her cheeks and neck are so fat, she looks as if she's gotten bee-stung."

She did look bad, Armand couldn't deny that. But pregnancy and vanity were not a good mix. Jean Baptiste should be looking at her through a haze of love.

But any haze cleared when the lovely Aida was helped out of her pirogue, showing an unmannerly amount of bare leg, Armand thought. And giggling about forgetting her gloves. What kind of woman went to a hulling bee with no gloves? The answer was simple, a woman who was more interested in being seen than in doing any work.

Aida Gaudet was silly, superficial, and useless compared to Félicité. And Jean Baptiste couldn't keep his eyes off her. It was frightening. Terrifying. If only Armand could speak up to him directly, man to man, and say, "Don't do this to your wife!" But he was afraid. Look at the mess careless words had already gotten him into. If he pointed things out to him, the situation might even get worse.

"Well, look who is here!"

The statement of surprise came from Emile Marchand.

Oscar Benoit sniggered under his breath. "Never known him to show up when there was real work going on."

A chuckle of agreement moved down the line of men like a contagion.

"*Bonjour*, Father Denis," Jean Baptiste said, stepping up to greet the man. "Welcome to my home."

The priest gave him a hasty, halfhearted blessing.

"Come and have coffee," Jean Baptiste continued. "You have walked so very far. If we had known you wanted to attend the hulling bee, we would have sent someone in a pirogue to fetch you."

"Hulling bee, is it?" the priest looked around him critically. "It looks more like a fishing party."

The men offered good-natured disagreement.

"Alas, our women keep warm and dry with the cotton," Hippolyte Arceneaux piped in sarcastically. "While we poor men are left outside with the gray and drizzle. Nothing to give us comfort but cold coffee and wet fish."

That comment evoked guffaws. Even Father Denis joined in.

"Would you care to linger with us, Father?" Jean

Baptiste asked. "Or would you prefer to join the women under a roof?"

"Oh no, I can't stay long," he said. "I only came to speak with your brother."

Jean Baptiste spotted Armand. "He's here to see you," he reported.

Of course Armand had heard Father Denis's words but he was quite reluctant to rush to the old priest's side. His unwillingness was not because he loved fishing, but rather a great aversion to having to deal with one more uneasy problem. Reluctantly he began pulling in his line.

"May I fish with your pole, Uncle Armand?" little Gaston asked excitedly. The boy's own had proved unlucky that morning. He'd not caught even one measly throwback.

Armand ruffled the boy's hair and handed him the pole.

"Clearly the fish are having trouble swimming around all this other bait," he said to Gaston, indicating the long line of fishermen. "My hook is always their favorite."

Around him the other men scoffed good-naturedly. The boy looked up at him, his trusting eyes wide.

"Give it just a tiny flick of the wrist when you toss it out," Armand suggested quietly. "No grand gesture, like a beau making bow to a mamselle, just a tiny flick, like a husband bidding his wife to dance."

Gaston nodded solemnly.

"The big catfish know that gesture," Armand assured him. "As soon as they see it they'll hurry to the end of your line."

Biting the side of his small mouth in concentration, the child attempted to follow his uncle's advice.

Armand squeezed his shoulder before turning toward the long-robed priest.

Armand offered a polite word in greeting. Father Denis answered with a blessing.

"What is it, Father?" he asked as the two stepped away from the riverbank. "You wished to speak with me?"

The cleric gave a quick disapproving look at the palmfrond hat that remained on Armand's head but made no comment.

"It is a beautiful day," Father Denis commented conversationally.

Armand raised an eyebrow. "It's drizzling rain."

The old priest shrugged. "Even the worst of times are the gift of our Father in heaven," he replied.

Armand shrugged a tacit agreement.

"Let us walk, shall we?"

Armand followed the priest's lead and they slowly made their way along the high ground path, pausing to turn inland when they reached the cypress *pieux* split rail fence.

"We have had cross words," the good father stated calmly as the two reached beyond the hearing distance of the others.

"It is not the first time, Father," Armand replied.

The years of tutelage and obedience were long in the past. Armand had long since spoken his mind with the priest and as often as not that frankness had brought discord.

"I have offended you somehow and in some way that I did not intend," the old man said. "And I find that I much need your help."

"If this is about the school, Father," Armand told him, "I have said all that I wish to upon the subject."

"But not all that needs to be said has been," he answered.

"Father, I will not—"

The old priest held up his hand.

"You are correct, my son, when you say that after twenty years I should understand your people better," he said.

Armand nodded agreement.

"I am a man of God, but I am also a Frenchman and will always be so. You and your people"—he shook his head—"they are a breed still strange to me, strange to most anyone, I think."

"We are not strange to ourselves, Father," Armand replied.

"Well said," the priest admitted. "It has been so many years that you have been away from anyone but your own. You have become distinct and strangely unique in your ways. The people here have grown less French in their ways than many of the Africans that have not one drop of French blood inside them."

Armand wondered how the father could know all this, then determinedly shrugged off what sounded to him very much like criticism. The two had reached the corner of the fencing and could walk no further. Armand leaned back against the cypress *pieu*, spreading his arms along the top railing and propping one bare foot upon the bottom.

"It is the French themselves who taught us that we are not French," he countered.

"Yes, yes, I know," Father Denis said patronizingly. "But that was all a very long time ago."

"A long time ago?" Armand's tone of voice lowered and intensified. "It was a very long time ago. But if we forget this wrong," he said, "if we say what is past is past, if we do not tell our children the story of how we came here and why, all that pain and rage and death will have been for naught.''

The priest's expression was solemn. "The Bible tells us to forgive our enemies, Armand. To bless them that cursed you and pray for them that despitefully used you.''

"And we do, Father," Armand told him. "We wage no war. We plot no revenge. Frenchmen, Englishmen, Spaniards, Creoles, or Americaines, they are all safe here in this place. We laugh, we dance, and we welcome strangers among us. We live on as God intended. But we will not, cannot, forget our past, and we shall not allow our children to do so.''

Father Denis observed his pained expression, but eventually nodded.

"All right, Armand," he said. "I will not ask you to bring your people around to my way of thinking.''

"Good.''

"But I still ask you to help me to start a school.''

Armand stopped in his tracks and huffed with indignation. "You have not heard a word that I have said.''

"I have heard every word," Father Denis replied. "But none of it convinces me that these children should not learn to read.''

"There is no need," Armand insisted.

"I would do nothing to turn the children against the old ways," the priest assured him. "You are right when you say that there is much evil in the world and that it is good to stand clear of it. But it is a perilous idea to believe that ignorance can be a protection. We must know what dangers lurk around us or we should never be on watch to avoid them.''

"To know the dangers of the world, Father, is to be tempted by them," Armand said.

"But without temptation there is no virtue, no choice to do right. We would all choose for children the good way, but in truth they each must at some time choose for themselves."

Father Denis glared at him sternly. "You always think that you know what is best, Armand Sonnier. That is always what you think. When I pushed you to become the judge, I did it because I believed in the strength of your mind. But your vanity has blossomed with your age."

The priest's words were soft, but their meaning was a condemnation.

"God has granted you much capacity for knowledge," he said. "I do not see yet that you have acquired much wisdom."

Dix

Aida Gaudet wanted to crawl into a rabbit hole and pull the dirt back over to cover herself up.

"Aida Gaudet to be the new treater?" Armand's tone was incredulous.

"I know it's a silly—" Aida began.

"It's my idea and a very good one, I am thinking," Orva said sharply.

Aida had mentioned Orva Landry's plan to no one, not even her own father. She knew that it would seem foolish, ridiculous. She was not a treater and she never would be. Women like her were not chosen for such tasks. Women like her were the decorations of a community, not the pinions.

Aida watched Armand. He looked down at Madame Landry, seated heavily upon a short stool in the middle of her garden and then over at Aida. He swallowed determinedly as if choosing his words and turned back to the older woman.

"I am not saying that Mademoiselle Gaudet could not be a fine help to you, *Nanan*," he said quietly. "She could be a companion, assist you in the garden. But learning the cures and charms?" He glanced toward Aida. And then smiled with genuine sympathy. "Why, *la demoiselle* has much too much to think about already."

Aida wanted to defend herself, but when she looked into his eyes she could not. Armand was correct. She was not nearly smart enough to become the treater. She'd known it all along. That Orva Landry even suggested that she could was ludicrous. But the old woman seemed wholly set upon it.

She sat stubbornly amid the remainders of her garden plot. The uncut corn was drying on the stalk, a few late tomatoes still hid among the vines, and a dozen brightly colored gourds were ripe enough to pick.

"The young woman has an interest," Orva insisted. "She has an interest and she shows an aptitude. That says enough for me. Would you have me ask *the voices* for your sake?"

Armand cleared his throat nervously. Clearly he did not want any sort of personal consultation with *the voices*.

"I wouldn't truly be the *traiteur*," Aida assured him with sincerity. "I would just grow the herbs. I can do that. It's simply gardening. And you will tell me how to put them together. You will keep the secrets of the charms and cures."

"Men don't keep those secrets," he told her.

"Of course they don't," Madame Landry agreed. "And I'm not asking you to keep them. Just to write them down. They need to be written down and I'm not the one to do it."

"It will never work," Armand insisted. "If you must apprentice someone, it must be someone who can *be* treater."

"There you go again! Thinking that you know everything." Orva huffed in disgust. "Has this current load of lessons you've been burdened with taught you nothing at all?"

Young Monsieur Sonnier appeared distinctly uncomfortable.

"I would think," the old woman continued, "that between that fat old priest's book teachings and my personal guidance, the brightest young man on the Vermillion River would have learned that things are not always exactly as they appear. But no. You believe you know best for yourself, best for everyone. It's a conceit, young man, very much a conceit."

Aida watched as Armand's cheeks reddened. She felt immediate empathy for him. How strange that a man as smart as Armand could be made to feel as silly and foolish as she often did herself. He looked strong and determined, his blue eyes intense. Without thinking she reached out to touch his arm.

He flinched slightly beneath her fingers and glanced up at her, startled.

"Excuse us for a moment," she said to Madame Landry. "I need to speak a word with Monsieur Sonnier."

The treater nodded and Aida led a reluctant Armand out of earshot. She regretted her action almost instantly. She could not offer wisdom or even reason. He would think she had gotten far above herself if she did. All she could speak was the truth.

"I know that I am no choice for this burden," she whispered to him. She kept her head high. She would not be ashamed of who she was, not in front of him. "I don't know a lot. I lose things. And I don't have a very good memory."

Armand said nothing. It would have been polite if he had begged to differ with her. But she took it as a compliment that he didn't immediately agree.

"Surely a true treater will come along and Madame Landry will recognize her straightaway," she continued. "It is a strange idea, indeed, that I could be of any help to Madame Landry. But she thinks it will be so."

"It is not for me to say who the treater should be," Armand said finally as he watched the determined set of her shoulders. "I just thought that it would be . . . it would be someone other than you."

"I agree completely," Aida told him, grateful that he was not openly derisive of her. "It's not a job I would want. And I am sure that another woman will come along who will be perfect for it. But until she does . . . it is only an afternoon or two spent in the old woman's presence. Will it be so much work to write down what she has to say?"

"No, I suppose not," he admitted.

"Until the true treater comes along, I can listen and learn what I can. That will not hurt anyone," she said. "And it will be a good thing to have the cures written down on papers, don't you think?"

He shrugged, but appeared to be conceding. "It could be a good thing," he agreed finally. "A written record is always a hedge against disaster or uncertainty."

"Then you will help me?" she asked. "You will listen while she tells me and you will write it down?"

"All right."

"Thank you, monsieur. Thank you so much." Aida smiled broadly at him, inordinately happy and pleased.

Armand gave her a strange look. "You have a chipped tooth," he said.

Aida covered her mouth, embarrassed.

"Yes, monsieur," she admitted. "I fell when I was ten."

"Pardon, mamselle, I don't know where I lost my manners to speak of it. I had merely never noticed it before. It is not at all distracting."

Aida was still blushing.

"I . . . I, too, have one cracked," he said, showing her a lower incisor. "Laron once hit me in the mouth with a poling tool."

She smiled broadly.

"You must learn to duck," she told him.

Her humor was unexpectedly contagious and Armand actually grinned back. "With my lack of height, mamselle, I had never before needed to!"

She actually giggled at his joke.

It was a warm, pleasant moment. Reminiscent of the friendship long past. Perhaps Monsieur Sonnier did not really like her, but he was willing to tolerate her ignorance for the sake of Prairie l'Acadie and Orva Landry. And he had seen her, he had seen her flaw. Strangely she found that pleased her.

"I promise to do my best to learn what Madame Landry tries to teach me," Aida vowed to him. "And for your sake, I will not act any more silly than I can help."

Those words raised his eyebrows and Aida wished she could call them back. She would look smarter, of course, to pretend that she didn't know that she wasn't smart. Oh how she wished he were more like the other fellows, like Placide or Ignace or even Laron. If she could just tease and flirt with him then it would be so easy. But Armand Sonnier was much too intelligent to be fooled by such nonsense. And nonsense was all that she had to offer.

"Are you two conjuring up a love affair?" Orva Landry called out to them.

Armand jumped back as if a shot had been fired, clearly horrified. Aida swallowed hard and kept her chin high as inwardly she writhed in humiliation, wondering if Madame Landry had somehow known the direction of her thoughts.

With deliberate purpose she forced a little giggle from her throat. "Oh, we are going to be much too busy for that this morning," she said. "You have promised to show me how to lessen Poppa's joint pain with potato shavings."

"That I will," the old woman said. "I will indeed. Well, *mon fils*," she said to Armand. "Go fetch your pen and paper if you are to write down my words."

"*Oui*, madame," he answered and headed for the house.

Aida watched him go for a moment and then moved to Madame Landry's side, seating herself in the cool earth at her feet.

"I am so glad he is going to help me," she said. "I could never remember all this."

"Of course he will help," Orva said waving away her concern.

"I was afraid for a moment that he would not," Aida admitted.

The old woman smiled vaguely. "Things always work out exactly how they are meant," she said. "Remember that, young one, exactly how they are meant. Fate. It's just that at times we are so stubborn, we cannot trust in that to be."

Aida frowned at her words, not understanding. *The voices* themselves couldn't be any harder to comprehend. She hoped that Madame Landry would speak more plainly. It was going to be difficult enough to fathom the treatey's knowledge without the rarities of language.

In fact, the afternoon proved to be a lot less difficult for Aida than she would have imagined. She was honestly surprised at how much she already knew about the herbs. Santolina and tansy. Marjoram and feverfew. They were as familiar to her as jasmine and marigold. And even the cures themselves seemed rather straightforward and commonsense. Not at all the strange spiritual world that she imagined.

"To get rid of head lice, you wash the hair in whiskey and powder it with sand," the old woman explained. "The lice will get drunk on the whiskey and the sand will make them think they are down on the ground. They'll fight each other to the death over territory."

"Really." Aida shook her head in amazement. Then resolutely committed the story to memory. Drunk lice will fight on sand.

"Now if it's body lice," Madame Landry continued, "it's a completely different problem.

Aida nodded, listening, deliberately trying to commit Madame Landry's words to memory. It was challenging and very difficult. She was so very grateful that Monsieur Sonnier was writing everything down.

She glanced momentarily in his direction. He was sitting nearby them on a cane-seat chair. His legs were crossed, right ankle on left knee, with the breadboard he'd appropriated from Madame Landry's kitchen serving as a writing surface.

The tiny bottle of blue-black ink was uncorked and held securely with the two fingers that also steadied the paper. He was obviously listening, but he kept his eyes on his efforts, writing continuously, with only occasional hesitations to re-ink his point.

His face, shaded by the wide-brimmed hat, was not visible to her. So Aida allowed herself to look more closely at the rest of him. From her place on the ground and with the distance separating them, Armand didn't appear little or boyish. It was curious actually how people talked of him as if he were a small, frail man. He may have been ill in his youth, but now, in fact, he looked to Aida to be anything but.

Normally he wore trousers, which Aida generally preferred on men, being so much more fashionable. Today however he was clad in Acadian *culotte* and buttonless cottonade shirt. The traditional costume suited him somehow. He looked natural. He looked attractive. Aida was somewhat surprised at her own thought. She scrutinized his appearance more carefully as if checking her conclusion.

His shoulders were actually quite broad. Oh, certainly not as broad as perhaps Laron's, but much broader than his hips, which were narrow and lean. The afternoon sun was warm and the sweat-dampened cottonade of his clothing clung tightly to his form. Aida found herself measuring the length of his torso and the width of his chest. He was fit and healthy, robust even. There was no evidence of the sickly scholar.

Her glance skittered past the frighteningly foreign territory at the crotch of his pants, lingering along the thick muscled length of his thigh, at the very top of which she could detect just the hint of a round masculine backside. Oh how she would love to touch it.

The idea shot through her like the heat of lightning and she wiggled a bit uncomfortably on the hard ground where she sat. What a strange notion to have!

Determinedly she tried to concentrate once more on what Madame Landry was saying.

"Put a small piece of mutton tallow to a jigger of snake oil and set it near the fire. When it's melted, add in twelve drops of attar of roses."

Aida's attention once more strayed to the man seated at a distance from her. Primly she withdrew her gaze from the not quite proper perusal of his nether person to the much more socially acceptable view of his limbs.

His *culotte* was tied neatly at the base of his knee. Below them his calves were bare, or mostly so. Even at a rail length or more, Aida could see the profusion of tawny brown hair that festooned the well-muscled curve of his leg.

Aida swallowed, but her mouth was surprisingly dry.

Short men should have short legs, stubby legs, she thought to herself. But Armand was not built so. He was perfectly proportioned, as if his growth had not been stunted as everyone said, but as if God intended for him to look exactly the way that he did. And what God made, He made perfectly.

Aida allowed her eyes to wander the length of his naked limbs, curious and admiring. With the wearing of *culottes* Aida was familiar with the shape of men's legs. At the *fais-dodo* or special dances the younger fellows often tried to draw attention to them by tying multicolored bows at their knees, occasionally with flowing streamers. Even in the coldest part of winter when their nakedness was covered by durable thigh-high Indian moccasins, leather fringes were attached to draw the eye. And the action of the gentlemen's bow was obviously designed to show the male limb to best advantage. Aida had cast her glance on many legs, but none had ever before held her attention.

The intriguing fleece of masculine hair stopped abruptly upon the top of his foot, which was rather long and narrow. His toes were well-shaped and lean, the second one slightly longer than the first. The sole she observed was callused and rough, a testament to the roads he traveled. His instep was high-arched and graceful, somehow giving the perception of both beauty and strength.

Beauty and strength. She had never associated either word with this man. No, not Armand Sonnier. Yet somehow, suddenly now, she knew both words described him. She allowed her gaze to wander back over the length of leg, the thighs covered in closely clinging cottonade, the curve of his handsome derrière, the strong muscled chest, the deceptively broad shoulders, the noble jut of his chin, those brightly honest blue eyes. His—

Brightly honest blue eyes!

He was staring straight at her.

Aida lowered her gaze immediately, but couldn't keep it down. Glancing up again, she saw she had been right. He was looking at her, straight at her, right at her. She couldn't turn away. He must have seen her watching him, examining him. He must be able to see right inside her. He must know what she was thinking, what she was feeling. The flesh on her body mottled with goosebumps. Her womb quivered like jelly. Her bosom was tight and high, the nipples puckered beneath the covering of her clothes. She didn't even know what she was thinking or feeling. Aida wasn't sure if she could still breathe. Her lips parted, inviting air into her lungs, but the lower one trembled, trembled with something akin to fear.

"Of course, if all else fails you can rub parsley into it. Armand? Are you not writing this down?"

Madame Landry's words penetrated to both of them. When he glanced away, Aida found that she could, too. Determinedly she concentrated her attention upon her own lap. She ached there. It was unfamiliar, unfathomable, and physical. Her hands were trembling. She clasped them together.

He didn't like her, she reminded herself. He thought her foolish and frivolous. He wanted her to marry his best friend. But what did that look, that intensity, what did it mean? She was the most beautiful woman on the Vermillion River. A lot of men had looked at her. But no man had ever looked at her like that.

Tears welled in her eyes. She wasn't sure if the emotion she felt was sadness or joy. Armand Sonnier looked at her and her whole world was changed.

"Now to make a charm against it," Orva continued, "you slice a real thin piece of old smoked bacon, the older the better. You stitch it into a piece of flannel and blacken it all over with pepper. Warm it until it's all as one and then fasten it with a string right into the craw of a man's throat."

"We are going to the *fais–dodo*," Armand told Laron determinedly. "And you are going to patch things up with Aida Gaudet."

Laron was poling the pirogue in the right direction, the evening's entertainment was to be at the home of Thertule Guidry, but he was distinctly uninterested in the outing.

Armand was sitting in the bottom of the boat. Armand was his best friend in the whole world. But Armand didn't have any idea of the way things were in his heart.

"I will go," Laron told him. "This is my community and family. I never want to be separated from them. But I no longer intend to wed Aida Gaudet. I will have Helga, Armand. I will have Helga or no one at all. You are my friend and the sooner you accept that, the better it will be for everyone."

Armand shook his head. "Laron, it just cannot be. I know that you love her. I have known that for a very long time. But you cannot have her."

"You once said that I could."

Armand nodded. "I did say it, careless words, I said. But I was wrong."

"Perhaps you are wrong now," Laron suggested.

"I don't think so," he answered. "I don't think so. She is married, Laron. That cannot be changed. He may have been no good, he may have left her, but he is still her husband and there is just no way that it can ever be undone."

Laron didn't reply. There was a way it could be

undone. Laron had thought long and hard about that way. But he did not mention it to Armand. There were things a man knew about himself that he could not reveal even to his best friend. Laron knew that he was going to have Helga Shotz, openly, honestly, sanctioned by God and man. She was going to bear his name and he was going to be her husband. He knew that.

And he also knew the only way for it to happen was for her to be a German widow indeed. Laron had decided. He must kill Helmut Shotz.

"I think you have underestimated Mademoiselle Gaudet," Armand continued. "She is so very pretty that we have all failed to notice all the other fine things about her."

"Hmmm." Laron was noncommittal.

"I myself have been guilty of this. Certainly the woman is no great intellect. But I have allowed myself to be so blinded by her physical appearance that I have not noticed her innate good sense. I told you that Madame Landry is teaching her the charms and cures."

"So I have heard."

"She may not be clever, but she is diligent and determined," Armand continued. "It is the most a person could expect of another human being."

Laron was no longer listening. He was remembering.

He had tried to stay away. He knew that it was the thing to do. Until he could offer himself, until he had something to offer, he should keep his distance. Not just for her sake, or for his own, but for the children.

He ached for Jakob's loving little-boy kisses, for Elsa's wide-eyed admiration, even for Karl's oft-times sullen companionship. The children loved and needed him and he realized, perhaps too late, that they were part of his heart.

But even more he required Helga. He could not recall the day, the hour, the moment when he first knew that he loved her. But he did and there was no stepping back from it.

The previous day he had been able to stand it no longer. He'd poled his way up Bayou Tortue hoping for a glimpse of her. He could be content with not even a word but he was starving for the sight of her. But it was not to be.

As he approached the house a longing stirred inside him as familiarity warred with separation. He noticed a section of rotting shingles on the roof and thought to himself that he'd get Jean Baptiste and Armand to help him replace them. Then like a direct blow to the chest he recalled that it was not his house and that his help, even his presence, was no longer welcome. Who would help Helga now? Who would see that the roof over her head was sturdy and that she had stores for the winter?

Elsa was in the yard pounding grain with the *pile et pilon*. She was young and strong and straight. A daughter any man would be proud to call his own. Her blond braids swung and slapped her back like ropes as her arms worked the pestle up and down into the hollowed-out log mortar. Across the distance of the water, Laron could hear the pop and shatter of corn being cracked. In memory he could taste once more that strange German version of fried *coushe-coushe* that Helga had so often served him for breakfast.

"Oncle! Oncle!"

Laron heard the cry before he saw the little fellow

who uttered it. Jakob had come around from the far side of the house. He carried a carved gourd crawfish trap, but he cast it aside carelessly and raced to the end of the dock when he spotted Laron.

"*Oncle*, where have you been?" he called out. "We have missed you so much."

Elsa, too, had set her work aside and followed her brother, a little uneasily, to the end of the dock.

Laron had not intended to stop. He had thought merely to pass by, to see from a distance those joys that he used to hold close with such casual unconcern. But he could not merely pass by. Not with young Jakob jumping up and down with delight on the dock. He steered the pirogue in the direction of the children. He even cast the line to Jakob to secure for him, but he did not disembark.

That did not matter to the little boy who eagerly threw himself into Laron's arms. It took all his balance to keep the pirogue from tipping, but he wouldn't put the boy aside. It felt much too good to hold him close. Tightly the child hugged his neck, punctuated by a smacking kiss at his temple.

"Mama said that you would not come back," he told Laron. "But I knew that you would. You love us and I told her so."

"I do love you," Laron whispered as he felt the tears well up in his eyes. "I do love you all, and that is forever."

"Karl said you are going to be like our poppa," he continued. "Not dead really, but as good as dead to us."

"I am not at all and in no way like your poppa," Laron assured him, deciding for himself as the words came from his mouth. "No matter what happens between your mother and me, I will never be dead to you until I am dead in fact."

"Oh Monsieur Boudreau!" Elsa tearfully threw herself into his arms also. "Mama is so unhappy. Now you are back and everything will be wonderful again."

The misery in her tone belied the hope in her words, but Laron could only press her tightly against him and pray that it could be so.

"Get in the house!"

The command was forceful and abrupt. All three looked up to see Helga's oldest son standing on the porch steps; the flintlock rifle Laron had given them for protection was in Karl's hands at the ready.

"You children get in the house!" he repeated.

"Shut up, Karl," Elsa hollered back. "Who made you the boss of anything?"

"*Oncle* is here," Jakob told him. "I'm not going into the house without him."

"You two mind your brother," Laron told them quietly. "Go on into the house. He and I need to talk."

"He thinks he's the man of the house," Elsa complained. "Ordering us all around and Mama crying every night."

"Go on inside, *princesse*," Laron said. "Your mother is in the house, is she not? She may need you beside her."

Reluctantly the two stepped away. Elsa took Jakob's hand and they made their way past their older brother. Elsa didn't resist snapping one more word of dissent at Karl. Jakob took that opportunity to look back in longing at Laron, still standing in his pirogue.

The children hesitated momentarily on the porch

and then passed through the curtained doorway into the house.

"Hello, Karl," Laron said finally.

"Mama wants you gone from here," the boy answered.

"Did she tell you to bring the gun?"

The youngster was momentarily nonplussed. "It's your gun, I know. Do you want it back?"

Laron shook his head. "No, no, certainly not. But it is meant for killing game and birds, not Acadians."

Karl raised both his chin and the rifle muzzle in challenge. "Any Acadian who comes here to make my mother cry deserves killing."

Laron almost smiled. The boy was a defender, a protector of the family. A man could ask no greater thing from a son.

"I am leaving now," Laron told him. "But I wish you to give a message to your mother."

Karl looked skeptical but nodded.

"Tell her that I am going to make it all right. Once and for all time, I am going to make it right."

And he would, Laron vowed silently once more as he poled himself and Armand toward the ever increasing volume of music along the river. He was going to make it right.

"She is very sweet and genuine, actually," Armand was saying. "Certainly a man cannot look at her without feeling a degree of lust, but it is not as if she draws it to herself or even desires that attention. A woman cannot be held responsible for her own beauty any more than she can be condemned for plainness."

"If you think she is so wonderful, Armand," Laron

interrupted, "then perhaps you should set your own sights in that direction. I am no longer interested."

"But Laron—"

"We are here already," he announced. "I fully intend to talk to her, my friend, so please do not bend my ear any further about it."

The *fais-dodo* was in full swing. Dancers twirled on the most even spot of the Guidrys' high ground. A huge fire was lit in the outside hearth, but it was not as much for cooking as for fending off the November chill in the air. The space at the end of the dock was overcrowded; the two men stepped out of the pirogue and were forced to wade the last steps to the bank, dragging the boat up behind them.

"I'm getting wet," Armand complained.

Laron laughed at him. "If you insist on wearing those resplendent Creole trousers, then you must learn to live with your damp pant legs."

His friend growled back at him good-naturedly.

They were met upon the bank by friends and neighbors with happy greetings and slaps upon the back. Laron, who had not been seen among them since his now well-known foray to the Bayou Blonde, was greeted with both warmth and curiosity. He'd stepped over the bounds, but he was back in the fold. All were willing to forgive and forget, and could do so easily.

Laron laughed and talked and communed with them. He enjoyed these people and this place. He cherished being a part of them. They were his family, some literally and others in his heart. He loved them. But he loved Helga more and he had things to accomplish. It was time to do those things.

He made his way to the edge of the dancers, his eyes taking in, with pleasure, the beauty of Aida Gaudet. On Granger's arm she danced with delicate grace. She was a treasure to behold, all light and prettiness as shiny as morning. She was a swirl of eye-catching color, all red and blue and yellow. Any man's attention would be drawn to her. He understood how his own once had been, too. He had thought to possess her. To press that lovely body against his own and fill it with his seed. He no longer had the desire to do that. He could look at her dispassionately now and know that she was human. He could be sorry that he was going to abandon her, but he would not regret the loss.

The music ended and the dancers clapped politely. Aida spotted him in that moment and paled. He never approached her early in the evening. He always watched her have her fun until he was ready to take his obligatory dance. Tonight he stepped forward immediately.

As if knowing that a *Passepied* was not Laron's main interest, Ony Guidry took that moment to put down the fiddle and seek out a cup of coffee.

"We must talk," he said to her.

"Yes," she answered, nodding.

Laron hesitated momentarily. Should he take her into the relative privacy of the nearby trees, or would that be unconscionable for a couple who were just about to become unengaged?

He led her a little away from the other young people, but kept in full sight of every person present. He wished suddenly that he had practiced what he had to say, but he hadn't truly gotten much past the decision to say it.

"My dear Mademoiselle Gaudet," he began formally. "It seems that I have done you a great wrong. I—"

Laron hesitated. Aida wasn't even looking at him, she was searching for something inside her sleeve.

"We have known each other from childhood," he continued a little warily. "And we have been betrothed for some time so I feel that I must speak plainly. I . . ."

She was still trying to retrieve something from her sleeve.

"Mamselle?"

"I have it here someplace," she said. "I purposely put it right here in my right sleeve so I would not lose it."

Laron's brow furrowed with curiosity. "I believe that is your left sleeve," he whispered.

Aida looked up at him wide-eyed. "Yes, yes it is. Oh dear, sometimes I just get so rattled. Just one minute. I have it here—"

She began immediately digging inside the other brightly colored sleeve. A moment later she pulled out what appeared to be a wad of multicolored rags. She pressed them in his hands.

"I know what you are going to say, or at least I think that I do and it is not necessary. I . . . I cannot marry you, Monsieur Boudreau, because I . . . think I may love someone else. And I believe that you do also. I think, however, that I should call it off. Everyone will think it is because of your adventure at the Bayou Blonde. That should keep the gossips occupied and we can try to sort out our lives as best we can."

Laron spread the wad of rags across his hands. It

was a miniature collection of male clothing. A tiny shirt, a little coat, and a pair of *culotte* that would more likely fit a mouse than a man. He had been sacked, handed his *vêtements*. In the traditional way, he had become the rejected suitor. He had shown himself too small in her eyes.

Strangely he caressed the tiny blue jacket and then looked up at her. She was very young, very pretty, and very anxious.

"I didn't realize that you could sew," he said.

"I can do anything that I have to do," she answered.

There was a gasp beside them and they both spotted Ruby beside them, staring in horror at the jilting suit. The small sound had captured the attention of others around her and within a moment's time there was a complete silence in the company and every eye was staring at the couple with shock and disbelief.

Laron leaned closer, not willing for any to hear.

"Thank you, Aida," he whispered. "I'm going away this night and won't be here to face the gossips with you."

"I can handle them," she answered. Her brow furrowed in concern. "Where are you going? Not to Bayou Blonde."

He shook his head. "Down the river to the German coast," he answered. "I'd rather no one knew, but I have business there."

She nodded. "Best of luck with your business, monsieur," she said.

He took her hand and brought it to his lips. "And best of luck to you, mademoiselle. I think I will find you more agreeable as a friend than I would have as wife."

She smiled at him, that tiny shy smile that could slay the heart of any man on the Vermillion River.

"Indeed I think you shall," she answered.

He stepped back, bowed formally, and walked away. The silence around the gaily lit party was near complete. Laron walked straight to his pirogue, looking neither to the left nor to the right. No one spoke a word or moved to stop him.

Suddenly Armand broke free from the group and hurried after him calling his name. Laron kept walking. He kept his face devoid of expression but he wanted to scream for joy. Free! He was free! Now it was left only to make her free also.

"Laron!"

Armand was hurrying behind him. He would not let him merely go without a word. But Laron was already ankle-deep in water before he finally forced himself to turn and speak to his friend.

"I am leaving," he said simply. "Do not be concerned for me. And tell my sisters not to worry. I won't be at Bayou Blonde."

"Laron, you cannot do this," Armand insisted. "I will not allow you to throw you life away. You cannot break this engagement."

He held up his handful of little clothes. "I did not break it, she did. It seems, my friend, that the lovely Aida thinks she loves someone else."

Onze

Armand had great hopes for the *fais-dodo*. It had taken a bit of arm twisting to get Laron to attend, but he'd done it. Armand was certain that familiarity, duty, and the lure of the most beautiful woman on the Vermillion River would do the rest.

As Laron had watched the lovely Aida dance, Armand made his way to the fire. He pretended an interest in the conversation going on there. In fact, he stood near the blaze in the hope of drying out his pant legs. He enjoyed the companionship of the fire until the fiddle stopped playing and the din of conversation increased dramatically.

Not far from him, smoking a pipe with Oscar Benoit and Hippolyte Arceneaux, his brother Jean Baptiste was telling a very crude joke that Armand had already heard about a woman whose entrance was stretched so big, her husband donned a miner's hat to mount her.

Jean Baptiste should have stayed at home, he thought. Félicité wasn't feeling well enough to come. Her husband should be there at her side, not here telling raucous jokes to other jaded husbands, probably no more steadfast than himself.

Armand had glanced back again at Laron and Aida.

Come on, my friend, he urged silently. *Make it up with her, marry her, and we can all be happy again.*

"Armand, my son, it is good to see you again."

He felt the priest's hand upon his shoulder and it was all Armand could do not to moan aloud.

"Good evening, Father Denis," he said. "I hope you are doing well."

"Tolerably so, thank you," he answered. "But of course I would do better if I were to hear that you have reconsidered your ill-thought-out position on the school."

"Father, I believe I have already said everything that is to be said on that subject," Armand stated stiffly.

The old priest smiled. "Yes, I suppose you have rather thoroughly articulated your wrong-minded view." He snorted and shook his head. "The idea that somehow the absence of knowledge could be an advantage and savior rather than a burden and affliction."

Father Denis's words were a little too close to the truth for comfort. Armand didn't actually believe it that way, or he didn't mean it quite as the priest portrayed. Still he hung on to his position with stubbornness.

"You will not be able to change my mind," he said.

Father Denis nodded. "Yes, I've come to that conclusion myself." He sighed and then smiled down at Armand. "This is another of those situations where I just have to trust in God to change it for me."

"What?"

"He works His will in our lives," the priest answered. "All we need is the patience to allow Him to do so."

Armand felt something familiar pull at him inside. It was a vague, uneasy, untenable feeling and he shrank from it. Fortunately his attention was immediately averted by the sound of a startled gasp.

Like everyone else he turned toward the sound. It had come out of the mouth of Ruby Babin, but unerringly he followed her gaze to the contents of Laron Boudreau's hands.

At first his brow furrowed in curiosity, then he realized what his friend held. Jilting clothes, sized to fit the man a fellow would think himself to be after being thrown over by his betrothed.

Armand was stunned into disbelief. What was happening? Aida was sending him away. That just couldn't be. It just wouldn't do. Armand was frozen in place, stunned into silence like those around him.

He watched Laron walking calmly, head unbowed, toward his pirogue. His heart ached for his friend. First to lose Helga and now Aida. It was not to be borne. Laron was leaving. Alone.

Armand broke away from the crowd and hurried after him.

"Laron!" he called out. His voice sounded unusually loud in the silence around him. "Laron wait!"

He finally caught up with him just when Laron was getting to the boat. Laron turned. His words were calm, but his expression was unfathomable.

"I am leaving. Do not be concerned for me. And tell my sisters not to worry. I won't be at Bayou Blonde."

"Laron, you cannot do this," Armand insisted. "I will not allow you to throw your life away. You cannot break this engagement."

Laron held up his handful of little clothes for his inspection. Armand still couldn't believe it and shook his head. "I did not break it," Laron pointed out, "she did." Laron actually smiled. "It seems, my friend, that the lovely Aida thinks she loves someone else."

He had turned then, unsecured the line, and waded out to his pirogue. Armand watched him go, stunned and silent. How could he fix this? How could he make it right?

Armand's inability to answer those questions led him down the path to renewed fear. Laron's words echoed inside him.

She thinks she loves someone else.

Armand turned quickly to face the muttering crowd of people behind him. Unerringly his eyes sought out and found his brother.

"Jean Baptiste." It was whispered, prayerful.

He was still standing with Arceneaux and Benoit. He was still safe.

With deliberate determination Armand walked back up the bank and into the crowd. People were talking all around him, asking him questions.

"What did he say?"

"Where is he going?"

"He's back to Bayou Blonde, no doubt."

"I wonder if he'll take that German widow with him?"

"Shush! Don't speak of her in front of the young women, Rosemond!"

"Have you seen that youngest of hers?"

"Doesn't favor him much?"

"Lucky. Very lucky."

"Why did she do it?"

"The widow?"

"Aida."

"Wouldn't want to set up house with a drunken galant."

"She could have brought him around."

"Good blood the Boudreaus have."

"Anatole must be spinning in his grave!"

"That old man had an eye for the ladies, he just married up with the prettiest one."

"And Laron had meant to do the same."

"What a shame. What a sad, sad shame."

Armand willed himself not to hear, not to think. He moved through them, not speaking, not reacting. He moved toward the clearing where the dancers stood. He had to get to Aida. He had to convince her that she'd made a mistake.

Finally he was standing in front of her. She looked scared and pale, but in control. A tearful Ruby was holding her arm. Nearby Granger and Marchand hovered uncertainly.

"I must talk with you," he said.

"Dance with me."

It was not an invitation but a demand.

"What?"

"Dance with me."

"I cannot."

"You cannot dance?"

"Of course I can dance, but not with you."

"Why not?"

"Because . . . because you stand taller than I."

"At this moment it seems a rather foolish concern."

He looked at her then, truly looked at her and realized how thin her layer of composure was. Even if she was about to break up his brother's marriage, she shouldn't be subjected to such a public humiliation.

"Monsieur Guidry!" Armand called out. "A *Rigaudon* if you will, the young lady wishes to dance."

The old fiddler was jolted out of his reverie and immediately struck up a lively tune. Armand bowed over Aida's hand and led her out. Several other couples joined them immediately and they quickly formed a ring and commenced the steps.

He had noticed before that she was a graceful dancer. She felt even more so in his arms. They spun and twirled and passed again. And when the step called for nearness and hands clasped, it did not seem all that intolerable that he was the shorter of the two. They moved together with ease and grace and when the ritual of the dance decreed that he place his hand at her waist for a half-spin, he did it. The need to wrap his arms around her and pull her tight against him was a desire that he didn't give in to. He forced himself to think about what he must do. She'd told Laron that she thought herself perhaps in love already. He must do whatever was necessary to protect her from Jean Baptiste. Or rather, he hastily corrected himself, to protect Jean Baptiste from her. That is what it was. She was beautiful and desirable and Jean Baptiste was merely weak.

Aida had broken with Laron no doubt because of Bayou Blonde. Clearly that was understandable. It was a disreputable place with disreputable people. No woman would want to think that the man she planned to husband her would dally among such coarseness and the dangers of disease. He must make her understand that Laron's inconstancy was a temporary aberration. Once she forgave him and they married, he would always be a good and faithful husband.

The ladies moved in front of him in a circle. He stepped forward, crossed his hands before him, and took Aida with his left and Mademoiselle Douchet with his right. He spun the two females simultaneously two turns before passing the extra, Mademoiselle Douchet, on to the next gentleman.

Momentarily, as he glanced down to see the lovely Aida's pretty hands in his own, he wondered if what he was planning to say would be true. Could his friend, loving one woman, be faithful in marriage to another? And what about himself? When the time came and some lovely little female from some other parish vowed to be his bride, would he still pine for Aida Gaudet?

The thought caused him to trip in his step. Aida looked over at him curiously as he recovered his balance, but not his composure.

He loved her, yearned for her, but it could never be. She was not for him, not at all.

The memory of the afternoon in Madame Landry's garden assailed him. She had been sitting, cross-legged and curious, in the dirt. Not precisely the prim, pretty Aida with which he was familiar. Her enthusiasm was buoyant and her wit surprising. He had been unable to keep his eyes off her.

And then she had caught him. Caught him straightaway, staring at her as if she were a feast and he a starving man. Well, maybe she was a feast and he could be described as extremely hungry, but there was no place for him at that dinner table.

It seemed forever before the tune was done, yet the time went too quickly. He bowed to her formally and then reluctantly released her hand.

He stepped closer to speak more privately.

"We must talk, mamselle," he whispered.

"No, I cannot, monsieur," she answered. "I cannot talk tonight. Tonight I must dance."

Armand was annoyed. It was important that he speak with her and as soon as possible. But if she would not, he could not. He moved to step away and spied his brother edging up closer to the dancers.

"If you wish to dance, Mademoiselle Gaudet," Armand said hastily, "then I would be your partner for the evening long."

Her eyes widened in surprise. "It is not done."

"Afraid of the gossips?" he asked. "Can they chatter faster than they are already?"

She giggled then. It was a delightful, warm, winning sound. Armand fought the urge to pull her into his arms.

"I am yours, monsieur, all yours for the night."

The words, offered lightly, had a jolting effect on Armand's body. He managed a wan smile. Oh how he wished that it was true.

Aida stood in the last glimmering light of the Saturday night moon washing dishes. Her poppa was already snoring in the other room as she leaned out the *tablette* window where her dishpan sat and scrubbed the dried-on remains of supper, grateful that the Acadian-styled lean-out wash shelf allowed her occasional inattention only to splash water on the ground below the window.

She'd forgotten all about the dishes, of course. In the excitement of going to the *fais-dodo* and her intention to hand Laron the jilting clothes, she'd allowed the mundane task to slip her mind. And she was unpleasantly surprised to come home and discover that she hadn't even cleared the supper table. This was just the sort of thing, she was certain, that led to people believing she was silly and scatterbrained. Well, perhaps that was she exactly. She certainly was acting that way.

She had thrown over Laron Boudreau, the most handsome man in the parish, because . . . because . . . because . . . There was really no answer. The people of the parish had decided long ago that the most beautiful woman on the Vermillion River should marry the most attractive man. That man was Laron Boudreau and nothing that had happened, not the German widow, the Bayou Blonde, or his seeming disaffection, had changed that.

But she had cast him off and she was not at all certain why. She had told him that she thought she was in love with someone else. Even remembering her own words brought a blush of embarrassment.

She had been thinking about Armand Sonnier, of course. It seemed that lately all she did think about was sweet, patient Armand Sonnier. As if such a pairing could ever occur.

He wasn't truly handsome at all, even if she squinted until she could barely make him out. And he was short, desperately short. A woman should never love a man whom she could stand next to and criticize the straightness of the part in his hair.

Of course, the other day in the garden, he had actually appeared quite attractive. And, strangely, dancing with him was exceptionally pleasant. She had not been uncomfortably aware of his lack of height, but rather enjoyed his very graceful movement and the way he twirled and led her with such precision and skill. A lazy, languid smile drifted over her face as she imagined once more those bright blue eyes as they looked at her with such intensity.

It could not mean what she thought, she assured herself. Armand Sonnier was not a man to be flirted with and wooed with false wiles. When he looked at her, he saw the real Aida. And if he did not turn away, that was a compliment in itself.

But no, he could not be in love with her. He was wise, knowledgeable, and literate. He was like a regular man, with a rather irregular mind. Yes, that was it. She smiled at the cleverness of her apt description. That was it exactly. And she could never hope to appeal to him.

Aida stilled suddenly. She'd heard something. Her soapy hands lay unmoving in the dishwater as she listened . . . listened . . . listened. She had heard something. Something. Her heart was pounding. Her blood was surging.

Don't be silly! she scolded herself. It was her own heart she was hearing. It was her own heart and nothing more. Still she held herself stiff and poised in expectation.

Aida had been one of those rare children who hated scary things. While her little friends had relished tales of pirate ghosts, swamp monsters, and peg-legged Englishmen, she had always cried at such stories and hidden her head. Even games like "got-you" and "boo" were not to her liking. She saw nothing fun about being frightened. And she was frightened now.

Deliberately, slowly, she pulled her hands from the dishwater and wiped them on her apron. She listened. Listened.

In the next room her father was snoring. The crickets kept up their noisy chatter. The world was far from silent, not holding its breath in fear as some bear or cat or giant beast approached. No Baritaria pirate, wild Indian, Americaine outlaw or escaped slave lurked in the darkness. The sounds were all there, they were all normal. It was nothing, nothing at all. She had simply taken a silly fantasy, she assured herself. There was nothing to fear.

She forced herself to release her breath. It was nothing, nothing.

She heard it again.

No, not heard it. She felt it. It was on her. In her. Cold. It—they were here in the room. They were in the room with her.

Aida was no longer paralyzed with fear. She ran. She ran as if all the devils of hell were after her.

She was through the curtained door and down the porch. Her bare feet slapped the cypress planks in a rhythm of panic. Too terrified to scream, she raced away, away from them. She had to get away. They pursued her. She had to get away.

At the end of the dock she stopped abruptly. There was no further that she could go. There was no path to get away. She could not run on water. She was trapped, cornered. There was no way out. No, of course there was not.

Aida trembled. She quaked and trembled at the end of the dock. She should call out for her father. But no, she knew her father could not help her now. There was nothing about this that her father could even understand.

She folded her arms across her chest, offering herself what little comfort she could. She bit her lip, wanting to cry, but she couldn't. They were here. They had followed her outside. They were all around her here, too. Somehow that wasn't quite so frightening. It was not so close here as in the house and the water was here. The evil, if it came, could be cast into the water. They were not evil. She knew that. Still her knees were shaking so badly that she could no longer stand and lowered herself to sit, curled as tightly as a ball at the end of the dock.

Cold. Cold. The coldness made her shiver. They were speaking to her now. Speaking to her. But not in words. They were speaking in pictures. She closed her eyes tightly, but she couldn't blot out the sight before her. It was bright, vivid, otherworldly, yet so very much familiar.

She was standing in a field by Laron. Poor Laron. He looked so very unhappy. Had she made him so? No, it was not she, she knew with certainty. It was something else that made him so. He was unhappy, but determined. She wanted to speak to him, but she could not. It was as if he did not know that she was there. It was as if she really was not there. But she could clearly see him, closer than she had ever seen him before.

He was working. Harvesting grain. The sun beat

down upon him, hot and unmerciful. Aida watched the sweat pouring off his brow like drops of blood. But he kept working. With great rhythm and force he moved the scythe blade back and forth, back and forth, back and forth.

Aida watched, mesmerized. Then the strangeness of the scene struck her. There was no grain. The land he worked was completely shorn, all of it had already been cut and left lying in windrows waiting for someone to gather it up. There was nothing, nothing at all, to harvest. Still he worked on, tirelessly, as if he could not see the chore was completed.

She tried to tell him, but of course she could not speak. She was not actually there.

Her gaze was caught by a movement off in the distance. A horseman was riding toward them. She strained and squinted, trying to make him out. But she did not recognize him. Even as the sleek, fine-flanked chestnut pulled up next to Laron's side, it took her a moment to identify the rider. It was Armand. Her Armand.

He looked in a way he had never appeared before. He looked older, wiser than she knew him to be. Atop the horse he was majestic and glorious, as if he had somehow overnight acquired tremendous wealth and fortune. His clothes were startling and radiant, finer than any plantation Creole's. The long trousers were jet-black, beaded along the seams with gold thread. His shirt glittered and shined as if light were pouring out from his chest, illuminating him. Over it he had donned a long cape of brilliant red that spread out so grandly it protected both him and the magnificent horse. Incongruously, he still wore his Acadian-style palmetto hat, but stuck in the band was a strange bright feather cockade, such as Aida had never seen before.

Aida could hear nothing the two men said, but clearly they were arguing. Armand pointed many times to the scythe, obviously trying to dissuade his friend from its fruitless use. But Laron would not quit the task.

It was foolish to try to talk Laron out of it, she realized. Armand needed only to point out the windrows. Men were rarely persuaded by moral admonitions. Once he understood that the result was achieved, the grain had already been cut, the two of them could gather it all in and be ready for winter. Aida must tell Armand that, she thought to herself. Somehow she must make him understand. That was what *they* wanted her to do. They, *the voices*, were expecting that of her. She must speak to Armand. She must make him understand.

And then they were gone. Aida gave a little startled cry as they left. The first sound she had uttered. She knew immediately she was alone once more.

She looked around her in the dark night, curious now rather than afraid. A peaceful weariness settled upon her heavily like a huge blanket. Aida sighed in relief and lay down flat on the dock, relaxing. She breathed deeply several times, allowing that sense of calm and peace to seep inside her and about her, comforting her, warming her.

"I simply have to explain it to Armand," she heard herself say aloud.

She lay several minutes at the end of the dock and then rose to her feet and made her way into the house. She was humming quietly, contentedly, as she entered into the familiar safety of the little home.

Inside, her father continued snoring peacefully. The candle had burned down and sputtered out, but the darkness was somehow welcome. Aida tucked away the doorway curtains and pulled the front doors together and latched them. She made her way to her room and stripped down to her nightclothes and burrowed under the warm quilted covers. She closed her eyes and immediately drifted off to deep, serene and renewing sleep.

The gray light of dawn was creeping through the windows when she awoke. Immediately she recalled the strangeness, Armand atop the horse, Laron working the shorn field.

She yawned and shook her head.

"What a dream!" she said to herself.

It didn't make any sense. But then, it was just a dream. She had fallen asleep, she told herself. Fallen asleep without realizing. That was what it was. She had thought that she was awake. She had thought she was being pursued by . . . by, well it didn't bear thinking about. But of course that had been part of the dream also.

That explanation made perfect sense. Comforted, she rose to wash and dress and begin her day. What a strange, strange dream! But dream was what it was.

It was only when she saw her cold dishwater sitting on the *tablette* shelf that her certainty faltered.

Douze

The morning was chilly and gray. Aida wrapped her shawl around her more tightly and pulled little Marie Sonnier closer to her side. Aida was happy. Armand, who was poling the pirogue, clearly was not. Although the downstream direction was no great strain and he was able to use the pole more as rudder than as impetus, he was in an obviously disagreeable temper.

"Where exactly are we going?" he asked Madame Landry.

The old woman dissembled easily. "Oh not far," she answered.

Aida had first learned about the trip when the boatload, Armand, Madame Landry, and the two older Sonnier children, Gaston and Marie, arrived at her home.

"We have an errand to run and we need you," the old woman had called out.

Her father had grumbled about her leaving him without having remembered to cook him any breakfast. But Jesper Gaudet had been grumbling almost continuously since the *fais-dodo* two nights previous. She had jilted her betrothed and spent the rest of the night laughing and dancing with another man.

Father Denis had not been particularly happy, either. His words on Sunday had chastised her harshly for her unforgiving heart. She had made no attempt to explain herself. She wasn't even sure that she could.

She had not been upset about Laron's visit to the Bayou Blonde. She did believe that he would be a good and faithful husband to any woman he married. And she had always thought that he would suit her perfectly. She no longer felt certain about that. Her uncertainty was not something that she chose to examine too closely. And the old priest's insistence that she do so went unheeded. After all, she had the *dream* or whatever it was to think about. And it seemed much more immediate and important than her former betrothal.

Orva began singing a little children's song about getting washed and dressed. Gaston and Marie both knew it, or knew most of it, and they eagerly joined in. The tiny girl wiggled out of Aida's arms to go sit with Madame Landry. The three voices contrasted vividly and actually sounded sweet and soothing to the ears.

The old woman had apparently insisted that Armand take her out in the pirogue and that the children come also. Félicité and Jean Baptiste needed some time together, she had said. Aida assumed that to be quite true, but couldn't quite shake the feeling that Madame Landry had some other purpose for their presence.

"We have to talk." Armand leaned down and spoke the words close to her. She startled from the feel of his warm breath so close to her neck.

He was right, they did need to talk. She needed to tell him about her *dream* somehow. She needed to make him understand that he must talk to Laron, he must make Laron see . . . He must make him see . . . something. What exactly, Aida wasn't certain of herself. But he was right, indeed they did have to talk.

"Must we?" she asked, nearly whining as she begged to put off the inevitable. "It is such a beautiful day."

"Beautiful day?" Armand looked at her as if she had lost her mind. "It's cold and gray and looks ready to rain down upon us any minute."

Aida giggled, feeling especially silly. "So it is." It was the only reasonable comment to make. "I suppose it must seem beautiful to me because I am just so happy."

The words out of Aida's mouth surprised her, but they seemed to have genuinely angered him. Armand's jaw hardened.

"How can you be happy when you jilted a fine and good man?"

Aida glanced, embarrassed, toward Orva Landry, who appeared to be deliberately inattentive to their conversation.

"He wanted his freedom as much as I," she said. "I know that he has been seeing the German widow. Perhaps he loves her; certainly he cares more for her than me. You are his friend, surely you know that to be true."

"I am sorry that you found out about Madame Shotz," Armand said quietly. "I am sure that it was a blow to your pride."

"My pride?" Aida looked at him curiously and

shook her head. "Perhaps a little, but I genuinely like Monsieur Boudreau. I want him to have the life that he wants."

"What a man wants and what is truly good for him are most often very different things," he said.

"Sometimes perhaps, but not most often," she disagreed. "I believe that you have not a high enough opinion of your gender."

"I believe, mamselle, that I might know more about such things than yourself," he said.

Uncharacteristically she bristled at his words. "I do not claim to be as intelligent as yourself, monsieur," she said. "But about love, perhaps a person does not have to be intelligent to be smart."

"And you believe that you have been *smart* about love?" he asked.

Aida's cheeks were flushed, but she held her chin high. "I do know that a marriage between two people who do not love each other is a very unfortunate thing."

His jaw hardened and his bright blue eyes sparked with anger. "Love has many seasons and cycles. What looks to you like a loveless marriage may just be a difficult period for a couple who truly cares about their vows."

His words seemed fierce. Aida drew back from his fury as her brow furrowed in curiosity. What on earth was the man talking about? A loveless marriage? A couple who cares about their vows? Clearly Armand was quite angry, but about what exactly, Aida was confused.

"I am no expert in love," she told him quietly, intent on calming his rancor. "But I think I would know if I were in it and I am not in love with Laron Boudreau."

"So I understand," Armand replied snidely. "You told him that you loved someone else."

Aida's fair face fired with humiliation. Laron had told him that, he had told Armand. She looked away from him, flustered, and desperately sought a reasonable reply.

"I simply told him that to ease the moment," she sputtered. "I never meant it."

"Then it's not true?" Armand's gaze was penetrating.

"That is what I just said," she answered.

Armand nodded slowly, but his gaze narrowed. "Yes, it *is* what you said, but you are unable to look me in the eye when you say it."

Aida swallowed, but determinedly raised her chin to face him. "You may be a great friend to the priest," she said sarcastically. "But it is Father Denis who is my confessor and not yourself."

He looked away from her then. Clearly still angry.

Aida was writhing in her own embarrassment, but couldn't quite fathom from where his displeasure came. It was impossible, she was sure, for him to believe that she cared about him. Why, she wasn't even certain herself that it was true. Still he was decidedly angry about something. Unhappily Aida surmised that she was just too silly to understand what.

In Madame Landry's lap, the children continued their happy exuberant singing. Thankfully it kept away the sullen silence that surrounded the young couple at the other end of the pirogue. Aida thought once again of the *dream* that was, of course, not a dream. Perhaps she should tell him now. It might serve to diffuse his anger and it would certainly change the subject from why and whom she loved.

"I had a very strange dream the other night," she said, leaning toward him slightly. "I need to tell you about it."

"A dream?" He appeared momentarily disconcerted. "Madame Landry sometimes interprets dreams, perhaps you should tell her."

"No, no," Aida said with certainty. "I must tell you because you were in the dream. There was something about it that was very important, I think."

Armand shrugged with unconcern. "It is nothing, I'm sure. I've always thought most dreams to be just too much coffee after supper."

"This one was not coffee. In fact, it was not a dream, not exactly."

"What do you mean?"

"I mean that I was not asleep when it happened."

Armand's brow furrowed in puzzlement. "You weren't asleep?"

Aida shook her head and cast a hasty glance in Orva Landry's direction before answering. "I was washing dishes," she said quietly. "I . . . I was washing dishes and a . . . a feeling came over me. I had a . . . well, a vision." The last was spoken with a low whisper.

"A vision?" Armand was incredulous. "Mademoiselle Gaudet, this attempt at being *traiteur* has gotten out of hand. Madame Landry has visions, you do not."

Aida was stung by his dismissal.

"It *was* a vision. I did not ask for it and I did not

want it, but I got it all the same. And there is something in it that I am supposed to relate to you."

"Mademoiselle Gaudet, I don't think—"

"Just listen," she told him. Deliberately she took a deep breath and tried, as best she could, to convey the importance and urgency she'd felt in her *dream*.

"I saw Laron cutting a field," she said. "But there was no grain there to cut. It had all been shorn and was lying in wait to be gathered."

Armand's eyes narrowed thoughtfully as he considered her words.

"I wanted to tell him that he should put away the scythe and gather up what was on the ground," she said. "But it was as if I was not there. He could not see or hear me."

Aida regarded Armand steadily. "You rode up on a big chestnut horse."

She hesitated momentarily. Somehow she didn't want to describe how handsome and noble he had appeared. In her memory he seemed strong and brave and infinitely hers. She was not willing to share that.

"You began talking to him," she said. "Trying to get him to stop scything at nothing. You continued to intone him, argue with him, plead with him, but you never once pointed out that the grain lay cut on the ground. Somehow I know that if he realized that it was already cut, he would go on about gathering it up."

There was silence between them for a long minute. Finally Armand pushed his hat back slightly, using his sleeve to wipe the sweat that had inexplicably gathered there in the cool morning.

"I don't believe for a moment," he said, "that this

was a vision. But whatever it was, it seems easy enough to interpret."

Aida swallowed hard and forced herself to look up at him questioningly. "And how do you interpret it?" she asked tartly.

"Well," he answered. "It is obviously about the broken betrothal. The German widow is the grain that Laron is trying to cut. He needs a wife and he is trying to find one. But that woman is already married. She is not available to him. You are the cut grain already shorn and waiting to be gathered up."

"What were you telling him then?" she asked.

"The same thing that I am telling you. The marriage between you two is the right thing and the sooner you go through with it, the better it will be for everyone concerned."

Aida considered his words for a long minute.

"That isn't what it means," she said finally.

Armand was immediately annoyed. "If that is not it, then what does it mean?" he asked, annoyed.

"I'm not sure. But I believe that you have spoken too quickly. Perhaps if you think about it longer, you will see some meaning more plausible."

"I think the meaning I have come up with is more than plausible," he said. "You must marry Laron Boudreau. It is exactly what you are meant to do."

"I will not do that," she stated flatly. "I do not love him."

"But you *should*, Mademoiselle Gaudet," he said. "You should."

She looked at him askance. "Do you believe, monsieur, that a person can force such a feeling?"

"I am not trying to tell you where to love," Armand said firmly. "I do suppose that is something that is out of a person's control. But I do think that a person, a man or woman, can decide on the simple things, the very important things, that could ensure or deny happiness. Those elements that they will and will not accept."

"What do you mean?"

"Well . . . like the prospective mate has a nasty temper or . . . or that he doesn't like children."

She scoffed. "I can't imagine many women falling in love with a nasty-tempered man who doesn't like children."

"Of course not, but you see my meaning. Standards are set."

"And you believe that Laron Boudreau and I would meet the standards of each other?"

"Perfectly," Armand answered. "He will be a handsome, generous, supportive husband. What more could you want?"

"And for him?"

"You are . . . well, you are not married to someone else," he said.

Aida thought it was very little to recommend a woman.

"Have you set standards, monsieur?" she asked.

"Certainly I have."

"What kind?" Her question was more than idle curiosity.

"Hmmm." Armand was thoughtful for a long moment. "The woman I wed doesn't have to be pretty," he said. "But I would be pleased if she had some attractive aspect. Nice eyes or soft hair or something that I would feel drawn to."

"All women have some desirable feature," Aida pointed out.

He nodded. "Yes, I think you're probably right. I'd also like to be able to talk to her. She doesn't have to be a keen wit or a brilliant thinker, but I would want her to have an opinion."

"Still that is nothing," Aida said. "Even I have an opinion. Is there nothing else?"

"Naturally she would have to be small."

"Small?"

"Yes, shorter than I. Certainly I would never consider a marriage to a woman who was taller than me."

"That's silly."

"It is not."

"It is. It's the most ridiculous idea I've ever heard."

"Then you don't often listen, mamselle. Everyone in the parish agrees with me. People are always suggesting to me young female relatives and acquaintances that are small in stature. It is accepted that the husband should be taller than the wife."

"I thought you could read both the law and the Bible?"

Armand eyed her curiously. "I can," he said.

"Is that written either place?"

"Of course not, but—"

"I know that I am not very bright, monsieur," she interrupted. "But if I were to love someone . . ." Her voice became soft, almost dreamy as she spoke. "If I were to love someone, I would let nothing that anybody thought or said dissuade me from my lover."

Armand's eyes widened in genuine concern. "But a person must always listen to their friends, their relatives, the people of their community."

"And why must I do that?" she asked. "A marriage

is between two people, a man and a woman. No one else must live day by day for the rest of time with that person. So no one else should have a say in it."

"So you would go against your family, your friends, your people?" His tone was angry, disapproving.

Aida Gaudet looked up at him, standing in the pirogue. Her chin was high and her words determined.

"For the man I love, monsieur, I would go against God Himself."

Armand was nearly shaking from the import of Aida's words. For the man she loved, she would go against God Himself. Certainly she was preparing her conscience for the break with church and community and family. She might not even realize it yet herself, but she was preparing to break up his brother's marriage and bring pain and misery upon all of them.

He glanced over at Gaston and Marie, still happy and contented in Madame Landry's lap. Earlier he had seen Aida hold the little girl tenderly in her arms. How could a woman do that? Be gentle with a child whose life she planned to ruin?

"Take this stream right here," Orva Landry ordered, breaking into Armand's thoughts.

"Bayou Tortue?" He looked at the old woman questioningly.

"Yes, this way," she said, indicating the narrow waterway named for its abundance of turtles.

"Madame Landry," Armand spoke up sternly. "You have no business up there."

Orva gave him a long, deliberate stare, nearly cool enough to frost his eyelashes.

"Bayou Tortue, young man. There is a person up that way with whom I must speak."

He hesitated only a moment, casting a quick glance at Aida, who was wide-eyed. Madame Landry was going to speak to the German widow. The prospect did not please him. Then he thought once more of Mademoiselle Gaudet's strange vision. Perhaps the old woman, too, had a plan to tell Aida that she must marry Laron.

With mild trepidation, Armand guided the pirogue into the turn and began the more laborious task of poling it and five people upstream.

The bayou was much narrower than the river, and the huge cypress and stately tupelos shaded the water so that it felt chill and dark. The verdant duckweed and water lettuce was thick and surrounded the boat like an unimpeded effluvium. Armand had been up this way, hunting and fishing many times in the past. The pervasive feeling of the place had never been as it was now. It was as if there were a sadness that seeped even from the vegetation.

"Something must be done," Orva said aloud, breaking the strange silence that had settled upon them. "Something must be done and soon."

Armand's pirogue covered the stretch between the river and the German widow's settlement in good time. The occupants of the boat, including the children, kept quiet and watchful until the small, well-worn cypress landing came into view.

"Look! It's a boy!" Gaston exclaimed as he spotted Helga Shotz's youngest handfishing from the end of the dock with a length of cotton cord.

The little boy looked up, his eyes curious and a little wary.

"Bonjour!" he called out to them. The sound of his French, as familiar as their own, was in stark contrast to his appearance. He was as blond as a human could be, the fairness of his hair and eyebrows almost the exact color of his skin. And he was dressed in the German fashion of very short wide-legged pants of homespun with shoulder galluses bibbed together with a block of the same material. He was small and strange and very foreign, but he appeared eager and friendly.

"Bonjour," Armand called back.

"Put the boat in," Orva told him. "I wish to disembark."

With some skill Armand eased the pirogue next to the boat. Gaston threw the rope out to the boy and he attempted ineffectually to tie it to the pillar.

A young girl came rushing down the dock. Her long blond braids were as thick as sweetgum saplings.

"Let me do it," she told the little one without criticism. She easily pulled through the good knots, without requiring the help of Armand, who had set the pole firmly in the bayou floor and bounded onto the cypress to assist.

"Good morning," he said formally to the newcomer and her brother. "I am Armand Sonnier. This is Madame Landry, Mademoiselle Gaudet, and my niece and nephew, Marie and Gaston."

The young girl gave a credible curtsy, nodding. "I am Elsa Shotz and this is my brother Jakob. Welcome to our home." Her smile was sweet and winning. "I have heard of you, monsieur," she said. "I have heard of all of you. You are acquaintances of our friend Monsieur Boudreau."

"He's not our friend," the little boy argued. "He is our uncle."

The little girl's cheeks flushed with embarrassment and she opened her mouth to dispute her brother's words, but Armand forestalled her.

"Indeed?" he said, sounding delighted. "Monsieur Boudreau is as well a cousin to Madame Landry, who is also my godmother. So it seems we are all almost family."

Armand deliberately avoided any mention of what his friend's relationship with Mademoiselle Gaudet might be.

More might have been said had not, at that moment, Helga Shotz stepped out on her porch. Her threadbare workdress was scrupulously clean, her hair exceptionally tidy, and her face as white as death.

"Has something happened?" she asked anxiously. "Has something happened to Laron?"

The use of his given name said volumes about the nature of the woman's relationship with Boudreau as well as her current state of apprehension.

"No no," Orva said, waving assurance. "I have only come for a visit. *Mon fils,* help me from the boat."

The children scrambled to the dock and Armand hurried to assist the old woman. He then offered a hand to Aida and the two of them followed the old woman up the ramp to the small house.

In front of him the children chattered together as if they were old friends.

"This bayou is so gloomy," Gaston commented to Elsa.

The little girl shrugged without comment, but her brother piped in a comment.

"Only since *Oncle* has gone away. We were all so happy before," he said.

Armand cast a quick glance at Aida before the two of them stepped inside.

Helga Shotz bustled around nervously, apologizing for the state of her home. In fact, the little cabin was scrupulously clean and the fragrance of fresh-baked bread emanated from the row of big bowl-shaped loaves cooling upon the shelf.

Her accent was heavy, forcing the listeners to pay close attention to her words, but her understanding of the language was estimable. The woman cast several surreptitious glances at Aida. Armand wondered what she was thinking. How would a plain, almost haggard-looking housewife regard the beautiful woman who was to be her lover's bride?

Aida, in fact, appeared more uncomfortable than Madame Shotz. She kept her body still and her eyes lowered as if she were trying to make herself disappear.

"Would you like coffee?" Helga asked. "I am afraid I do not make it so good, but I can make it."

Orva smiled broadly at her. "Do make us coffee," she said. "And do not worry about the quality of it. If an Acadian wants coffee he will drink any kind. And if he doesn't want coffee, then he's probably drinking *sazerac!*"

The joking comment dispelled some of the tension in the room.

As Helga busied herself brewing the aromatic *café noir*, Orva chattered along in what sounded much like idle conversation.

"I knew the man who built this house," she said. "It was empty for years before your husband bought it. But I knew the fellow who had it first."

"Really?" Helga's question was politeness devoid of interest.

Orva took no notice. "He was a Spaniard, a strange little man," she continued. "He lived alone here, needed no one and talked to no one. He trapped in the back prairies for thirty years before our people arrived."

"What happened to him?" Helga asked.

Orva shrugged. "No one knows. Some say he moved on to less peopled hunting grounds. Some say he was killed in a drunken brawl with a trader in Opelousas. Years back old Arceneaux killed a gator and found a silver belt buckle in his belly. It looked a whole lot like the one that Spaniard always wore."

"Oh dear." Helga's eyes widened in shock.

"The *syndic* we had then." She pointed to Armand. "The fellow who served as judge under the Spanish, he finally had to simply declare the man dead."

Orva tutted almost to herself and shook her head sadly.

"When a man has made a life where no one knows or cares about him, often when he leaves it, there is not so much as a ripple in 'the water to show his passing."

The coffee, when presented, was certainly drinkable, and the strange German bread was surprising tasteful, though a little coarse for their tastes.

Madame Landry kept up an unending stream of conversation, seemingly in no direction at all. Armand waited patiently for her to get to the point of their visit but the old woman seemed content to just drink coffee and chat.

With Helga's admonition to Elsa to watch the little ones, the children played together outside. Their loud boisterous play belied the fact that they had never set eyes upon each other before that morning.

The only disruption in what appeared to be an amiable social call was the abrupt arrival of Karl Shotz, Helga's oldest son. The burly twelve-year-old burst through the back door, clearly believing that something was amiss. Then he glared unhappily at the room full of strangers who had come for coffee.

His mother introduced her guests and the youngster offered polite greetings in a slightly belligerent monotone.

Helga suggested that he help his sister supervise the younger children. Instead he pulled up a chair and seated himself between his mother and Madame Landry.

"Do you know who I am?" Orva asked him.

"You are the fortune teller," he answered.

Madame Landry's eyebrows shot up.

"No, that is not quite correct," she told him calmly. "I am a treater. I do what I can to aid the sick and injured. For that job, I often have the help of voices and visions. At times, it is true, I can tell a person what his future will be."

He gave the old woman a slow, almost insolent look.

"Then tell me my future," he demanded.

Armand was startled by the young man's antagonism, but even more surprised by Orva's calm response. From his own experience, Armand knew that

Madame Landry did not tolerate insolence or disrespect. Yet she continued to talk to the boy as if she did not notice the offensiveness of his tone.

"You have a very bright future," she said to him. "But you think that it begins now. It does not."

The young boy's brow furrowed. "What does that mean?" he asked.

Madame Landry smiled. "It means that it is still time to leave the judgments of elders to elders." She reached over and patted his arm. "Soon enough you will be such a one yourself."

Karl angrily jerked his arm from her and stormed out of the room.

Helga's face was flushed with humiliation. "I must apologize," she said. "My son has been very short of temper these days, but I cannot excuse his rudeness."

"Let it be," Orva said, waving away the woman's concern. "It is a difficult time for your family. And a difficult step in childhood."

"Yes, I suppose so," Helga agreed.

"A boy, especially at his age," Madame Landry continued, "well, he needs a father. He needs a man to show him how to do and be."

Helga's face paled visibly.

Armand shifted uncomfortably in his chair.

"A mother must do her best," Orva stated. "But a boy learns to be a man by watching a man."

Madame Shotz lowered her eyes guiltily.

Aida's were wide.

Armand wanted the floor to open and swallow them up. Why was Madame Landry deliberately bringing up this most painful of subjects?

The old woman continued. "It is up to a mother to

ensure that the man he watches is the man that she wishes her son to grow up to be."

"Sometimes that is not possible," Helga said quietly.

Madame Landry shrugged and nodded. "Yes, sometimes it is not," she agreed.

"Madame Landry is teaching me to be the *traiteur*," Aida blurted out suddenly. They were virtually the first words she had spoken. "Of course I cannot remember the cures and charms so Monsieur Sonnier is writing it all down."

"That is wonderful," Helga said.

"I had never thought to be a person so responsible as a treater," she said. "And I know that I am not worthy, but it seems that it is what I shall be."

"How nice."

"Of course I have always loved to work with herbs, but I am not very smart and I have a very bad memory."

Madame Landry chuckled. "Mademoiselle Gaudet often sees her shortcomings, but fails to understand how they benefit her."

The cryptic words caused a momentary pause, but Aida had effectively rescued the conversation from the uncomfortable direction in which it had been headed.

Within another quarter-hour the coffee was finished and Madame Landry made to leave. Helga walked them to the dock, calling to the formerly rowdy, now tired children.

She touched Aida on the arm, drawing her aside. Her words were low but Armand could hear them.

"Thank you for coming by, mademoiselle," she

said. "Though perhaps we cannot be friends, I do not wish to be your enemy."

"I would be happy to be your friend, Madame Shotz," Aida answered with obvious sincerity.

Helga was flushed, obviously embarrassed by the situation.

"Please give my regards to Monsieur Boudreau. I will not be seeing him in the future."

"I may not see much of him, either," Aida said. "I broke off our betrothal last Saturday."

Helga's eyes widened in shock at Aida's words. "You broke it off?"

Aida nodded.

The children rushed upon them like a plague, all laughing and pushing and talking at the same time. A plunge from the dock by little Marie was barely averted.

Armand handed Aida into the boat and then the two children after her. He turned to aid Madame Landry into the pirogue, but the old woman ignored him, speaking to Helga Shotz once more.

"Do you know what we call you? How we refer to you?" she asked.

Helga blushed bright red and glanced nervously at her children as if expecting a vulgar derisive term.

"We call you the *veuve allemande*," she said. "The German widow."

Helga's brow furrowed. "I have told no lies about my marital status, madame," she said defensively.

Orva nodded. "I know that you have not. Actually, they got that from me. I was the first to call you that."

She turned then to Armand. "Help me into the pirogue," she said.

Once the old woman was settled, Elsa and Jakob

managed the rope and cast it to Armand as he pushed off.

"Monsieur," the little boy called out. "Please tell *Oncle* to come and see me."

"He is gone away right now," Armand called back. "I will speak to him when I see him."

"Where has he gone?" Jakob asked.

Armand shrugged, unknowing.

"To the German coast." The reply was called out by Aida.

Armand was surprised at the answer. Madame Shotz appeared stunned.

Treize

Aida showed up as requested at Madame Landry's home for another day of learning. She was rapidly becoming accustomed to the idea. Certainly she still was not smart enough, and she still had trouble remembering where she'd left her shoes, her shawl, or her sunbonnet, but since the vision she was beginning to believe that it was true that she should be the treater.

Only three days earlier, on that surprisingly uneventful visit to Helga Shotz, she had stated with conviction for the first time that she was to be the new treater. Her words had been spoken only in an attempt to cover an awkward moment. Yet she had felt a strange sense of confidence. The burden of responsibility bolstered her in a way that her physical beauty never had.

Of course, there was still Armand. He still seemed less than convinced of her abilities, but while she valued his opinion, it somehow did not matter as much as it once had. If he thought her unsuited for the task—well, he was in many ways correct. If he was not willing to believe that her vision was real, well, in that he was wrong.

Aida stood alone with her thoughts inside the quiet

solemnity of Madame Landry's house. Alternately she watched out the front door for Armand's arrival on the river, glanced at the old woman alone in her garden, and eyed a large luscious blueberry tart cooling on the table.

Madame Landry was in a strange mood that morning, pale and almost listless; she requested to be left to herself awhile.

Aida respected her wishes and therefore paced alone in the house. She wondered if the old woman was communicating with *the voices.* The idea was momentarily frightening to Aida. Then she recalled the warm sense of calm and peace that had settled upon her after the strange vision she'd experienced. Perhaps one could become accustomed to such. Especially knowing that it was meant to help people in the community, heal the sick, ward off disaster.

If only Armand had taken her more seriously. Aida shook her head as the vivid memory of the field of shorn grain troubled her once again. There was something important that Armand must tell Laron. Somehow Armand was the key; he had the answer and he could not see it.

Of course there was still time. Laron had not yet returned from the German coast. Aida ruminated momentarily on what business he might have there and then let the thought go by. Laron would be back within days, undoubtedly. Maybe by that time she could convince Armand to speak with him.

A low murmur of voices caught her attention. Aida walked eagerly to the doorway to look out through the curtains toward the bayou.

Jean Baptiste Sonnier was poling the pirogue near

to shore. Armand adeptly jumped to the dock. He carried under his arm the tools of his trade, a polished wooden box containing his paper, ink, and plume. Safely on the bank, he turned to wave his brother off.

Jean Baptiste waved back and then apparently caught sight of Aida in the doorway. He doffed his hat and gave a half-bow.

"As beautiful as always, Mademoiselle Gaudet!" he called out.

Armand turned to look at her, his expression black.

Aida's heart sank. Another bad mood day, she thought. Could Armand Sonnier never just be happy?

He stomped up the porch steps and in through the door.

"Where is Madame Landry?" he asked grumpily.

"She's in the garden," Aida told him. "She wanted to be alone for a while."

Armand's brow furrowed in momentary concern. "Is she all right?"

"Yes I think so. Perhaps she is . . . well, communing with *the voices*."

Armand looked askance. "Surely not," he said firmly. "That certainly must only occur when she is alone or at night or—"

"Why would you think that?"

He shrugged without answering. "It just seems more likely."

"Nothing about *the voices* is likely," Aida pointed out.

Armand considered her words. "Well, I'm sure you know more about it than I do."

THE LOVE CHARM · 237

"I *do* know more about it," Aida said argumentatively.

"I just said you did."

"But you did not mean it," she accused. "You are all angry and puffed up again for no reason."

"Am I?"

"Yes you are!"

She stood nearly toe to toe with him, nearly shouting the words in his face. Her behavior surprised both of them. Embarrassed, she stepped back. An apology was on her lips, but he spoke first.

"I am sorry," Armand said. His tone was sincere, as was his expression. "I am grumpy as a bear this morning, I think. It is no cause to take it out on you."

"Thank you," Aida said, her voice not sounding nearly as meek as she felt.

"I have been thinking about all this," he admitted. "I do believe that you can be *traiteur* and I cannot wholly discount your vision."

"Then you will talk to Laron?" she asked.

"If I can decipher what to say. Clearly the vision seems to me to be concerned with the fruitlessness of his relationship with Madame Shotz."

"I liked her," Aida said.

Armand nodded almost sadly. "I did, too."

The quiet moment between the two of them lengthened.

"Ummm, look at this!"

Armand walked to the table, noticing the blueberry tart for the first time.

Aida smiled, grateful for the distraction. "I saw it already. In fact, your arrival probably saved it from mysteriously disappearing."

"Mysteriously disappearing?" Armand looked at her, his eyes almost twinkling.

"No one would have ever seen or heard of it again," Aida whispered dramatically. "And all that would be left would be a blueberry stain on my lips."

Armand picked up the game easily. "Show the judge your mouth, mamselle," he ordered in a haughty demanding voice. "Let us see if you are guilty or innocent."

Aida stuck her tongue out at him playfully.

"The woman is a saint," he declared in an impressive tone. "She is innocent of sweet thievery, although I believe she did lust after it in her heart already."

Aida gave a tiny giggle of delight at both his risque comment and his comedic tone.

"You are so funny," she said, delighted.

"I have amused you?" he said, his words feigning surprise. "I thought only handsome fellows spouting odes to your eyelashes entertained you, mamselle."

"And I thought you had become so stuffy and sensible that you wouldn't know a laugh if it hit you full face," she replied.

Armand raised his brow in surprise. "Mademoiselle Gaudet, I am known as a man who can tell a good joke."

"And I am known as a woman who appreciates one," she countered.

"Well, it seems that this lovely tart has brought us to a new understanding of each other," he said.

"It seems so."

"Then I believe that, in celebration of that happy conclusion, we should eat it."

"We can't." Aida's eyes were wide with scandalized amusement.

"Are you fearing Madame Landry's wrath?"

"She would not be happy to lose such a delicious looking pie," Aida said with certainty.

Armand nodded. "I've stolen sweets from her before," he admitted. "As a young boy I was scolded for such a sin more than once."

"And did you learn your lesson?" she asked.

He sighed with feigned despair. "Apparently not," he replied. "For looking at this beautiful bit of blueberry all I can recall with certainty is my half-burned, overchewy *coushe-coushe* that I left half-eaten. My brother and I allowed my sister-in-law to lie abed this morning while we cooked breakfast for ourselves and the children."

"I forgot about the morning meal completely," Aida admitted. "Poor Poppa slathered some mayhaw preserves on yesterday's cold biscuit."

"Then surely," Armand suggested, "this tart was meant to be devoured by you and me."

Aida tutted in warning. "Are you trying to tempt me, monsieur?"

"Oh no, mamselle, I would not do such a thing," he said with great hauteur.

"But you *are* going to taste it," she said.

"Just the edges," he assured her as he broke off a fairly generous portion of a corner. "I'll just try it, in order to convince us that it is not something that we really want to eat."

The hot blueberry filling was oozing out of the crust and would have dripped on the table if Aida had not reached over and allowed the heavy dollop to slide upon her finger.

"Thank you for saving that," he said. "We could not allow it to fall upon the table and make it sticky."

She giggled before burying the blueberry-covered digit in her mouth.

"Mmm," was her only comment.

Armand tasted his portion and offered a similar opinion.

"It's wonderful," she said.

"Maybe it is my hunger," he said. "But I don't believe that I have ever tasted better."

"I have never been overfond of Madame Landry's cooking," Aida said. "But this is wonderful."

"We have to have another bite, don't we?" he asked.

Aida looked longingly at the tart.

"Just a little one," she said. "I haven't even tried the crust."

Armand broke off another corner and shared it with her.

Once more they made sounds of pleasurable satisfaction as they consumed the sweet blueberry filling and light crust of Madame Landry's tart.

"How is Félicité?" Aida asked him conversationally. "Her time is getting very close."

Armand nodded as he licked his fingers. "She is doing well, I think. She is more tired these days than I recall with the other babies, but maybe I was not paying as much attention."

Aida broke off the third corner and shared it with him.

"I don't know much about birthing," she told him. "Madame Landry has said that I shall be with her to assist at the next lying-in. That undoubtedly will be Madame Sonnier."

Armand's brow furrowed as he scooped out a bit more of the hot, oozing center of the tart with his fingers.

"It is very unusual for an unwed lady to attend a birthing," he said.

Aida nodded agreement. "I said that very thing to her."

"What did she say?"

"It was really very strange," Aida told him. "She just gave this unexpected, almost shrieking laugh and said that she didn't think that my being a maiden would be a problem."

Armand shrugged. "Maybe she thinks that since you have been chosen as *traiteur* the normal sensibilities simply do not apply."

"Perhaps so."

The two of them dug fingers into the last corner of the tart and giggled guiltily as they split it between them.

"Do you think she will forgive us?" Aida asked.

"Certainly. She is a reasonable woman and she will understand how seductive a blueberry tart can be to two hungry young people."

"Then you are going to confess."

Armand grinned. "No need to rush into anything. Let her notice it is missing and scold me first."

Aida laughed.

"Children! Children! Come here!"

The call came from the direction of the garden.

"Children? I suppose that's us," Aida said.

"I think so," Armand agreed. "Do I have blueberry on my face?"

Aida looked him over, laughing. "No, monsieur, but don't let her see your tongue. What about me?"

"You appear as angelic and innocent as if no blueberry tart could ever tempt you," he said.

He offered his arm formally and the two headed out the back doorway to the garden. "We are coming, *Nanan*," Armand called out.

Aida felt warm and happy and content at his side. They were friends. He did at least seem to like and respect her. It was a lot for a woman who so admired him.

Madame Landry was seated as usual among the remains of her garden. The curled and discolored leaves and vines of autumn were all around her, deteriorating so very slowly to dust. She had a peculiar expression on her face, but she appeared quite happy.

"Well good morning to you, *mon fils*," she said, greeting Armand for the first time.

"I have my paper and ink," he said. "And Mademoiselle Gaudet and I await your lessons."

"No lessons today," she said, surprising both of them. "I have things to think on and consider and I have no time for teaching."

If Armand was annoyed at losing a day's lesson and having made a futile trip to her home, he didn't say so.

"It has been a long time since you sent me away to play," he said.

"But you always loved those days of play," she said. The old woman's smile was secretive, as if there was some joke to which the others were not privy.

"You two run along now, you can make your way home, of course," she said.

"Certainly," Armand told her. "My brother dropped me off on his way to visit the Héberts; we can walk up there and get the pirogue to take Mademoiselle Gaudet.''

"Good, good," the old woman said. "You do that. And let me get you that tart."

"Tart?" Armand asked, casting Aida a quick guilty grin.

"I made a blueberry tart for your brother," she said. "As I recall he was always partial to blueberry."

"The tart is for Jean Baptiste?" Armand's question was curious.

Old Madame Landry nodded. "Perhaps you have not noticed," she said. "But your brother seems to be going through a difficult time now. He is not altogether happy about the new baby and is not as devoted to dear Félicité as he once was."

Armand visibly paled, but he did not dispute her words.

"And you think baking him a blueberry tart will make him more devoted to his wife?" His tone was doubtful.

"Oh, the one I made him will," Orva assured him. "I laced it heavily with a very effective love charm."

Armand and Aida knelt beside the riverbank, choking, gagging, coughing as both thrust fingers down their own throats time and time again to no effect.

"I cannot vomit!" Aida wailed. "She must have put an antiemetic in it also."

Armand had discovered the same incontrovertible fact but had not yet voiced it.

"What can we do?" Armand asked her. "Is there no remedy?"

"You have been there when she has taught me,"

Aida answered. "Not once has she even mentioned love charms. How am I to know if there is an antidote?"

"How do you feel?" he asked. "Do you think it is going to start working right away or later today or . . . ?"

Aida was still and self-absorbed for a moment and then shook her head.

"I don't feel anything except frightened and anxious," she said. "That must be more the effects of knowing that I've swallowed the charm than the charm itself."

Armand nodded agreement. He felt exactly the same.

"Perhaps it takes time before it starts to take effect," she said. "Maybe we should just go home and be alone so there is no one to fall in love with."

"The charm might be specifically for husbands," Armand suggested. "It may very well do nothing to us."

"We should go home and tend to our usual business and simply pretend that this did not happen."

"Yes, I think that really might work," Armand agreed. "We will just go home and stay by ourselves."

"Until . . . ah . . . until tomorrow?"

"How long can a charm like this last?" he asked.

"Surely no longer than a day or so," she told him hopefully. "It couldn't stay in the body very long."

"Then we will go home and stay alone and nothing will happen. Nothing can happen," he assured her.

"Good," she agreed. "Very good. Everything will be fine."

"Yes, everything will be fine."

Aida sighed as if in great relief, and Armand momentarily felt sorry for her. It was his fault, after all. She hadn't eaten the tart until he started.

"Well then, let us get going," she said. "We'll head for the Héberts."

"The Héberts!" Panic momentarily seized him.

"Yes, isn't that where your pirogue is? The sooner we get it the sooner we get home," she said. "We can't know when this charm might begin."

"We can't go to the Héberts! Jean Baptiste is there."

"Jean Baptiste?" Aida looked at him puzzled. "He doesn't know that we ate his tart."

"No! Jean Baptiste will . . . Oh never mind, it's just that we can't go there."

"But we must."

"We cannot."

"Then how will we get home?"

It was a question for which Armand didn't have a ready answer. His time was surely running out, but he could not risk taking Aida Gaudet to the Hébert place, where his brother was. He loved his brother and Félicité. He couldn't take the risk that Aida Gaudet might fall for Jean Baptiste and lure him from his wife.

But he had to do something. Something. He had to get her home so that she would fall in love with no one. Or he had to find someone appropriate for her to fall in love with. Laron was down on the German coast. Who else was there?

Perhaps it was the effect of the charm or maybe Armand just saw things clearly for the first time. But within a fraction of a heartbeat he knew whom he wanted the beautiful Aida to love.

He reached out and took her arm and pulled her into his own.

"Armand?"

Hearing her speak his given name was like a spark to kindling.

"Kiss me!" he demanded.

With almost no hesitation she brought her mouth to his. He met her lips with his own. Warm. Plump. Sweet. It was everything that he had ever imagined. Everything that he had ever longed for.

He pulled back and looked into her eyes. They were wide with surprise, perhaps fear, but also there was desire. He saw it and recognized it and it urged him forward.

He half-led, half-dragged her into the shade and safety of a stand of cottonwoods. He wrapped his arms around her and pulled her close again, angling his kiss to fit more closely and opening his mouth upon hers, seeking, tasting.

He had never held a woman before, never kissed one. But he suffered no reluctance or hesitation. Aida Gaudet felt right in his arms. Her body fit with perfection against his own. Her lips seemed familiar rather than foreign. After all, he had loved her for so very long a time.

"My Aida," he declared in a whisper as he nipped her lower lip lightly and explored her mouth once more.

She felt so right against him, all her soft curves of her body corresponding accurately with the sharp angles of his own. Her high round bosom, long admired at a distance, was now pressed so firmly against his chest. And unexpectedly she wrapped an eager limb around the leg of his trouser, stroking the back of his calf with her heel.

"Mmm yes," he encouraged against her lips. "Mmm."

They broke apart only momentarily to draw in breath and gaze at each other in heightening lustful longing. Then they recklessly kissed again, this time deeper, their tongues dancing in exquisite tenderness.

Keeping her tightly against him, Armand allowed his kiss to wander from the generous warmth of her lips to the vulnerability of her pale throat. She gave a gasp of pleasure and shock as he, like a rutting stallion, nipped her there. Her reaction only served to encourage him. She threw back her head like a spirited mare, offering him easier access to her smooth slim neck.

Armand's hands did not remain idle. He much enjoyed the tight embrace that pressed her breasts so firmly against him. But he could not resist the long, straight length of her back. He soothed and eased her as he kissed and caressed. When the direction of his exploration led him to the curve of her waist and then to the flair of her derrière, his heart pounded like a hammer.

He traced the shape of her buttocks, round and high as if daring a man to touch them, pulling her up against him intimately.

Aida cried out, partly in surprise, partly in pleasure. Then she squirmed against him, desperate to get closer.

Armand's body flashed like fire. He, too, felt an almost frenzied need to meld with her flesh.

"I don't think I can stand up," she whispered against his hair. In truth her body leaned against his heavily. "My legs are no sturdier than the filling of the blueberry tart."

Armand also felt like jelly. That is, except for the hard throbbing ache in the front of his trousers.

"Let's lie down," he said, astonished at the surprisingly normal tone of his voice. His breathing was quick and labored, his heart pounding like a drum, and the heat of desire surging through his veins like lightning in a stormy sky. "We'll just rest here on the ground."

Rest was the furthest thing from either's mind. Without relinquishing their embrace the two lowered to their knees. Armand eased her back onto the yellow Indian grass, still slightly moist from the morning dew. He lay atop her, which was even better than pulling her close. No longer did he have to use his arms to embrace her, but could allow his hands to wander where they would.

Aida's hands also were free and she measured the width of his shoulders and the length of his spine. She coaxed and kissed him and called out his name.

He could feel the curve of her breast through the covering of her clothing and caressed her.

She purred like a cat and thrust her bosom forward, pleading for more. Armand squeezed and kneaded and stroked through the rigid restraint of her boned bodice, but it was not enough.

"Take it off," she whined. "Help me take it off."

Enthusiastically Armand began pulling at the front laces of her corset vest, loosening her from the stiff confines.

He sought the softness of her skin and managed to get a hand beneath her blouse. The warm, smooth feel of her naked flesh was far too enticing to resist. A moment later he held her firm, plump breast, the nipple at its peak, thick and hard.

"Oh my God!" he exclaimed in whisper. "Aida, my sweet, sweet Aida, I never thought it would be like this."

"Kiss me," she pleaded.

He did. He kissed her lips, her neck, her throat. He kissed her again and again and again. The pressure of his erection became more insistent. He just couldn't get close enough. He just wasn't quite close enough.

Aida must have felt similarly as she squirmed and wiggled beneath him, fanning the flames of Armand's desire and making tiny curious sounds of passion that spurred his lust.

With a growl that was almost beastlike he rolled over on his back, pulling her with him. Aida's skirt hiked up considerably and the feel of her bare legs straddling him made Armand moan aloud.

It was a little better this way. The hot, damp haven at the crux of her legs was poised immediately over his throbbing ache. It was closer, nearer, but it was still not enough.

He ran his hands up the backs of her bare thighs and under her skirts. The round nakedness of her buttocks was perfection beneath his touch. He caressed her, kneading and squeezing her generous backside. Then he bucked and clutched her close, grinding his body against hers.

She gave a little cry of delight and half sat up, arching her back, meeting his pressure with her own.

With eager, almost desperate hands she cast away her unlaced bodice and jerked her blouse off over her head.

Armand's breath caught in his throat as he gazed at her unadorned breasts above him, like two big luscious peaches hanging just within reach and clearly meant for him. Eagerly he sampled the proffered fruit, tasting the sweet, salty flavor of her skin and worrying the stiffened nipples with his teeth.

Aida buried her hands in his hair and held his head against her, aiding him in his homage to her.

She was squirming again. Squirming and wiggling atop him as if she were riding an untamed horse.

"Oh please, please," she began to whimper. "Oh please Armand, my love, my love."

She begged please, and to please her was what he wanted most in the world. He didn't know where first to touch, where to probe. He wanted to kiss and caress her everywhere, everywhere at once. His mouth on her right breast, his hand on her left. He continued to stroke her bottom, but he was drawn to the hot recesses between her thighs. He slipped his hand through the back of her legs and possessively clutched her intimately. She was damp, eager, and she squirmed against his hand.

Armand was not far from begging himself. His heart was thundering in his chest. His breathing was rapid and labored. And his erection was hard, heavy, and pressing painfully to be free of clothing.

He relinquished her breast to pull at the buttons on his trousers. Aida tried to help, but the touch of her small hand upon him had him calling out in pleasured anguish.

She jerked at her skirts, gathering them about her waist. She was naked against him. Nothing now separated them except the thin layer of cottonade that covered him. Nothing else separated them. Nothing else except vows and honor and holy wedlock.

"Oh no! I can't stop!" The words were screamed in agony and directed at his own conscience. It had gone too far. He had meant for her to *fall* in love with him, not to *make* love with him. She was not herself, she was under the effects of the love potion. And he was painfully aroused, living out a dream. He had desired her from afar so long and so secretly, and now she was in his arms, nearly his.

"I can't stop," he moaned again. "I can't stop now."

But he did.

He rolled over and laid her upon the ground. Slipping out of her embrace, he widened the distance between them.

"Armand?" She spoke his name, her voice husky with desire. It was almost his undoing.

"Don't move, Aida," he told her. "Please just lie still a moment; don't speak and don't move."

He sat up, still struggling to catch his breath and slow the beating of his heart. He covered his face with his hands and tried to imagine poling down the river in springtime when the hyacinth were in bloom.

"Armand?"

Her question was plaintive. He ached to press himself against her once more.

"We can't," he told her. "We can't do this, Aida."

"We can," she told him. "I want to."

"It's the charm making you want me this way,

think this way," he said. "But the charm will wear off and if we continue, we'll be compromised beyond going back."

"I don't want to go back!" she insisted.

"But you will," he told her. "You'll regret this very much and want to go back."

Her silence condemned him. He opened his eyes and turned to look at her. Her hair was wild, her dress was mussed, she had never been more beautiful.

"Oh Aida," he whispered. "I am so sorry."

"You don't want me," she said. "Not even my body. You don't even want my body."

He could see her lip trembling; her whole body began to shake likewise. He couldn't ignore her, leave her trembling. Armand scooted over to her and enfolded her in his arms.

"Shhh, shhh." He whispered the words as he stroked her back. "I do want you, all of you. How could I not? Shhh, sweet Aida. It will be all right, somehow we will make it all right."

He must hold her like a brother, Armand cautioned himself. If he allowed passion to flare again, perhaps he would not be able to stop it. He must hold her like a brother, a friend. Though she was in his arms, he kept the lower portion of their bodies separated by a distance. He must comfort her but protect her, from the charm and from himself.

"Hold me close, Armand," she pleaded. "Hold me close and kiss me again."

"Keep very still and I will hold you," he promised. "I will hold you until this feeling passes."

She snuggled against him. He steeled himself not to react.

"I love you, Armand," she told him. "I really love you."

The words sounded so sweet, so precious to him, he felt unwelcome tears well up in his eyes. How he wished it could be true. How he secretly longed for those words. But they were false. All of this was false.

"No you don't, Aida. You don't love me," he answered. "It's the charm. Be still now and let this feeling pass. It is just the love charm."

Quatorze

Helga Shotz and her children worked together gathering fruit into baskets in the brightly colored persimmon woods. Each child gathered what he could reach of the purplish orange fruit known as *plaquemines*.

"Have we got enough yet, Mama?" Jakob asked her.

"We must fill up all the baskets," she told him. "We'll get everything we can carry."

Helga had not known persimmons until coming to this bayou. And her first experience had not been good. Unripe, the fruit had puckered her lips. It was the most sour and bitter flavor she had ever tasted and had lingered for hours. Miraculously, she discovered, when they ripened, the persimmon was the sweetest fruit ever tasted. Dried and ground with mortar and pestle, it was sprinkled onto sweets and baked into cakes. Although cane grew in grand abundance on plantations down the river, cut and squeezed and cooked into sugar by African slaves, for her children and many others among the prairies, the only sugar was persimmon sugar.

Of course, ripe persimmons were good to eat right off the tree, they dried easily and grew in such abundance that they were used for livestock fodder. But for Helga, one of the best parts of gathering the fruit was the excursions to the persimmon grove. They always took on an almost picnic tone and were much enjoyed by her children. These days joy was something she couldn't offer her little ones much of.

Karl helped his baby brother up on his shoulders so that Jakob could pick "up high," an unceasing ambition of the littlest child. Karl pretended that the weight was too much and feigned staggering with mock danger. Jakob squealed with delight and had all of them laughing together. It was good to hear laughter once more.

Helga knew that she'd done the right thing. She'd had to break it off with Laron. A woman might choose for herself a life of sin, a life beyond the edges of accepted society. But a mother could not, should not, force that life upon her children. Karl did not deserve to cringe with shame hearing his mother's name on another boy's lips. And Elsa was growing up. What chance would she have of finding a nice, kind man to love her if her mother was beyond the pale?

And more than all of that, how could she expect, demand, the upright standards that she knew would make her children's lives better, happier, if her children did not see *her*, their mother, living that example?

Jakob was whooping now, pulling persimmons from high limbs at a wild hectic pace.

"Don't throw them, my baby," she cautioned. "We don't want them bruised."

She knew that she was doing right. Still, she could not hide the sorrow, the emptiness that filled her since Laron had said goodbye. Each day she told herself that tomorrow it would be better. But day after day the ache, the grief, the hollowness inside her welled up once more.

She tried to recall how she had felt when her husband walked out. She had been frightened. Overwhelmed with the responsibility, uncertain of the future, she had been all those things. But under that, she had been relieved, relieved and even glad.

Helga could not work up any gladness about the leaving of Laron Boudreau. His absence was like a mortal wound. It continued to bleed strength from her day after day. She needed him so much. She needed just to look at him, to laugh with him. She needed to be enfolded in his arms, garnering strength and sharing sorrow.

She should never have become involved with him. That was what she told herself a dozen times a day. If she'd kept her wits and her morals about her, she'd never have gotten herself in such an unhappy position. But in truth, even in her most self-critical moments she could not wish away the happiness of the last three years. Not for herself and not for her children.

Laron had been a father for them as Helmut had never been. He loved them wholly and unconditionally with a naturalness that even Helga could envy. It was the way that he had been loved by his parents and in honesty, Helga thought it a wonderful legacy. Something that she could not help but want for her own children.

And they missed him, too. She'd told herself that they would be fine, that he would slip from their young memories as easily as their father had. But she knew it was not true. The day that he'd shown up at their dock had been the best since he'd left. Jakob had been laughing and happy all the way up to bedtime. And Elsa had not been compelled to argue with her older brother over anything. Only Karl had been silent. But then, only Karl was torn by the knowledge that the two people he loved most, the two people whom he had begun to think of as his parents, were joined in an alliance that was condemned by the church, by the community, and by the very rules that they themselves had taught him to respect and honor.

Karl had begun to feign staggering once more under the tremendous weight of little Jakob. Elsa pretended that she was trying to help, and the three-year-old so high on his brother's shoulders giggled with enthusiasm. Finally Karl gently and conveniently "fell" into a soft patch of grass. The two immediately began to wrestle, Karl pretending that he was furiously angry at losing his balance. He allowed the little fellow to get him in a stranglehold while Elsa cheered them on.

They would be all right, Helga assured herself. They would go on, grow up, and live their lives. They would see Laron from time to time, that was unavoidable, but they would get used to not having him around. Children could get used to anything. She wondered if she would be so lucky.

The excitement of the wrestling match was waning. Helga gave a calculating glance at the location of the sun and decided it was time for luncheon.

"Could I interest anyone in food?" she asked.

Whoops of approval erupted from the three of them and they abandoned their rough-and-tumble play for the food hamper. "Don't let me see one dirty hand sneaking into that basket," she told them.

As one they hurried to the small *coulée* at the edge of the grove to wash up. Helga finished transferring persimmons from the gathering bins to the carrying baskets before she headed in the same direction. Elsa and Jakob met her coming back.

"Spread out the cloth in that sunny spot," she told Elsa. "And not one bite for either of you until we've said grace."

Jakob moaned and grabbed his belly, pretending that he was near to fainting from hunger. Helga smiled at him, remembering that because of Laron, her youngest had never once known that feeling.

She hurried on to the water to wash up herself. Karl was hesitating there, his mind obviously on neither food nor fun. Helga suffered a momentary twinge of cowardice and wanted to turn and walk the other direction. With her thoughts so much on Laron, the last thing that she was ready for today was a confrontation with her oldest son.

Deliberately she plastered a smile upon her face. "It's a wonderful day for gathering persimmons," she told him.

Karl nodded, but his brow was still furrowed. He looked so German when he worried, Helga thought. He looked so much like her brother, lost to her so long ago.

"Mama," he said. "There is something that I think that I should tell you."

Helga almost sighed aloud in exasperation. She wanted to pretend everything was all right, if only for the children's sake and if only for one day. Apparently Karl was not going to let her do that.

She squatted before the *coulée* and began to wash her hands. "What must you tell me, Karl?" she asked, purposely keeping her eyes averted.

"It may be of no importance," the boy said. "It may be something that I should keep to myself." He hesitated thoughtfully a moment before continuing. "But I told him that I would tell you, so I suppose I must keep my word."

I told him that I would tell you. The words echoed in her head. It had to be Laron. The other day when he'd been there on the dock, he'd talked to Karl. There had been some message for her? Her son had said nothing. In some part of her heart, she wished that his silence would continue.

"If you promised to tell me," she said, "then you must. A man always keeps his word, Karl."

She turned to look at him then and her son nodded.

"It wasn't that I was trying to keep anything from you, Mama," he said.

Helga nodded.

"I just hate to see you cry," the boy admitted.

"I haven't been crying," Helga insisted.

Karl looked at her and shook his head. "Not in front of us, Mama," he agreed. "But don't you think we know why you go off by yourself so much and why your eyes look so red and sad?"

Helga's eyes welled at that very moment. She bit down on her lip to control the emotion.

"I'm getting better," she said. "Please try not to worry about me. I'll be fine, my darling."

"I do worry," her son said. "I know it's all my fault that he went away."

"No, it was not," Helga said. "You know that we . . . we were living in sin. We were wrong to do that and once you were old enough to understand, we could not continue."

Karl looked down at the ground and then up at her. His own eyes were glistening with moisture. "I like him so much, Mama. And he likes me, too. It's not pretend with him, he really likes me."

"Monsieur Boudreau loves you, Karl," she said. "And he always will. Nothing that has happened between him and me will change how he feels about you and the children."

Her son nodded, acknowledging the truth.

"What he told me to tell you," he continued. "Mama, I want to believe it, but I just don't know how."

"What did he tell you?"

"He said that he was going to make it all right," Karl said. "He said for once and all time he was going to make it all right."

Helga's brow furrowed as she stared at her son, trying to comprehend his words. How could Laron make it right? How could he make it right for them to be together for all time?

In memory she saw once more the group of people drinking coffee. The old woman with two little children beside her in the pirogue. The shortish young man who was, she knew, Laron's best friend, stood poling the craft from shore. And the lovely woman who had been his intended called out to her where Laron had gone.

The German coast.

Helga's eyes widened in horror.

"Oh my God!"

"What Mama?" Karl's tone reflected the terror in her own.

"Get the children," she ordered. "We must get help to stop him."

Aida didn't know whether to scream or cry. She lay in Armand's arms but the true distance between them yawned like an unbridgeable chasm. She had retrieved her blouse to cover herself, but had yet to bother with the lacings of her corset vest. Modesty seemed a little enough concern at this point.

He desired her. That she knew at least. With the help of a love charm and every feminine wile she possessed, he desired her. It was a start, she argued to herself. At least it was a start. But she was not sure that the young man's honor would even allow him to pursue the direction.

His honor. That was what a judge was called. And with Armand it was an apt description. If only they'd gone just a little further. If only they'd managed to get past the point of no return. His honor would have compelled him to marry her. And dishonorably, she wanted nothing else more.

"Are you all right, Aida?" he whispered close to her ear.

She nodded, not quite trusting her voice to speak.

"I cannot . . . cannot begin to apologize enough for what I've done to you," he said. "I can only be grateful that some last shred of sanity we possessed prevented us from going further."

He hesitated as if waiting for her to agree with him. Aida couldn't find her voice to do so.

"I can promise you," he continued finally. "That no word of this will ever be spoken."

She believed him. He would never say a word. He would probably forget the incident completely. But she, Aida knew, would remember him for her whole life long.

"We both were out of our heads," he went on. "The charm made us behave as we never would have. It made us say and do things that we would never otherwise."

That was true, Aida realized. For him at least, it must have been true. In fact, she had not felt any strange effects of the charm. She had wanted him, certainly. But she knew that there was always a strange weightiness of the effects of drug and herb. There had been none of that for her. He must have gotten all the charm and she none. Because she knew that what she felt for him was real and true and from the heart.

"Speak to me, Aida," Armand pleaded. "Are you truly all right?"

She turned in his arms then and looked straight at him. Those wonderful blue eyes, so precious and familiar to her, were dark with worry. In a few moments they would sit up and then stand up and then walk away from this place. And she knew that once they did so, she would never be this close to him again. If only they had not been able to stop. If only—

A wave of sheer slyness settled over her and gave her voice at last.

"You must marry me," she said.

"What?"

He sat up immediately and brought her with him.

"You must marry me," she insisted once more.

He gave her a long look and then glanced away, clearly ill-at-ease.

"There is no need for that," he said.

"You have compromised me and you must make it right."

Armand ran a nervous hand through his hair and chose his words carefully. "Mademoiselle Gaudet, you are obviously very innocent of the ways of . . . of human procreation," he said. "What we did here, though unarguably sinful, was not, in total, the marriage act. You are in no danger of producing a child. I can assure you, mamselle, that there is no need to wed."

Aida hardened her resolve and raised her chin. "So you are now back to calling me mamselle," she said sarcastically. "You used my given name, monsieur, when you touched me as no man but a husband has a right."

Armand's mouth dropped open in shock. Aida couldn't look him in the eyes. She feared he would see the deception in her own.

"I think you must marry me, monsieur," she continued. "And I am certain that if I described what happened this afternoon to my father, he would most likely insist on the same."

"He would most likely kill me outright."

"And even if I were to try to keep the truth from

him," she said, sighing. "I will certainly not be able to keep it from my confession. Father Denis will not be pleased to hear this at all."

"You would tell Father Denis?"

"Certainly. I will have to. As will you also, monsieur."

He looked horrified. Coming to his feet he offered his hand to help her up and then turned away. He walked around the small clearing. Finding his hat, discarded, he picked it up and began dusting and shaping it as if it were the most important thing on earth.

Aida concentrated on doing the lacings on her corset vest. She wanted to scream, she wanted to cry. It was strange to think that love could be so closely allied with humiliation. She was having to beg, actually beg him to wed her.

Perhaps it was a kind of justice, she thought. For years men had sighed after her so longingly and she had so casually rejected them. Now, at last, she had fallen in love herself. Would she be as casually discarded as her former swains? But none of them had ever loved her. She knew that as surely as she knew anything. They had loved her beauty, but no one had ever loved her. She glanced again toward Armand, still turned from her. Maybe no one could.

She was not very bright; she was only pretty. That was the truth and everyone including her knew it. But, she declared to herself stubbornly, bright or pretty were not the only choices. A woman might be hardworking, like Félicité Sonnier, or she might be humorous, like Yvonne Hébert. She might have Estelle LeBlanc's tremendous pride. Perhaps she heard voices, like Orva Landry, or was a resourceful and exemplary mother like the German widow. Ruby Babin was only herself and that was sufficient. Aida was no longer willing to live with self-aspersion.

Armand turned back to face her once more. She stiffened her back to face him.

"Mademoiselle Gaudet, my . . . dear Aida," he said, hesitating. "I do not know what to say to you."

She knew exactly what he should say and raised her chin, glaring at him decisively.

"I believe I have indicated, monsieur, that a marriage proposal is in order."

She was now completely dressed. She found her discarded sunbonnet on the ground and picked it up as she began walking away.

"Where are you going?"

"To the church," she answered. "If you will not marry me, then I must . . . I must be a nun or . . . or Father Denis will know what I must do. I am compromised. I must go to the church."

"Aida wait!" he called out.

She kept walking.

He ran after her. "Wait," he called again.

She did not.

When he reached her side he grabbed her hand. He hesitated only a moment before dropping to his knees. His held his hat in his right hand and used both to cover his heart as he gazed up at her. He appeared more worried and anxious than ardent and lovestruck. But the words he spoke at least sounded sincere.

"Mademoiselle Gaudet, you would show me great honor and afford me much happiness if you would consent to be my bride."

It was an ordinary offer of betrothal, traditional

and customary. The kind of proposal any man might make to anyone. A simple speech with no flowery words of praise or declarations of undying devotion.

"Very well, then I will," she answered, wishing he had said more.

He rose to his feet and took her hand in his; he brought it to his mouth and gently kissed her fingers. A silence settled between them that was distinctly sorrowful. To break it, he placed his hands upon her shoulders, leaned forward, and kissed her cheek.

"I will try to make you happy, Aida," he said. "I cannot promise that you will be, but I can swear to be dutiful, faithful, and a good provider."

"What more could I want?" she asked them both, feeling the totally unreasonable and unacceptable desire to burst into tears.

Aida Gaudet had won the man of her choice. It had taken a love charm and a complaint of compromise, but she had won. Somehow the victory seemed hollow.

He continued to hold her hand as she turned and walked. He walked beside her.

"We are going the wrong direction," he said finally. "We should return to Madame Landry's place and wait for a pirogue."

Aida raised her chin, determined. "We are on our way to church," she told him. "When I said that I wished to be married, monsieur, I did not mean tomorrow."

Quinze

Father Denis had awakened late and it was obvious to Armand the minute that he came to the door that the old priest had not yet even had his breakfast. His robe was hastily donned and his thin gray hair stood straight up on his head, bent from sleep.

"*Bonjour!*" he said, surprised to find the young couple at his door. "*Bonjour*, Aida, Armand."

"We did not mean to wake you," Armand told him.

"It looks to be nearly mid-morning," the priest admitted. "I have not been sleeping well of late. The need for a school keeps me in prayer long after the last candle of evening has gutted and died."

The statement was directed at Armand, but he let it pass without comment.

"What brings you to church on Thursday morn?"

Aida looked in Armand's direction, questioningly. He swallowed nervously. He was the one who ought to speak, it was customary. But he knew without doubt that if he did not, she would.

Unwilling to be bowed in shame, he raised his head and faced the priest with a near hint of arrogance.

"We are here to marry, Father," he said finally.

267

The cleric looked momentarily confused. "To marry? To marry whom?" he asked.

"To marry each other," Armand answered quietly.

The priest's jaw dropped open in shock and he gazed at the two in stunned surprise.

"You are joking!" he accused.

"That we are not, Father," Armand insisted. "We are here to wed. And we are here to wed each other."

He shook his head and gazed at Aida soberly. "You wish to marry Armand Sonnier?" he asked.

She nodded mutely.

"We all know that you have just finished your betrothal with Monsieur Boudreau," he said. "And I saw at the *fais-dodo* that you dance well together. But you are still young and lovely, my dear; there is no need to jump hastily into marriage."

"I am not being hasty," she assured him. "I have thought it through a good deal."

The old priest chuckled as if she had said something humorous. "*You* have thought it through. Dear, dear Aida, your pretty little head was not meant for weighty thoughts. Does your poppa know of this wedding plan? It must be he who thinks such a decision through. There must be banns read and an engagement party . . ."

"No Father," she admitted. "It . . . we . . ." She gave Armand an embarrassed glance. "I am compromised, Father. I wish to wed before I speak to Poppa."

"Compromised!"

The priest's expression was one of total disbelief that quickly turned to anger. Armand stood silent, guilty, his hands behind his back. He wished fervently that the earth could open and swallow him up.

Father Denis did not even ask him to deny the

accusation. The former mentor looked at him as if he were a worm, a worm beneath his feet.

"You will marry immediately," he said. "Immediately!" The old priest's voice rose to a bellow.

"Yes, Father," both agreed meekly.

The furious cleric wrung his hands and pursed his lips in unspoken frustration.

"Allow me a few moments to ready myself and I will hear your confession."

"Confession?" Aida almost squeaked out the word.

"Of course, my daughter," the priest answered. "You would not wish to wed with this sin upon you."

Armand watched her from the corner of his eye. She swallowed nervously. He wanted to wrap his arm around her and tell her it was all right. It wasn't much of a sin, as sins go, he wanted to assure her.

"All right, Father," she said, sounding almost frightened.

The priest went to wash and comb his hair and ready the sanctuary. Armand and Aida were left alone, uncomfortable with each other. Aida was very anxious and fidgety. He wanted to comfort her.

"It will be fine," he told her calmly. "Please don't worry. It will all be fine."

She nodded, but her expression still showed concern. Armand's brow furrowed thoughtfully.

He used his hat to fan away the dust on the step and then offered the place to her. She seated herself and gazed out at the river before them, as if too embarrassed to look at him directly.

Hoping to offer reassurance, Armand took her hand in his own. It was a simple, tender gesture. She glanced at him but then turned away in obvious shame.

Certainly there were explanations to be made. And with the unexpected betrothal, speculation would be rampant. But they would get through that. And Armand would see that she was protected from the mass of snide gossip or uncomfortable questions. Mentally Armand readied himself for that task.

He knew that he should be remorseful about what happened. Aida felt compromised. The fact that she was not was no great credit to their restraint. And it could not, in total, be blamed upon the love charm. He had not felt drugged or entranced. He had known exactly what he had been doing.

She felt compromised, but he was certain that would pass. But they would still be wed. He would have her as his own, forever. He should have tried harder to talk her out of this, but he hadn't. He hadn't wanted to. He wanted to marry her, he realized. He had always wanted to marry her.

And why shouldn't he do it? Laron didn't want her and she didn't want Laron. Jean Baptiste might want her, but his vows were made and the breaking of them could only bring sorrow to everyone, including Aida. Armand *did* want her and he was not spoken for elsewhere.

It could all work out perfectly, he told himself. He had taken the opportunity when it presented itself. It could all work out perfectly, for him at least.

He was not at all sure that it would work out perfectly for Aida. He had taken advantage of the circumstances and of her charm-inspired passion. He should feel shame. He did feel shame. But more than that, Armand admitted to himself in honesty, he felt grateful.

"It's going to be fine," Armand told Aida, who sat so anxiously beside him.

He brought her clasped hand to his lips. It was the first kiss since they left the stand of cottonwoods.

She turned to face him. With the index finger of his other hand he gently traced the lines of worry that had formed on her forehead.

"It's going to be fine," he repeated.

Of course she was frightened, he thought to himself, noting the paleness of her complexion. This was supposed to be the happiest day of her life and instead it had been confusing and embarrassing, and if they were not lucky, they might both be still on their knees doing penance until nightfall. But then they would be together.

Silently Armand vowed that though he hadn't tried harder to talk her out of the idea, he would try hard to make her happy.

"I do vow this moment, Aida Gaudet, to be a good husband to you," he said. "I know I am not your choice, but even without Madame Landry's love charm, I will always show you the greatest respect and affection. In that there is no cause for concern."

His words seemed to upset her even more.

Of course people were going to talk. Armand knew that. The folks in the community would be certain to speculate on how the lovely Aida Gaudet came to be wed to short, ordinary Armand Sonnier, but he would never reveal the truth to a soul. Whether a bride was caught by love or guile, the wedding was just as valid.

"Armand—" Her voice broke like thin glass. "Armand, I must confess—"

The door to the church reopened. Father Denis was ready.

"You must confess what you must," he told her. "Do you wish me to go first?"

She shook her head. "I'm ready," she said to the priest.

Standing alone, he watched her go. She turned to give one last longing look at him before Father Denis closed the door.

Armand sat down once more on the church step and contemplated the future. The house he had planned to build this winter, well, he would certainly have to build it now. Aida would be a part of that. It would be her house, too.

Unless, of course, she wanted them to live with her father. That is what she and Laron had planned. Armand was not so fond of that idea. But, he decided, it was better than the two of them living with Jean Baptiste and Félicité. Not that Armand was worried about his brother and Aida. Jean Baptiste might risk his own marriage vows, but he would never disrespect his brother's. That house was simply too crowded and would be even more so with the arrival of the new baby.

Perhaps they could live with her father for a while and then decide whether to build their own house or stay to take care of the old man.

Armand shook his head in momentary disbelief. Jesper Gaudet, the wealthiest farmer in the parish, the owner of the grist mill, was to be his father-in-law and his responsibility. Most men would have considered that a great stroke of good luck. As husband to the lovely Aida, he would have almost an excess of riches.

The door behind him opened and Father Denis called his name.

The old priest showed none of the ill-disguised anger of only moments before. Armand concluded that once hearing the truth about what happened from Aida's lips, he was less outraged.

He walked inside and spotted Aida kneeling at one of the pews near the front of the church, obviously offering her penance. Her head was bent in fervent sorrow. Armand felt drawn to her and wished he could grant her comfort.

In the far back corner of the church two chairs sat side by side. One was finely carved and scrolled, the other as plain as any in the parish. Between them stood an ornate frame hung with a delicate lace curtain.

Father Denis took his seat in the fine chair. Armand sat in the plain one on the other side of the curtain.

"Forgive me, Father, for I have sinned," he said in a hurried almost singsong manner, born of much familiarity. "It has been . . . ten, no eleven days since my last confession."

With clear, unhalting words Armand told of his lustful thoughts, his stolen kisses. And he told of his deliberateness, how he could have resisted the temptation to draw her to himself, but he had not.

When he had finished, there was a long thoughtful pause on the other side of the curtain.

"Is that all of it?" the priest asked.

"Yes, Father," Armand answered.

Again hesitation.

"Do you love her, my son?"

"I love her," he admitted simply.

"Ah."

It was a sigh that sounded like relief.

Father Denis forgave him and blessed him and to Armand's surprise the penance he was given was exceedingly light.

He walked to the front of the church as Aida was rising from her prayers. They looked at each other.

She was beautiful, Armand thought, beautiful and uncertain. She looked like the lovely Aida. She looked the way she had always looked. Armand realized in a flash that what he had always taken for silliness and vanity was a lack of self-assurance. He could give her that. If he had anything in great abundance to offer, it was confidence.

He winked at her.

Her expression registered immediate shock, followed by a smile. He would keep her smiling forever, he vowed.

Armand did his penance in rapid time and with a light heart. God knew how he felt about Aida. God had known it always. Somehow it would be right. Somehow it just had to be.

When he finished he headed toward the church door. Hearing voices outside, he hesitated in midstride. He knew from the tone that something was wrong.

Immediately, protectively, he thought of Aida and rushed to her rescue. If anyone, her father included, tried to disrupt this wedding, they would have to do over his body!

Before he even stepped outside he realized that it was Orva's voice that he heard. Momentarily he was wary. She had undoubtedly found the remains of the blueberry tart and had probably drawn her own conclusions. But Madame Landry, he declared in silent fervency, was not going to stand between him and his marriage.

It was not Orva, however, whom he spied first from the church doorway, but Helga Shotz. She stood in the churchyard, her children all around her, wide-eyed and scared. Tied up at the end of the dock was a leaky old skiff that Armand recognized as the one Orva Landry sometimes used on her solitary night trips along the river.

"Madame Shotz? What are you doing here?" Armand asked.

The woman didn't have a moment to answer. Her youngest came hurrying toward him, eagerly running and talking at the same time.

"We come all the way from the persimmon grove to the treater woman's house," little Jakob announced. "And we left our persimmons there."

"Madame Shotz has come for our help," Orva told Armand. She stood next to Father Denis and was giving the old priest a look that was cold enough to freeze mosquitoes on the trees in July. "She needs our help and it is our Christian duty to provide it."

"Please, please, you must help me," Helga pleaded. Her tone was more heavily laden with strong German speech than Armand remembered. "I did not know where else to come."

She sounded desperate. Armand tousled the hair of the little boy who stood at his feet.

"Of course we will help you," he answered. "What is it? What is wrong?"

Glancing down at her children, Helga appeared momentarily hesitant to speak. She said something to the oldest in German and he immediately hustled the other two away toward the dock so that she could speak more privately. When the three were beyond hearing distance she turned back to answer the question.

"It's Laron," she answered. "I'm frightened for Laron."

A cold chill of fear quivered down Armand's back. "What has happened?" he asked.

"Nothing I hope," she answered. "But I am afraid that something terrible might."

"Tell me."

She gave an uneasy glance toward Father Denis, Madame Landry, and Aida. "Are you aware that I have been allowing Monsieur Boudreau to visit me?" she asked nervously.

Armand nodded.

She swallowed, obviously embarrassed. "I have broken it off with him," she said. "I have . . . have no excuse for allowing it to continue as long as I did." She turned her apologetic gaze upon the priest. "But finally . . . finally I broke it off."

"Laron told me, madame," Armand answered. "He told me both about the past and that you had broken it off."

She nodded, grateful. "It was because of the children," she said, her voice rife with self-derision. "It was not that I regained my good sense. I simply could not continue such a . . . such a sinful liaison in front of them. Not if I want to teach them right and goodness."

"Amen!" Father Denis pronounced.

"It is hard to teach a lesson one does not live," Madame Landry agreed.

"It has been so terrible without him," Helga continued. "And I know he must feel the same, missing us, myself and the children."

"He loves you very much," Armand told her honestly.

Behind him Armand heard Father Denis tutting with disapproval.

"Yes, I know. But love does not always make things right. Sometimes it is not enough to do that."

Her eyes welled with tears, but she visibly stiffened her lip and raised her chin. "We cannot be together. I have made vows. I am still married."

"God can forgive your sin," the priest proclaimed. "And as He counseled another caught in adultery, you must 'go and sin no more.'"

"That will not be enough," she explained.

Helga's expression was rife with misery, and grief choked her words. Aida moved closer and wrapped her arm around the woman's waist, offering what comfort she could.

"He came by our place last week," she said. "He talked to the children, made them laugh again. I didn't go out to speak to him. I couldn't."

Aida patted her with understanding.

"He told Karl to give me a message," she continued. "He said that he was going to make it right. That he was going to make it right for us to be together once and for all."

Armand's brow furrowed. "What can he mean?"

She turned to Aida, clasping her hand. "You said that he has gone to the German coast."

"That is what he told me," Aida answered. "The night we broke our betrothal he said he was going there. He said that he had business there."

Helga nodded. "It is that *business* that concerns me."

She turned to look at Armand, her tearful gaze full of fear. "I told Laron, long long ago, that the last I heard of my husband, he was in St. Charles Parish on the German coast."

Aida's eyes widened. Madame Landry tutted with worry. Helga continued to look at Armand in anguish.

"I am afraid," she whispered, as if fearing God Himself might hear. "I am afraid that he has gone there to kill my husband."

Father Denis gasped and offered up a hasty prayer to the saints.

Armand moved into action. "I must stop him," he said decisively. "I will follow him to the German coast and somehow I will stop him."

"*We* must stop him," Helga corrected. "You cannot go alone. You will be a stranger there. You do not speak the language. You won't be able to ask questions. And even if you find Laron, he is not thinking as himself. It may take both of us to convince him that this is not the way."

Armand nodded. He didn't like the idea of taking the woman out of the safety of Prairie l'Acadie, but he thought she might well be right. He did not know German words or German ways and he remembered how determined Laron had been, how certain and sure. If Laron had completely lost all sense of rightness it might take Helga herself to convince him murder was no answer.

"Aida, take her children to my brother's house,"

Armand ordered. "Tell them that we will return as soon as we can."

"No," Orva interrupted. "Aida must go with you."

Armand gave the old woman a puzzled look. Aida's expression was equally surprised.

"It is not the thing to travel alone with this woman," Madame Landry said. "Aida, as your wife, must be there with you."

"Wife?" Helga's question was rife with surprise. "I did not know you two had married."

"We haven't yet," Armand said.

"Then hurry up, old fat priest," Orva said, directing her words to Father Denis. "There is no time for dallying; they must find Laron before he does something he will regret all his life."

"These two need not marry today," Father Denis declared. "They can marry when Armand returns," he promised. "Then it will be a fine wedding with a full Mass and flowers and family."

"What if they do not return?" Orva asked. Her question cut raw at the moment.

"I want to marry now!" Aida declared.

Armand found himself unwilling to argue with her.

"Aida will not slow you down," she continued. "And you may need her. If anyone is hurt or injured, she will be able to help. I would go with you myself, but I have duty here that I must attend."

Father Denis might have protested, but he had learned from long experience that it was easier to give in to Madame Landry than to argue with her.

The wedding ceremony on the steps of the church was brief and to the point. Armand promised to love and cherish. Aida promised to honor and obey. Madame Landry and Helga Shotz and her children served as witnesses. It was over before Armand had time to regret the haste.

He gave her the briefest kiss on the cheek as they were pronounced man and wife and immediately turned to go.

"We must hurry," he said. "If we push very hard we can make the mouth of the river by dark. Then into the east bayous and to the German coast by late tomorrow."

"Leave the children here with me," Father Denis said. "I will take them up to your home, Armand. Your sister-in-law will care for them."

"No," Orva disagreed. "They will stay with the Héberts. Laron's sister will look after them, do not worry."

"Father Denis can take them to my brother's house," Armand said. "Félicité will be glad to watch them."

The old woman shook her head. "Not this night," she said. "They will stay with Yvonne. Hurry now, go."

"We have no boat," Armand said. "We cannot go anywhere before we find a boat."

"You will take the skiff," Orva told him.

"That old thing?" Armand's voice was incredulous. "We will be killed with the first wave of rough water."

"It's neither as swift nor sure as a pirogue, but moves across the water with no great wake. I've learned many things sitting inside it. And on this trip there will be many lessons to learn."

* * *

Laron Boudreau carefully lit the small driftwood fire on the sand-covered stretch of beach on Vermillion Bay. He was sober. As the fire blazed up he added more wood. It wouldn't be a good cooking fire until there were sufficient burning coals at its base. He eased his pot of fresh water near the edge. It would take time to get it boiling. He moved a few feet away and watched the rolling surf and colors of the late afternoon as the sun eased its way toward the sea.

He'd been to the German coast. He had traveled the length of the river and set out along the coastal passages. In his tiny pirogue he'd faced the mighty waters of the gulf. At Grand Terre he'd headed back north up into the swamps and bayous that had been the province of pirates. Through the marshes called Barataria and the fiefdom of Jean Lafitte. He had found the New Orleans backwaters claimed by the Germans. But he had not found Helmut Shotz. And he had not done his deed. He had not killed the man who stood between him and the happiness of the woman and children that he loved.

The place had been nothing like he'd thought it was going to be. Somehow he'd imagined it like Bayou Blonde. The people would be strange and foreign. The German coast would be dirty, ill-kept, and intrinsically wicked.

It had not been that at all. It was wet bayou country, not nearly as good for cattle as his own desolate Prairie l'Acadie, but it was cropland. And it had been populated by farmers and fishermen. They dressed different and talked different, but were, in their lives, not so very different from him.

They had a look about them that he had found

oddly comforting. Neat and starched. The men in the familiar garb occasionally sported by Karl and little Jakob. The women in their pale, nearly colorless, staid dresses. Probably all wearing drawers, he thought to himself and smiled.

It was not until now that he realized that what was so comforting, what was so familiar, was that they reminded him of Helga. Their faces, their hair, their sturdiness. It was their peculiar look. He had thought of it as Helga's look. He realized that it was the look of Germans.

Only a few spoke a smattering of French, and that nearly indecipherable and liberally laced with English. Though the language barrier had been formidable, the people themselves had been generally open and welcoming. That is, until he'd mentioned the name of Helmut Shotz. Immediately he'd become suspect. It had taken only a short conversation to get the message clear. If he were a friend of Shotz, he was no friend of theirs.

Helga's husband had come to the coast three years earlier. He had wintered with them, causing more than his share of trouble and grief. He'd taken up courting a wealthy old widow, they said.

"He was courting a widow?" he'd asked, shocked. "The man is married."

The farmer had shrugged. "His wife was not with him," he said. "We are Lutherans, you know. And divorce is legal in Louisiana."

The widow, however, had seen through his fast talking and charming manners and sent him on his way. Shortly thereafter her life savings, safely tucked in her mattress tick, had been confirmed as missing.

Shotz had been highly suspected, but nothing

could be proved. One of the woman's kin asked to search his belongings. When he refused, the man tried anyway. Shotz attacked him, gutting him from throat to belly button in front of witnesses. Then he had fled.

They found the money in his pack but he was gone.

By spring there was word that he had been seen in Texas. He was tried in absentia, found guilty, and sentenced to death. There was a price on his head in the state of Louisiana. But no one had seen or heard of him again.

Laron had asked for and been given directions to a couple of new German settlements where it was likely that Shotz might find refuge. He'd hurried out to the coast, Texas-bound. Now he stood on the gulf shore, staring out at the water to cross. Behind him was the mouth of the Vermillion River. His route back home. He could simply return home.

Sighing thoughtfully he checked his pot of water. It was just beginning to boil. He was hungry. The thought of fresh boiled crabs had his mouth watering.

A few feet from the fire was the catch of the day. He'd poled the pirogue into the shore early to avoid the pull of the outgoing tide. He'd been immediately rewarded by the sight of a huge tidal crab scurrying onto the beach intent on burying itself in the safety of the sand. Laron had chased the eager fellow down and tapped upon it lightly with his knuckles. The crab had frozen in fear and been easily plunked from the sand for supper. He'd dug up two others while gathering wood for the fire and the three were now impatiently awaiting their fate in a small bucket.

Laron squatted in the sand to stare in the bucket, admiring his catch. They were all of similar size and

color and for the life of him he couldn't tell the one
who'd raced on the beach with him from the others.
He noted that they were attempting escape. But
success did not seem close within their grasp. One
would use the others to climb up the side of the
bucket. But when it would just get the barest claw
grip on the edge, the second would hang upon it
wanting to follow it up. It seemed likely that they
would make it, likely that they would see freedom
once more. Then the third crab would get a grip on
the second and all three would fall back in the bucket
and start all over.

Laron watched this futile effort for several moments, curious. They were trapped. Victims of their
fate. It was not that there was no escape, he realized.
It was that they could not *all* escape. If one of them
would sacrifice itself, become a ladder for the other
two, then those two could get free.

He watched and watched. But crabs weren't as
smart as humans. Or perhaps they simply did not
know love. A man who loved would sacrifice himself
to free the others.

Sacrifice. That is what he planned to do. To make a
sacrifice of himself. Laron turned his gaze to the
lowering sun in the western sky. Texas. He was going
to Texas to kill a man. Not that he thought that killing
Helmut Shotz was going to set them free, make them
all happy. He'd thought that when he'd left Prairie
l'Acadie, but he believed it no more. Days alone to
ponder and question had made it clear. He could kill
the man, but he would still not have what he wanted.
Helga and the children could be free, but they could
not be his. They could have the safety of the sand, but
like the crab, he would remain trapped in the bucket.

The world was not so lawless that he could commit murder and expect to get away free. Even a worthless man like Helmut Shotz was allowed his life. Taking it would not be permitted. Laron would be hunted down, caught, tried, executed. He could not expect the deed to be forgotten.

Even if he managed to flee the scene, to get away to avoid the capture, even if he slunk back to the secluded safety of Prairie l'Acadie, he could never hide from such a secret.

Helga would know. He would know. And eventually the children would have to know, too.

The children, Karl, Elsa, and Jakob. Laron closed his eyes as he thought of them, yearned for them. Did a man love the children of his own loins more than he loved these? Laron could not imagine it.

Helga wanted the children to grow up rightly, to learn to do good and to be good. She wanted to teach them the morals that would make their lives better. Teaching was done by words, but more forcefully by example. She and Laron had cast off their love for each other because it could not be shown within the sanctity of marriage. How much more wrong would it be to devalue the sanctity of life by killing a man who stood in their way?

The children would see only great violence and great wrong in the people that they most loved. Their lives would be forever torn. Divided always in their hearts between the man who was a father to them and a murderer, and the man who fathered them and was murdered.

Laron continued to gaze at the crabs.

"Sacrifice." He whispered the word silently to himself.

He had planned to make himself a sacrifice. Truly he could see no other option. Was it right or wrong? He no longer knew. But he did know that he would forever be alone.

Seize

Aida Gaudet had never been more than a few miles from her home. This day, the day of her wedding, she was traveling to the very end of the Vermillion River, but this was no wondrous and exciting wedding journey. This was a dangerous and harrowing errand to keep a man from making a horrible mistake. Strangely she felt not the slightest fear. A peace had settled upon her as she'd seated herself on the flat bottom boards in the old worn cypress skiff. It was going to be all right.

The day had been a long one. As evening approached it was difficult to remember that just this morning they had eaten the blueberry tart. Just this morning she had almost, but not quite lost her innocence. And just this morning, as she had insisted, Armand Sonnier had married her.

Now she ran headlong and heedless with him and Madame Shotz in a race for Laron's honor and perhaps Monsieur Shotz's life.

She glanced at Armand, standing at the back of the boat. His poling stick moved with care and efficiency, being both propulsion and rudder. He was a scholar, she thought. But there was nothing of the sickly, studious fellow now. He was a man on a mission. A mission to save his friend. And he was as strong and ready and able as the task required. She felt proud to call him husband.

The day had been fair and cool and the sun had shone brightly, but hadn't warmed the nip in the air. Armand, however, was drenched in sweat as he poled relentlessly, unwilling to allow the speed of the river alone to pull them downstream. They had made tremendously good time, he'd assured them. And now that they were low in the river, the evening tide was pulling them toward the sea in a very rapid pace.

They had good cause to be afraid. The tiny, less than seaworthy skiff was all but flying over the top of the water. An immersed log or a jutting rock just below the surface could tip them into the water at any moment. And the nests of gators got thicker and more numerous as they approached the sea.

But strangely she was not fearful. She was safe with Armand. She was safe with him, and sure. Anywhere that he chose to go, she would follow him there. Anyplace that he took her, she knew that he would give his life to protect her. And if the fates decreed this to be her last day on earth, then she would go to heaven at his side, content.

It was a strange sensation, this newfound trust, this certainty. Was it merely that she had wed him? Or was it because she loved, truly loved this man? Perhaps it was a foolish, female fancy, but never had confidence and assurance filled her so fully. He had seen her, truly her, not just the outside but her silly thinking and her chipped tooth. He had seen her and he had not turned away. It was a warm, comforting feeling and one for which she was grateful.

She glanced up at him again. She loved Armand Sonnier. He might not truly have wanted to marry her, but she determined that she would never give him cause to regret it.

Across from her Helga Shotz anxiously scanned the river and the bank. Aida was fearful for Laron, because Laron was dear to her, but Helga loved Laron as she loved Armand. She tried to imagine what she might feel if it were he who was in such danger. What if it were Armand bent on ruining his life? The idea twisted inside her, churning like nausea. She reached over to take the German woman's hand and squeezed it comfortingly.

"We will find him," she whispered. "I am sure of it."

"Have you had a vision of it?" she asked.

Aida shook her head. The only vision she'd seen had been the one of Laron cutting the shorn field. That one was for Armand, if she could ever make him understand. She had no comfort to offer Helga.

"But we will find him, I feel sure," she said.

Helga nodded, but her face continued to be lined with anxiety.

"Laron is a serious and thoughtful man," Aida told her. "Occasionally he gets mistaken ideas, like the plan to marry up with me. But once he has thought it through, he always knows the right way to go. It will be the same this time."

Helga nodded hopefully. "I pray you are right," she said and then shook her head with worry once more. "But love clouds the judgment, does it not?"

Her words were an unwelcome reminder of the morning in Armand's arms. She, loving him, had easily thrown caution to the wind. It was only his clear-eyed good sense that had prevailed upon them to resist sinful temptation. And she, loving him, had forced him to take vows that perhaps he did not want to make. Love did cloud the judgment, but she could not wish it away and would not if she could.

Aida forced her thoughts back to Helga and patted the woman's hand comfortingly. "Try not to worry," she said.

Helga smiled. "You are too kind to me," she said. "I have wronged you greatly and still you are kind."

Aida shook her head. "You have wronged no one but yourself, I think," she answered. "Things will be fine, I know that they will."

The woman gave her a wan smile, not believing, but grateful for the words nonetheless.

"He said that you were pretty," she told Aida. "I think he did not do you justice. You are very beautiful."

Aida shrugged. "The river here is beautiful and this country that we travel through. But I cannot love it. We can admire what we see. But we can only love what we truly know."

"Yes, you are right. And I can see that your Armand does truly know your heart," she said.

Aida blushed with shame at her words. If only what she said were the truth.

"Hold on to the sides of the skiff," Armand ordered, startling them both from their reverie. "We are drawing into the bay now and must put over before we are swept to sea."

A poling stick was only good when the water was shallow enough to catch the bottom with it. Armand deliberately kept close to shore where he had control, pulling with great strength and determination against the relentlessness of the sea.

"Once we get to the east shore," Armand told them. "We will pull up until the tide turns. We need rest and food anyway."

The two women clinging determinedly to the tiny skiff could not help but agree. As they approached the beach the danger lessened and the waves no longer seemed likely to tip the boat.

"Look," Helga called out. "There is a fire on the beach."

Aida followed her gaze and could see the blaze and one man standing on the sand.

"This is a desolate area," Armand said. "It could be an outlaw or pirate."

"It is Laron!"

Helga spoke the words with absolutely certainty that belied the distance that separated them from the man.

Aida shook her head disbelieving and then spied the long, cypress pirogue pulled up on the beach. Someone had braved the gulf waters in such an inconsequential craft?

"I think she's right."

Armand pulled toward the fire.

"Ho! The beach!" he called out in French.

The man in the distance turned toward them, waved, and called back.

Orva Landry was smiling to herself as she sat alone on the end of the dock in front of her house. She'd packed her bag, everything that she would need, and calmly she waited. Father Denis had taken the children to the Héberts. Jesper Gaudet had been by to pick up his daughter and had been startled and furious and near mad as a rabid dog to learn that not only had she married without permission, she had run off with her new husband without so much as a word.

Orva had finally made him see the sense of all of it and was sitting, waiting, humming to herself with pleasure. In the distance she already spied a pirogue headed in her direction. She waited knowing with certainty that Jean Baptiste would arrive shortly.

Beside her on the worn cypress planks was the blueberry tart that she'd made him. She'd left it cooling in the back of the cupboard, careful to keep it separate from the one she'd made for her own supper. She certainly hadn't wanted to get the two mixed up. This one contained a dangerous potion that she personally had no wish to ingest.

Of course, there had been no danger of that. Those naughty children, Armand and Aida, had eaten up every bite of hers. She should have hid it equally as well, she thought.

She shook her head thinking of those two. What a surprise they turned out to be. No matter how long she lived a woman could never tell who would ultimately end up with whom. Those two had been in the soup for a good long time now. All they had needed was a little push.

That was what Jean Baptiste was getting tonight, she thought. Just a little push.

"Heave to the boat, Jean Baptiste!" she called out. "I'm going upstream with you."

"*Bonsoir*, Madame Landry!" the young man said, surprised as he eased his pirogue closer to her dock. "It would be my pleasure to take you up."

"What a day it has been," she said. "I suppose you have heard."

"Just now," he said. "They say that my brother has married Aida Gaudet and the two have gone down the river with the German widow to find Laron Boudreau."

Orva nodded. "They should be all the way down-river by nightfall," she answered.

Jean Baptiste maneuvered closer, ultimately getting close enough to throw the old woman the rope. She deftly tied the boat and stood, ready to board.

"I cannot think how such a thing has come to pass," he told her.

The old woman chuckled.

"Strange times are brewing," she replied.

The young man helped her into the pirogue and settled her in front before untying and easing off from the dock.

"I made you this blueberry tart," she said, indicating the dish beneath the white cloth.

"For me, madame?"

"Just for you," she told him, nodding as she pulled back the towel that covered it allowing him to admire the treat.

Jean Baptiste's eyes widened with appreciation. "It looks wonderful. I suspect I'd better save it for after supper."

"Yes," she agreed. "Definitely you must wait until after supper."

"Where are you headed tonight, madame?" he asked.

"Well, first to your place," she said. "Then beyond. I aim to take your children upriver with me."

"My children?" He looked at her questioningly.

294 · PAMELA MORSI

"Your old Tante Celeste hasn't seen those little ones in a month of Sundays. I heard *the voices* tell me that tonight is the night to visit."

Jean Baptiste's expression turned grave. Anytime *the voices* spoke of anyone, there was cause for concern.

"You don't think the old woman is ill, do you?" he asked. "Perhaps we should all go and spend time with her, Félicité and I, too."

"No, indeed not," Orva insisted. "Félicité's time is too near. And you'll need to be with her. I'm to go and take your three little ones. You are to merely drop us off and return to your wife. Jacque Savoy will bring us back tomorrow or the next day."

Jean Baptiste nodded a little uncertainly. Tante Celeste lived very far up the river, they'd be lucky to make it there by nightfall. If it seemed a very long trip for one or two days, however, the young man was not brave enough to question the *traiteur* about it.

"Pierre, too?" he asked curiously. "You want to take the baby also?"

Orva nodded. "All three of your children will go with me."

"I'm not sure Félicité will like that," he said honestly. "He's yet very small and still taking tit from time to time."

Madame Landry laughed. It sounded almost like a cackle. "Don't worry, Tante Celeste and I will manage fine. And Félicité will do as I tell her. It's time that you two spent an evening alone together. Sometimes it's necessary for a couple to learn the truth about how important they are to each other."

Jean Baptiste looked at her, speculation now evident in his eyes.

"You are up to something, are you not?" he said.

She smiled up at him. "That I am."

He hesitated, his brow furrowing in worry. "Are you to tell me, or must I be kept in suspense?" he asked.

She shrugged. "Actually, I intended for Armand to speak of it, but as I suppose he cannot I must do it myself."

"What was Armand to tell me?" Jean Baptiste asked.

Orva gazed at the young man for a moment and then chose her words carefully.

"Armand was to say that there is a love charm in this tart."

Jean Baptiste looked at her astounded and then laughed out loud.

"A love charm?" He shook his head, disbelieving. "You've made me up a love charm? Old woman, I've been married five years and have nearly four children. Do you think I am in need of such a nostrum?"

She smiled slyly. "I think you need what's in this tart."

Jean Baptiste still shook his head.

"I love my wife, madame," he said.

"I never doubted it," she answered.

"Then why make a love charm?"

"Are you not interested in making love?"

Her question brought him to blush. They passed the rest of the trip up to his house in near silence. Orva was smiling to herself. She knew enough about life, and about men and women, to closely guess at the young man's thoughts. He had married young, much in love, and now saw himself burdened with duty and responsibility. He would willingly take the opportunity to have an evening alone with his wife. An evening when they might pretend, for a few hours, that they were the carefree lovers of their past.

True to expectations, Félicité was not keen on allowing the children to go off overnight with her. But Orva insisted and Jean Baptiste was even more adamant. In just a few moments the Sonnier children, baby Pierre included, were sitting in the pirogue, heading upriver for an unexpected visit to Tante Celeste. Félicité stood at the end of the dock watching and waving to them as they left.

"Don't give these little ones so much as a moment's worry," Orva told her. "There will be plenty to think about this night, I promise."

Madame Landry cuddled the little ones close to her and kept them quiet and calm as she told them stories. It was a curious fact that the youngest of the community loved Orva and were drawn to her. Once they came to understand the ways of the *traiteur* and *the voices* and the notion of spirits and charms, a fearful distance was created that could never quite be bridged. For that reason, Madame Landry, always took the early opportunities to love and be close to the little ones of the parish.

Orva had never had children of her own. She'd actually been married twice, but there had been no issue from either union. She did not regret that, nor was she saddened by it. Her life was filled with important tasks to be accomplished. It was uncertain if she could have been as effective as a treater if she had also been a mother. The nearest she had come to motherhood herself was being godmother to Armand.

Vividly she remembered the small, sickly little

baby that they had brought her. No one had believed that baby would live. Truthfully she hadn't believed it herself. But she had been determined. Why had God given her the treater's skills if He had not meant her to be able to save this special little life that had been placed in her arms?

She had saved him and she had made him strong. And she had watched him grow into a wise and just man. She was proud of him. As proud as any true parent might be. And she loved him. She had every hope that his new life, his married life, would bring him much happiness. And what she did this night was as much for him as it was for Jean Baptiste and Félicité.

It was full dark when they arrived at the little shack up high in the dark bayou. They almost missed the place. Tante Celeste had long since gone to bed and there was no light to spot the location.

Jean Baptiste had seen it, fortunately, and with a little maneuvering and a lot of noise, they had managed to tie up the boat at the broken-down old dock.

Tante Celeste came out of her house, shucked down to her smallclothes to see what was going on.

"I couldn't be more surprised if tree frost turned into real silver," the old woman declared.

"We've come to pass-a-time with you," Orva told her. "I brought these little children and the two of us will have to try to take care of them for a day or two."

Tante Celeste ushered the sleepy children into the house as Jean Baptiste hastened off.

"You go on home now," Orva said. "And soon as you get to the house you eat up that tart I made for you."

He chuckled. "I hope you know what you're doing."

"I mostly always do," she replied.

"Maybe I should share a bite of it with my wife," he suggested.

"No, don't do that," Orva cautioned.

"Félicité's not been interested in laying close with me for some time," he confided quietly.

Orva shook her head firmly. "Every bite of that tart is for you. Don't let that woman have even so much as a taste of the crust."

Jean Baptiste nodded agreement.

"Heaven will be taking charge of your wife's body this night, telling it exactly what to do. You'll not have to worry on that account," Orva said. "This charm is meant strictly for you."

In the moonlight Orva couldn't plainly make out his face, but she sensed his embarrassment.

"Madam," he whispered his reply. "I don't know what you've been thinking but my . . . my body has never failed me in that way. I can always . . ."

"Yes, yes, I'm sure you can," Orva conceded. "This treatment is not for curing impotence. I know full well that is not the problem. It's something entirely different. You just go on home to your wife, Jean Baptiste. Eat up every bite of that tart. And believe me, within a few minutes the way your body will be acting is going to be like nothing you've ever felt in your life."

With a lighthearted chuckle and a shake of his head, Jean Baptiste stepped into his pirogue.

"So it is your aim to make a memorable night for us," he said as he pushed off from the dock.

Orva nodded and waved as she called out to him.

"Young man, your whole life long I don't believe that you will ever forget it."

As Jean Baptiste and the little pirogue headed downstream in the full dark of moonlight, Orva could hear the young man whistling.

She almost felt like whistling herself.

Dix-sept

"Laron!" Helga stood in the pirogue calling out his name while they were still buffeted by the surf. She waved eagerly to him and she jumped from the skiff to the beach, heedless of the water.

He stared for a long moment and then ran into her arms.

"Helga! My love, my own sweet love."

He gripped her against his chest almost desperately close to him and whispered her name over and over.

She was crying with pent-up anxiety and relief.

"Are you all right?" he asked. "Are the children all right? Has anything . . . anything happened?"

"Only that I missed you," she answered. "Only that I missed you so much."

Armand helped Aida onto the beach and together they pulled the skiff safely out of the tow. By unspoken agreement, the two successfully managed to keep their eyes on each other, affording Laron and Helga a brief moment of privacy.

"How did you get here? Where are the children?"

"We came after you," she told him. "The children are with your sister. Madame Landry said for her to care for them."

"Madame Landry?"

"I didn't know where else to go," Helga admitted. "I thought her the person most likely to know what to do."

Laron nodded tacit agreement.

"We left her place just this morning."

"You came all this way today?"

"We were headed for the German coast," Helga said.

"In that worn-out old skiff?" Laron directed that question to Armand. "You would have never made it."

"It was all we had," he answered.

"Perhaps Madame Landry knew that we need only make it here," Aida suggested.

"Mademoiselle Gaudet?" Laron noticed her for the first time. "What are you doing here?"

"I . . ." She hesitated and then glanced over at Armand. The sight of him seemed to give her courage. "I am Mademoiselle Gaudet no longer," she said. "I am Madame Sonnier."

Laron's jaw dropped open in disbelief and then he leaned over and heartily slapped Armand on the back.

"*Bon Dieu!*" Laron exclaimed. "My friend, you never said a word."

"There was no word to say," Armand admitted. "I asked her to wed me and she has."

Laron took Aida's hand and leaned over to kiss her on the cheek. "Best wishes, madame," he said.

"Thank you," she replied, almost shy. "We . . . we just decided recently."

"It must have been very recently," he agreed. "So it was Armand who was the other man you loved."

Aida blushed a vivid scarlet and did not reply.

Laron turned to regard Armand once more. "And when were you wed?" he asked.

Armand gave Aida a little guilty glance. "Today, this morning."

"What?" Laron was genuinely shocked. "And this is how you choose to spend your wedding night?"

"You are my friend." He gave a nod toward Aida. "Our friend. Madame Shotz needed to go in search of you. So of course we wanted to help."

"Your people and your friends have been very kind to me," Helga said. "I would have come to you, come to find you, if I'd had to swim. Thankfully there was that little boat. Monsieur Sonnier made it fly over the water. For that I will always be grateful."

Armand shrugged.

Laron reached out and shook Armand's hand. "Thank you," he said simply. "I will always be grateful, too. If something happened to Helga, I . . ."

His voice wavered and he could say no more.

Silence settled upon them. In the western sky the sun was sinking into the water like a bright red ball. There was much to say, but much to do also.

"We'd best make camp while we can still see," Armand said, breaking through the spell of quiet thoughtfulness.

"And I'm starving," Aida said.

Her tone was so much the spoiled Aida that Armand thought he once knew that he couldn't help smiling at her.

"When Madame Sonnier gets hungry," he declared with feigned gravity, "then food must be prepared."

He was rewarded for his humor with a swift elbow

in his ribs, but he only laughed and the others joined in.

"I've got some crabs I was about to cook," Laron told them, his tone considerably lightened by their humor. "They aren't enough for four people, but I'm willing to share."

"Madame Landry packed us dinner," Helga said. "With that and the crabs, we will surely eat well enough."

"That's assuming the old woman provides a better meal than she does a boat," Armand said.

For the next half-hour the four of them set to work, making camp, preparing food, joking and talking as if they were on a carefree picnic. Just below the surface of this happy laughter was the concern and anxiety that was as yet still unspoken.

The wind off the water was blustery and cool. Laron and Armand built a wind break, half-burying the two poling sticks from their boats at an angle and criss-crossing the space between them with piles of driftwood and brush. It was not much of a shelter, but it kept the worst of the wind from them. And the area between it and the fire was most comfortably warm and toasty.

Laron took the chance to privately thank him for helping Helga.

"She is everything," he told Armand. "More precious to me than you can understand." He looked over at Armand and his gaze was questioning. "Or perhaps you do understand. Are you in love with Aida?"

Armand shrugged. "Who would not love Aida?"

Laron gave him an even look. "I did not," he answered simply.

The two men stood together for a long moment. Armand finally gave him the response he sought.

"I love her," he said. "I love her and I am very pleased to be married to her."

Slowly Laron's stern expression warmed to a grin and he slapped his friend on the back.

"*Felicitations, mon ami,*" he said. "Congratulations on your marriage, my friend."

Although Helga took charge of boiling the crabs, Aida used some oil and flour to mix up a hot roux. Once the crustaceans were cooked and cracked, Aida dribbled the tasty sauce over the meat.

Armand had never thought of Aida as being much of a cook. But it made sense that a woman who knew and understood herbs might have talents that lay in that direction. He glanced at her from time to time, surprised by how at home she seemed in front of the primitive campfire.

The food was either exceptionally good or the four of them were very hungry. They ate in complete silence except for the occasional wordless expression of appreciation. The spicy flavored crab had them licking their fingers. And the last of the tangy roux sauce was mopped up with Madame Landry's only slightly stale bread.

"This is the best food I've eaten in a week," Laron declared.

"Don't tell me that they did not feed you on the German coast," Helga said.

He smiled warmly at her. "An old farmer's wife did make me some goose liver and dumplings, but it was not nearly so fine as your own."

There was no tart in their basket, but Aida did find a handful of fresh blueberries and divvied them out.

The taste was a sweet, pleasant reminder to Armand of the wonder of the morning. He had held Aida Gaudet in his arms, kissed and caressed her, and he could have possessed her. He had married her. He caught her eye momentarily and watched her blush. Aida Gaudet was blushing for him. The very idea of it had his heart pounding.

Deliberately he pushed the delightful thought to the back of his mind. There was no time now for a flight of fancy. It was time to speak with Laron, to find out if what they suspected was true. And if it was, to dissuade him from his course of action.

The night around them had turned dark and chill. The fire crackled brightly, the orange glow warming them and displaying their faces as they slowly sobered their thoughts and gazed at it introspectively.

"You do know what Helga has been thinking," Armand began at last.

Laron raised his eyes to his friend and then turned to regard the woman he loved.

"He has gone to Texas," Laron said, answering the unasked question. "Years ago now. There is a price on his head. He won't be back. I know of settlements there, but I cannot know where he might be."

"You mustn't go after him," Helga declared. "You must come home with me, Laron." The German woman's tone was firm. "I was wrong. I was very wrong, I see that now. The children love you and will come to understand. They will understand everything. I want you back."

Laron looked down at her, his heart in his eyes, but he made no promises.

"It is foolishness to kill him," she continued. "As I

told you, I was wrong. I want you to come home with me."

Laron looked at her a long time and then shook his head.

"I cannot, Helga," he said. "I cannot live with you again as we have. You were not wrong. It *was* wrong. It was the wrong example for the children."

"The children will learn to understand," she insisted.

"To understand? To understand that the world is a cruel and evil place? To understand that for all their lives they must be outcasts to pay the price for their parents' happiness?" He shook his head determinedly. "We can live with our sin, Helga, because our love is stronger than it," he said. "But we cannot force them to live with it, too."

Her eyes welled with unshed tears.

"You saw it before I did," Laron told her. "We selfishly loved and thereby hurt the innocents who love us. We cannot change the past, but there is no future for us together."

She paled as if he had struck her, but she nodded.

"Then if we cannot, we cannot," she said. "But you must not do this thing. I cannot allow it. You must not search him down and kill him."

"She's right," Armand told him. "No matter what we think of him, the law never sees killing as justified except in self-defense. And he would be the one with that right."

"I do wish he were dead," Helga declared forcefully. "If he were dead, I would marry you in a moment. But you cannot kill him, Laron. If you did, you would not be the man that I love."

Laron sighed heavily. "It wouldn't solve anything, would it?"

It was a statement rather than a question.

Helga's answer was a nod.

"Maybe there is some other way?" Aida piped in. "Surely there is some other way for you two to be together."

She looked at Armand hopefully. He stared back at her mutely. There were no words to be spoken. There was no way for them to be together, except illicitly. Still he searched his mind, his thoughts, his memory for some answer. Aida believed that he could find one.

"You could divorce," Armand said finally. "The German church permits divorce and the law provides for it."

"But our ways do not," Laron said. "If she were to divorce him, the people in Prairie l'Acadie would see her still as ineligible. Father Denis would never marry us."

He reached out and took her hand, expressing the thoughts in his heart wordlessly.

"Prairie l'Acadie is not the only place in the world," Armand said. "You could live elsewhere."

"Perhaps . . ." Laron looked toward Helga hopefully.

"But you could not leave your home," she said. "All of your family, all the people you love are there."

"You and your children are the people that I love," he replied.

Helga shook her head. "No," she declared. "I could never let you leave. It is beyond imagining. Your home is there. I have heard you tell the stories, the stories about your people. How they were torn from their homes and scattered to the four winds. They have made such sacrifices, paid such prices in blood and pain so that they could be together. You cannot throw that away. That is who you are."

"She is right," Armand agreed. "If you went away it would be like . . . like death for all of us."

The faint glimmer of hope that had been fire in Laron's eyes sputtered and died out.

"We must simply part," Helga said. "We must simply promise to keep away from each other. Try to go on with our lives as if we had never met."

"I don't know how I will bear it," Laron said. "It is one thing to make a vow to keep my distance from you when I am sitting so near. It is another to keep that vow when you are out of my sight, less than an hour away."

Helga nodded understanding. "It is misery to be so near and forever separated. It is I who should go away."

Laron was stunned by her words. "But where could you go?" he asked.

"To . . . to . . ." She hesitated thoughtfully. "I could go to this German coast. You did say that it was a nice place. If my husband is no longer there, I could go there and start a new life. The children would be welcomed and we could begin again."

Laron considered her words.

"I don't know if I could bear that any better," he admitted.

Helga's expression showed agreement, but her voice was decisively firm. "It will be easier if I am not so near," she said. "And I do not mind going. The children will grow up among their own kind."

Laron shrugged. "Truthfully they speak their French as well as their German."

She smiled proudly.

"What about your place?" Laron asked. "You've put so much work into it. Would you sell it?"

"*We've* put so much work into it," she said with emphasis. "And I suppose I must just leave it. It belongs to my husband. I cannot sell it, or trade it, or truly even own it."

Laron glanced toward Armand for verification; he nodded slightly. Only a real widow had rights over her husband's property.

"If I go away," she said. "You will be able to forget me."

"No Helga," he told her honestly. "I do not believe I could ever forget you."

The lovers gazed into each other's eyes with sorrow and intensity that was almost palpable. Armand was nearly cut to the quick by the sight. He hastily rose to his feet, offering his hand to the woman beside him.

"Aida and I will walk," he announced. "She is very fond of long leisurely walks. It will be some time before we return."

If the two took note of his words, they made no sign.

Aida grabbed up a blanket and wrapped it about her shoulders like a shawl.

"It's cold tonight," Armand agreed.

She nodded and allowed him to wrap his arm around her as he led her away from the fire and into the darkness.

As soon as they were out of earshot, Aida spoke up. "We can't let this happen," she said. "There is something that we can do. I know that there must be."

"There is nothing," Armand assured her sadly. "This is best, undoubtedly. She will go to the German coast and he will go on with his life."

Aida shook her head. "Something," she said. "There must be something. Think of the vision."

"The vision meant nothing, I'm afraid," he answered. "I know it was your vision, Aida, and your very first one. But I think it meant nothing."

She shook her head. "It's not possible that it serves no purpose at all. It was too real, too vivid. It was too important."

"Perhaps it was, but how can we decipher its meaning?"

"We simply must," she insisted. "We need to think about it and think about it until we understand what it meant."

"Aida, I—"

"You are the answer, Armand," she said. "Of that I am certain. In some way, somehow, you are the answer."

Her words harkened back to those spoken by Madame Landry and gave him pause. He repeated the words softly aloud.

"A careless word spoken is like a tree falling into a mighty river. When the water is low and the yonder bank delicate, sometimes the river will swirl around the tree with some force, wear away the weak side and cause the flow to meander in a new direction."

Aida's brow furrowed.

"It was something Madame Landry said to me," he explained.

"What does it mean?"

Armand shrugged, shaking his head.

Aida shivered.

"You're cold," he said.

"It was better by the fire," she admitted. "But I think we are right to leave them alone for now."

Armand nodded in agreement and then drew her into his arms.

"Let me try to keep you warm," he said, holding her close against him.

"Oh yes," she whispered to him. "That is much better."

"I don't know how he will say goodbye to her. I think that I . . . I think that I didn't know entirely how much she must mean to him. Not until . . . until this morning."

"Armand," she whispered against his cheek. "Do you regret marrying me?"

He was still for a long moment, considering her words.

"What a question to ask a man on his wedding night," he answered finally. "No, Aida. Not unless you do."

"I don't. I was just afraid that perhaps you thought that . . . that I pushed you into it."

"I didn't think that."

"But I did push you into it," she admitted.

"You felt compromised," he countered.

"But I was not truly compromised," she said.

"Aida." He turned and drew her close, kissing her in the way that he had wanted to that morning in front of the church. A long, lingering, loving kiss. "It's done now," he told her at last. "I am your husband. And my only regret is that we must spend our night standing on a cold beach instead of a flower-filled bower."

"A flower-filled bower?" She laughed. "Monsieur Sonnier, where would we get flowers this time of year?"

He laughed with her and they began to walk once more, arms wrapped around each other as much for the pleasure of it as for the warmth it afforded.

"It is not much of a wedding night," he said.

She shrugged, unconcerned.

"Unlike most young women I have spent more time being fearful of my wedding night than anxious for it," she said.

"Fearful?" His brow furrowed in concern. "You have been afraid your husband would hurt you?"

"No, not that. I . . . I've been afraid of his being disappointed."

"Disappointed?" Armand's look was incredulous. "How could any man be disappointed with you?"

She dissembled prettily and at first he thought that she would not answer, but she did.

"I . . . I am like a fancy store-bought gift," she said. "All bright and shiny-looking tied up with a bow."

"That you are," Armand agreed quietly.

"But I have always been afraid that when . . . when I am divested of my wrappings and ribbon," she said, "I will be nothing but an empty box."

"An empty box?" Armand stopped, stunned, shook his head, and looked straight into her eyes. "Aida, my sweet and lovely Aida," he said. "You are in no way empty. You are full of joy and brightness and care. I have seen it in the way you laugh at yourself, the way you charm the old men as easily as

the young, the way you defer to Madame Landry.
And the way that you look at me and make me
believe that I am strong and wise. You are not at all
empty. You are filled, filled nearly to bursting with
everything that a man could want. At least with
everything that *this* man wants."

Jean Baptiste finished up the last bite of the blueberry tart and wiped his mouth. It hadn't been the
best dessert that he'd ever eaten. In fact it had a rather
unpleasant undertaste, but he'd ignored that, assuming it to be the ingredients of the love charm. And a
love charm, he'd decided, was a welcome idea.

Félicité was on her hands and knees with a cleaning rag finishing up the floor. Jean Baptiste shook his
head and marveled to himself as he watched her. The
first evening she'd been alone with him in years and
she'd taken it into her head to scrub the house from
back porch to the rafters.

He wasn't sure when it had happened or how it
had happened, but things had changed between
them. They had grown up together, friends long
before they were sweethearts. He had planned for her
to be his wife when he was little more than a boy. At
age seven they'd taken first Communion together and
he had informed her, accurately as it turned out, that
the next time they were both dressed so finely and
headed for church would be their wedding day.

He'd tried to call upon her two years before her
father allowed her to sit Sundays with suitors. They
had a secret agreement to wed of which neither
family was aware. And they could hardly wait until
her parents deemed her old enough to be a bride.

Jean Baptiste recalled their wedding as an afternoon of absolute perfection. They danced and laughed and looked deeply into each other's eyes. Happily ever after was not merely a well-used phrase, but their reality.

The night that followed was equally blissful. Both were total innocents, but they were much in love and flawlessly in tune. There had been plenty of fumbling and a few surprises, but there was no fear and a lot of giggling.

They discovered sex as if they had made it all up from scratch. They learned by curiosity and practice how to please themselves and pleasure their partner. And they discovered how to make babies.

True love's road, however, strewn with pregnancies, babies, and hard work, had turned out to be surprisingly disappointing. Jean Baptiste still felt young, vital, energetic. He wanted to laugh and be free and have fun. And Félicité . . . well, his wife was somebody's mama.

Perhaps a love charm was exactly what they needed to get them back to the place where they were still young and sex was still fun. Jean Baptiste felt the longing for those times well up in him both physically and emotionally.

He walked over to the corner of room near the doorway and stood directly in front of her. She continued washing the floor. Just before the damp rag was to wipe across his feet, she stopped and looked up at him.

"Jean Baptiste, you'd best get out of the way if I'm to finish cleaning this house tonight."

"*T amie*," he coaxed, using his pet name for her, little friend. "*T amie*, I think that you are getting very tired working here on the floor." He leaned down and took the rag from her hand and gave her a long meaningful look. "Wouldn't you like to go lie down in that nice warm bed with your *cher époux.*"

He ran one finger lingeringly down the length of her jaw and then traced the shape of her lower lip with his thumb.

Félicité retrieved the damp cloth and sighed heavily. "Please, Jean Baptiste, I am very busy."

She immediately recommenced her scrubbing and her husband stared at her in disbelief. Hadn't Madame Landry promised him something entirely different?

"I was just thinking about Armand and Aida Gaudet," he said. "This is their wedding night."

"Yes, I suppose it is," she agreed.

"Do you remember our wedding night?" he asked. "Do you remember how many times it was before we collapsed in exhaustion?"

"No, not really," she answered. "At least we were inside and warm. I doubt those two can say the same."

"You remember how it was," Jean Baptiste teased. "A pair can make a lot of warmth together."

"I suppose so," she said.

"I *know* so. Now little friend," he continued, coaxing. "Why don't we go warm ourselves?"

"Jean Baptiste, I am cleaning the house."

"All this dust and grime you're fighting against will still be here tomorrow." He deliberately gave her what she often referred to as his little-boy grin. She'd always found it irresistible. "Come to bed with me, sweetheart, and maybe we can stir up something real dirty in there."

"Not tonight," she said simply.

"Oh yes, yes, please tonight," Jean Baptiste insisted, a whiny tone to his voice.

"No."

"Félicité—"

She sat back on her heels and regarded him unfavorably. "Look at me!" she demanded. "I am nine months' pregnant. I am as big as a cow and twice as clumsy."

He shrugged and spoke in a voice as smooth as molasses. "To me you are beautiful, *chèrie*."

She rolled her eyes and huffed in disbelief. "Well, I don't feel beautiful," she said. "My back hurts, my legs hurt, my feet hurt."

"What about your yum-yum?" he asked, his tone playful, teasing. "You remember how your *cher époux* loves your yum-yum. Does your yum-yum hurt?"

"Jean Baptiste—"

"Maybe we can make it hurt. Remember when we would play *bon coucher?*"

Félicité sighed tolerantly. "My *yum-yum* is getting ready to bring another baby in the world. I know from past experience that it will be hurting plenty for several weeks thereafter."

"But that's a bad hurt," Jean Baptiste told her. "I want to make it good hurt, like we used to, remember?"

"That was three, almost four, children ago."

"But there are no children here now," he said.

"Not tonight," she stated firmly.

He fought annoyance. Sex offered just about the only pleasure that married life still afforded. But even that had lost a good deal of its luster and was not nearly so available as he had thought it would be when he'd wed.

"Come on, 'T, he pleaded. "Come on, 'T amie, maybe I should tickle you. Would that do it? Do you want me to tickle you?"

"No, please."

Jean Baptiste ignored her answer and squatted down next to her with full intention of tickling her into surrender.

A sickly feeling flashed over him, cold then hot. Momentarily he ignored it, but when it sped through him again the resulting weakness caused him to drop all the way into a sitting position on the floor, momentarily faint.

"Please just leave me alone," his wife was saying. "I haven't had time to really get these corners cleaned for weeks. Having the children gone gives me a great opportunity to get some things done around here. And I just really don't feel like doing any sort of bed play with you tonight."

It was as if she were speaking to him from a great distance. A very strange and very unpleasant nausea was building up inside Jean Baptiste. He was never sick, never. The children, from time to time, came down with all sorts of bilious illnesses. And Félicité suffered nausea with every pregnancy. But he was never bothered in any way by sick stomach. Yet he knew, without question, that he was about to lose his supper.

"Oh God!" he exclaimed as he jumped to his feet.

He just made it outside in time and lost his dinner off the side of the porch. His retching was ferocious and unceasing. A half-dozen tremendous heaves brought him down to his knees. Still he felt no relief.

Exhausted he lay down on the porch boards, allow-ing the cool cypress planks to soothe his fevered brow. He was weak as a newborn kitten. His hands trembled.

What was happening to him? He had felt fine only moments ago. This illness had taken him with sudden tremendous force. Was it something spoiled in his dinner? It couldn't have been; Félicité had fed the children the same before they left. Besides he'd hardly eaten his supper, so anxious he had been to consume the blueberry tart with the love charm.

The love charm? Could the love charm have made him this sick?

Jean Baptiste had little time to consider the possibility. The queasiness came over him again. This time he could not run, or even walk, to the edge of the porch. He crawled forward far enough to hang his head over the side and vomited.

After the upheaval, he rested. He wondered why his wife had not come to his side. She always knew when he needed her. She was always there for him. Félicité must not be aware that he was ill, he decided.

He needed to get back into the house where she could take care of him. He considered crawling, but after a few deep breaths, he assured himself that he could stand on two feet and make it inside. Once there, he was certain Félicité would care for him.

He sighed with anticipation. She would put him to bed, wash him with a cool rag, and make him feel better again. Félicité would care for him.

He lurched uneasily to his feet and made his way to the door. He pushed his way through the curtains and leaned heavily upon the doorframe as he spoke.

"I'm sick," he said.

She didn't answer. He raised his eyes to look at her. She was standing just where he'd left her. But the hem of her dress was wet and soaked and there was a murky, red-streaked stain on the floor that she'd just cleaned.

"Did you spill something?" he asked.

She looked up at him in stunned surprise and answered, "My water broke."

Dix-huit

"Oh, Armand, you are going to make the most wonderful husband," Aida said with a sigh.

The two walked arm in arm together along the darkened beach. "You make me want to try," he told her.

She looked into his eyes and knew he was telling the truth. He might not love her, but he did want her, he did believe in her.

"It's strange," she said thoughtfully, "that of all the men on the river, you were the one who made me feel most nervous, most unsure of myself. But now I am not afraid at all."

"Good," he said, hugging her close to him.

"I mean," she told him in a softer almost conspiratorial tone, "that I'm not afraid of having a wedding night with you."

They stopped walking and stood together. Aida deliberately fitted herself as closely to him as she could. She saw his eyes widen and he pulled away from her.

"Aida, you don't mean that," he said.

"Oh yes, I do mean it," she said. "I like having you hold me in your arms. I like it a lot."

"Well there is no reason why I can't hold you," he said, wrapping his arms more tightly around her.

"There is no reason that we can't do more."

He chuckled, but there was little humor in it. "No, my dear wife, no reason except that we have no bed, no floor, not even a roof."

"Do you think Adam and Eve had a roof?"

"They at least had a garden."

She giggled and hugged him tightly. She nuzzled against his hair and whispered into his ear. "I want to be your wife."

She felt the shiver that skittered through him.

"You *are* my wife," he stated.

"I want to be your wife in all ways."

"You will be. But we have no place to stay, not even any place to lie. There will be other nights, my love, many nights. We should wait until then."

"Why?"

"Because . . . because we should."

A niggling worry pursued her. She drew back slightly to look him in the face. "Is it because you think it won't be the same?" she asked.

"What do you mean?" he asked.

"I mean that . . . that perhaps you think that without the charm we won't . . . you won't want me."

"I won't want you!" He laughed. "Aida, I've had no charm tonight and I want you now very much."

"You do?"

"Can you not feel it?"

"Feel what?

He pressed more tightly against her. "Feel that?"

"Your leg?"

"Aida, that is not my leg." A strangled sound escaped him. "Good Lord, Aida, don't touch it!"

"You don't want me to touch it?"

"Not now I don't."

"This morning, when you touched me . . ." She lowered her eyes, momentarily shy. "When you touched me, I liked it very much."

"God grant me strength," he whispered before he covered her mouth with his own.

His mouth opened over hers and urged her lips apart. He tasted hot and spicy, and the gentle pressure and tugging drew her until she felt she was nearly inside him.

He relinquished the kiss and feathered tiny pecks and bites along her jaw and neck. Aida arched her throat, eagerly offering to him whatever territory he might wish to explore.

"Oh Aida, I want you so much," he whispered.

"I want you, too," she told him. "I want to touch you."

His breathing was forced and labored as if he'd been running down the beach instead of merely standing on it with her in his arms. She found that her own heart was pounding rapidly, pulses beating wildly in places she had never known she had.

"Make love to me, Armand," she pleaded. "Make love to me now."

"Not here, not now, my love."

"But I want you," she said.

"And I want you, too," he declared. "But it must be a good thing between us, a wonderful thing. You deserve that. You deserve a glowing candle and a warm bed and flowers."

"I don't want those things, Armand. I just want you."

"And you will have me," he said. "But not here, not now. That doesn't make any sense."

"Waiting doesn't make any sense," she said. "Look at Laron and Helga. They love each other, but they cannot be together. What if something comes along to keep us apart as it has them?"

"It's not likely."

"But it could happen. Why . . . why that old skiff could turn over tomorrow and we might be eaten by alligators."

"Aida—"

"Oh Armand, if I am to be eaten by alligators tomorrow, I want to be made love to tonight."

"But—"

"Hold me," she pleaded. "Please hold me and kiss me and touch me."

His better judgment had him hesitate one more moment and then he brought his mouth to hers. "All right, my love," he said. "We'll touch each other. Touching is good. We can touch. I'll touch you."

"Yes, yes, touch me, Armand."

He fumbled through the layers of the shawl-draped blanket and covered her breast with his hand.

Aida arched her back, pressing herself more firmly into his hand. He was caressing, kneading, weighing it. When his thumb slid over the hard, erect tip it jolted her.

"Harder, squeeze it harder," she demanded. "And the other one, too, Armand. Do it to the other one, too."

The blanket dropped behind her, forgotten, as he used both hands to massage her bosom.

"Do you remember this morning?" she whispered.

"This morning they were naked and you kissed them and sucked them. Do you remember that?"

"Aida, do you think I could ever forget it?"

He began to jerk determinedly at her laces, pulling at her blouse until one full round breast had escaped its confines.

"Kiss me, Armand. Kiss me there where I am naked."

He squatted slightly and wrapped his arms around her hips.

Aida gave a startled cry as he raised her feet from the ground, holding her high enough off the ground that his mouth found easy access to the soft round flesh that she offered.

Aida rested her elbows upon his shoulders and restlessly rubbed her cheek against the top of his head as he suckled and teased and nipped at her.

So naturally her legs wrapped around his chest. She dug her bare heels into his curve of his backside to give her leverage to move her body against him.

She strained and squirmed. He brought a hand to her backside to assist her.

In all her life she had never known that the tip of the nipple and the entrance to the womb were so closely linked. Every movement of his mouth on her breast roused an immediate and direct reaction between her thighs. The want, the need that she had experienced this morning was back in raw, profuse abundance. It had to be assuaged.

"Armand! Please touch me down there. Touch me down there."

Immediately he slid her down the front of his body. The instant her feet met the sand, his hand met the ache at the crux of her legs.

The touch of his fingers simultaneously eased her desire and made it worse. She was wet, lavishly wet. She whined and wiggled against the stroke of his hand. When his thumb found the rigid, pulsing nub buried in her curls, she ground out a sound that was animal and pleasurable.

She could hear him speaking to her; she could hear the passion in his own voice.

"You're so hot, you want it so much, you want me so much."

"Please! Please!" Her words of pleading were all she could manage.

"I'm going to put my finger inside you," he told her. "Just one finger. If it hurts I'll stop."

"Do it! Do it!"

A long index finger eased inside her. She gasped.

"Does it hurt? Have I hurt you?"

"More! More!" she begged.

A second finger followed the first, filling her, firing her.

"You are so tight," Armand whispered against her throat. "You are so hot and so tight."

"It feels so good."

"Aida, I'm dying here," he told her.

"Don't die, don't die now."

He began to withdraw his fingers. She reached down and grasped his hand.

"Don't take it out!"

"Easy, Aida, my sweet, my love," he soothed her. "I'm going to make it better."

He thrust back inside her, the heel of his hand grinding down on the soft plump flesh of her pubis.

A startled sound escaped her throat.

He did it again and again and again.

She began bucking her hips to meet his rhythm as the feel of it, the rough, spiraling feel of it drew her further and further and further.

"Let me see it, Aida." Armand's urging penetrated the primal pleasure that enveloped her. "Let me see it, Aida. Let me see you do it. Do it for me. Just for me."

She did.

She collapsed in his arms and together they dropped to their knees as the throbbing succession of clenching spasms drained her. They lay together on the cool sand as she drifted back to earth.

"Oh Armand, oh Armand," she whispered, nearly breathless. "Is it always like that?"

"If it's not," he answered, "then it should be."

She rolled over and pulled him close.

"My goodness, Armand," she said. "I can feel your . . . your leg now."

"Please Aida," he answered, his voice strained. "If you even touch me I will go off in my trousers like a green boy."

"Don't do that, Armand," she said, jerking her skirts up to her waist. "Come inside me, like an experienced husband."

The wanton invitation silenced his better judgment, but not his need to protect her. He slid one arm under her shoulder and the other beneath her knees and pulled her up into his arms. She was grateful not to have been asked to walk; satisfaction had settled in her legs like jelly and she was not certain that she could.

He carried her a little away from the shore to where the sand piled up into small dunes. Sea oats grew tall and in profusion, forming a private shelter from the cool wind off the water.

Armand threw down the blanket and then laid her upon it. Hastily he removed his jacket. Aida followed his lead, casting off her remaining clothing, eager to be naked in his arms.

"Oh my God!" she heard him whisper and she looked up to see him staring at her in awe.

She was chilled and covered only in goosebumps, but a strange surge of sensual power flooded through her, exhilarating her. She turned on her side and drew up one leg coyly. She touched her bottom lip with one fingernail.

"Are you cold up there, Monsieur? Perhaps you should lie here next to me. I'm very very warm."

Armand dropped to his knees beside her, pressed her back to the blanket, and spread her knees, opening her before him.

He tore the tie of his trousers, but managed to rid himself of them. In the faint gray silver of moonlight, she saw for the first time how God had built a man.

"Armand, that thing is bigger than you are."

He scrambled to lie between her spread thighs. "With you Aida, it is bigger than it has ever been before."

He stroked her and kissed her using the rough edge of his tongue to taste her for the first time. Aida's flesh alternately quivered and sizzled at his touch. She squirmed and wiggled beneath him, eager to please, anxious to get closer.

He grabbed her bottom in two hands and raised her slightly, positioning her for his entry.

"Aida," he whispered, snuggling up against her ear. "If I hurt you just tell me and I'll stop."

She purred and ran her fingernails along the smooth, pale curve of his buttocks. "And if I hurt you, speak up, also," she said.

Her humor broke some of the tension of the moment. He punished her with a teasing bite against her collarbone.

Armand was an eager but unselfish lover. He kissed, caressed, encouraged, and soothed as he inched his way inside her.

Aida reveled in it. She felt wonderful, powerful, beautiful. He was inside her. She wanted him inside her. The pressure and give of her body as he pushed through the thin barrier brought no pain at all, only openness and relief. He invaded her fully until he was buried to the hilt.

"I love you, Aida," he whispered against her. "There is no charm that could make me love you as I do this moment."

"I love you, Armand," she answered. "I always have."

It was a tender moment, but the heat of desire, the needs of the body, the lure of the flesh were honed too sharply to be denied.

"Move with me," he ordered. "Meet me and match me."

She did as he bid, greeting him stroke for stroke, flesh against flesh in an ancient rhythm that was both universally human and peculiarly their very own.

As they gained confidence in the pairing of their bodies, their tempo increased. Aida felt herself spiraling once more. She urged him on, begging, pleading. He was pounding now, pounding, thrusting. It was wild and rough and sweet, oh so sweet, as her body tightened like a wire. Pulled taut and more and more and more.

When she flew apart she cried out. And she heard him calling her name as if it were an echo.

"Félicité, I'm sick," Jean Baptiste told her. "I am sicker than I think I have ever been in my life."

As if to answer, she bent over nearly double, clutching her distended belly for a long moment.

"It's coming fast, it's coming very fast, the second pain nearly on top of the first."

Jean Baptiste's eyes widened in disbelief. " 'T amie, you can't have the baby tonight. I am sick."

She moaned and shook her head. "As if your will alone should stop it!" she told him. "Go get Madame Landry, go get me some help."

She doubled over in pain once more. Jean Baptiste shot outside as if the demons of hell were after him.

He made it all the way to the porch steps before another wave of nausea overtook him. He hesitated, praying that the ensuing weakness would pass. An instant later, everything went black.

"Jean Baptiste, Jean Baptiste."

He awakened to find her nudging him awake. She was holding on to the porch rail and prodding him with her bare foot.

"Wake up!" she demanded. "You have to wake up, I need you."

"I'm awake, Félicité," he said, moving slowly as he made his way to a sitting position. "I'm awake, and I'll get to the boat. I know I can get to the boat."

"There is no time for the boat now," she said. "There is no time for anything. Come into the house, Jean Baptiste. You are going to have to help me have this baby."

As if to emphasize her words another pain went

through her and her step faltered. For an instant Jean Baptiste thought that she might fall from the step and shot to his feet, hurrying to steady her.

She didn't fall, but he nearly did as lightheadedness assailed him once more. The smell of his own sickness and the vile bitter taste in his mouth was abhorrent. As he helped her back into the house, he began to explain his predicament.

"I think I can make it to the boat and even if I pass out there, it will drift downstream," he said. "I don't think that I can pole to Tante Celeste's for Madame Landry. But I can get some woman, somewhere surely."

"There is no time for you to go out looking for some woman," she said firmly. "This baby is going to be here very soon."

"It can't be this soon," he told her. "The other babies took hours and hours. Why, the day Marie was born Armand and I managed to put up the whole west fence while we were waiting."

Félicité moaned again and leaned heavily against him. Jean Baptiste held her, worried. Félicité had to be wrong. A baby shouldn't come this fast. If it did, something might be wrong. And whether there was something wrong or not, he absolutely, positively could not help her have a baby.

Once the contraction passed, she seemed exhausted.

"You'd better lie down," he said.

"Not yet, no not yet, it helps to walk. Help me walk." They began to move across the room.

"Jean Baptiste you are going to have to help me bring this child into the world," she said.

He shook his head. "I can't," he told her simply. "I haven't the vaguest idea of what to do."

They reached the far corner of the room and turned, heading back the way they came.

"I think I know what to do," she said. "I've had three, remember, this one can't be that different than those. Of course, Madame Landry said that each one is different."

Jean Baptiste's queasy stomach was beginning to trouble him again.

"That old witch!" he proclaimed angrily. She'd not only left his wife alone while she was in labor, she'd poisoned him as well.

"You'll need to put some water on to boil," she said. "In that basket near the bed I've been saving rags. Put that old oilcloth table cover over the bed, then cover it with a sheet. I don't mind a big pile of laundry, but I don't want to lose that bed tick. That old one was never the same after I spilled all over it with Gaston."

Jean Baptiste was going to vomit again. He knew that there could be nothing left in his stomach to heave, but he was going to have to heave it anyway. As he moved to run outside, Félicité gasped as the next contraction overtook her. It was much stronger than the last and she cried out loud.

She had clutched her belly and through the layers of clothing, Jean Baptiste could see the coursing wavelike movements.

"*Sacré!*" he whispered breathlessly to himself. He was holding her entire body weight in his arms and he felt as if his weak legs would give out from under him at any moment.

He tamped down determinedly on the nausea rising in his stomach. He was not about to throw up on his wife in labor.

The long agonizing pain passed and she straightened.

Immediately Jean Baptiste raced out to the porch and threw up the last bit of bitter brown bile in his craw. He was weak, weak and sick. He couldn't possibly do this. He should get on the pirogue and get Félicité some help. That's what he should do.

"Jean Baptiste!" she called out. "Come here, I need you."

He hurried back inside the house.

His wife was walking and moaning. She'd gathered up the harness straps for the bed and an old metal dishpan.

"He's already started to roll inside me," she said. "You'd best get the bed ready. We're going to need it soon, very soon."

Jean Baptiste ran a nervous hand through his hair. "Félicité, 'T amie, I can't do this."

She turned to stare at him.

"I simply can't. It is . . . I just cannot. Perhaps if I felt better I would try to . . ."

He watched his wife's face as it changed, as it changed very drastically. Her brow drew down, her jaw tightened, her eyes narrowed. Without further warning she hurled the dishpan at his head. Her aim was nearly true and she caught him smartly on the shoulder.

"You lousy, no-account, worthless swamp leech!" she screamed. "Just get out of this house, get out of my life and stay out of my bed. You can't do this, you can't do this!" she mocked his words. "Do you think that I can do this? Do you think I want to? I'll tell you what I want to do. If I could I'd go back to nine months ago. And when you pulled that big thing out of your pants, I'd beat you both senseless with an ax handle before I'd let it near me!"

She was crying now, yelling and crying.

"It's so easy for you," she told him. "You just put the baby in my belly and then get out of the way. Oh, you ask me if I'm fine and you tell me not to work too hard. But do you massage my back and rub my feet at night? Do you take on any of the work that is so hard for me? Do you just snuggle in bed and hold me close and kiss me without trying to get that thing inside again? No, you don't, Jean Baptiste, you never have and I guess I know that you never will. You lie up in that loft, dreaming of being a free man, dreaming of other women."

"I have never been unfaithful," he declared.

"Oh no, you wouldn't do that," she growled back. "You wouldn't openly bring shame upon me or lower yourself to indecency. But what you do is just as evil. You are irresolute in your heart."

"Félicité, I love you. I have always loved you."

She shook her head, but her tone softened. "You married me to be my lover. Having a lover is a great pleasure, but it is not a necessity. A woman doesn't need a lover, but a woman needs a husband. I need a husband. I need a husband this night and if you can't be one . . . If you can't . . ." Another pain commenced and it brought her to her knees.

"Oh God!"

Jean Baptiste ran to her rescue. He squatted on the

floor with her, holding her in his arms. She was screaming as he rubbed the spasms in her belly and whispered words of comfort.

"It will be fine," he heard himself whispering to her. "We . . . we can do this, we will do this and we will have a beautiful, beautiful baby. We love babies, Félicité. Remember how they are, 'T amie, they are so tiny and helpless and just so sweet that you can't look away from them. All this pain is going to bring us a sweet little baby."

As the pain passed, he helped her to her feet, still whispering words of comfort and kissing her brow tenderly.

"Can you stand right here?" he asked her, propping her up in the doorframe. "Or would you rather sit?"

"I'll stand."

"Let me get the bed made up. Where is that oilcloth table cover?"

"In the cedar chest," she answered.

Jean Baptiste hurried to it and opened the lid. When he bent over to search it out, his stomach revolted once more and he had to race to the window. He did a half-dozen wrenching dry heaves before his insides settled once more. Little stars spangled around the edges of his vision but he didn't believe that he was going to faint again. He returned to the chest to find the table cover.

"You're so pale, Jean Baptiste," Félicité said. He noted that she was not looking quite herself either.

"Just something I ate," he told her, smiling more bravely than he felt.

He immediately began to work, trying to do those

things that had to be done. He had not, in his lifetime, ever made up the bed and had to learn the mystery of it as he went along. Once he got the oilcloth securely tucked in, he turned with some pride to his wife, only to realize that she was beginning another contraction. He rushed to take her in his arms. He held and stroked her and encouraged her. She gnashed her teeth together and screamed.

"It's coming, Jean Baptiste," she told him, even before the spasm was completely past. "It's coming now."

He helped her remove her skirts and get into the bed. Her body looked huge, distended without its modest covering. The reality of what her body was capable of somehow became more real to him than ever before.

Quickly he harnessed the straps as she directed, one to the head and one to the foot of the bed. She would need them to pull against as she delivered.

"Get the hot water and rags," she told him.

Jean Baptiste left her and hurried to the fire. The water was just beginning to boil and using a mitt on the handle, he carried it into the bedroom.

Félicité was moaning and writhing on the bed.

"Have you got your knife?" she asked.

He pulled it out of his pocket.

"Drop it in the water, that's what Madame Landry always does."

Jean Baptiste hesitated a moment—water would rust a blade—then he dropped it with a splash into the pot. If his wife wanted a wet knife, then a wet knife was what she would get.

"Soak some of the rags in the water," she told him.

"And wring them out good, they should be hot rather than wet. And get that cotton cord out of the cupboard and bring that dishpan I threw at you."

He nodded and did as she asked. The nausea had eased somewhat. He laid the items he'd retrieved in easy reach on the floor by the bed, then he bent to check the cotton rags in the water.

They were hot, almost to scalding. He tossed the wet rag from hand to hand for a moment until it had cooled enough to hold.

Another pain gripped her.

Jean Baptiste used one of the warm rags to wipe her brow.

"Not there!" she growled. "A cool cloth for my forehead. The hot ones go down there."

He didn't ask her to elaborate but hurried to dip a cool cloth for her. Once more he talked to her through the pain, caressing her back and belly and urging her onward.

When the contraction subsided she turned sideways in the bed, hanging her feet off the side, and spread her legs so that he could stand between them.

"The hot rags go down there," she said. "On my . . . on my yum-yum."

Jean Baptiste raised a surprised eyebrow.

"They loosen up the flesh," she explained. "Help it give without tearing so badly."

He dipped his hand into the hot water and brought one out. It was almost too hot to wring.

"I'm afraid I'll scald you," he said.

Félicité shook her head. "It's better to scald than tear," she assured him.

He didn't scald her. He packed the hot rags around the opening of her body. Jean Baptiste barely had time to complete the task before the next pain was upon her.

This time she reached for the straps. He put them into her hands and she pulled against them. She threw her head back and the sound that came from her clenched teeth was almost a howl.

Jean Baptiste felt frightened, helpless. What if something was wrong? How would he know? What if this baby ripped her apart? How could he stop it? He was her husband, the only husband that she had. He had brought this pain, this danger to her, and he had no idea how to take it away.

He dropped to his knees in front of her, massaging her legs and thighs and talking, endlessly talking, reminding her of their three beautiful babies. Reminding her of their life together. Reminding her that no matter how he acted or how foolishly he had treated her, he loved her. He completely, totally, truly, and eternally loved her.

"It's time!" she hollered at him.

Jean Baptiste removed the hot rags that covered her and the truth of her words was revealed. His brow furrowed in momentary confusion as her intimate body appeared changed. There were tufts of hair inside?

Realization dawned with wonder.

"I can see him, *'T amie*," he told her. "I can see his little head."

Félicité didn't answer. She was gripping the harness straps with such force that the bed was shuddering with her effort. She was growling and snarling like an animal as she bore down heavily and pushed, pushed, pushed.

"Here he comes," Jean Baptiste told her.

The tiny head eased out of her and he held it in his hands. Félicité was grunting and puffing. The baby turned slightly to let its shoulder pass and then, with a startling whoosh, it was in Jean Baptiste's hands.

Immediately, unbelievably, it set up an angry wail.

"It's here, it's alive," Jean Baptiste said, his voice filled with wonder and incredulity. "It's . . . it's . . ." He glanced down to the baby's genitals. "It's a girl!"

"A girl?" Félicité's first words were weak and near breathless. "I thought it was a boy."

"It's a girl," he told her with certainty.

"You must tie the cord and cut it," she said.

He lay the slippery new little creature on Félicité's abdomen and used the cotton string to tie two knots a handspread apart. Then he fished the knife out of the hot water pot and forever separated his wife from his new daughter.

Dix-neuf

Helga and Laron sat up all night. It was, they knew, their last few hours alone together. Those couldn't be wasted with sleep. They gave little thought to Armand and Aida except to momentarily rue their own thoughtlessness.

"This is their wedding night," Helga said. "We should have let them have the shelter and the fire."

Laron nodded. "Or you would have thought that he and I were bright enough to know that we would need two fires and two shelters!"

"Do you think that they are truly happy?" she asked. "It was all so surprising and hurried."

Laron shrugged. "I don't know how it happened, but he says that he loves her. I have never known him to be a liar."

"She must love him, too," Helga said. "When she looks at him her face nearly glows."

They shrugged at each other at the unfathomable mismatch and then smiled. Laron wrapped his arm around her shoulder, pulling her closer.

"I can say that I envy my friend Armand this night," he told Helga.

She nodded. "Aida is most beautiful," she agreed.

"No, I don't envy him the possession of her. I envy that this is his first night with the woman he loves. For me and the woman I love, it is the last night."

Helga nodded, understanding. They kissed, almost dispassionately, storing a memory of taste and texture and feeling.

"We should not make love," she told him with firm conviction. "We have too many memories together already."

He agreed.

"It would be too bittersweet to claim you this night," he said. "And I need your words and your voice to soothe me as much as the feel of your body."

They lay together side by side, chastely, as friends. Talking, sharing, regretting the past, fearing the future. The hours passed.

As the night waned and the reality of their time together drew short, things changed between them. Over and over each cast anxious glances toward the eastern sky, fearful, apprehensive. Their kisses became more sensuous, more daring, more urgent. Suddenly and simultaneously they both became almost desperate for the touch of the other.

Laron ripped her drawers getting them off and she cursed their existence in expressive German. They made love forcefully, passionately, rashly. Biting. Scratching. Pleading. It was a frenzied coupling. Full of fire and lust and recklessness. As if the physicality of their love could drive away the reality of their lives.

Helga moaned his name as she shuddered with release. Laron moaned in agony as he was barely able to remove himself from her body in time.

They lay in each other's arms, quaking, shaking, humbled by the power their bodies could create in tune. But as the sweet ecstasy stole away from them, misery took its place.

Helga cried then. She cried wrenching, bitter tears. Laron held her close and whispered his love to her. He cried, too, his strong, solid chest heaving in grief.

Afterward, in the quiet of the storm's wake, they dried each other's eyes and kissed each other's cheeks. They joined their bodies again. There was no wildness this time, no primal insistence, only the sweet swell of love expressed, bodies connected. They moved slowly and languidly together, tiptoeing to the brink of passion and retreating again and again, until finally exhaustion alone spurred them to fulfill the climax.

Spent and sleepy, they lay wrapped together in a blanket sheltered by the windbreak of poles and brush. She rested her head on his chest. And he toyed with the sweet-smelling wildness of her loosened hair. As they faced the end of their time together, they reminisced about the beginning.

"I couldn't believe it," Laron admitted. "I was green and ignorant and just plain scared. I thought that it couldn't be true. You weren't really going to touch me, of that I was certain."

"You didn't make it easy for me," she told him.

"How could I?" he asked. "When you knelt down in front of me, I thought you were going to pray."

"I was praying. Praying I could go through with it," she said.

Laron shook his head, fondly recalling the night so long ago.

"When you took me in your hand I closed my eyes and convinced myself that I was imagining the whole thing."

"And I thought you closed your eyes because you liked it so much!"

"I liked it too much. I told myself that I was back in my own sleeping cot, dreaming of you and holding myself."

She chuckled. "Perhaps had it been your own hand, monsieur," she said with feigning complaint, "you would have comported yourself more ably."

Laron growled and pulled her closer to him. "You're never going to let me forget that, are you?"

She shook her head.

"Oh Helga, my sweet Helga," he said. "After three years I am still embarrassed and ashamed. Right in your face! One touch of your lips and I go off right in your face."

She began to giggle, remembering.

"You're laughing at me!" he complained and pointed an accusing finger. "You were laughing at me then."

She admitted as much.

"In truth, I think it was good that you were obviously so unfamiliar with the carnal," she told him.

"Why is that? Because you enjoyed being my teacher?"

Helga was thoughtful for a moment. "The years of my marriage I . . . well, I didn't enjoy sex. Helmut was often drunk and he was never . . . never tender. I had never initiated the act, not ever."

Laron rubbed her arms to ward off the chill he knew she always felt when she spoke of her husband.

"Helmut took what he wanted from me; I never gave anything," she said. "If you had been more knowledgeable, more demanding, perhaps I could not have given to you, either."

"I am more knowledgeable now, am I not?" Laron asked her.

She huffed irreverently. "You are far too clever a pupil for this teacher," she told him. "You have learned your lessons so quickly and so well, did I not know better I would think you were having a tutor on the side."

He pinched her backside playfully. "Careful, Madame Shotz," he said. "A woman making unfounded accusations may well find herself across my knee."

"Oh please *non*, monsieur," she said, her voice tiny and theatrically pleading. "My big derrière is still stinging from the last time!"

He laughed heartily and then pulled her close to look into her eyes. The mood sobered.

"What I intended to tell you," he whispered, "before you teasingly changed the subject, is that you should never believe that somehow you are responsible for the failure of your marriage with Helmut. It was not that he was domineering and that you needed to control. It was not that he was powerful and that you wanted that power for yourself. It was not that you required a lesser partner. Never, never think that. Now *I* am knowledgeable and *I* am demanding. Yet you still give to me fully and unhesitatingly. The difference, my Helga, is that while I take from you, I give also. That is the way it should be. So that one partner need never fear to end up empty."

"Empty," she repeated the word like an echo on her breath. "That is what I most fear about the years ahead. That without you they will be empty."

"You will have Karl and Elsa and Jakob," he told her. "And you will have the certainty that I have loved you truly and as God surely intended. And that love will be with us always though we never touch again."

"Perhaps when the children are gone, in our old age maybe—"

Laron placed a silencing finger against her lips.

"It is too dangerous to wait, to hope. Know that if heaven grants that I can be with you, I will. And I will know that if you ever feel that you are free, you will seek me out."

She kissed him then. And he held her tightly in his arms. The vaguest gray light of dawn was lightening the eastern sky. Their time together was almost a thing of the past. They clung to it and to each other, in their hearts both praying for a miracle.

Armand awakened slowly. He was cold, gritty, exhausted. The ground beneath him was harder than rock and every muscle in his body ached from misuse. He had never felt better.

In his arms lay the lovely Aida Gaudet, now Aida Sonnier. There was a strange rhythmic sound coming from her throat and he listened to it critically and grinned. The most beautiful woman on the Vermillion River was snoring.

Her hair was everywhere. Those long dark locks that he had never before seen completely loosened were upon him like silken ties, binding him to her forever.

The sun's warm glow had not yet reached the place where they lay, but it was morning nonetheless. The first morning of their married life.

She had been right, of course. He'd thought to remain chaste until they were in more suitable surroundings. He dreamed of her, loving her for the first time, atop a warm overstuffed mattress, on fresh cotton sheets strewn with herbs and the glow of one candle lit at the bedside.

Yes, that would have been nice. It still would be nice. He wanted to have her there. And he would. He would have her there. And he would have her on the floor in front of the fireplace. He would have her in the hayrick. Upon the kitchen table. In a prairie field. Could such a thing be done in a pirogue? If it could, they would.

The nature of his wicked thoughts was tightening the front of his trousers. She was sleeping so soundly. He disengaged himself from her embrace and moved away, careful to tuck the blanket in around her so she would not be chilled. He hesitated only long enough to place a gentle kiss upon her brow.

"Rest yourself, my love," he whispered. "You're going to need it."

He walked toward the shoreline, dusting the sand from his clothes as he went. She had been right. He had already been worried that her desire for him would have faded with the charm. Waiting another day or perhaps two would have made him far more pessimistic and unsure.

Perhaps it was that she had lived so long without confidence that she knew so well how to shore it up for others. He had never consciously worried about his ability with women. But she was no ordinary woman. And he wanted her to find him as no ordinary husband.

He had only meant to touch her, hold her. But

when he had seen her passion and watched her reach fulfillment with only the caress of his own hand, he had felt a power and a certainty that transformed him. In a flash of an instant as her body clenched against his hand he had changed from hesitant bridegroom to insatiable lover. It was a conversion that they could both appreciate.

Love. Sexual union. Procreation. Eternity.

Armand sighed with appreciation as he stared out at the waves rolling into Vermillion Bay and pondered their meaning. The sea was good for that. Good for pondering. And for men such as the Sonniers the sea was truly a link with life itself.

Far to the north in a place that existed now only in the memories passed down, Acadians had built their lives, their culture, on the Bay of Fundy. The sea had been their source of strength and hope and survival. The lands they had farmed had been culled from it. The ships sailing upon its surface gathered fish and lobster and crab. Their ways and seasons were prescribed by the tides. They were a seafaring people.

Even now, though they had been land-living, prairie people for two generations, the terms and phrases that flowed from their tongues were spawned from the sea. The prairie itself was like a sea of grass, slow-rolling like waves. They were creatures of the sea and it would always be with them, even if only in their hearts.

Armand stared out at the rolling water before him. Waves rose and broke and receded to rise once more. So much like life, he thought. The deceptive appearance of changelessness while change was constant.

He thought of Laron and Helga. His heart ached for them. He had been sympathetic to his friend before. He had felt sadness, but he had not been able to comprehend the agony. Now, knowing love, knowing the oneness of a man and his mate, he understood fully for the first time the harrowing pain of this parting. If only there were something that he could do.

His brow furrowed in thought. Aida had been right about their first night together. Perhaps she was also right about the vision. There was no question in his mind of what she had seen. And why would she have seen it if it meant nothing? Maybe there was some answer within it.

Calmly, deliberately, he seated himself on the edge of the water. Like a man mesmerized he stared out on the breaking waves and forced himself to think. He had to think. He simply had to think harder.

Deliberately in his mind he went over what Aida had seen again. Looking critically at each piece of the strange puzzle. Laron had been trying to cut grain that was already cut. Armand had gone to stop him. But Armand did not point out to him that the grain was lying in windrows around him. For some reason it was not possible for Laron to see that. But Armand could see it. Armand could see it plainly, or at least he could have if he had looked.

"Well now I am looking," he whispered quietly to himself. "Now I am looking as carefully and as fully as I have ever done in my life."

Armand leaned forward thoughtfully, elbow on his knee, chin in his hand.

A careless word—Madame Landry's voice lingered in memory. Careless words were everywhere, he realized. Careless words had set everything in motion and careless words might well be the key to setting it right again. It was all there in careless words. And careless words were all around him.

LARON: *I want to kill him.*
HELGA: *We cannot live in sin.*
AIDA: *There must be some other way.*
MADAME LANDRY: *Something must be done and soon.*
HELGA: *I do wish he was dead.*
AIDA: *You are the answer, Armand.*
LARON: *He had fled to Texas.*
HIMSELF: *A widow has rights over her husband's property.*
LARON: *I want to kill him.*
HELGA: *I wish he were dead.*
AIDA: *There must be some other way.*
MADAME LANDRY: *You,* mon fils, *are the center of it.*
LARON: *There is a price on his head. He won't be back.*
HELGA: *I would marry you in a moment.*
LARON: *I want to kill him.*
HELGA: *I wish he were dead.*
AIDA: *Armand, you are the answer.*
MADAME LANDRY: *They call you the* veuve allemande, *the German widow.*

Armand sat up immediately; he held himself still a long moment, thinking, waiting. Madame Landry was not one to speak careless words.

"*I have told no lies about my marital status,*" Helga had answered her.

"*It was I who first called you the German widow,*" the old woman replied.

Armand's eyes narrowed. She'd said something

else. Something else important. Something that day, that very day she had said something else.

Armand strained his memory trying to recall. They were still sitting at the fire. They were drinking the badly brewed coffee and chatting about the house and Madame Landry had said . . . she'd said . . .

"No one knows what happened to him. The syndic, *the judge we had then, had to declare him dead."*

"The Spaniard," Armand whispered to himself.

He'd moved on or was killed in a drunken brawl. His belt buckle was found in a gator's belly.

Armand sat there, still, silent, waiting, waiting for a long, long moment. Then he jumped to his feet and whooped for joy.

"Armand?"

He heard Aida call to him and he turned in her direction. She was sitting up wrapped in the blanket, looking sleepy disheveled, and incredibly desirable.

"Armand, what is it?"

"I've figured it out!" he hollered, running toward her. "I understand the vision!"

Vingt

Félicité had finally given in to sleep. And the new baby, the one his wife had decided to call Jeanette, for him, was tucked in and sleeping soundly in the little reed-woven *crèche* that had cradled her brothers and sister in their first weeks of life. Jean Baptiste had done what he had to do. He had cleaned up the baby, then his wife and the bed. He had taken the afterbirth and buried it in the fence row. He had fired off two rounds to announce to the neighbors that they had a new child, and it was a girl. He had done all this between frequent and hurried trips to the outhouse. The "love charm" that had been so unkind to his stomach intended, it seemed, to be equally unpleasant to his bowel.

"Are you still not feeling well?" his wife had asked him.

"I am fine," he told her, leaning down to brush her cheek. "I am as fine as any man can be."

"She's a pretty baby, isn't she?"

He nodded. "Oh yes, all our babies are."

"But she is especially so," Félicité insisted.

"She will always hold a special place in my heart," he said.

She smiled at him and her brow furrowed slightly. "I know that you were not happy about another baby so soon."

"I never said—"

"You don't have to say things, Jean Baptiste. I am your wife in all ways. I can sense how you feel."

"Well, I was wrong," he told her.

"I promise that we won't have another so soon."

"I don't recall that you are solely responsible for these children," he said. "And unless you wish to live apart from me I don't know how we are to stop them from arriving."

Félicité lowered her voice to a whisper, as if she feared the baby might hear. "Madame Landry says that I will not get pregnant if you pull yourself out before you expel the semen."

Jean Baptiste gave a wry shake of his head. "I begin to think that old woman doesn't like me much."

Félicité's expression registered surprise. "Why would you say that?"

"Never mind. I . . . I was aware that a man can . . . withdraw his seed . . . to spare a woman childbearing. Father Denis, of course, speaks against it. But when a wife is weak or ill . . . well, Acadian men say, what does a priest know of marriage?"

"I am not weak or ill," Félicité admitted.

"Do you want more children?"

"I want what you want."

"No Félicité, speak plain; you did so when you were in labor with our Jeanette. Speak plain to me now."

She swallowed hard and then looked him in the eye. "I love you, Jean Baptiste. I want you as my husband and I will do whatever it takes to keep you." She looked down at the tiny child she held in her arms. "I love babies. I love to hold them and touch them, they smell so good and smile so sweet. I would willingly have a dozen. But I can be content with these four if I have you in my arms."

He looked at her for a long, long moment. She was his Félicité. The girl that he had loved when they were too young to love. Yet she was not. She had become a woman. When he hadn't been watching, she had become a woman. If no other lesson was learned this night, he had understood at least that. She was a woman. And until now he had remained a boy.

He looked back over the last months, the last years, as time had left him untouched. He had longed for the warmth and security of marriage, but had grumbled under the weight of its responsibilities. He had relished the pleasure of having a wife and whined about the burden of keeping one. Not anymore.

"Félicité, do you ever worry about all those Boudreau children?"

"What?" She looked at him, puzzled at his question.

"Laron's parents, old Anatole and his wife, had fifteen children."

"Yes, I know."

"And all those children, except for Laron, are married now and having children of their own."

"So?"

"So who are all those Boudreau children going to marry, I ask you? They can't marry each other, and come mating time the Boudreau children are going to want to wed."

Félicité looked at him askance.

"Why, you get those frisky Boudreau boys desperate for loving," he continued, "and they are liable to marry some fat French woman or a Creole or, heaven forbid, an Americaine."

"Oh surely not."

"It could happen, my dear. It could happen." He leaned down and wrapped his arm around her shoulder, pulling her against him. "Who is going to marry up all those Boudreau children?"

"Who indeed?"

"Why, the Sonniers, of course," he answered.

"What exactly do you mean?" she asked.

"What I mean, my dear wife, is that perhaps it is our God-given duty to produce as many children as heaven sees fit to send our way."

"Jean Baptiste—"

"We won't do this selfishly, we'll do it for the poor Boudreau children."

Slowly, ever so slowly, she grinned. "I suppose we could, just for their sakes, of course."

"I love you, Félicité. Have I told you that recently?"

"Not recently enough."

"Well, madame, it is very true. I love you. I love being the father of your children. And if we have only these four or fourteen more, I will love and want and cherish each and every one."

"I love you, Jean Baptiste."

He kissed her then, really kissed her, in a way that he hadn't done in months.

She looked up at him and sighed, starry-eyed, and he leaned down to place a tiny kiss on little Jeanette.

"Sleep now and rest, my love," he told her. "There will be little time to do so later."

He was right about that and she followed his suggestion. Now with night waning Jean Baptiste sat in the small hide-seat chair and watched the two of them in quiet, almost reverent repose. As soon as the sun was up there would be friends and family everywhere. There would be noise and music and jubilation. But right now, in the little room where Jean Baptiste had been born, in the room where he'd brought his young bride, in the room where he had seen with his own eyes the miracle of his daughter Jeanette, in this room and in this time there was wonderful peace.

He bowed his head.

"Thank you, God," he whispered. "Thank you for my wife and my children. Thank you for all of this life you have given me. And thank you for Madame Landry who made me notice."

It was full dawn when the baby awakened and Jean Baptiste brought her to her mother to nurse.

"Jean Baptiste," she noted with concern, "you did not sleep at all and you were so ill earlier in the evening."

"Don't worry, it was only a passing thing, something I ate. I'm feeling much better," he assured her.

"You're still looking quite pale."

He shrugged and gestured toward the baby clinging greedily to her breast. "You two look very lovely."

Félicité blushed with pride.

The sound of a boat bumping against the dock captured their attention.

"Someone is here," Jean Baptiste said.

"Already? It's hardly morning."

"I'll see who it is and keep them at bay if I think I should," he said from the doorway, turning back to give her a teasing wink.

With all his running outside every few minutes through the night, he'd never bothered to close the door, and the curtains twirled lightly in the morning breeze.

"Poppa! Poppa!" He heard Gaston's voice before he saw him. Sure enough, Jacque Savoy was tying his pirogue at the dock. It was full to bursting with his three children, Madame Landry, and Tante Celeste.

"Monsieur Savoy says he heard the shots and that Mama has had the new baby and it's a girl," Gaston continued shouting.

"Gaston has Pierre, now I have someone, too," Marie declared. "What's her name, Poppa? What's her name?"

His two oldest children had jumped from the pirogue and were running toward him. Jean Baptiste hurried to meet them. Gaston got there first and he grabbed the boy up and kissed him. He did the same for little Marie, delightedly informing her that yes indeed the new baby was a girl like her and that her name was Jeanette.

"Jeanette!" Marie exclaimed. "That's pretty."

"And so is she," Jean Baptiste answered. "Your mama is feeding her, but if you tiptoe in and are very quiet, she will let you have a look."

The two scrambled toward the house.

Jean Baptiste leaned down to take Pierre from Tante Celeste's arms and helped her and then Madame Landry up onto the cypress planking.

"We could hardly believe the child came so soon," Tante Celeste told him. "We just had to hurry and see."

"Go ahead," he urged her, and the old woman followed the children with the hope of seeing the newborn.

"Mighty bad stroke of luck," Jacque Savoy commented. "Taking Madame Landry upriver on just the night you was going to need her. Did you find some other woman to help you?"

"No," he answered. "My wife and I managed on our own."

The man shook his head and wandered off in the direction of the house.

Jean Baptiste propped young Pierre on his hip and turned unhappily to face Madame Landry. She was grinning broadly.

"You're looking a little pale this morning, Jean Baptiste. Could it be something that you ate?"

"What the devil was in that 'love charm'?" he asked.

She snorted inelegantly. "There is no such thing as a love charm. Folks think that there is, but it's just foolishness."

"You said it was a love charm," he pointed out.

"Oh no, I said that I wanted Armand to *tell* you that it was a love charm."

"You wanted Armand to lie to me?"

"Yes."

"Why?"

"So you would eat it," she said.

"You knew it would make me sick," he said.

She nodded. "I knew it would make you sick," she admitted. "Just miserable sick, not sick unto death."

"Why would you want me to be sick?" he asked.

"I knew that your wife would be delivering last night; all the signs were there. Once you ate my little surprise, you'd be too sick to go for help, but not so sick as to be no use at all."

"Let me understand this," he said, getting testy. "You knew my wife was to give birth last night and you purposely went upriver where I couldn't get you and fed me something to make me sick?"

The old woman was thoughtful for a long moment. "Yes," she agreed. "That's about right."

"Why?"

"That's how love charms work."

"You said there is no love charm."

Madame Landry gave him a long look and chuckled. "You're in love with her again, aren't you?"

Jean Baptiste didn't answer.

They had reached the porch and he heard his wife telling Tante Celeste about the night's events.

"It was the easiest labor I ever had," she was saying. "Not more than a couple of hours altogether and the baby just slipped right out. I didn't even tear at all."

He felt his lips pulling into a grin. He glanced toward Orva Landry, who was still gazing speculatively at him.

"Oh yes, madame," he answered. "I am very much in love with her again."

It took two days to pole back up the Vermillion River to Prairie l'Acadie. Neither Armand nor Aida had cause to regret the time. They were together and it gave him ample opportunity to convince Laron and Helga that Armand's plan would work.

"The point is that he probably *is* dead," Armand told them. "Madame Landry obviously thinks that he is or she would not have taken to calling Helga the German widow. Madame Landry never does anything without purpose."

Armand's words were confident and certain. Aida felt sure that he had found the answer and that he would make it work out.

She gazed up at him, loving him.

They had tied the pirogue to the back of the skiff. While she and Helga sat in the middle, Armand and Laron on either side used their poles in unison to propel the little craft and its passengers back upstream.

They were going back together, together forever. She and Armand and, she trusted Armand enough to believe, Laron and Helga, too.

"A declaration of death is as legal and indisputable as a corpse in the churchyard," Armand told them. "More so, for the corpse could be misidentified. Once the paper is written up, signed, and filed, Helmut Shotz will be the deadest man in Louisiana."

Clearly the two lovers were trying not to be overly hopeful. They wanted to believe, but were too frightened of the potential for disappointment.

"You wanted to kill him, Laron," Armand said. "You cannot. Even if you were to find him, you are not the type to take another man's life. Well, as your friend, I want to kill him, too. And unlike you, I may kill him with impunity, no knife or bullet required."

Aida felt pride swell up inside her. A man need not be big and forceful and dangerous to protect his family, to help his friends. If a man was smart enough and used his good sense and the knowledge he'd gained in the world, he could be as effective as the most able and valiant fighter.

"As judge appointed to this parish," he explained to them. "I can honor or disallow contracts. I can probate wills. I can rule on disputes of property or violence. And I can certainly declare one missing German dead. I need only to inscribe the appropriate papers and send them by messenger to the office of parish governance in New Orleans."

Laron and Helga glanced at each other, not speaking. It was as if both were holding their breath.

"Once that is done, Helmut Shotz will officially be as dead to us as he truly is."

Laron reached over to take Helga's hand. She looked near tears, but she raised her chin bravely to ask Armand the question.

"What if he is not dead? What if he were to return here?"

Armand's tone was tender, but his words were sure. "Then we shall take him into custody and send him down the river to the German coast to be executed."

"But he would be alive again," Laron pointed out.

"Not long enough to even bother to change the paperwork," Armand assured him.

The men looked at each other, silently assessing. Aida remembered what people had said of the two as boys when they got into trouble. When Laron couldn't bust them out, Armand would talk them out.

Slowly, so slowly, Laron began to nod his head.

"Do it, Armand," he said finally.

Aida watched the grin spread across her husband's face. "Once we've declared him dead," Armand continued, "then all of his property becomes yours,

Helga, free and clear. You can remarry and your children can be adopted by your new husband."

"If you want to," Laron pointed out, his mood now teasing. "You can still reject me like any woman anywhere."

The look in her eyes said that she would not.

"Will . . ." Helga hesitated, worried. "Will Laron's family accept this, accept us?"

"My family loves me," Laron told her quickly. "Because I love you and the children, they will also."

"And the entire community will accept you once Father Denis has given you his blessing."

Father Denis. Aida felt a nervous flutter herself. The old man was difficult and a stickler. It would be very hard to convince him to do anything that he thought might be remotely in the wrong.

"The old priest is the rub," Laron said, voicing Aida's own concern and shaking his head. "How will you ever get Father Denis to bless us? To marry us?"

Armand's expression turned sly. "I have a plan," he assured them. "Oh yes, I have a plan."

Vingt et un

Armand had not been able to talk with Father Denis immediately upon their return. Facing old Jesper Gaudet's wrath at not being present at the wedding of his only daughter and learning that he had a new niece took up most of the first day back.

There were almost as many congratulations for him and Aida as for Jean Baptiste and Félicité.

"You sly devil," his brother said to him. "All these last weeks every time I'd mention that woman's name, you'd talk like you thought she was dumb as a post and bow-legged besides. Now I find out you were secretly stealing her away from Laron."

"There was nothing between us before their engagement was broken," Armand assured him.

Jean Baptiste grinned. "Nothing spoken I am certain. But I've known you too long, my brother. You do nothing on impulse. For you, things are always thought through."

Armand found that he couldn't deny that.

The two were standing together near the barn, surveying what they had on hand of timber and brick, pulleys and building materials. Jesper Gaudet had looked horrified when Aida had suggested that perhaps they live with him. Both she and Armand had thought the old man would be loath to allow his only child to move from home and leave him to fend for himself. To their surprise he indicated with absolute conviction that the newlyweds should have a separate house.

"I only wish for you and Aida," Jean Baptiste told him, "all the happiness that Félicité and I have."

His brother looked at him askance.

"You are happy with your marriage?"

Jean Baptiste looked momentarily chagrined. "I am very happy," he said. "You have worried about me, haven't you?"

Armand had no desire to mention the sleepless nights, the anxious days, and the hours of planning and scheming that he had been through. He simply nodded.

Jean Baptiste lowered his head guiltily. "Armand, the only piece of wisdom I can offer you about marriage is that it is not a line from here to happily ever after or from here to death do us part."

His brother was thoughtful for a moment, and then as if noticing it for the first time he held up the thick piece of braided hemp in his hands.

"Marriage is not a line at all," he said. "It's a series of loops or coils like the ones in this rope. At the top is total bliss, at the bottom abject misery. Sometimes you are high on the loop and sometimes low. Most of your life you are somewhere in between. At times you know how happy you are and believe that it must go on that way forever. At others you may think that you cannot bear the pain any longer and want to throw the coil away completely. What you must remember is that the loops are never ending. When you are low, so low you are agonizing, you must

simply have faith that the coils head upward next
toward happiness once more."

It seemed to Armand later that the coils he was
living through these days were very tightly wound.
One moment he was happy and jubilant, the next
deep in despair.

That night he had made love to his wife in a real
bed for the first time. It was Aida's own girlhood bed,
laid with fresh cotton sheets and strewn with sweet
herbs, and one candle glowed from the bedside.

They had reached the high desperate peak at the
same instant and had thrown themselves together
from that precipice. It had been exquisite. Afterward,
however, he had lain awake worried.

"Armand," she'd said sleepily beside him. "What
is wrong?"

"Nothing," he assured her.

"It is something. Is it about Laron and Helga?"

He turned to her and pulled her into his arms. "No,
my love. I was thinking about my brother."

"Jean Baptiste?" Her expression was curious. "He
seems very happy about the baby."

"Yes, he is," Armand told her.

He was quiet for a long time, looking into her eyes,
wanting, hoping.

"Do you mind very much that you are married to
me?" he asked.

She lowered her eyes, afraid to face him. "No,
Armand, I am happy about it."

With one finger he raised her chin, not allowing
her gaze to evade him.

"Do you love him still?"

Her brow furrowed momentarily. "Laron? No, I
told you. I did not love him at all."

"Not Laron, Jean Baptiste."

"Jean Baptiste?"

"Yes, Jean Baptiste."

Her brow furrowed in incredulity. "Your brother, Jean Baptiste?"

"We know no other."

Aida sat up in bed, pulling the sheet up to cover her nakedness, and stared at her husband in disbelief.

"You think that I loved your brother?"

"I know that you loved him," Armand said. "I cannot and will not ask you to change the past. But what I must know is do you love him still?"

Aida continued to stare at him.

"You see, Madame Landry warned me that my careless words to Laron were going to cause him to turn from you. It was only natural that you would fix your choice on another man. Jean Baptiste was there and he was so smitten with you. It would have been hard for you to resist that."

"You thought I would break up your brother's marriage?" Her tone was not pleasant.

"At first that's what I thought," he said. "Before I really knew you. I know now that of course you would never have done that. The two of you would have just been unrequited lovers. In anguish from afar."

Aida maintained her silence.

"But when we ate the love charm, I became really frightened. If you were under the spell of the charm and were to see Jean Baptiste, nothing might stop you from being together. So I . . . so I purposely drew you to me and kissed you. I must not have eaten any of the charm. I felt nothing but the . . . the desire that I have always had for you. I maneuvered you into this marriage and I will try to make you happy. But I must know. Do you still love him?"

Aida got up out of the bed. She didn't even bother to drag the sheet with her. Stark naked she stood in the room and gazed around as if looking for something.

"I wondered where this had gotten to," she said as she crossed the floor to pick up the wooden *battoir* with which she did the wash.

She turned and raised it high over her head. To Armand's total surprise she brought it down in fury, aimed right at the most vulnerable part of him.

"Aida!" he hollered, jumping out of range and then out the other side of the bed.

"You idiot! You fool! You . . . you . . . I can't think of anything bad enough to call you!"

She raced to the other side of the bed and swung the *battoir* at him once more. Thankfully missing again.

"I have always thought you were so smart, so smart," she snarled at him angrily. "But you are the most stupid, stupid man that I have ever met in my life."

She swung at him again. Armand was backed completely in the corner and frantically tried to appeal to her reason.

"Aida, please, put down your weapon and we'll talk."

"Talk! I never want to talk to you again, Armand Sonnier. I have always known that I am not as smart as you. But you always treated me as completely without sense at all. And this . . . this just proves that you believe it. I would not, ever, never, not in a million years fall in love with a man who was already married. That is the most stupid idea that any woman ever had and I would not have it. Do you understand me?"

"Yes, yes, my darling. Please put down the bat, my darling."

"And as for you maneuvering me into this marriage, you haven't enough sense," she declared. "I maneuvered you! I wasn't affected by that love charm, either. I knew I wanted you and when you kissed me and caressed me, I knew that if I were compromised you would have to marry me."

She ground the words out through clenched teeth.

"When you managed to restrain yourself, I wasn't disappointed just because I wanted you. I was afraid that you might get away. So I insisted that I *was* compromised. And I insisted that I *must* be married."

She threw the *battoir* from her. It clattered along the floor. Her fury and anger turned to other emotion as her beautiful eyes welled with tears.

"You have never thought me anything but some silly decorative flower. I have value beyond my appearance. I am . . . I am a flowering herb. I have beauty, but I have power, too. I loved you and I wanted you. When I broke my engagement to Laron, Armand, it was for you."

"Aida," he whispered and pulled her into his arms. "Aida, I have loved you all my life. Even when you were affianced to my best friend, I loved you. I spoke to you as if you were silly and treated you as if I didn't care for you because I was trying not to. I was trying not to love you as I always have."

"I love you, Armand," she whispered against him. "In all my life, the only man I have ever loved is you."

The next morning as he headed down to the church

to speak with Father Denis, Armand recalled his wife's sweet words and they brought a smile of satisfaction to his lips.

She loved him. He loved her. Now all that was to be done was to make things right for Helga and Laron.

"I cannot do it," Father Denis stated flatly.

"It is perfectly legal," Armand told him. "The law was made for situations exactly like this."

The old man tutted disapprovingly.

"I wanted you named as judge, Armand Sonnier, because I believed that you were honorable and principled."

"And I believe that I am, Father," he said. "I believe that what I am doing is the best thing, the right thing, and the perfect solution to the problem at hand."

The old priest's huff was skeptical.

"Laron and Helga love each other. They have been living in sin, but they want to repent of that, to 'go and sin no more.' We can give them the opportunity to do that.'

"It would compound sin upon sin to bless a marriage that is unlawful and bigamous."

"I have issued the declaration of death. It is therefore neither unlawful nor bigamous," Armand said.

Stubbornly the priest shook his head.

"Helmut Shotz is dead, absolutely and incontrovertibly dead to the state of Louisiana."

"What is truth for the state of Louisiana, young man," the priest answered, "is not the same as truth for the Holy Roman Catholic Church."

Armand's expression turned shrewd. In life, as in the game of bourré, it was best to let one's opponents take the easy tricks, puff up their confidence, so that one might more easily overwhelm them at the last. Father Denis had already thrown in his best cards. Armand moved to play his own.

"Father Denis, are you still praying very hard for your new school?"

The old man raised an eyebrow and regarded Armand questioningly.

"I know what it is you want," Armand said. "You want a school to teach our children about reading and writing and the world outside ours. But we are very leery of such teaching. We want our children to grow up just like us, farmers, cattle herders, fishermen. Most of us would not voluntarily send our children to school. But if it were the law, if the parish law required that all children attend school, no man or his family would go against it."

"You are telling me nothing that I do not know," Father Denis said.

"You need for me to make such a law, Father. You will never have your school unless I do. And I am loath to make it, because I worry about our children also."

"What are you saying?"

"If you will honor the death declaration and accept the marriage of Laron and Helga, I will decree that all parish children be given education."

"That is blackmail," Father Denis accused.

Armand grinned at him. "Father, the Lord works in mysterious ways."

The old priest was thoughtful, pensive, considering. Armand knew he had found the chink in his armor.

"Her husband *is* dead," Armand assured him.

"Madame Landry believes it to be so, and so do I. The paper only officially declares what we believe already."

He wasn't convinced.

"What we believe or want to believe is not equal to what we know to be true. There is no grave, no body, not even word that the man has died."

"But Madame Landry—"

"The old woman is an herb healer not a soothsayer," Father Denis insisted. "She cannot know things beyond us."

"She is the *traiteur*, Father. She talks to *the voices*," Armand said.

The old priest scoffed. "She thinks she hears Joan of Arc on the river. That is superstition and none of the Church."

"Who is to say what is real and is not?" Armand asked.

"I am to say it," Father Denis replied. "I am to say it and I do say it. Helmut Shotz is not dead until he is proven dead. You may declare him dead a hundred times, but until I see that he is dead, his widow will not be married in my church."

"They need not marry in your church, Father. They can marry elsewhere. You need only to accept their marriage, bless it, and regard it as true."

"You think some other priest would marry them quicker?" Father Denis asked incredulously.

"It need not be a priest, Father. Helmut Shotz was Lutheran, Helga's first marriage was in their church. She and Laron could wed there also."

Father Denis scoffed. "Wedding in a Lutheran church is the same as no wedding at all."

The two men stilled at the words. They stopped and stared at each other.

"She was married to this Shotz by a Lutheran minister?" Father Denis asked. "No Catholic priest or prelate officiated?"

Armand shook his head. "No, Father."

The old priest smiled. "Then as far as I am concerned, the woman has never been married at all."

Vingt-deux

The wedding of Helga Shotz and Laron Boudreau was one of the happiest ever celebrated in Prairie l'Acadie. The couple was dazzlingly attractive. Laron, as always, was resplendent in knee-length *culotte*, formally donned with silk hose and leather boots. His indigo-blue jacket was buttoned high, just to the knot of his yellow silk tie.

Helga looked startlingly different divested of her drab German clothes. With Aida's help, she had donned a striped skirt of pale green and purple and her corset vest was vivid red.

Virtually every human being within fifty leagues of the parish had shown up. The Boudreau family alone was a monumental crowd.

Father Denis officiated. After effecting Helga's conversion to Catholicism, he was eager to lead her out of sin and to bring her, much welcomed, into the fold.

The wedding was quiet and solemn. The Mass was said, the wine was tasted. The vows were made. It was not Armand but Karl Shotz who stood as *garçon d'honneur* beside the bridegroom. His chin was held high with pride, and the young boy's bearing was already much that of a man.

When Father Denis pronounced them husband and

371

wife a cheer of joy went up from the crowd. Laron kissed his bride, lovingly, longingly, lingeringly, until young Karl tapped him on the shoulder and reminded his new father that the couple was not alone. The well-wishers laughed uproariously. The happy couple blushed with chagrin and happiness.

Ony Guidry struck up the fiddle and the dancing began. Food for the feast had been brought from every household and the long planks that had been laid out were filled and weighted down with it.

The Shotz children had been totally taken in by the Boudreau family and at the wedding Jakob and Elsa found themselves completely surrounded by their new relatives, *tantes, oncles,* and *cousins,* many many cousins.

"How many cousins do I have?" Jakob had asked Father Denis, overwhelmed with his good fortune.

The old priest considered for a long time.

"That will be your first mathematics problem at the school, Jakob," he said. "When you can count high enough to get the number of all your cousins, I will award you a mark."

The little boy was industriously working on it. But he continued to have trouble with the numbers that began with twenty.

Aida danced with the new bridegroom, her brother-in-law, Marchand, Granger, Pierre Babin, and even old man Breaux. But mostly she danced with her husband, who twirled and twirled her on the floor, glorying in the pleasure of partnering her.

Aida was laughing and happy and having a wonderful time. When she spied Ruby, she motioned the young woman over to her.

"Ruby, you look lovely tonight," she said. "And so very very happy. What is it?"

Her friend smiled back. "Oh, you are joking with me. You must have heard," she said.

"Heard what?" Aida asked.

"I am engaged."

Aida's mouth dropped open in disbelief and then she squealed with delight and hugged her friend.

"Who? Who is it?" she asked.

"Surely you know?"

"No, I haven't any idea."

"But you must," Ruby insisted. "You invited me Sunday after Sunday to sit upon your porch. Why else would you have done that? Surely you planned for me to marry him."

"Who? Placide? Ignace?"

Ruby wrinkled her nose and giggled with disbelief. "Of course not, silly. I'm to wed Monsieur Gaudet."

"Who?

"Monsieur Gaudet, your father."

"My father?"

"Yes, as soon as he heard you had wed Armand, he came over to ask me. He said that he had waited so long because he wanted you safely wed and didn't think it fair to bring another woman into the house while you still lived there."

"That's why he is so anxious for us to move," Aida said to herself.

"You do not mind, do you? I thought you would be happy for us. That you had planned it for us. But if you—"

Aida hushed her with a kiss.

"I could not be more happy. You and Poppa, I . . . I am delighted."

"He is so handsome, do you not think so?" Ruby gushed. "And such a gentleman. He makes me feel so pretty. He says that I am the most beautiful woman in his heart. Is that not lovely? And Maman is so thrilled because he is such a great catch for me. He is wealthy, the wealthiest man in the parish, you know. Of course he is much older than I," Ruby admitted, but then leaned closer to speak more privately. "But when I agreed to wed him, Aida, he kissed me. And then he did not seem old at all."

It was after much dancing and laughter and celebration that Laron and Helga boarded their wedding pirogue. The little boat sported a fresh coat of pine tar and was festooned with ribbons and berries and prettied up in a manner befitting a bride.

Once the bride was seated and they pulled away from shore, the rowdy young men waded into the water, teasingly threatening to tip them into the river. As Helga squealed Laron kept them at bay with his pole until they were out into the river far enough to be safe.

Aida felt a hand enjoin with hers and glanced back to find her husband at her side. He gave her a wink and surreptitiously pulled her away from the crowd. Hand in hand they ran away from the rollick along the river and into the privacy of the wooded glade beyond the church.

Alone at last, Armand backed her against a sturdy cottonwood and kissed her passionately.

"I love you, Aida Sonnier," he said. "I love you more than anything or anyone in the world."

"Mmm, and I love you, my Armand, my wonderful, wonderful Armand," she answered.

Their mouths and bodies fit together perfectly.

Both because they were made that way, and because of much recent practice. Their kiss was hot and urgent with pent-up longing.

"I want you, Aida," he whispered. "I don't think I can wait until we get home."

She giggled against his neck. "Well, it is almost full dark," she said. "Surely if we are quiet, no one will find us out."

"I don't know if I can be quiet," he said as his hands began to roam the geography that he had already learned so well.

Aida moaned aloud. "I'm not sure I can be quiet myself," she admitted.

"What the devil do you have on?" Armand asked suddenly, the timber of his voice rising as he was startled out of his revelry.

"They are called drawers," Aida answered. "Helga gave them to me. All the German women wear them and they have become quite the fashion among the Creoles and the Americaines, she assures me."

"I don't like them," he said bluntly.

"They are a wonderful invention," Aida said. "They are warm and pretty and a woman need not live in mortal fear of every gust of wind that comes her way."

"But Aida, I can't get to you through these," he complained.

"Then, Monsieur Sonnier, you will just have to learn how to take them off."

Jakob watched and waved at the departing pirogue long after the music and dancing had resumed. His *oncle* was now his poppa, which was how he had always dreamed it would be.

Tonight they would spend in the cabin on Bayou Tortue by themselves. Tomorrow Monsieur Hébert, or rather Oncle Ozeme, would take him and Elsa and Karl home and they would live forever with Mama and Poppa. And Jakob's name would not be Shotz anymore. It would be Boudreau, just like Mama's and Poppa's and like so many of his cousins.

He squinted to catch the last glimpse of the prettily festooned boat in the distance, the happy couple within it so very much in love. He closed his eyes to try to press the sight upon his memory forever. He succeeded admirably.

Twenty years later he was to recall it with perfect clarity as he decorated his own pirogue with blooming hyacinth and real satin ribbons brought all the way from New Orleans by steam packet. It was right to have it done up so pretty as his bride, Mademoiselle Sonnier, was extremely so. In fact people said of his lovely Jeanette that she was the most beautiful woman on the Vermillion River.

America Loves Lindsey!

The Timeless Romances
of #1 Bestselling Author

Johanna Lindsey

KEEPER OF THE HEART	77493-3/$6.99 US/$8.99 Can
THE MAGIC OF YOU	75629-3/$5.99 US/$6.99 Can
ANGEL	75628-5/$6.99 US/$8.99 Can
PRISONER OF MY DESIRE	75627-7/$6.99 US/$8.99 Can
ONCE A PRINCESS	75625-0/$6.50 US/$8.50 Can
WARRIOR'S WOMAN	75301-4/$6.99 US/$8.99 Can
MAN OF MY DREAMS	75626-9/$6.50 US/$8.50 Can
SURRENDER MY LOVE	76256-0/$6.50 US/$7.50 Can
YOU BELONG TO ME	76258-7/$6.99 US/$8.99 Can
UNTIL FOREVER	76259-5/$6.50 US/$8.50 Can

Coming Soon in Hardcover
SAY YOU LOVE ME